"[Caitlín R. Kiernan has] a gift for language that borders on the scary. Deeply, wonderfully, magnificently nasty." **—Neil Gaiman**

Praise for the Novels of Caitlín R. Kiernan

Daughter of Hounds

"Kiernan's handling of underworld figures is impressive, and this book proves she's as adept at writing crime as she is dark fantasy. . . . A thrilling page-turner that also features the depth, complexity, and unflinching willingness to contemplate the dark that we've come to expect from her books."

—*Locus*

"A hell-raising dark fantasy replete with ghouls, changelings, and eerie intimations of a macabre otherworld. . . . The complex plot springs abundant surprises . . . on its juggernaut roll to a memorable finale . . . an effective mix of atmosphere and action."

—*Publishers Weekly*

"Kiernan's storytelling is stellar, and the misunderstandings and lies of stories within the main story evoke a satisfying tension in the characters."

—*Booklist*

"Caitlín R. Kiernan pays homage to Lovecraft in the scary *Daughter of Hounds*. There is a sense of the foreboding Gothic that creeps out the audience and the antagonists who set much of the pace seem freaky and deadly. Reminiscent of Poppy Z. Brite's darkest thrillers, Ms. Kiernan provides Goth horror fans with a suspense-laden tale that keeps readers' attention."

—*Midwest Book Review*

"Kiernan's writing is what really makes the book special. . . . [It's] best described as 'What if John Bellairs had written *Pulp Fiction*?' Erudite discussions and entrancing descriptions intertwine with snappy, punchy dialogue that is as often as not laced with Tarantino-esque rhythmic profanity. All of this adds up to a pretty explosive and captivating read . . . highly recommended."

—Green Man Review

continued . . .

"Readers who like their Lovecraft armed to the teeth, dressed in black leather and ready to rumble had best get crackin' on down to the bookstore before said beings yank this title off the shelves.

"Kiernan more than most has a handle on what Lovecraft did and did well. Kiernan knows how to conjure the outside, the ancient, those forces that are so different from us so as to cause madness. She started her journey into an unknowable past with *Threshold*, and with each successive novel she's become better and better at conjuring both the actions and the emotions—or lack thereof—of those who encounter it. To my mind, *Daughter of Hounds* is her best yet, one of those novels where you can pick it up and open it to almost any page and find yourself immersed in images that summon the outer darkness into your snug little life.

"But *Daughter of Hounds* does a lot more than just bring on the deep chills. Kiernan's really, really furious this time around. Kiernan is always good at the slow-burning prose, the kind of coiled power that one might imagine comes from swallowing fishhooks. *Daughter of Hounds* displays her skill at creating a densely layered and carefully orchestrated plot, chockablock with lots of hideous monsters and scenes of incipient madness. . . . Her work does bring to mind the sorts of terror that are eating up our world, bit by bit, bite by bite." —The Agony Column

"Kiernan has a superb hand in writing detailed and extremely heart-pounding fight scenes and I admit to not being able to stop the pages from turning. The descriptions of the areas in which the readers found themselves were astounding and the meticulous bits of flavor given to the simplest of tasks were mind-bending." —Book Fetish

Murder of Angels

"I love a book like this that happily blends genres, highlighting the best from each, but delivering them in new configurations. . . . In *Murder of Angels*, the darkness is poetic, the fantasy is gritty, and the real-world sections are rooted in deep and true emotions. Lyrical and earthy, *Murder of Angels* is that rare book that gets everything right."

—Charles de Lint

"[Kiernan's] punk-rock prose, and the brutally realistic portrayal of addiction and mental illness, makes *Angels* fly."

—*Entertainment Weekly* (A-)

Low Red Moon

"The story is fast-paced, emotionally wrenching, and thoroughly captivating. . . . Kiernan only grows in versatility, and readers should continue to expect great things from her." —*Locus*

"*Low Red Moon* fully unleashes the hounds of horror, and the read is eerie and breathtaking. . . . The familiar caveat 'not for the faint of heart' is appropriate here—the novel is one of sustained dread punctuated by explosions of unmitigated terror." —*Irish Literary Review*

Threshold

"*Threshold* is a bonfire proclaiming Caitlín Kiernan's elevated position in the annals of contemporary literature. It is an exceptional novel you mustn't miss. Highly recommended." —*Cemetery Dance*

"*Threshold* confirms Kiernan's reputation as one of dark fiction's premier stylists. Her poetic descriptions ring true and evoke a sense of cosmic dread to rival Lovecraft. Her writing envelops the reader in a fog concealing barely glimpsed horrors that frighten all the more for being just out of sight." —*Gauntlet Magazine*

Silk

Winner of the International Horror Guild Award for Best First Novel
Finalist for the Bram Stoker Award for Best First Novel
Nominated for the British Fantasy Award

"[Kiernan's] tightly focused, unsparing, entranced gaze finds significance and beauty in the landscape it surveys." —Peter Straub

"A remarkable novel . . . deeply, wonderfully, magnificently nasty." —Neil Gaiman

"A daring vision and an extraordinary achievement." —Clive Barker

Novels by Caitlín R. Kiernan

Silk

Threshold

Low Red Moon

Murder of Angels

Daughter of Hounds

The Red Tree

The Red Tree

Caitlín R. Kiernan

A ROC BOOK

ROC
Published by New American Library, a division of
Penguin Group (USA) Inc., 375 Hudson Street,
New York, New York 10014, USA
Penguin Group (Canada), 90 Eglinton Avenue East, Suite 700, Toronto,
Ontario M4P 2Y3, Canada (a division of Pearson Penguin Canada Inc.)
Penguin Books Ltd., 80 Strand, London WC2R 0RL, England
Penguin Ireland, 25 St. Stephen's Green, Dublin 2,
Ireland (a division of Penguin Books Ltd.)
Penguin Group (Australia), 250 Camberwell Road, Camberwell, Victoria 3124,
Australia (a division of Pearson Australia Group Pty. Ltd.)
Penguin Books India Pvt. Ltd., 11 Community Centre, Panchsheel Park,
New Delhi - 110 017, India
Penguin Group (NZ), 67 Apollo Drive, Rosedale, North Shore 0632,
New Zealand (a division of Pearson New Zealand Ltd.)
Penguin Books (South Africa) (Pty.) Ltd., 24 Sturdee Avenue,
Rosebank, Johannesburg 2196, South Africa

Penguin Books Ltd., Registered Offices:
80 Strand, London WC2R 0RL, England

First published by Roc, an imprint of New American Library,
a division of Penguin Group (USA) Inc.

First Printing, August 2009
10 9 8 7 6 5 4 3 2 1

"*Pony*" was previously published in *Tales from the Woeful Platypus* (Subterranean Press, 2007).
Epistolae morales ad Lucilium translation copyright © Sonya Taaffe, 2009

REGISTERED TRADEMARK—MARCA REGISTRADA

LIBRARY OF CONGRESS CATALOGING-IN-PUBLICATION DATA:

Kiernan, Caitlín R.
The red tree/Caitlín R. Kiernan.
p. cm.
ISBN 978-0-451-46276-3
1. Manuscripts—Fiction. 2. Trees—Fiction. 3. Psychological fiction. [1. Rhode Island—Fiction.] I. Title.
PS3561.I358R43 2009
813'.54—dc22 2009015105

Set in Adobe Caslon
Designed by Spring Hoteling

Printed in the United States of America

For Dr. Richard B. Pollnac and Carol Hanson Pollnac,
for making this novel possible.

In memory of Elizabeth Tillman Aldridge (1970–1995).
Sic transit gloria mundi.

THE RED TREE

by
Sarah Crowe
and
Dr. Charles L. Harvey

"The true harvest of my life is intangible—a little star dust caught, a portion of the rainbow I have clutched."
Henry David Thoreau,
Walden, or, A Life in the Woods (1854)

"If ever you have happened on a grove set close with ancient trees grown beyond the common height, the pleaching of their branches one upon the other screening out sight of the sky, that loftiness of forest and solitude of place and sense of wonder at so dense and undisturbed a shade out in the open, will convince you of the presence of a god."

Seneca the Elder,
Epistolae morales ad Lucilium (CE 64)

EDITOR'S PREFACE

I have visited the old Wight Farm and its "red tree," there where the house squats ancient and neglected below the bogs that lie at the southern edge of Ramswool Pond. So, I have been. I have seen it for myself, but just once. Having accepted the task of editing *The Red Tree* for posthumous publication, it seemed, somehow, like a necessary pilgrimage. A sort of duty, required of me if I were to gain any insight at all into Sarah Crowe's state of mind in those last months of her life. So, I went, and I even went alone.

I made the drive up from Manhattan in the spring, many months after receiving the typescript. The day was bright and crisp, a cider day in late April, the sky laid out wide and blue, and the land just beginning to go green with the first signs of spring. There was nothing the least bit foreboding about that day, but already my expectations had been colored by the pages of a suicide's long ordeal and confession, and by the "secret history" of the Wight place that Sarah had discovered in yet another manuscript, this one having purportedly been left behind by the farmhouse's previous tenant, a man who, as it happens, had also died there, half a decade before her arrival. The day of my visit fell, almost precisely, one year subsequent to Sarah's arrival at the farm in April of 2008.

I will endeavor to keep this brief, as it is not *my* story being told here. I am, at most, that story's reluctant caretaker.

After an early lunch in Providence with a college acquaintance I'd not seen in some time, I took Route 6 west out of the city, past North Scituate, then, at the intersection with State 102, I turned south, through Chopmist and Rockland, crossing the Ponaganset River where it spills into the great gullet of the Scituate Reservoir, then drove on to Clayville and the Plainfield Pike. At the Providence–Kent county line, I turned northwest onto Moosup Valley Road. I was unfamiliar with this part of the state—I largely still am—and allowed myself to spend an hour or so looking about a couple of cemeteries in Moosup and the old church (ca 1864–1865) now claimed by a congregation of the United Church of Christ. I also had a look about the Grange Hall and the Tyler Free Library (the latter, ca 1896–1900), before continuing on to the intersection with Barbs Hill Road, just west of town.

The road is kept up moderately well, as there are many homes and farms spread out along its length, but it does change over from asphalt to "tar-and-chip" almost immediately. The turnoff to the Wight Farm is located just past a small pond, no more than a sixth of a mile from the north end of Barbs Hill Road. Surprisingly, unlike many of the assorted side roads, driveways, and footpaths, it isn't gated. I'd rented a Jeep Cherokee for the trip; otherwise, I'd never have made it much farther than the Blanchard place. The Blanchard family has owned the Wight Farm since 1979, and I'd cleared my visit with them the week before, explaining that I was editing Sarah Crowe's final book and needed to see the house where she'd lived while writing it, which also happened to be the house where she'd died. Mr. Samson Blanchard, her former landlord, was neither as curious nor as suspicious as I'd expected from my scant, secondhand knowledge of the Yankees of western Rhode Island. I gave him my publisher's contact information, but, later, I'd discover that he never even made the call. I credit this, in part, to the fact that the Blanchards suffered virtually no media attention following Sarah's death. And, oddly (or so it seems to me), there is little evidence that local teens and other curiosity seekers have targeted the Wight Farm for nightly visitations, vandalism, or, to employ the vernacular of folklorists, "legend-tripping."[1] Indeed, given local traditions of ghosts, witches, and even vampires,[2] I find the general absence of "urban myth" surrounding the farm nothing short of remarkable.

The afternoon was growing late as I bumped and

---

1 See the relevant entry, "legend trip," in Jan Brunvand's *American Folklore: An Encyclopedia* (Garland Reference Library of the Humanities, Vol. 1551), pp. 439-440.

2 Michael E. Bell, *Food for the Dead: On the Trail of New England's Vampires* (2001, Carroll & Graf Publishers).

bounced my way along the narrow, winding path leading south and east through the woods to the Wight place. I couldn't drive the whole way, as the road dead-ends and there's a turnaround less than two hundred feet from the house itself. I parked there, then crossed an alarmingly rickety wooden bridge on foot. It fords the unnamed creek that flows out of Ramswool Pond, joining other streams off towards Vaughn's Hollow, before finally emptying into Briggs Pond after half a mile or so. Most of the trees here are oak, of one sort or another, interspersed with white pine, hickory, and red maple, and they threw long shadows across the clear, slow-moving water. The weedy banks were thick with reeking growths of skunk cabbage, the fleshy, purplish flowers open to attract bees and stoneflies. I noted the fading daylight, the late hour, and so walked quickly on to the house itself.

I wish I could say that during the two hours I spent poking about the place I felt some disquieting supernatural presence, a demonic or preternatural threat, or that I witnessed anything at all I am now unable to explain. I'm sure, if I had, this would make a far more interesting and satisfying preface to what follows. But the truth is, I didn't. Beyond a general air of loneliness and the dim melancholy that such locales have always elicited from me, I didn't feel much at all. I had honestly *expected* to find the visit unnerving, and had even considered delaying it a week until my husband could accompany me.

Mr. Blanchard had mailed me the keys to the house, and I went inside and walked through all the rooms of the house, one by one. It was still furnished with an assortment of antiques and junk, just as it had been when Sarah took up residence there. I saw the manual typewriter she'd produced her manuscript on, the same typewriter that had supposedly been used to type out the older manuscript she'd eventually found. I went up to the small attic, which, according to Sarah, was used that summer as a studio by the painter Constance Hopkins, before Hopkins returned to Los Angeles.[3] The house was cold and dank and smelled musty, but no more or less so than any very old house built on such boggy land would after standing uninhabited for so many months.

I did not enter the enormous basement, as I'd forgotten to bring a flashlight, and Blanchard had not gone to the trouble and expense of having the power turned on just for the sake of my brief visit. However, I will say that I very much *wanted* to go down those flimsy stairs and see how much truth there was (or wasn't) to what Sarah had written about the space below the house. It seems, to me, to lie very much at the heart of the matter. I stood at the basement door, and I even opened it, gazing down into that solid,

---

3 It should here be noted that while I have been successful in acquiring the necessary releases allowing me to speak of Hopkins and her part in this strange affair, and to publish everything Sarah wrote about her, Ms. Hopkins has repeatedly refused my requests to be interviewed. The only published work concerning Hopkins, aside from what follows and her website, was a brief profile and review in *Culver City Artscape* (September 2009) following her installation at a gallery on La Cienega Boulevard last summer, a show which apparently included several of the canvases mentioned herein.

formidable darkness, smelling the fetid air wafting up from below. But I am not the least bit ashamed to admit you couldn't have paid me enough to make that descent alone. The basement is a mystery I will leave for someone else to answer, some more intrepid soul, a would-be Lara Croft or Indiana Jones.

After the house, I peeked into the sagging, dilapidated barn, and a couple of the other outbuildings, before following one of the fieldstone walls seventy-five yards or so to that enormous red oak[4] that had formed so much of Sarah Crowe's fatal obsession. Along the way, I noted that a break in the wall, mentioned repeatedly by Sarah, had recently been repaired. Far more than the house and the surrounding landscape, the tree, and what I found near it, made an impression on me. To whatever degree she might have hallucinated, imagined or exaggerated her experiences at the Wight Farm, I can say with certainty that she did *not* overstate the imposing presence of this one tree. It stands at least a hundred and thirty feet tall, and at the base its trunk is easily six feet in diameter,[5] dwarfing all other trees in the vicinity. I will not here waste time describing the tree itself, as Sarah's manuscript does a far better job of that than I ever could. The branches seemed very stark that day, very grimly drawn against that April sky, despite a cheery spray

4 *Quercus rubra*(=*Q. borealis*), known as the Northern Red Oak and Champion Oak; also see Donald Cultoss Peattie's *A Natural History of Trees of Eastern and Central North America* (Houghton Mifflin Co., 1950, with a 2nd ed. in 1966).

5 These measurements were given me by Mr. Samson Blanchard, a few weeks after my visit.

of new leaves coming in. But, again, I'd cite my expectations, more than any objective attribute of the tree itself, as the source of this impression. Here and there, names and dates had been carved into the bark. The oldest that I spotted was from 1888 (which Sarah also mentions), but there may well have been much older graffiti that I missed.

Set out about the circumference of those gnarled roots, I found many dozens of small glazed ceramic figurines, mostly of the exact sort one gets free inside boxes of Red Rose teabags.[6] There were animals, circus performers, and characters from nursery rhymes, some balanced on the knotty wood, or tucked into crevices in the bark, others set out on the mossy ground surrounding the oak. It was an unexpected and startling sight, and I stood there for some time, studying the figurines. I did not take any of them away with me, or even touch them, thinking that, perhaps, they had been left here by the Blanchards' grandchildren, who I understand frequently visit and have been known to wander as far as the Wight place. There was something reminiscent of a shrine or reliquary in the arrangement of the tiny ceramic animals, which are never mentioned in Sarah Crowe's manuscript. I assume, therefore, that they

6 Manufactured by George Wade Pottery in Burslem, Staffordshire, England, Red Rose Tea has included these "whimsies" since 1967, beginning as a short-term promotion in Quebec. The first American figures were offered in 1983. To quote the company's website, "To date, it is estimated that more than 300 million Wade figurines have been given away in packages of tea in America." See also *The World of Wade* by Ian Warner and Mike Posgay (Schiffer Publishing, 2003).

were placed here following her death. I'd forgotten my camera that morning, so I am forced to rely on memory, but two of the figurines I recall quite clearly—a sepia-colored rabbit and a pinkish wild boar, both date back to the very first American series of animal figurines offered by Red Rose Tea (1983–1985). At any rate, dusk was coming on fast, and I still had to cross the rickety bridge and then navigate the rutted dirt path leading back to Barbs Hill Road and Moosup Valley. By the time I got to the Jeep, the air was filled with the eerie calls of owls and other night birds, and I was glad that I had not lingered longer at the red oak. I made it back to New York around ten-thirty that evening.

And that was my pilgrimage, the dues I felt that I should pay before the privilege of writing this preface. And, now, having written it down, the day seems even more unremarkable and underwhelming than before. The mystery posed by the final months of Sarah's life, the red oak, and the manuscript she left behind are to be found in the pages that follow, not this account of my "legend-trip" to the Wight Farm.

I must also confess that I still do not fully understand the circumstances that led to that odd typescript landing on my desk, hardly a month after her funeral. It was wrapped in brown butcher's paper and bore a Providence postmark, but no return address. In fact, it was accompanied by no cover letter, nor word of explanation whatsoever. Having served as her editor on two novels, and having considered Sarah—if not a close friend—at least a good acquaintance, part of me wished that the whole thing would quickly prove to be no more than an elaborate hoax.

But as I read it, I recognized her there on every page. Even if, for whatever reason, some other author had perfectly aped her voice, most of the pages bear notes and proofreader's marks in Sarah's own unmistakable handwriting. Regardless, I requested that it be examined by a graphologist certified by the American Board of Forensic Document Examiners, Inc., who concluded, without any reasonable doubt, that Sarah Crowe did, in fact, produce at least the handwritten portion of the manuscript. I also discovered several pages bearing distinct fingerprints, presumably made when a ribbon in the old typewriter was being changed, and submitted those for fingerprint analysis by a private investigator (name withheld by request). Again, the results were positive. So, regardless of whether or not she actually conceived and composed *The Red Tree,* there can be very little doubt that she did, in fact, frequently handle the typescript and make notations to it. Ergo, if this is an elaborate forgery, it's one she literally had a hand in.

That last summer of her life, Sarah Crowe lived in a self-imposed seclusion, only infrequently reaching out to make contact with others. A few calls to her agent, a handful of emails to me, asking for more time on a long overdue and never completed novel. She had become, like the heroines of her novels, a haunted woman, drawing in upon herself, shutting away the world, wrapping herself ever more tightly in what I am forced to concede were shrouds of delusion and depression. A lifelong Southerner (who frequently claimed to loathe everything about the South), she abruptly fled to rural Rhode Island, seeking, perhaps, a new beginning. Perhaps peace. Perhaps some closure to what she saw as a chaotic and misspent life. There is never any definitive, conclusive statement in *The Red Tree,* only frustrating hints. We know that she had recently been diagnosed with a chronic neurological disorder that caused seizures and that may or may not have been a form of epilepsy. We know her tumultuous relationship with "Amanda Tyrell"[7] had come to an ugly end, and that Sarah blamed herself for not having managed to somehow save her lover. We know that she was unable to write a contracted novel, and that she eventually found herself writing *The Red Tree,* in journal form, instead. Once a sociable, outgoing woman, at the end she'd become withdrawn and secretive. She was only rarely seen by either the Blanchards or the people of Moosup Valley. We know how she died, and that a coroner's inquest ruled her death to be a suicide. We know that Sarah had always had a violent disdain for her own work, referring to it, for example, as "tiresome hackery"[8] and "genre drivel."[9] And we know that the generally positive reviews and the praise of her peers did little to change this opinion, which seems to have been bolstered by the poor sales of her novels. In the end, this amounts to very little,

7 Sarah chose this pseudonym for her former lover, and I have chosen to respect her decision to do so by never using "Amanda's" true name. However, it is not difficult to learn, if one is so disposed.
8 *Atlanta Journal-Constitution,* December 14, 2001.
9 *Publishers Weekly,* March 3, 1999.

this rough assortment of facts, and a poor way to sum up a life. But, then, I must remind myself this is *not* a eulogy I am writing, but a preface to a very odd book.

As I've said, the same day I visited the Wight Farm and saw the red tree for myself, I stopped by the Tyler Free Library in Moosup Valley. The small white building is hardly a quarter mile northeast of the old farm, and I knew that Sarah had visited it several times in those final months. More than anything, I think I was curious to see if this modest country library had any of her books, and I was pleasantly surprised to find that they did have on their shelves a single copy of her second short-story collection, *Silent Riots*.[10] I took it to a reading table and flipped through the pages, a little embarrassed that, though I was her present editor, I'd never read any of her short fiction. I made a mental note to get a copy of the book as soon as I got back to Manhattan, and was about to return it to the shelves when I noticed something scribbled (with blue ink) in Sarah's hand on one of the otherwise-blank end pages. I sat there for maybe five or ten minutes, marveling at this scrap of graffiti, which read, simply, "Joke's on you. But please do try not to take it too personally.—Signed, The Author (7/18/08)."

That day, it just seemed sort of odd and funny, if you understood Sarah's rough, usually self-deprecating sense of humor. And it seemed a little sad, also, that, only weeks before her suicide, she'd taken a moment to deface this library

10 HarperCollins, 1998.

copy of a book of hers she'd publicly and privately claimed, time and again, to despise. Now I find myself wondering if, in that moment, in that act of vandalism, she didn't give us an epigraph that might well serve both *The Red Tree* and her fiction-writing career as a whole. Maybe even her life as a whole, if one could only look back upon it from her own unique perspective.

One final word: the typescript I received was not broken up into chapters, but consisted, rather, of a single continuous narrative. I have made the chapter divisions myself, somewhat arbitrarily, for the sake of convention. Also, I have added a postscript, an excerpt from Sarah's novel *A Long Way to Morning*. It strikes me as apt commentary on what follows, and almost as foreshadowing.

Sharon D. Halperin

October 4, 2009

New York, New York

CHAPTER ONE

7 May 2008 (Wednesday, 9:38 a.m.)

I'm almost awake now, starting in on my second cup of coffee, sitting here at the kitchen table, and writing this in the spiral-bound notebook I purchased down in Coventry, a little over a week ago. I only bought it as an afterthought, really, with some vague notion that I might begin keeping a diary, or maybe scribble down a list of the birds and wild animals and snakes I see around the house, something of the sort. Until this morning, I'd not even taken it out of the brown paper bag from the pharmacy. There were thunderstorms last night, and this morning there's a heavy, lingering mist, but, even so, from this window I can see all the way north to the flooded gravel quarry the locals call Ramswool Pond. The pond is about a hundred yards from the house, I'm guessing, past two of the ubiquitous dry-stack fieldstone walls. I've not yet bothered to walk down that way, because I haven't noticed a trail, just a lot of poison ivy, wild grapes, and greenbriers. From here, the water is the color of slate, that same flat charcoal gray, framed in shades of green branches and yellow-brown grass and the leaden sky hanging overhead. The way it shimmers, I can tell that the wind is whipping up tiny wavelets on the surface. I was told, by the landlord—whose name is Sam Blanchard—that the pond used to be a granite quarry, dating from the twenties until sometime in the 1950s or 1960s. It was abandoned, then, and flooded as groundwater gradually seeped up and filled in the great, ugly wound scraped into the earth over all those decades by men and their digging machines. I have no idea how deep it might be, but I'm guessing pretty deep. I suppose that on hot summer days it might become a swimming hole, and maybe someone's bothered to stock it with fish. Again, I'm just guessing. And this is not a hot summer day. This is a chilly, misty morning in early May. I imagine deer come down to the pond to drink, deer and raccoons and skunks; the woods around the old farm are full of deer, and I've heard there are even bobcats and black bears in these woods.

I have written nothing, nothing at all, since leaving Atlanta and coming to Rhode Island, and the truth is I have not *tried* to write anything. And before that, I suppose I'd written nothing worth mentioning since finishing that last short story, which means it's been a good seven months or so. More than half a year, come and gone. So much time, flowing up to fill in those empty, wasted days the way the slate-colored water has filled in an old quarry. I haven't even unpacked my pens, so I'm using a yellow No. 2 pencil I found in one of the kitchen cupboards. I have always hated writing with pencils, ever since grammar school, and the heel of my hand is already smudged with graphite. What's left of the pink eraser hardly even makes a decent stub, but lazy women take whatever they can find, I suppose.

The coffee is bitter and good, but I wish I had a cigarette. Sitting here, looking out at the dense tangle of weeds and saplings behind the old farmhouse, looking away towards Ramswool Pond, the dream is already starting to disintegrate, breaking apart and fading, burning off the way this mist will do in only another hour or so. And I won't lie. I'm glad for that. Hell, I would even be thankful, if there were anyone or anything I believed in enough to offer up my thanks. I rescued the notebook from the drugstore bag and found the pencil and sat down at the table to write out all I could recall of the dream, and now I am glad that all I can recall are fleeting glimpses and impressions. More how it made me feel, than whatever actually happened in the nightmare. Yes, of course, the dream was a nightmare. They are *all* nightmares now. It's been a long, long time since I had any other sort of dream, even longer than it's been since I've written anything worth reading.

Sometimes, in the mornings and evenings, the deer come out of the trees to graze near the house, and I sit here and watch them. They amaze me, I think. I've lived most of my life in the cement sprawl and jumble of Southern cities, places where pigeons and squirrels and maybe the occasional opossum pass for wildlife. Watching them, the deer, I feel, constantly, that they are conscious of my scrutiny, of the attention of alien eyes. They are nervous, wary beasts, seeming always on the verge of bolting back into the cover of the oaks and pines and the tall straw-colored grass, back to those shaded, secret places where I cannot watch them. This morning, though, there are no deer, though I saw a fat groundhog earlier, before I started writing, trundling along near the barn. There are rabbits here, a veritable plague of rabbits, it seems, and I've seen hawks and bluebirds. I saw a *rafter* of turkeys a few days back. I had no idea that one refers to a flock of turkeys as anything but a flock of turkeys, that there was a collective noun for turkeys, until I looked it up online. A bouquet of pheasants, a murder of crows, a lamentation of swans, and a rafter of turkeys. Oh, unless the turkeys are immature, in which case they are a *brood*.

Here I am, three pages into this notebook, the heel of my right hand smudged silvery gray, and I have hardly said a word about the nightmare. Am I stalling, or do I simply not care enough to trouble myself with it? Has it faded to the point where I couldn't remember enough of it to put down, anyway? It was nothing remarkable, one of the regulars, some alternate version of the night that Amanda finally walked out on me. I think I have dreamt at least a thousand permutations of that night. Sometimes, she doesn't leave. Sometimes, she doesn't tell me where she's going is none of my business. Sometimes, she doesn't die. And yet, somehow, even *those* dreams are nightmares. Perhaps because, subconsciously, I know that they are lies. There is one truth to the matter, just one truth, and all the rest is only my silly fucking regret trying to make it play out some other way.

While I've been sitting here, writing all my nothings-in-particular, the mist has thinned a bit, but it has also drifted out across the nearer end of Ramswool Pond. I can no longer clearly make out the wavelets rippling across the surface of the flooded quarry. But, I see the wind rustling the leaves and the weeds, so know that they're still there, those small waves. And now, I think, I know what I am going to write here, instead of the bad dream. I'll write the bad dream after its next inevitable permutation, possibly. It can wait. The pond has reminded me of something I don't think I've thought about in a very long time, and that's what I'm going to write. After I get my third cup of coffee.

I suffered through the better part of my childhood and my teenage years in a stunted little town about fifteen miles east of Birmingham, Alabama. Back in the seventies, that place was still clinging rather resolutely to the forties and fifties, I suspect. Hanging on for dear fucking life as the world rushed forward without it. I've given interviews where I made jokes about *The Andy Griffith Show* and such, calling my "hometown" things like Hooterville or Dogpatch or Mayberry on crack. Not so very far off the mark, no matter how snarky it might sound. I'm told that the town's public library removed my books from its shelves after I said something to that effect in an interview with the *Atlanta Journal-Constitution*. Whatever. Fuck them if they can't take a joke . . . or face the truth. But, I digress. Always, I digress. It's my superpower. Some asshole at the *New York Times Book Review* once said that my novels would benefit tremendously from "an editor willing to rein in my unfortunate propensity for digression." Or *something* along those lines. I suppose I shouldn't use quotation marks when paraphrasing from an unreliable memory.

Anyway, a couple of miles from my house, there was an old chert pit, long since abandoned and flooded, just like Ramswool Pond out there. I used to go to that old pit—which had no name that I was ever aware of. Most often, I went alone, sometimes to hunt the trilobite and crinoid fossils you could find there, sometimes to chuck rocks into the water or sneak cigarettes or shoot BB guns, sometimes just to get the hell away from my mother and father and my kid sister for a while. There were all sorts of local stories and folktales about the place. Supposedly, bootleggers had run a still out there during Prohibition, and it had ended badly with a shoot-out between the moonshiners and Revenue men. Careless swimmers were said to have drowned in the greenish, murky waters. Some claimed that the pit was connected to an underground river, and that giant, man-eating salamanders and bullhead catfish and fuck knows what else were swimming around down there. Car thieves were reputed to dump the carcasses of the automobiles they stripped into the pit, and I tended to believe that part, because here and there you could spot the rusted hood of a pickup truck or the roof of a car just below the water. I don't recollect all of the stories. There were so many, but this is, I think, the first time that I have ever told my own.

It was the end of the summer of 1977, and in a couple weeks more I'd be starting high school. Wait. I have to find a knife and sharpen this damn pencil again. Okay, pencil sharpened. So, summer of '77, and the radio was awash with the Eagles' "Hotel California" and the Bee Gees "How Deep Is Your Love" and "Blinded by the Light" by Manfred Mann's Earth Band . . . all that crap, though mostly I was listening to Pink Floyd and David Bowie back then. Carter was president. *The Bionic Woman* and *The Rockford Files* were my favorite TV shows. I knew I was going to hell, because I had a bitch of a crush on Lindsay Wagner.

And here I go, digressing again. Regardless, I'm pretty sure that on the August day in question, I was out looking for trilobites, because I'd sent some of mine off to the state geological survey in Tuscaloosa, and I'd gotten back a letter asking if I could please send more. Which meant I had to *find* more. Years later, a paleontologist in Birmingham described my trilobites as a new species, and I hope I spell this right—*Griffithides croweii,* naming them after me. That was my first brush with fame, I suppose, though I doubt anyone at "home" even knew. By then, I'd left Mayberry and was living with a girlfriend up in Nashville, but the paleontologist tracked me down, and she sent me a copy of the scientific paper. Her name was Matthews, Esther Matthews, I think. I still have it somewhere, that paper. I still have one of the trilobites, too. It's about as big as my thumbnail, a shiny copper-tinted bug stretched out on a bit of brownish-orange chert. As I have admitted, in two or three interviews now, I'd have gone into geology or paleontology, instead of becoming an author, if only I'd been any good with math. If I ever had a "calling," that was it. I took a few courses in college, and, to this day, a sizable portion of the nonfiction I read is books on paleontology and earth history. I often dream of fossil hunting, which, I suppose, is my subconscious mind working through regret. But, hey, at least I have the trilobite.

The rain is starting again. I suppose this may keep up all damn day.

So, that particular August afternoon in 1977, thirty-one years ago, it must have been about a hundred and two in the shade. I was clambering about the steep, crumbly edges of the quarry, turning over chunks of the hard stone, cracking it open with a brick hammer that had once belonged to my grandfather, but not finding much of interest—seashells, corals, crinoid stems, no trilobites—and probably wishing I had a cold Coca-Cola or a Mountain Dew or something. I might have been thinking about stripping off my jeans and risking the giant catfish of legend for a swim or perhaps giving up, calling it a day, and walking back through the kudzu to the place where I'd left my bicycle.

My bicycle, by the way, was a lot like that town. It had actually belonged to my mother when she was a girl, back in the fifties. It was a mottle of rust and flaking blue paint, and the seat tended to fall off anytime you hit a pothole or went over a curb. I have no idea whatever became of it.

But, anyway, there I was, crouched right down at the waterline, on this narrow, mossy ledge surrounded by cattails and whatnot, sweating like a pig and trying to keep a weather eye out for copperheads *and* trilobite fossils at the same time. I must have heard something, maybe the sudden splash of a frightened, fleeing bullfrog that I'd disturbed, or maybe something else, and I looked up. And way over on the other side of the pit, directly across from me, which would have been at least a good forty or fifty feet away, I saw this girl standing in the rushes, naked as the day she was born, the muddy water up to her knees. She was staring back at me, and I just froze, the way the deer around here freeze when they get spooked, just before they dash back into the woods. I remember that she had the blackest hair I think I'd ever seen, hair like ink, and I wasn't so far away that I couldn't tell she was pretty. I mean, fucking *unearthly* pretty, beautiful, not what passed for pretty in that little Alabama town. There I was, fourteen years old and just beginning to suspect I might be a dyke, and there *she* was, and all I could do was stay very, very still and watch. I was thinking, *Why don't I know you? Why haven't I ever seen you before?*, because everyone in that town knew everyone else, at least by sight. And if I'd ever seen her, I sure as shit would not have forgotten her. She might have been smiling at me, but I couldn't be sure. My mouth was so dry, I still recall that, the dry mouth and parched throat, and my heart pounding like a goddamn kettledrum in my chest. And then she took a step or two towards me, the water rising up to her waist, hiding the ebony thatch of her sex, and she held her arms up and out like maybe she wanted to give me a hug or something.

Back then, I had blessed few points of reference, but now I'd point to any number of the Pre-Raphaelite and Victorian painters. *They* knew women with faces like hers, knew them or invented them. They set them down on canvas. In particular, I'd point to Thomas Millie Dow's *The Kelpie,* which I first saw in college, years after that afternoon at the chert pit, and which still makes me uneasy.

When the water was as high as her chest, she must have reached a drop-off. The pit was at least a hundred feet deep, and the submerged walls were very steep. Most spots, it got deep fast. She took another step forward and just sank straight down, like a rock. There was a little swirl of water where she'd been, and then the surface grew still again. I crouched there, waiting, and I swear to god (now, there's a joke) I must have waited fifteen or twenty minutes for her to come up again. But she never did. Not even any air bubbles. She just stepped out into the pit and sank . . . vanished. And then, suddenly, the stifling summer air, which had been filled with the droning scream of cicadas, went silent, and I mean completely fucking silent. It was that way for a few minutes, maybe . . . no insects, no birds, nothing at all. That's when I realized I was scared, probably more scared than I'd ever been in my life, and a few seconds later the whippoorwills started in. Now, back then, growing up in bumblefuck Alabama, you might not learn about Pre-Raphaelite sirens, but you heard all about what whippoorwills are supposed to mean. Harbingers of death, ill omens, psychopomps, etc. and etc. Never mind that you could hear whippoorwills just about *any* summer evening or morning, because the old folks said they were bad fucking juju. And at that particular moment, waiting for the naked, black-haired girl to come up for air, with what sounded like a whole army of whippoorwills whistling in the underbrush—"WHIP puwiw WEEW, WHIP puwiw WEEW, WHIP puwiw WEEW"—I believed it. I just started running—and this part I don't really remember at all. Just that I made it back to my bicycle and was at least halfway home before I even slowed down, much less looked over my shoulder. But I never went back to the chert pit, not ever. It's still there, I suppose.

So there, that's my only "true-life" ghost story or whatever you want to call it. My Wednesday morning confession to this drugstore notebook. No doubt, I must have come up with all sorts of rationalizations for what I'd seen that day. Maybe the girl was from another town—Moody or Odenville or Trussville—and that's why I'd never seen her before. Maybe she was committing suicide, and she never came back up because she'd tied concrete blocks around her ankles. Maybe she *did* come back up, and I just missed it, somehow. Possibly, I was suffering the effects of hallucinations brought on by the heat.

And it's raining even harder now. I can hardly see the slaty smudge of Ramswool Pond anymore. It's lost out there somewhere in this cold and soggy Rhode Island morning. Days like this one, I have a lot of trouble remembering why the hell it was I left Atlanta. But then I remember Amanda and all the rest, and this dreary goddamn weather seems a small price to pay to finally be so far and away from our old place in Candler Park. Yes, I *am* running, and this is where I have run to, thank you very much. I put out a housing-wanted add on Craigslist, and one thing led to another, connect the fucking dots, and here I am, crappy weather, sodden groundhogs, and all. No regrets. Not yet. Boredom, yeah, and nightmares, and a dwindling bank balance, but life goes on. And now I have a hand cramp, so enough's enough. Maybe I'll just stick this notebook *back* in the bag from the drugstore, dump it in the trash, because right now, I truly wish I'd been content to sit here and drink my coffee and wait for the deer to come out.

9 May 2008 (Friday, 8:47 p.m.)

The thing I can't seem to get around is the boredom. Or maybe I mean the solitude. Perhaps I am not particularly adept at distinguishing these two conditions one from the other. I didn't have to plop myself down in the least populated part of the state. I could easily have found something in Providence or some place near the sea, like Westerly or Narragansett. Coming here was, I suppose, an impulse move. Seemed like a good idea at the time. And there's TV and the internet (by way of two different satellite dishes, I'll note), and I have stacks of DVDs and CDs, my cell phone and the books I brought that I've been meaning to read for . . . well, some of them for years. But I've been here two weeks, and mostly I just wander about the property, never straying very far from the house, or I drink coffee and stare out the windows. Or I drink beer and bourbon, even though that's a big no-no with the antiseizure meds. I've taken a couple or three long drives through South County, but I've never been much for sightseeing and scenery. Last week, I drove all the way out to Point Judith. There's a lighthouse there and picnic tables and a big paved parking lot, though, fortunately, it's early enough in the season that there weren't tourists. I understand they are like unto an Old Testament plague of locusts, descending on the state from Connecticut, Massachusetts, New Jersey, New York, other places, too, no doubt. The siren song of the fucking beaches, I suppose. I saw a bumper sticker during one of my drives that read "They call it 'tourist season,' so why can't we shoot them?" And yet, I expect that all of South County and much of this state has, sadly, become dependent on the income from tourism. The curse is the blessing is the curse. But, yeah, I sat there at one of the tables at Point Judith, and I watched what I suppose were fishing boats coming and going, fishing or lobster boats, a few sailboats, headed into the bay or out to sea or down to Block Island. The gulls were everywhere, noisy and not the least bit afraid of people, and that made me think of Hitchcock, of course. The tide was out, and there was a smell not unlike raw sewage on the wind.

Yesterday, I drove up to Moosup Valley, which is a little ways north of here, much closer than either Coventry or Foster. I saw the library, but only went in long enough to grab a photocopied flyer about its history. I don't like being in libraries any more than I like being in bookstores, and I haven't liked going into bookstores since my first novel came out fourteen years ago. Here's a bit about the library from the flyer: "The History of the Tyler Free Library began when the people of Moosup Valley acquired Casey B. Tyler's private collection of about 2000 books and therefore needed to build a structure to house it. The Tyler Free Library was formally organized in January of 1896, and a Librarian was hired. The Library opened and fifteen cards were issued on March 31, 1900. Local residents organized the books and the Library was open on Saturday afternoons." The flyer goes on to say that the rather austere whitewashed building was moved from one side of Moosup Valley Road to the other, north to south, in 1965. And why the hell am I writing all this crap down? Oh yeah, boredom.

I also stopped at an old store on Plain Woods Road, to buy cigarettes and a few other things. I'm smoking again, and that wouldn't make my doctor back in Atlanta any happier than would all the whiskey and bottles of Bass Ale. Like just about everything else around here, the store is ancient, and like the library, it, too, bears the name of Tyler. I always heard all that stuff about how closemouthed and secretive New Englanders are, especially when you get way out in the boonies like this, and especially towards outsiders, but either the stereotype is false or I keep running into atypically garrulous Yankees. There was an old woman working in the Tyler Store, and she told me it was built in 1834, though the west end wasn't added on until 1870. Most of what she said I don't recall, but she did know (I don't know how, some local gossip's grapevine, I suppose) that I was the "lady author boarding out at the old Wight place." And then she said it was such a shame about the last tenant, and when I asked her what she meant, she just stared at me a moment or two, her eyes huge, magnified behind trifocal lenses.

"You don't *know*?" she asked.

"I don't know," I replied.

"Then it's not for me to tell you, I suspect. But you ask Mr. Blanchard. You got a right to know."

I told her that Blanchard, the landlord, is away on some sort of farm-related business, a fertilizer convention or sheep-dippers' conference or something of the sort, and that I wouldn't be seeing him again for at least a week, and probably longer than that (he lives up in Foster and hardly ever comes out this way). But, no dice. She wouldn't say more, and returned, instead, to the history of the old store, and a cider mill that used to be somewhere nearby, and something about the cemetery where her father is buried, and all that sort of thing. Local color. And I listened politely, deciding I shouldn't press her regarding the former tenant, whatever it was about him or her I should know, that she felt I had a right to know. All Blanchard ever said was that a professor from URI rented the place before I came along, but I know it'd sat empty for more than two years.

Not long after I got back to the house, there was a phone call (because I forgot to turn off my damned cell), Dorothy wanting to know if I was settled in, how I was getting on out here, was I homesick, and, finally, when she could no longer put it off, had I made any progress on the novel. I almost hung up, because she knows I have not even *started* the goddamn novel. But, Dorothy is a good agent, and those don't grow on trees, and I might still need her someday. She reminded me, tactfully, but unhelpfully, that publishers who have paid out sizable portions of sizable advances eventually expect manuscripts in return, no matter how much money I might already have made for them on my previous books. I could have lied and said the writing was going well and not to worry. But where's the fucking point? The deadline is only six weeks off now, and that's not the original deadline. That's the extension on the original deadline, and so then we talked about the feasibility of a *second* extension, say six or eight months. Dorothy gets this tone in her voice at times like that, and I feel like I'm a kid again, talking to my mother. But she said she would call my editor next week. At least she didn't ask about my health. At least that's something.

Oh, I finally unpacked my Waterman pens. I'm using the "diamond-black" Edson I bought in Denver last year. I have consigned the yellow pencil stub to a drawer. On a whim, I seriously considered burying the damned thing, but then I started worrying over whether the graphite (a form of carbon, I believe) would be bad for the earthworms and moles and such. I *think* I read somewhere that residual graphite is harmless, but I've already got enough on my conscience without having to worry about whether I've poisoned the grubs. I'll do my best to keep making entries in this notebook. The pens make it much easier, and it's not like I've got a hell of a lot else to do, is it?

11 May 2008 (7:29 a.m.)

I have been awake maybe twenty minutes, and the nightmare is still buzzing about my skull like a hungry swarm of mosquitoes. Nothing, though, that I can conveniently swat away. Also, I have misplaced my glasses, and, no matter how hard I squint, the blue college-ruled lines on this page shift and sway, grudgingly resolving for a few seconds at a time before they fade and blur again. Still, fuck the coffee, I'm going to get this down before I lose it. Last night, I read back over my two previous entries, and hell, they don't even sound like me. They sound like some pale ghost of my voice. Not even a decent echo. What does a writer become when she can no longer write? What's left over when the words don't come when called? What did Echo become after she was slaughtered for spurning Pan, or after her collusion with Zeus was discovered and so she was punished by Hera, or after her rejection by Narcissus? Those pages seem, at best, my *own* echo, a waning, directionless cry in this wilderness to which I have exiled myself. But, the dream. Write down the dream and save the rest for later. Write down what you can recall about the dream.

I was at the kitchen table, just as I am now, smoking and staring out at the shadows gathering as the sun set, the afternoon melting into twilight. I could see the dark smudge of Ramswool Pond, and the low, rocky hills around the farm, the trees pressing in, new-growth trees where once there were fields for grazing sheep and apple orchards and whatever else. I was sitting here, smoking, and the longer I watched, the more unnerving the shadows became, as the coming night drew them ever sharper. I felt as though they were becoming substantial, corporeal things, and that the sun's retreat westward was releasing them from unseen prisons, below the ground or from out of unseen dimensions which exist, always, alongside this visible world. There were no lights on in the house, I think, and it had already fallen into darkness around and behind me, and that darkness seemed inhabited, populated by dozens of muttering men and women. I would try to make out what they were saying, but always their words slipped away from me. And all the while, I suspected the murmuring was meant to distract me from all that lay outside the kitchen window. With hindsight, I might even be so reckless as to guess that this intent was merciful. But, since I could not make head nor tails of the murmurers' attempts at communication, I watched the window, instead. I realized here that I was not sitting in the kitchen of Mr. Blanchard's old farmhouse, but in a small screening room, a movie theater, and the window was, in truth, a screen. It's a cheap fucking trick, the kind of unimaginative, low-budget legerdemain at which dreaming minds seem to excel or in which they only compulsively indulge. I sat in my theater seat and stared out the window, which was now, of course, merely the projected image from concealed mechanisms hidden somewhere behind me, flickering moments fused to celluloid. The muttering voice had become other members of the audience, though I could not actually see any of them (and I am not certain that I tried). I don't often go to the movies. But Amanda liked to, so she usually went without me. That was something else we might have shared, but I couldn't be bothered.

On the screen, I see the kitchen's window frame, and

the fallow, overgrown land beyond, and I see the shadows growing bolder. And then I see *you,* Amanda, and you're standing with your back to me, but, still, I know it's you. You're standing at the first of the stone walls, staring out towards the flooded granite quarry. Your shoulders are slumped, your head down, almost bowed, and you're wearing a simple yellow dress, and even though you are too far away for me to make out such details, I can see that the fabric has been imprinted with tiny flowers of one sort or another, a yellow calico. Your long hair hangs down as though you wear a veil, and it's matted and tangled, as if you haven't combed it in days and days. That's so unlike you, and I began, here, to suspect I was only dreaming, because you'd never be out with your hair in such a dreadful state, not out where someone might *see* you.

And then the deer are coming out of the shadows gathered beneath the trees, and there are other animals, though it's hard for me to be sure what they are. Animals. Things smaller than the deer, things that move swiftly, mostly creeping along nearer to the ground. I think the deer are all coming *to* you, that possibly you have called them somehow, and I think, for a second or two, I am delighted at the thought and wonder why you never told me you knew how to call deer. I think back on the stories you told me about your childhood in Georgia, that your father was a hunter, so I consider that maybe it was a talent you learned from him. And it occurs to me now that, a page or two back, I shifted fucking tense, past to present. I fucking *hate* that, but I'm still so asleep and afraid I'll forget something important—that I have already forgotten—if I wait and try to wake up before putting this down.

In the dream, I think the deer are being called to you, the deer and those other animals. But you do not raise your head to greet them, do not make any sign whatsoever to acknowledge their approach. And I think, *Maybe she knows that would only scare them away.* The movie has a soundtrack, though I think I only become aware of it as the animals approach. I can hear their feet crunching softly in the grass, can hear wind, and what I think might be you singing very softly to yourself. All this time my girlfriend could sing to deer, and I had no idea. How crazy is that? And before much longer, those nervous, long-leggedy beasts and their damp noses would be pressing in all about you, and in that instant you seemed to me some uncanonized Catholic saint. Our Lady of the Bucks and Does and Fawns. And here, I think, I am grown quite certain that I am dreaming, but it hardly seems to matter, because there you are, so perfect, and I need to see you, and I need to know what is about to happen.

And here, too, the dream shifts again, canvas and plywood backdrops swapped and costumes changed in a seamless, unmarked segue. Now it is some *other* evening, and I am not in the kitchen of the rented farmhouse off Barbs Hill Road, and I am not in that anonymous theater, either. Amanda is with me now, and we are no longer divided by windowpanes or silver screens or time. I am telling her how sorry I am, how it'll never happen again, and she's on her knees, huddled on a sidewalk washed in the sodium-arc glow of a nearby streetlight. She holds a stick of chalk gripped tightly in her left hand, drawing something on the concrete at my feet. By slow degrees, I scrape up enough comprehension to see that what she's making resembles the squares of a child's hopscotch game, only instead of numbers, each square contains a line from the magpie rhyme, with the first square marked *Earth*. In the second she has written "One for anger," and in the third "Two for mirth." She is only just beginning to fill in the fourth square, the chalk loudly scratching and squeaking against the pavement, and as I talk she shakes her head, *no, no, no*. She will not listen, will not hear me, and it does not matter whether I am a liar or sincere, for we have already come to a place where actions have forever eliminated even the possibility of forgiveness and reconciliation.

"Three for a wedding," she says.

And all the things that I said, I've lost those words, had forgotten them by the time I awoke. But in the dream I speak them with such a wild desperation that I have begun to cry, and still she shakes her head—*No, Sarah, no.*

"Four for a birth," she says, and doesn't look up at me. There are enormous, rumbling vehicles rushing and rattling by, neither trucks nor cars, precisely, but I only catch fleeting glimpses of them from the corners of my eyes, for I know they are abominable things that no one is meant to gaze upon directly. The air smells like exhaust and something lying dead at the side of the road, and "Five for rich," Amanda says and laughs.

Her chalk breaks, splintering against the sidewalk, and

again I am only sitting in the kitchen, in this same chair. Again, I am watching her as the deer and other animals approach from the cover of trees and lengthening shadows. Head bowed, she is still singing, her voice calling out clearly across the dusk. Every living thing perks its ears to hear, and the sky above is battered black with the wings of owls and catbirds and seagulls. And it is here that I realize, too late, that the deer are not actually deer at all. Their eyes glint iridescent green and gold in the failing day, and they smile. Those long legs, so like jointed stilts, pick their way through brambles and over stones, and your song invites them. Perhaps, even, Amanda's song has somehow *created* them, weaving them into being from nothingness. Or no, not from nothingness, but fashioning them from the fabric of my own fear and remorse and guilt. Maybe they are only shards of me, stalking towards her in the gloom. I rise to shout a warning, but no sound escapes my throat, and my fists cannot reach the glass to pound against the window. They smile their vicious smiles, these long-leggedy things, and the house murmurs, and she is still singing her summoning, weaving song when, one by one, they fall, merciless and greedy, upon her.

Fuck it. Fuck it all to hell.

I know I'll look back at these pages in a few hours, and all this will sound like nonsense. It'll sound like utter horseshit. The sun will hang high and brilliant in the sky, and my only clear recollection of the nightmare will be what I have written down here. I'll laugh at the foolish woman I have allowed myself to become, jumping at these shoddy specters spat up by my sleeping mind, then wasting good ink to consign them to paper. It will fade, and I will laugh. More than anything, I'll be annoyed at that fucking tense shift. But, Sarah, this raises a question, one that I am still too asleep to have the good sense to avoid. If I can write about Amanda through a child's allegorical, symbolic horrors, then can I not also bring myself to write about the truth of it? This dream and all those I *haven't* written down and likely never will, they are only a coward's confession, indirect visions seen through distorting mirrors, mere "shadows of the world," because I do not seem to possess the requisite courage to look over my shoulder and face my own failures. Is that who I have become? And if so, how long can I stand the sour stink of my own fear? And hey, here's another question. Have I stopped writing, not because I no longer know what to write about, but because I know *exactly* what I need to be writing? They were always only me, the short stories and novels, only scraps of me coughed up and disguised as fiction, autobiography tarted up and disguised as figment and reverie.

Maybe I'll have another long, long drive today. Maybe I'll get into the car and head back to that lighthouse and those picnic tables overlooking Point Judith and the bay. Or I'll fill up the tank and hit the interstate and not stop until I'm in Boston. I *won't* drive south and west, because that way lies Manhattan, sooner or later, and Manhattan has come to signify nothing to me but looming deadlines and impatient publishers. At any rate, enough of this. Lay down the pen and shut the hell up for a while. Give it a rest, old woman.

`14 May 2008 (3:29 p.m.)`

So, turns out, the poorhouse will be avoided just a little fucking longer. Dorothy called from Manhattan about an hour ago. I was in the bathroom, but heard my cell phone ringing here on the kitchen table. My backlist was just picked up by a German-language publisher, the whole thing, which will make for a tidy little advance. Lucky me. The check from Berlin should arrive just about the same time things start looking genuinely bleak in my bank account. I know she could hear the relief in my voice, because I'm lousy at hiding that sort of thing. No poker face here. Anyway, after the news, there was a moment of awkward silence, then an even more awkward bit of chitchat—how's the weather, are you feeling well, etc.—before she asked the inescapable question. Never mind she'd just asked a few days back.

"Any progress with the writing?"

I'd offer to send her this notebook, but I don't think that she'd appreciate the humor. What I *wanted* to ask Dorothy, but didn't, is when we're finally going to admit the truth to one another and stop playing this game of wishful thinking. The day will come. I see that now more than ever. The hour will come when she asks, and instead of making my usual excuses or dodging it altogether by changing the subject or making a joke of the whole mess, I'll just tell her it's not going to happen. Sorry. The well is dry, and sorry it took me so long to summon the courage to say so. Is that how it happens? How a writer stops being a writer?

Can it actually be as simple as a few words spoken into a cell phone?

I just read back over that last entry, the dream of Amanda and the animals and the game of hopscotch. I'm really not so glad I wrote it down. If I hadn't, most of the damned thing would have faded by now. I'd recall very little beyond the mood that it evoked, that almost smothering sense of dread, and I wouldn't be sitting here gnawing it over. Or sitting here while *it* gnaws at *me*. Have I come all the way to this musty old house at the end of the world to be whittled away by nightmares and obsession? Merely running from ruin to dissolution? I can picture those nightmares and memories as termites, or maggots, or some cancerous growth, slowly consuming me, bit by bit. And maybe I've done nothing but make myself more palatable.

16 May 2008 (9:47 p.m.)

I met Amanda Tyrell on Friday the 13th, at a party I didn't want to attend, where I hardly knew anyone else in attendance. And it wasn't just any Friday the 13th, but Friday the 13th in October 2006. For the first time since January 13th, 1520, four hundred and seventy-six years earlier, the digits in the numerical notation for the day added up to thirteen (1+1+3+2+6=13). By the way, there's a tradition that on January 13th, 1520, Ferdinand Magellan reached the banks of the Rio de la Plata and proclaimed, *"Monte vide eu!"* It's probably apocryphal, and I only know it because of the goddamn internet, which makes historians of anyone with enough motivation and intellgince to tap at a computer keyboard. But it all sounds rather prophetic, right? Sounds like I should have done the math, read the signs, and then wisely looked the other way. It's easy to say shit like that in retrospect. Hell, at the time, all I knew was that it was Friday the 13th, and I found most of the people who'd shown up for this CD-release thing to be utterly loathsome. I knew a girl in the band, had once dated her, in point of fact, and that's the only reason I was there. I didn't even particularly care for the music, sort of a countrypolitan revival thing, the whole business trying much too hard to sound like Patsy Cline and Skeeter Davis and Jim Reeves. I was drunk, nothing unusual there (except that I was drunk on *free* booze), and kept wondering if maybe I'd wandered onto the set of a David Lynch film, circa *Lost Highway*. Cowboy hats and twangy guitars and some stripper who could not only drink from a Budweiser can held between her grotesquely artificial breasts, but could then crush the can with those same great mounds of flesh and fat and silicone. "*Monte vide eu,*" indeed.

I sat there, brooding in the smoke and honky-tonk roar, the din of all those chattering voices and laughter, and Amanda was sitting on the other end of the sofa from me. She said she knew who I was, that she'd read *The Ark of Poseidon* and, what's more, she hadn't really liked it. And nothing gets me wet like literary rejection. And, too, I probably hadn't been laid in the last six months. She was wearing this skimpy wifebeater A-shirt and jeans, and there was nothing the least bit artificial about her breasts. Though, honest to fucking god, it was the talk that got me, at least at the start. I mean, she just sat down and started telling me how I'd screwed up that novel, like I'd asked her opinion or something. She was smoking clove cigarettes and drinking Jack and Coke, and it amazes me now that I can remember either of those details, given it's been two years, and I was very, very drunk at the time.

"I wouldn't go so far to say that it's overwritten," she said. Well, no. I don't remember precisely *what* she said, but that was the sentiment. "But it could have been a lot less wordy." I do recall that she said *wordy,* and that she laughed afterwards.

"Is that a fact?" I might have asked, and maybe she nodded and took a drag off her cigarette.

"Also," she said, "the shell in Titian's *Venus Anadyomene* is most emphatically not an oyster shell, but a scallop. And the painting was owned by John Sutherland Egerton, who was the 6th Duke of Sutherland, not by the 5th Duke of Sutherland." And no, that's not really what she said. I have no idea what she really said, but it was exactly that pedantic and irrelevant to both the theme and plot of the novel.

"Yeah? So, sue the copy editor," I replied, and she laughed again.

"You ever even been to Greece?" she may have asked next, and I may have replied, "You're an audacious little cunt, aren't you?"

"Audacity," she said (or let's say she did). "Yeah, I am audacious. But, as Cocteau said, 'Tact in audacity is knowing how far you can go without going too far.' "

"I think I must have missed the tact."

"Then you aren't paying attention."

I finished a bottle of Michelob and set the empty on the table beside the sofa. And she just sat there, smoking and watching me with those fucking gray-green eyes of hers, eyes like lichen clinging to boulders on Rocky Mountain tundra or alpine meadows, like something unpleasant growing in the back of the fridge, eyes that were cold and hard, but very much alive.

"Sorry about that," I said. "I'm drunk. Drunk and confronted with tactless audacity."

And then she smiled at me and said, "In every artist there is a touch of audacity, without which no talent is conceivable."

"Oh, so you're an artist?"

"Depends."

"On what? On what does it depend?"

"On how one chooses to define art."

I glanced towards the bar, wanting another beer, but lacking the requisite motivation to walk that far. Besides, she might leave if I got up.

"Who the hell said that, anyway?" I asked her. " 'In every artist there is a touch of audacity,' I mean."

"Disraeli," she replied. "But you still haven't answered my question, Miss Crowe."

"Do *not* call me *Miss Crowe*. Jesus, I'm not *that* much older than you, am I?" Only later would I learn that I was (get this) thirteen years older than Amanda, and that we shared the same birthday.

"Have you ever been to Greece?"

"Yes," I lied. "Two years before I wrote the book," and then I began ticking off what I could recall of Greek geography on my fingers. "Athens, Lamia, Crete, Peloponnese, Thessaly . . . did the whole tour. I never write about a place unless I've spent time there. And you know what I recall the most—I mean besides the ouzo and legal prostitution?"

She said that she didn't, of course, and by this point I'd forgotten all about wanting another beer and was in full-on tall-tale mode.

"I was out walking on a beach one morning, and don't ask me where because I don't remember exactly. Maybe Thessaloniki. Maybe Kavala. But I was out walking off a bull bitch of a hangover, and I came across this enormous dead sea turtle on the sand. It had this awful gash in its shell, and I figured that was probably from a propeller blade. Figured that's what killed the poor fucker."

"You went to Greece, and what you remember most is a dead turtle?" she asked, and those gray-green eyes flashed skeptically. "Besides the ouzo and the whores, that is."

"Yes," I said, jabbing a finger at her for emphasis. "Yes, that's what I remember most. That poor, dead fucking sea turtle, spread out there on the beach. It was big, like something from dinosaur times, bigger than any turtle I'd ever seen. It was, I learned later on, a loggerhead, an endangered species. And there it was, fucking murdered by some asshole's outboard motor, and I just sat down in the sand beside it and cried."

I stopped talking, and she sat staring at me a moment. I stared back, mostly at her breasts. And then she said, "So, Sarah, you went all the way to Greece, and then you wrote a book about it. But you left out that thing that made the greatest impression upon you?"

"Irony," I replied, without missing a beat. "Besides, I thought putting the turtle in the book would cheapen it. The novel, I mean. Not the sea turtle. Matter of fact, hell, I've never told anyone but you that story."

"See where audacity gets you?" she asked. "Anyway, the novel you wrote before that one, it was much better."

"A Long Way To Morning?"

"Yeah, that's the one. I remember now, because it sounds like an Ernest Hemingway title." And then she asked if I wanted anything else from the bar, because she'd just finished her Jack and Coke and was sucking on an ice cube.

"I can go," I offered. "I'm not so drunk I can't walk."

"No, I'll go," and she glanced at the bottle on the table. "Michelob?"

"Michelob *Amber Bock,*" I said, and she nodded, standing up, vanishing into the crowd, all those hipster idiots in cowboy boots and rhinestone-studded shirts. I thought sure that was that, all she wrote, and I'd never see her again. But, still, I did congratulate myself on the improvised sea-turtle yarn, thinking it might make a halfway decent short story one day. But she did come back, maybe ten minutes later. I was sitting there peeling the label off my empty bottle, trying to decide if I'd endured enough of the party that it wouldn't look too bad if I left. There were tattered scraps of foil all over the floor at my feet, on my shoes, a few on the table. I set the empty down and accepted the fresh bottle when she held it out to me.

"Thanks," I said, and Amanda Tyrell just smiled and shrugged and sat down again, but this time she sat down quite a bit closer to me than before. And then I broached The Question, because, even sober, I'd made The Embarrassing Mistake too many times in the past. Never assume. Never, ever fucking assume.

"You *are* a lesbian," I said, and that earned more laughter.

"Is that an inquiry or a command?"

"That's a question," I said, sipping my beer, "because I think I'm getting signals here, and I don't want to make a goddamn fool out of myself if you're straight."

She stared at me a moment, just long enough, I think, that she knew I'd be getting nervous. And then she nodded.

"Guilty as charged," she told me. "A lesbian is what I am. Last time I screwed a guy—first and last time, by the way—I was fourteen."

"Well, then, that's a relief," and I laughed, probably for the first time since we'd begun talking.

"But, I have a confession to make," Amanda continued, so I'm thinking, yeah, here comes the other shoe. She's in a relationship. Or she's celibate, or I'm just not her fucking type. Something of the sort surely, but then she says, "I haven't actually read *The Ark of Poseidon*. Or anything else you've ever written."

I probably laughed very loud then. Maybe beer even squirted out my nostrils. Maybe my sinuses burned all night.

"I got those questions about your book from Tracy," and she pointed into the constantly shifting crush of bodies. Tracy, by the way, was the girl in the band, whom I'd been dating back when I was writing *The Ark of Poseidon*, and she'd even helped out proofreading the galley pages. I felt set up and relieved at the same time.

"Cute," I told her, though I didn't think it the least bit cute. Mostly, I was wondering what the hell Tracy was playing at, if she thought I was so pathetic I needed her sending fish my way (which, at that point, I probably was), or if she was just messing with my head.

"You think so?"

"No, but it's more pleasant than if I tell you what I'm really feeling right now."

Her eyes dimmed and her smile faded a bit then, and I started to feel like maybe I was, by dint of her confession, regaining the upper hand. This assumes I ever *had* the upper hand, that I'd enchanted her with my fib of a dead sea turtle on a Grecian shore. I stared at the crowd, at that place where Tracy might be, observing her handiwork, and took a couple of swallows of the cold beer.

"Well, I hope I haven't pissed you off," Amanda said, after a minute or so.

"Nah, you haven't pissed me off," I assured her. "When you're a writer, you learn to live by dirty tricks, or you don't last very long."

"You think that was a dirty trick?"

"Near enough," I replied, and then, changing the subject, because I was still a lot hornier than I was angry, I said, "So, it depends on what I consider art. Whether or not you're an artist."

There was a brief pause, long enough that I had time for another swallow of beer, before she nodded her head. "Photography," she said. "Well, it's sort of photo-montage, lots of compositing, Photoshopping, image manipulation. You know, that sort of thing."

"And that's not art?" I asked, having more than half expected her to tell me she was into body modification (despite any visible evidence to that effect) or flash mobs or action poetry, something more along those lines.

"I think it's probably my subject matter that gets me into trouble," she said. "Too dark, I think. Too dark for most people, anyway. I used to do a little freelance magazine illustration, but now I mostly just do commissions."

I nodded, trying to think of what I would say next, as I knew almost nothing about photography or photomontage. And, finally, trying to sound interested, I asked, "Is it lucrative, the commissions?"

Amanda seemed to perk up a little then, so I guess I'd said the right thing, or at least avoided saying the wrong thing. Six of one, half dozen of the other. She set her glass down on a cocktail napkin.

"It pays the bills, most of the time. Mainly, I have clients, private collectors who are into what I do, and I take requests. They ask for some specific image, and I create it.

Images you can't get with just a camera, but that they carry around in their heads. And there's some pretty dark stuff in people's heads. They bring me their sick shit, and I make it visible."

"Perverts?" I asked.

"Yeah. Some of them, sure. But not all. Some of them are just . . ." And she paused, frowning and stirring her drink with a swizzle stick. "Some of them just need to see with their eyes these images that they've already seen in their *mind's* eye. Sometimes, it seems like I'm a sort of therapist, or a midwife. They might want a photorealistic unicorn, or a woman might want a photo of herself, naked, riding a unicorn, or—"

"A photo of herself fucking that unicorn," I said.

"Pretty much," she nodded. "It can get sexually explicit, and intense, and most times it's a lot grimmer than unicorns and fairies and mermaids and what have you. But that's the way I happen to lean, anyway. A true disciple of Francis Bacon, Diane Arbus, Goya, Sidney Sime, of the Mütter Museum, Eighteenth-Century anatomical and obstetric wax models, and so forth. I've actually *been* to the Josephinum in Vienna, and, dude, that was like I'd died and gone to fucking heaven."

The way she said *Josephinum,* coupled with that line about dying and going to heaven, I could tell that I should be impressed—or at least that she *hoped* I'd be impressed—so I made some appreciative sound, then, and apparently did a decent enough job of feigning whatever she needed to see. Truth is, though, she'd lost me after Goya.

"If I had my laptop with me, I could show you some of my work," she told me, still using the swizzle stick to rearrange the ice cubes in her glass.

"A shame," I said, more than half meaning it, because she'd managed to pique my interest, even through the obscuring haze of alcohol and horniness.

"It's not all that far from here, my apartment, which is also my studio. Just down in Grant Park, on Ormewood, not too far from the zoo. I mean, if you'd really like to see. If you're not just saying that."

"Are you kidding?" I asked Amanda Tyrell. "Women screwing unicorns? Unicorns exchanging the favor? How often does a girl get an opportunity like that? Besides, this fucking music," and I pointed to a huge speaker mounted on the wall.

"Yeah, I don't like it much, either," she said. "But the open bar, you know. An open bar and those little Swedish meatballs on toothpicks, they get me every time."

And right about then, suspecting I'd lucked out and hit the jackpot, I was wondering if I could find Tracy the fucking busybody, wherever she was tucked away in that noisy, faux-cornpone crowd to thank her and buy her a goddamn drink or maybe a line of cocaine, if that was still her deal. And then, hoping I didn't seem *too* eager, *too* obvious, I asked Amanda if she had a car, and no, she said, she'd come with a friend, and, by the way, if we were going to leave the party, she needed to find said friend and tell her, so she wouldn't worry. Fine, I said, sipping my beer.

"I'll be waiting right here," I promised. "Sure as hell got nowhere else to go."

"I won't be long. She's here somewhere. And, yeah, it'll be cool, you'll see."

The party was in some East Atlanta dive, the sort of place that works hard at *being* a dive, and we would have taken Moreland Avenue down to Ormewood Avenue SE, I suppose. I don't recall, precisely. I was too drunk to be driving in the first damn place, but my old Ford truck was a stick, and when she saw it, Amanda informed me that she could only drive automatics. Later, I would learn this was a lie, but, let's save later for later. And that was *much* later. Not too many concrete memories about our conversation on that drive. I was trying too hard to focus on the road and the street signs and not getting pulled over by the boys and girls of the APD.

Turned out Amanda lived in a huge old Victorian that had been converted into three apartments—first floor, second floor, and the attic. She had the attic, of course. The drive from the club to that house, it's all a blur of streetlights and traffic lights, stop signs and yellow center lines. The great jungle of urban squalor and gentrification south of I-20. Yuppie condos and million-dollar flip jobs rubbing shoulders with ghetto pawnshops, fast-food restaurants, crack dens, and gangbangers. The neighborhood got a little bit better after we turned onto Ormewood, approaching that great swath of sculpted urban wilderness known as Grant Park. In 1890, a mere twenty-six years after Sherman ordered his troops to burn the city to the ground, the

Olmsted Brothers of Brookline, Massachusetts—sons of the great Frederick Law Olmsted—were hired to design Grant Park. But I digress. . . .

Always, I digress. I may have mentioned that already.

So, I followed Amanda up wobbly back stairs and into her apartment. It was small, but nicer than what I'd expected. She complained about roaches and her downstairs neighbors, whom she said were Scientologists. She also claimed they abused their dog, a golden Lab named Shackelford. Amanda said they frequently beat the dog, and that she'd called the cops about it a couple of times. She offered me coffee, and I gladly accepted, wanting to be sober. I sat in a kitchen chair (she had no table), and I suppose we talked about nothing in particular until the coffee was done. I asked for milk, no sugar, and when she wanted to know if half-and-half would do, I said sure. Half-and-half would do just fine.

I followed her down a short, narrow hallway, then, into the room where she said she did most of her work. The walls were painted a deep cranberry shade of red, and there was an assortment of Macintosh computers, scanners, a light table, several expensive-looking cameras (both digital and the old-fashioned analog sort), and so forth. She said she used another room, farther down the hallway, for her clients' photo shoots, and that the bathroom doubled as her darkroom.

"Where do you sleep?" I asked, sipping my coffee, aware that I was asking another question entirely.

"I don't sleep," she replied. "Not much, anyway. But there's a futon in the front."

"Insomnia?"

"Not exactly. I go to sleep just fine, when I let myself. My psychologist calls it an NREM parasomnia, an arousal disorder that takes place between the third and fourth stages of NREM sleep. Same thing as night terrors. You've heard of that, yeah?"

"Yeah," I told her. "I've heard of that."

"Moderately rare in adults. Maybe three percent or so suffer from it as badly as I do. Oh, and I also grind my teeth. You should *see* my dental bills. Fucking brutal. I'll have dentures by forty at this rate."

And then she sat down in front of one of the big iMac G5s and flipped it on. It hummed to life, and her desktop image, near as I could tell, was a color photograph of a dissected cat. There wasn't another chair anywhere in the room, so I stood while she explained that she had printouts, of course, hard copies of everything, but that she really preferred the way her art looked on an LED screen.

"When I was a kid, I always wanted a Lite-Brite, but it never happened. These babies here"—and she paused to kiss the white monitor—"are my inner child's vengeance against unresponsive parents."

And then she started opening files, one after another, the pale plastic bulb of her mouse clicking icons to reveal impossible creatures engaged in unspeakable acts. And for a while I forgot about pretty much everything else but those sublime, grotesque, and beautiful images. Centaurs and satyrs, dryads, a host of dragons and merfolk, Siamese twins, men and women so completely undressed that every muscle, every tendon, was clearly visible. There were werewolves, wereleopards, weretigers engaged in acts of feeding and copulation, and sometimes both at once. There were women tattooed from head to toe, endless debaucheries of fairies and trolls and goblins, genderless beings and hermaphrodites, alabaster-skinned vampires, and rotting zombies. Women with the serrate teeth of sharks and men with blind, toothsome eels where their cocks should have been. There were unnamable masses of tentacles and polyps and eyes, escapees from a Lovecraft story or a John Carpenter film, their human elements all but obscured. I'd honestly never thought of myself as much of a deviant, beyond the way that my upbringing had trained me to view my lesbianism, of course. But standing in that cranberry room, seeing all those fabulous beasts, those impossible, exquisitely rendered hybrids born from the melding of Amanda's skill and imagination with the secret fantasies of her "clients," I found myself growing light-headed with excitement, sweating, my heart beating too fast, too hard, my mouth gone dry. And if, at the time, my reaction *disturbed* me (and often the hybrids and the things they were doing were undeniably disturbing), it hardly mattered to my libido.

"Most of the compositing is done from photographs," she said, opening a new file, something that was more machine than woman, "but I also work with a couple of local makeup artists, from time to time."

I said something, and maybe it made sense, but more likely it didn't. Regardless, she didn't seem to notice.

"For some, it's just a kink. You know, a fetish. For some others, there really isn't much of a sexual component involved. But I do get some pretty serious cases, from time to time. The self-described therianthropes, for example. The Otherkin. The Transhumanists and parahumanists. The occasional necrophile. But, when you come right down to it, they're all auto-voyeurs. They're all Narcissus staring into that damn pool, you know."

"Frankly," I said, and I think my voice was trembling, "I have no idea what you're talking about, Amanda, but, right now, I'd really like to fuck your brains out. If the futon's good for that, I mean."

"If not, there's always the floor," she said, and there was no change in her expression or the tone of her voice, no change whatsoever. She closed Photoshop, then shut off the computer, and led me to a room near the front of the attic apartment. The walls were lined with bookshelves. There was a television and VCR and an X-Box (even through the lust clogging my higher brain activities, the X-Box surprised me). There was an assortment of animal skulls, set on the shelves or hung above them on the walls: coyote, horse, antelopes with spiraling horns, the fully articulated skeleton of a monkey of some sort. There was a single window—no blinds or curtains—looking down on Ormewood Avenue. We didn't bother with the futon. Because, just like she'd said, there was always the floor.

"Take your clothes off," she said, and while I struggled with the zipper of my jeans, she took a very realistic dildo out of a box beneath the futon, the dildo and the leather harness she fitted it into. I stopped fighting with the disagreeable zipper and the buttons on my shirt and watched, speechless, while she undressed, letting her clothes fall in a pile at her feet. Her nipples were erect and the color of walnut shells. Maybe I can't remember what we talked about on the way from the club to her apartment, but I recall the exact shade of brown of Amanda's nipples. They looked almost hard enough to slice me.

Maybe that's all I ever actually wanted from her, for those walnut nipples to cut me open. Make me *bleed*. Maybe, Amanda, that's the one thing you were never able to understand, because I was never able to articulate the desire.

She fastened the leather harness firmly about her small waist, the molded silicone phallus drooping obscenely between her thighs, and then she undressed me herself. I do not know how many times I came that night, or how many times she came. It seemed to go on forever, our lovemaking, the hammering of our sweaty bodies one against the other, even if there was no love there anywhere. Finally, towards dawn, I slept, and awoke hours later, hungover and disoriented, staring out that attic window at the sky above Grant Park. She was still sleeping there on the floor beside me, snoring very softly. And that was the night I met Amanda Tyrell. October 13th, 2006. Never mind if I don't genuinely recollect even half the shit I've written down here, if I've just made stuff up to fill in the gaping mnemonic crevices. Whatever. A necessary fiction, and if the facts are compromised by my lousy memory, I don't think the *truth* is any worse for it.

You want words, Dorothy? Well, you could have these. Maybe they're not Shakespeare or Updike or Stephen goddamn King, but they *are* sincere and sincerely unexpected. Jesus fuck, how long's it been since I've written this much at one sitting? I don't even know. My wrist has stopped aching and is going numb. And there are pages and pages and pages. I didn't notice the sun go down, and that was almost two hours ago.

Here you are, Amanda, like a wasp sealed in a hard, translucent nugget of Baltic amber, like a pearl, like a splinter wedged beneath a fingernail. Here you are, recorded for future demonologists to summon or puzzle over or merely fear. I need food. I need a goddamn drink.

CHAPTER TWO

Editor's Note: A full twenty-six days elapsed between Sarah Crowe's last entry in that part of the manuscript I've labeled "Chapter One" and the first entry in the section I've titled "Chapter Two." Almost all that is known of her activities and experiences during this hiatus—almost a full month—is what she's chosen to set down on paper. I have confirmed that some of this time was spent at the Tyler Free Library in Moosup Valley, and there were a few emails and phone calls to her agent in New York. Beyond that, we must rely on her account. It should be noted that it was not unusual for Sarah to put a manuscript aside for weeks at a time before returning to it, and, in that respect, the gap is not unexpected, however frustrating it might be to the reader approaching this work as a novel, rather than what can more accurately be described as a journal or diary.

June 25, 2008 (8:37 p.m.)

A fucking hot day today. Only a fool thinks she's escaping the heat of summer by coming to New England. There was rain last night, the first rain in days, but it only seems to have made matters worse. Everything outside the kitchen window is soaked in the scalding-white sun, and the humidity must be at least ninety percent. You live and learn, Miss Crowe, you live and fucking learn.

Two days ago, day before yesterday evening, while trying to escape the heat, I made my first trip down into the cellar of this house. I don't know why it didn't occur to me to do so earlier. The cellar door is just off the kitchen, in a sort of alcove near the hallway that leads to the bedroom and bathroom. It's an exceptionally small doorway, even by the standards of this place. What do you call the top of a doorframe? I know there's a word for it. I measured it with a yardstick I found in the attic. Just an inch more than five feet, top to bottom, so I have to stoop a bit to keep from smacking my head. The ten steps down to the hard-packed dirt floor are narrow, and the cellar air is (no surprise) rank, as you'd imagine. Still, there's no air-conditioning in this dump, and Blanchard won't spring for window units. All I have are two useless box fans I bought in Foster, and, truthfully, it was a waste of good money, because they only manage to stir the hot air round and round. Sweat soup, I would call it. Anyway, I took a chair down there, one of the chairs from the kitchen table, and a flashlight and the book I'm reading. Fortunately, the cellar ceiling is not nearly so low as the doorway down to the cellar, though I've never been claustrophobic. I think that cellar would be a claustrophobic's nightmare. There are shelves heaped and crammed and sagging with the weight with all manner of junk dating back fuck knows how far—decades, more than a century, I can't yet say. And then there's the stuff that's just been piled directly on the floor. I parked my chair near the foot of the stairs and tried not to think about rats, spiders, and toxic mold spores. I'm guessing it was no more than sixty degrees down there, so it was heaven, really, after the broiling oven that this house becomes every afternoon, every night. I ignored the musty air, the stink like dirt and mushrooms and wet newspapers, though it was genuinely cloying.

Anyway, after only a couple of hours, I grew bored with the novel—it really isn't very good, worse than one of mine—and started poking around in the refuse. I think maybe an antiques dealer or a historian would have a field day down there. Then again, there's so much accumulated filth and mildew, deposited in thick, tacky gray strata, perhaps anything of significant value is beyond salvaging at this point. However, I did come across an old manual typewriter buried beneath a bath towel on one of the shelves. The thing weighs, I don't know, I'm guessing twenty or twenty-five pounds, though it was marketed in the forties as a portable. I found one like it on a website devoted to the history of typewriters. It's a 1941 Quiet Deluxe portable, manufactured by the Royal Typewriter Company of Hartford (later known as the Royal McBee Typewriter Company) just like Hemingway used at his home in Key West. "The Snows of Kilimanjaro," *For Whom the Bell Tolls,* and *Death in the Afternoon* were all written on a Royal typewriter of this very same make and model. I saw one in mint condition online for $475, though the one from Blanchard's cellar is, sadly, far from mint.

But it *does* type fairly well, the keys only sticking now and then. Conveniently, there was also a padded manila envelope stored with it, containing several inked silk ribbons that fit the machine. The envelope is lying here beside me. It was shipped from a company called Vintage American Typers from a P.O. box in Burke, Virginia, to a Dr. Charles L. Harvey at the Department of Sociology and Anthropology at the University of Rhode Island's Kingston campus. The Burke postmark is dated January 12, 2003. More than five years ago. There was even a single page still in the typewriter's carriage, a sheet of onionskin paper, cockled finish and all. I don't know if you can even still *buy* onionskin paper. It makes me think of the *Oxford English Dictionary* and Bibles and such. Anyway, the page reads as follows:

something distinctly Fortean about "bloody apple" affair, though I have searched through all four of Fort's books and found no record of the tale in any of them, nor any variant of this phenomenon. Indeed, there is little to go on beyond the article in Yankee (collected in Austin N. Stevens' Mysterious New England; Yankee Books, 1971), though the legend of the tainted "Mikes" appears well-known locally. This one certainly seems right up Mr. Fort's alley, young boys biting into shiny red apples only to discover globules of blood at the cores. Also, there is an echo here of H. P. Lovecraft's short story "The Colour Out of Space," recalling the poisoned orchards of Nahum Gardner following the fall of a meteorite-like object on his farm. Indeed, Lovecraft might well have known of Franklin's "bloody apples," though I can find no direct evidence that he did. The tree from which the apples are said to have grown was purportedly felled by the Great New England Hurricane of 1938, so would have been extant in March 1927 when Lovecraft wrote his story (not published until September of that year, in Amazing Stories; Vol. 2, No. 6, pp. 557-67). In the absence of any document linking the "bloody apples" of the Micah

And yes, it just ends right there, with the name *Micah,* about halfway down the single-spaced page. However, I was fortunate to discover a copy of *Mysterious New England* at the library in Moosup, and, sure enough, the story is on page 156—"Franklin's 'Blood' Apples" by Joseph A. Owens. It corroborates everything on the typed page, which I can only assume must have been written by the same Dr. Harvey to whom the package of ribbons was addressed back in 2003. A nice little mystery, something to take the edge off the monotony of the last month, yeah? Well, it gets better.

Remember that woman at the store on the Plain Woods Road, the one who thought I had a "right" to know about this place's previous tenant, but then wouldn't actually *tell* me what she was talking about? Well, after finding the typewriter and the envelope of ribbons, after reading that page, I put two and two together, whiz-bang, and figured that she must have been speaking of Dr. Charles Harvey, as I'd already been told by Blanchard that the house's former tenant had been a professor at URI. It seemed an unlikely coincidence. *That* professor pretty much *had* to be the same professor who'd written about the blood-filled apples. I googled the guy's name and discovered that, yes, he did live here for almost three years, 2001 to 2003. Harvey was a folklorist and anthropologist with an interest in urban legends and occultism in the Maritime and New England. Born in Eugene, Oregon, in 1942, he received his doctoral from UC Berkeley in 1969. Dr. Harvey was on an extended sabbatical from the university, supposedly writing a book on the evolution and propagation of "fakelore" in Connecticut, Rhode Island, and Massachusetts when he died *here*, in Blanchard's house, on August 7th, 2003. Well, no. Not actually *in* the house, but on the property. The obits were sketchy on details, but it seems he hung himself from a tree somewhere within the boundaries of the Wight Farm. He'd divorced his wife years before, and his only daughter lives up in Maine. That's the stuff I was able to glean from the internet. But I also phoned Blanchard this morning, to tell him I'd likely be a couple of days late on July's rent (still waiting for that damned check from Germany), and, as tactfully as I could, I broached the subject of Charles Harvey. I made notes during the conversation, pretty much a word-for-word transcript of that part of the call:

Me: So, anyway, I just found out about that Harvey fellow, Charles Harvey, the suicide.

(long silence)

Me: The URI professor? Rented the place before me.

Blanchard: Yeah. I know who you mean. The man wasn't right. So, what. You angry I didn't tell you about him?

Me: No, I'm not angry. I'm just curious.

Blanchard: I'm the one found him, you know.

Me: No, I didn't know that. None of the obituaries or articles I found online mentioned that.

Blanchard: Well, ain't like it's the sort of thing they hand out medals for, finding a man strung up in one of your trees. But I did. I found him not far from the house.

Me: *This* house?

Blanchard: Yeah. Used an extension cord, not rope, but it worked just fine. He'd been up there four or five days, the coroner said. That's what they told me. It was hot weather, and that wasn't a pretty thing to come upon. Birds had been at him, and the maggots, and whatnot.

Me: I had no idea.

Blanchard (sounding defensive): Hardly the sort of thing you go around advertising when you want to lease a house. Not the sort of thing attracts the element I want to be renting the place out to.

Me: No, I guess not. Still, you know, it *was* a bit of a shock. I have to admit that.

Blanchard: You're not angry about this, are you?

Me (laughs): No, no. It's fine. Really. I was just curious, that's all. Poor man.

Blanchard: I suppose you gotta have sympathy for situations like that. Still, he wasn't right, and he croaked himself owing me two months back rent. His girl up in Portland offered to pay, but hell, what kind of asshole would I have looked like taking the money from her?

Me: He was writing a book. That's what I read.

Blanchard: Yeah, he was writing a book. You don't come across like the superstitious sort to me, Miss Crowe.

Me: No, I'm not superstitious.

Blanchard: So, sure you're not sore I didn't tell you about him?

Me: I'm sure. Why didn't the daughter take his typewriter with the rest of his belongings?

Blanchard: Daughter didn't take none of his stuff. My wife sent a bunch of it off to the Goodwill, and I just threw most of the rest out. I thought someone might be able to use that typewriter someday, so I put it in the basement.

Me: And the ribbons?

Blanchard: Ribbons? You lost me.

Me: There was an envelope with ribbons for the typewriter. Several of them. I found those, too.

Blanchard: Yeah. There was an envelope. That's right.

Me: So, what happened to his book? The manuscript, I mean. There was a page still in the typewriter. I assume he died with it unfinished.

Blanchard: Listen, Miss Crowe, can we please talk about this later? I don't want to be rude, but I got business over in Wakefield this afternoon, and I'm already running late as it is.

I told him not to worry, that I was probably being nosy and that I hate nosiness, especially when I'm the guilty party. I promised again to have the rent to him by the 10th of the month, and he thanked me for letting him know I'd be late with the check, then hung up first. I switched off the cell phone, and promptly hid it from myself. Maybe I'll find it later. Maybe not. If anyone wants to harass me, they can use the landline.

Anyway, I'm left to conclude that the late Dr. Harvey's unfinished book, in all likelihood, went to the local landfill or a bonfire or whatever, *if* it's true that the daughter in Maine claimed none of his effects. I can't imagine why Blanchard would have lied about something like that. All that survives is that one peculiar page, incomplete reflections on "bloody apples" from a tree that died seventy years ago. I've been thinking about driving down to Connecticut, to Franklin (formerly Norwich), where Micah Hood's cursed fruit is said to have sprouted some three hundred years ago. If I'm lucky, I might can get a magazine article or short story out of this.

And that reminds me, I got the extension on the novel. The extension on the *original* extension. The guillotine will just have to wait another six months. Dorothy's a miracle worker, but I gather my publisher is magnificently displeased, and I've had to promise this will never, ever happen again and so forth. Which is rather like promising you'll never get the flu again, or let it rain on the Fourth of

July. Do they think I'm doing this shit on purpose, just to foul up their publishing schedule? Right now, I'd probably give all the fingers on my left hand (I type mostly with my right) for a finished manuscript to appease my editor and fulfill my contractual obligations. Something I could trade in for a decent goddamn payday. Anyway, maybe if I can give Dorry a short story to peddle, everyone will leave me alone for a while. Also, I think this will be the last entry I make in the notebook. I've got half a mind to dust off Dr. Harvey's old Royal machine, feed it a little oil to loosen up the sticky keys and suchlike, and transcribe everything from the spiral-bound notebook to typescript. It's something to do. And I haven't felt like going near the laptop for anything but the web (mostly porn, I will admit) since I got here.

June 26, 2008 (3:04 p.m.)

Blanchard called at some ungodly hour this morning and woke me up to tell me he's letting the upstairs, the attic, out to some artist from California. What the fuck? I think I actually said that to him. He pointed out that the lease permitted him to do so, that, as it happens, I'd only rented the downstairs portion of the house. I asked him to hold on while I read through the lease, and yeah, the bastard's telling the truth. It's right there, which is what I get for not bothering to read the things I sign before (or after) I sign them. He offered to let me out of my lease, like I have anywhere to go. I declined. I half think he *wants* me to leave. Likely, I'm just being paranoid, but maybe I shouldn't have brought up the subject of the dearly departed Dr. Harvey. The woman arrives next fucking week. So much for solitude.

I have now typed everything from the notebook. It comes to sixty-five pages, all stacked neatly on the table beside me and the bottle of Jack I've been working on since yesterday. From here on, I'll keep this journal—which is what it seems to have become—on the dead man's typewriter and give my pens a rest. I had to drive all the way to Foster to get paper, a pack of five hundred sheets. So, I cannot type more than five hundred pages. Oh, and the woman, this painter from California, is named Constance Hopkins. My luck, she'll be straight. Watch and see.

June 27, 2008 (6:57 p.m.)

Spent most of the day in the basement, hiding from the heat and trying not to think about the imminent arrival of the dreaded attic lodger. Also, I got to thinking that just maybe, when Blanchard stowed the old typewriter and the envelope of ribbons down there, possibly he did the same with the anthropologist's unfinished manuscript. So, hours spent picking through all the moldering junk. I tried to be systematic, beginning at the shelf where I found the typewriter. It wasn't there, just empty Mason jars, cardboard boxes of grimy machine parts, a busted electric fan that surely must have dated back to the twenties, a plastic milk crate filled with bundled copper wiring, three broken claw hammers, and so forth. I moved from one slouching plywood and cinder-block shelf to the next, venturing deeper into the basement than I ever had before. After about an hour and a half, I came across a low archway of fieldstones and mortar, and realized it marked the northern periphery of the house, below the kitchen table. I shone my flashlight through the arch, and it was clear that more shelves, more boxes, more indistinguishable mountains of refuse, lay on the other side. I thought about giving up the search and heading back to the stairs. Surely, Blanchard would have put the manuscript near the typewriter, had he decided to keep the thing (which was beginning to seem unlikely). I lingered there at the place where the house ends, where the merely dank basement seemed to give way to a genuine clamminess. There was a draft, air that was not cool, but cold, cold and unpleasantly damp, leaking through the archway, and I spotted a rusty iron horseshoe mounted on the keystone. A few of the nails had come loose, and it was hanging down, not up, and the first thing I thought of was Blanchard's question on the phone—"You're not a superstitious woman, are you?" or however he phrased it. The remaining nail had a distinctly square head, so I'm guessing that horseshoe's been up there quite some time. There was a red-brown ghost of rust on the granite from when it *had* hung with the two ends pointing upwards towards the ceiling, so the overall impression was of something like an hourglass. I thought of the red bellies of female black widow spiders, and tried to recall if they live as far north as Rhode Island. And then I remembered when Amanda and I went to England (a sort of working vacation), how she'd laughed at me because I wouldn't follow her into some damned abandoned railway tunnel that she wanted to explore. I chickened out and let her go in alone. I looked it up online, the tunnel, before I started writing this entry; it was, in fact, the Morewell Tunnel at Tavistock in West Devon (N 50° 31.154 W 004° 09.997). It had been a passenger rail, closed down since the 1960s, and was overgrown when we visited. There was a gate you had to scale to get inside—to *trespass,* as I'd pointed out to Amanda. She made clucking noises and scrambled nimbly over the chain link.

"All right," she'd said. "But if I break my neck, you're to blame."

I think I told her to get bent, go fuck herself, something like that. Words that only made her laugh harder, her laughter echoing off the tunnel walls as she vanished from sight. That day, the tunnel entrance struck me as an open mouth—the most obvious analogy possible, I suppose. Specifically, I thought of the gaping, open mouths of predatory water things, like snapping turtles and anglerfish, lying in wait for a curious, tasty morsel to come along and have a look inside before those jaws slammed closed. I stood there shivering, while the miserable English sky drizzled, waiting for the tunnel to snap shut. *Are* you superstitious, Sarah Crowe? Maybe just a *little*?

Anyway, the memory of Amanda mocking me that day was enough to get me moving again and through the cellar archway, past that horseshoe, that rust hourglass. The temperature seemed to drop a good ten degrees, and the hard-packed dirt floor gave way to a somewhat muddy, uneven floor, with native rocks showing through, here and there. I shone the flashlight at the ceiling. It was a foot or so lower than in the basement proper, and countless roots and rootlets had penetrated from above, giving it an ugly, hairy appearance.

There was a rough-hewn stone threshold, too, dividing those portions of the basement to the south and north of the archway. It wasn't granite or schist or phyllite or whatever, but some dark, slaty rock that reminded me of the older headstones I've seen in local cemeteries, the picturesque ones dating back to the seventeenth and eighteenth centuries. I kneeled down for a better look, playing the incandescent beam over the stone. I'm going to have to go back with my camera and get some photographs. The damned thing is inscribed with an assortment of crude designs. At first glance, I thought I was just seeing graffiti. Maybe something Blanchard's kids or grandkids had done, or something done, who knows, a hundred, two hundred years ago by someone else's kids. But I quickly recognized a few of the symbols, that they *were* symbols. Astrological, alchemical, Cabbalistic—really a nonsensical jumble, which put me in mind of the hexes you can still see painted on barns in Pennsylvania's Dutch Country. The planetary symbol for both Pluto and Jupiter, various presumably Christian crosses and Hindu swastikas, letters from the Hebrew alphabet, a pentagram—a hodgepodge, as though either some *very* superstitious person had decided to cover all of his or her bases, or, more likely, a teenager armed with a book on the occult. And yeah, sure, I can admit that it gave me the creeps, and yeah, I can also admit I had second thoughts about exploring the darkness beyond the horseshoe-guarded archway. I'm a big girl, and I can admit when something gives me the heebies. And when I'm being silly. But there was Amanda, the fucking ghost of Amanda, my goddamn memories of her standing in the maw of the Morewell Tunnel, laughing at me. I turned away from the threshold, turning, I noted, towards Ramswool Pond, and let the light play across this newfound vacuity below the old farmstead.

I do not believe, at this point, that I was still searching for Dr. Harvey's manuscript. I think, more likely, I was only trying to show myself that Amanda had been wrong all along. That day in Tavistock, and all those other days and nights. I was *not* afraid of the dark, or of the hunger of abandoned places, or, for that matter, of anything else that she might have accused me of. That she is dead (there, I've said it, I've *written* it), and so would always have the last laugh as regards all these little grudges and jabs, hardly seemed relevant. It was not in vain, because if I was proving something to Amanda, I was also proving something to myself. Jesus fuck, Amanda. No one we knew ever believed that there was anything between us but the sex and some virulent allure, my dirty dishwater circling the drain of you. Not a very pretty comparison, but maybe it's the best we'll ever deserve, either one of us. Anyway, I went into that stinking, muddy darkness because, once upon a time, she thought I was a coward. Two little girls bickering because neither of us ever learned to love, and this was my latest chance to give you the finger, Amanda, posthumous though it may be.

The ground made a soft, squelching sound beneath my sneakers, and I slipped once or twice, almost falling. I hastily looked over the contents of the shelf nearest the archway, which held very little besides row after row of ancient canned goods (mostly cucumber pickles, I think, but the fuzzy clots of mold in the jars made it hard to be sure) and disintegrating bales of *The Farmer's Almanac* and *Field and Stream*. I paused, shining my light north, towards the place where the darkness ought to have ended in another wall, probably earthen. But the batteries were getting weak, and the beam would not penetrate that far, however far that might be. And this is when I saw the grimy chifforobe missing all its drawers, sitting just a few feet farther in, and on top of it was a cardboard box, not so different from the manuscript boxes I get from Staples or Office Depot. I grabbed it, suddenly wishing to be anywhere at all but that slimy hole in the world, wanting to be outside, beneath the summer sun again. Better the sweat and glare and stifling, relentless heat than that clinging damp and darkness. I tripped climbing the stairs and have a nice yellow-green bruise on my left shin to show for it. I'm sure, if Amanda *had* a soul, and if it somehow survived her body, she was cackling at panicked, fraidy-cat me from whichever afterlife or underworld she's consigned herself. I bolted the basement door behind me, and sat down on the floor. I actually kicked the cellar door hard, two or three times, leaving muddy footprints that I'm gonna have to wash away. I thought for a moment I was going to knock the goddamned thing off its hinges. It was all anger, the force behind those kicks—anger at my own kid fears and my memories and Amanda's suicide and the goddamn overdue novel I'm not getting written. I lay on the floor a while, grateful for the muggy kitchen, the stagnant air that did not stink of mold. I lay there until my heart stopped racing. And then I sat up and looked inside the box.

It was taped shut, but most of the adhesive had dried out long ago, and I didn't need a knife to get it open. Inside was page after page of the same onionskin paper I'd found in the Royal's carriage, and so there I was, returned fucking victorious from my own personal katabasis, Hecate back from the bloody bowels of hell with rescued Persephone, what the fuck ever. I'd done the deed, and now I held the prize, and seeing it there, my fury quickly, calmly, melted away. Not caring that my dirty fingers would leave smudges, I lifted the first page from the box, and then the second, and then the third, reading over them as quickly as I could. After maybe ten or fifteen minutes, I finally had the presence of mind to get up and carry the box to the kitchen table, where, after half a decade, I reunited it with Harvey's typewriter.

I got a beer from the refrigerator (because, already, the heat was feeling a lot less welcome than I'd imagined it would be while I was still in the basement) and then sat down to reread, more carefully, those first few pages. The first was simply a title page—THE RED TREE by Dr. Charles L. Harvey and all that. The usual. The second page was occupied by two epigraphs, one from Thoreau, the other from Seneca the Elder. Neither meant very much to me, but perhaps they will later, once I've had a chance to get through the manuscript. The third page was blank, but the fourth bore the heading—CHAPTER ONE: THE CURSED ACORN—only THE CURSED ACORN was crossed out (~~THE CURSED ACORN~~), and a string of question marks had been scrawled in directly above it in red ink. I sat there, sipping at my beer, the amber bottle perspiring and growing slick in my hand. Despite the things I'd read online, nothing *here,* before me, pointed to Harvey's unfinished book being a study of regional "fakelore." Rather, it looked to be concerned with local traditions regarding a tree on the plot of land now known as the Wight place. What's more, it quickly became evident that this tradition amounted to stories of murder, witchcraft, lycanthropy, cannibalism, and a miscellany of other unpleasantries, dating back to the first decade of the Eighteenth Century. Scanning those thin, hand-corrected pages, the typescript and Harvey's annotations, I got goose bumps—swear to fuck, I truly did—and found myself pausing repeatedly to glance out the window at the farmland gone fallow and brushy, the oaks and pines pressing in around the dark expanse of Ramswool Pond.

Hardly the sort of shit you advertise when you're trying to rent out a house, indeed.

June 28, 2008 (4:47 a.m.)

Jesus fuck, the goddamn nightmares. Screw the seizures. Please just give me a pill for these goddamned bad dreams.

I awoke from one about fifteen minutes ago, and stumbled out here from the bedroom for a drink (bourbon, yes, but I did cut it with water). I stood at the big window in the den for a few minutes, watching the eastern sky. The birds are awake and chittering away in the trees and bushes, and I know the sun will be along before too much longer—already, the sky is lightening—but the way I feel right now, soon can't come soon enough. Maybe it *won't* be so bad having someone else in the house, even an artist from California. Even if she's straight.

So, yeah, here I sit, typing on Harvey's Royal after a measly four hours' sleep. Not sleeping is one of the triggers; for the fits, I mean, so this can't become a habit. I *have* to sleep, bad dreams or no bad dreams. I have to sleep, but I just couldn't stay in bed after that, couldn't say "Fuck it" and pop another Ambien. I need to be awake. I need to be awake and in *this* world. And I think I really am going to write down what I can recall about the dream, with the dimmest hope that it will loosen its grip on me. I *know* I am awake now, and not merely stranded in some mundane intermission between one terror and the next. I *know* the sun is coming. I know I can get a nap later, when the day is all around me, and I don't have to go back down to sleep beneath the starry canopy of the fucking night.

It's another oft-cited, so-called weakness of my writing, by the way. All the dream sequences. The "reliance" on dream sequences, and, some of the stuff I've seen said, you'd think I'd *invented* the blasted things. As though the reviewers (and here I refer particularly to those self-styled reviewers who leave comments at Amazon and suchlike) have managed to get through high school and college (big assumption here, I admit) without ever encountering such a basic narrative technique. Let them pick on Pushkin or Shaw or Mary Shelley or goddamn Shakespeare and leave *my* sorry midlist ass the hell alone. I've actually had my agent suggest that my novels would come across as more accessible and I might increase my readership if I avoided so many dream sequences. And I am appalled at authors and critics alike who brand the use of dreams in fiction as a "cheat," used only by writers who cannot "figure out," in a waking narrative, some other means of saying what he or she has to say.

This attitude denies so much of . . . yes, I have digressed, and I am on my goddamned soapbox. But, honestly, honestly . . . I have lost track of the times readers have complained that they couldn't follow the "story" because they weren't clear what was "really happening" and what was "only" a dream. Right now, from where I fucking sit, it's all a dream, marked by varying degrees of lucidity. Get with the program or stick to television (though, it must be noted that film and TV rely very, very heavily on dream sequences, so you'd think—if for no other reason—the lowest common denominator would have long since become accustomed or desensitized or whatever to writers employing dreams to expand and further the story). Whatever. I did *not* sit down here to complain about readers who cannot be bothered to be literate. Yeats said (and this one I know from memory, and let it stand as my sleep-addled defense, if any defense is needed):

I have spread my dreams beneath your feet;
Tread softly because you tread on my dreams.

Outside, the sky continues to brighten. The sky is the color of blueberry yogurt. Harvey's unfinished manuscript is still in its box, here beside the typewriter. I've read the first two chapters. And that probably wasn't so terribly bright of me, not after I figured out what his book is about, but curiosity and cats and all that. My dreams be damned, how would I *not* read it?

Look at this. Two and a half pages already, and I've managed not to get to the point. I have managed to *skirt* the point, to dance around the *periphery* of the point. Stop writing about dreams, Sarah, and writing *about* writing about dreams, and just *write* the dream.

The sky is going milky. . . .

I cannot recall the beginning of it, but I was back in the basement with my flashlight. I know that I wasn't looking for Harvey's manuscript, because I clearly recall setting it down on one of the sagging shelves of pickles or machine parts or whatever, so I'd have a hand free. I was on the other side of the archway, past that odd threshold and its preposterous array of glyphs. I was somewhere past the threshold, trying to locate the north wall of the basement, pacing off my steps, one after the other, doing my best not to lose track and have to start over again. I realized that I must have walked very far beyond the house, and the footing beneath me grew increasingly wet. There were stagnant pools of black water standing here and there, pools whose depth it was impossible to judge, and I did my best not to step too near any of them. They seemed . . . unwholesome. Yes, that's the word. Of course, truthfully, the whole damned place seemed unwholesome, as if I had somehow stumbled into an actual gangrenous abscess in the ground, a geological infection that had hollowed out this cavity below and within Blanchard's land.

Here, where the pools of water began, there were far fewer shelves, and all of them contained nothing but antique books, volumes swollen from the moisture, their covers warped and spines splitting open like overripe berries. I did not stop to examine them, to learn any of their titles. I didn't want to know, any more than I wanted to approach those motionless obsidian puddles. And this is when I realized that I was not alone. I heard footsteps first, and looking over my shoulder, I saw Amanda. Only, in death (and she *was* dead, of that I am certain) she had taken on aspects of various of her photomontages, the sick fantasies of her pervert clients. She had the ridged and lyre-shaped horns of a male impala sprouting from her skull, and her eyes were as black as the pools of stagnant water. When she came closer, I could see that her cheeks and the backs of her hands were flushed with tiny scales that appeared to shimmer with some internal light all their own.

"Changed your mind, did you?" she asked, and when I nodded yes, she laughed—and it was so much *her* laugh, in no way distorted by the dream. It was simply Amanda laughing, and I was grateful to hear it again. And then she asked, "So, was it inquisitiveness, or was it peer pressure? Or maybe you just got to thinking I wouldn't want to fuck a woman who was afraid of the dark."

"I am *not* afraid of the dark," I replied, a little too emphatically. "It isn't safe down here. They seal these places for a reason."

"So, you've come to *save* me?" and she laughed again, but the sound was neither as pure nor as welcome as before. "Are you my Lancelot? Are you the kindly huntsman come to rescue me from all the big bad wolves?"

And I told her no, it wasn't anything like that, that I was only trying to find the north wall of the basement, because I knew it had to be there somewhere. I explained that if there were no north wall, then there'd be nothing to hold back Ramswool Pond. And since the basement clearly wasn't flooded, it stood to reason the wall was there somewhere.

She shrugged and pointed at one of the puddles, not far from her muddy, bare feet. "You never can tell," she said, "what goes on down below. Given any thought to where these fuckers might lead?"

"They're mud holes," I replied, growing impatient with the argumentative ghost of my argumentative lover. "They don't lead anywhere."

She smiled the sort of smile that maybe dead people commonly smile, and said, "You always were a woman of unfounded assumptions, Sarah."

And around us, then, suddenly there were fireflies, and swirling motes of unidentifiable bioluminescence that seemed to make the darkness no less dark. The ceiling of the basement was draped with more than roots, I saw, with the sticky silken threads of larval glow worms, and I imagined there were zodiac constellations drawn in the arrangement of their deadly lures. Amanda held up her arms, as though she'd summoned this swarm, as though she worshipped or made herself an offering to it. And the basement had, I saw, grown into a cavern, something straight out of *A Journey to the Center of the Earth,* and forests of oyster-colored mushrooms the size of redwoods towered all around us. I heard the crashing waves of a not-so-distant sea, and Amanda sat down on a rock, and, slowly, she lowered her arms.

"So, what. You think this is usual?" she asked me, or some question very near to that, and I turned, trying to see the way back to the arch, and, past that, the foot of the stairs leading to a place that was only a basement.

"I don't know what I think anymore," I lied.

"Perhaps you ought to put it back," and I knew she meant the manuscript, Harvey's manuscript, without having to ask. "Perhaps you're not ready for this."

"That's not for you to say," I told her.

"And the typewriter, too," she continued, as though I'd not even spoken. She did that a lot, when we were both alive. "It can't be healthy, Sarah, having it around like this, *working* with it, a thing that has recently borne such strange fruit." And if her allusion was lost on me in the dream, it's not lost on me now.

The impala horns abruptly dropped from her head, and where they'd been nothing was left but two bloody stumps. She sat looking at them, the horns, and her expression was not so much sad as wistful, I think.

"Kind of makes you wonder," she said, nodding at the shed horns. I waited for her to elaborate, but she never did. And I saw then that a variety of pale fungi had begun to sprout from her flesh, from her jeans and T-shirt, not so much devouring as simply *augmenting*, and I knew that, in this dream, I was neither a knight-errant nor a woodsman who saves lost girls from hungry wolves . . . nor from parasitic toadstools and yeasts, molds and agarics. I had already told her that, but as I watched Amanda's body slowly, steadily bloom with the progeny of unseen spores, any doubt I might have harbored in this regard vanished.

There was more, what seems like hours and hours more, a roiling tumble of nonsense and phantasmagoria, a flight through that subterranean forest to the shores of Verne's *Mare Internum*, his Liedenbrock Sea, perhaps. It may be I sailed a plesiosaur-infested ocean, or maybe I only sat on that alien shore, gazing up at a sunless, electric sky. But, however it proceeded, I don't think I'm up to writing the rest. Whatever I might remember of the rest. The compulsion that drove me from my bed to this chair and the typewriter of Dr. Harvey has deserted me.

Since coming here, I have written two dreams, and damned little else, and in each one, of course, I encounter you, Amanda. In each one, I have no say in what becomes of you, so, in that respect, at least these are true dreams.

Then again, in each one, you seem somehow imperiled, when I find it hard to believe there was ever any threat to you beyond your own penchant for self-destruction. So, paradoxically, the dreams may also be lies. Or both things are equally true—a particle and a wave, as it were—and I'm only being narrow-minded. A woman of unfounded assumptions, a woman of either-or.

But sitting here, watching the day coming on—a morning pregnant with the promises of yet another scorcher—it occurs to me that perhaps I should consider passing Harvey's manuscript along to someone. I really don't know who. Perhaps URI would want it, some former colleague or his department or the library or something, if his daughter in Maine truly has no interest. I surely do not need this new source of morbidity. I brought more than enough here *with* me. Maybe today I'll try to call the university. I could drive it over, the manuscript, if there's anyone there who wants it. If no one at the school is interested, maybe I'll contact Brown or the Providence Athenaeum. At this point, I'd appreciate what I could deem a valid excuse to blow a tank of gas on the road trip and get away from this place for a day. And I can't imagine that Blanchard would mind my getting rid of the manuscript. Not that I'll bother to ask him, not after the way he's foisted this new impending upstairs neighbor upon me. I googled her, by the by, and got nothing at all.

I suppose I could even try to track down the daughter; I doubt it would be very hard to do. I have her name from the obits. But there's something, I think, inherently creepy and stalkerish about doing that. Unless Blanchard's lying, she had a chance to claim her father's work and passed. Who knows what that relationship was like? Maybe she's glad the old man croaked himself, and maybe she even has a *right* to be. Maybe he was a complete bastard, and the last thing she needs is some stranger butting in. It just seems somehow wrong that this manuscript has languished in the basement of a farmhouse for half a decade. Then again, this all supposes there's something here worth saving. But I suspect I'm hardly qualified to make that call, and the same is likely true of Dr. Harvey's disinterested daughter.

I need coffee. I need coffee, and I need to drive into Coventry for groceries. I'm down to my last can of Campbell's Chicken and Stars soup and a little bit of peanut butter. And I'm awake now, and the sun is shining. I'm bleary as hell, and maybe the slightest bit drunk, but at least the damned dream has stopped feeling like anything more than another permutation of the Nightmare.

June 29, 2008 (10:27 p.m.)

The first bad seizure yesterday since leaving Atlanta. In Which Our Heroine is Lulled into a False Sense of Security. Yes, I've been drinking since I got here, a little, but I've been religious about my meds, and I think I had actually allowed myself to believe that shit was over and done with. Then, yesterday evening, after I got back from the market, after the trip to Coventry, I was washing dishes and . . . it occurs to me, now, I've never tried to describe one of these things. Vincent van Gogh, my favorite fellow epileptic, wrote in a letter to his brother, Theo:

> *"In my mental or nervous fever, or madness—I am not too sure how to put it or what to call it—my thoughts sailed over many seas. I even dreamed of the phantom Dutch ship and of Le Horla, and it seems that, while thinking what the woman rocking the cradle sang to rock the sailors to sleep, I, who on occasions cannot sing a note, came out with an old nursery tune, something I had tried to express in an arrangement of colours before I fell ill, because I don't know the music of Berlioz."*

Hell, that makes it seem almost a desirable experience. Me, I have nothing so romantic nor pleasant to report. I was standing at the kitchen sink, setting the coffee cups out to dry on a dish towel, and then I was lying on the floor, staring up at the ceiling. Maybe ten minutes had passed. There was a small cut on my left hand from a broken cup, and I'd bitten my lip pretty badly, so my mouth tasted like blood. I lay there for a while, because sometimes they come in clusters. Sometimes it's BAM—BAM—BAM. I lay there feeling sick and hungover and disoriented, dazed, stupid. I lay there, thinking about the *first* time, the first time to my knowledge, at least, and how badly it scared Amanda. I think it scared her a whole lot more than it scared me. She cried. It wasn't the only time I saw her cry, but it *was* one of the few times. She told me she thought that I was dying, and then there were all the goddamn specialists and tests I didn't have health insurance to cover, and that's what she *should* have cried over. I spent most of the evening on the sofa, feeling Not Quite Right. I watched television and tried to read. I fell asleep and woke hours later with a crick in my neck, but feeling somewhat less strung-out.

Anyway, enough about that, the raging electrical storms behind my eyes. I thought maybe I had something to say here, something to match the grand dreamquest of Monsieur Vincent van Gogh, but I don't. I have a broken cup, a bandage on my hand, a swollen lip, a few bruises . . . missing time. I have the knowledge that this *thing* is still with me, this shaking malady, my tarantella, and I can sit here all night long wondering what part it played in Amanda's death, and what part it is playing now in my inability to write anything more than these meandering entries on the typewriter of Dr. Harvey. For the first time since coming to this house, I wish there were someone else with me. Right now, for whatever reason, I don't want to be alone. It's not so much the fear, though I'd be lying if I said I'm not scared. I'm sick of my own company. I am weary of my own voice, of talking to myself, of talking and there being no one to answer me, but me. Then again, it's really nothing I haven't earned.

30 June 2008 (3:12 p.m.)

I spent the better part of the morning on the phone, mostly with people at URI, trying to find a final resting place for the manuscript. After being passed from one office to another to another and back again, from one secretary or administrative assistant or grad student or professor to another, round and round the goddamn mulberry bush, I finally found someone in the Dept. of Sociology and Anthropology interested in the manuscript. Only, she's leaving for a vacation tomorrow and won't be back in until after the Fourth, but I don't suppose that matters a great deal. The box sat in the dank and the dark on that chifforobe for five years. Another week's hardly going to make much difference. And it gives me time to finish reading the thing, even if Dr. Harvey couldn't been bothered to finish writing it before stringing himself up. It's grimly fascinating stuff, as promised by that first page I found, the bit about the "bloody apples." Oh, sure, it's grim stuff I no doubt shouldn't *be* reading, out here with only the woods and the deer and my fits for company, but if I pretend it's only fiction, how does it differ from any number of the novels in that stack I have not yet managed to read? I'm tempted to have it photocopied at the library in Moosup, just so I'll have a record. I'm certainly not going to sit here and retype the whole damned thing. But I will transcribe the following passage, from Chapter One, because it gets straight to the heart of the matter, and I'll confess it's made me start thinking about looking for some other place to live (though the Coming of the Attic Artist already had me thinking along those lines). Harvey writes (on page 8 of the manuscript):

I will admit, since taking up residence here, I have considered on more than one occasion simply cutting the damned thing down myself. There is a chain saw at my disposal. I have thought of burning the tree, or salting the earth at its roots. But it is only a tree, I remind myself, and these are only stories. There are days and nights when I have given my imagination freer rein than is healthy, evenings when I've spent too long trying to tease history from legend, truth from fancy. Is it only the power of suggestion, having read these letters, diaries, and newspaper accounts, that leave me lying awake at night, listening (though for what I cannot say)? Is it only having so submerged myself in the native lore surrounding the oak that repeatedly draws me down to sit on the wall nearest it and contemplate the seemingly purposeful interweave of those monstrous roots?

And, as long as I'm typing this, I may as well also include *this,* from ms. pages 3–5:

In this case, my personal introduction to the curious and often grisly lore surrounding the 'Red Tree of Barbs Hill' is the odd story of William Ames, second son of a wealthy English merchant. Following his father's death, Ames emigrated from Weymouth to Boston in 1832, seeking his fortune in America. He soon found himself in Providence, having invested a considerable portion of his inheritance in one of the many new cotton mills springing up across New England in the wake of Samuel Slater's refinements to the design of the water-powered spinning mill (1793). By all accounts, this enterprise was a great success, securing Ames a position among the city's industrial elite. It is something of a mystery, then, why, in October 1836, William Ames sold his interest in the mill to his partners, having decided, instead, to try his hand at agriculture in the western part of the state. He purchased a large tract of land just south of Moosup, and built a house there on the foundation of an older house (indeed, the very same house in which I am composing this book).

There is little information regarding Ames' life after his departure from Providence, though it seems that his farming endeavors met with far less success than his milling venture. He married a local woman, Susan Beth Vaughan of Foster, in 1838, but their marriage was to be a short and troubled one. Unable to bear her husband children, Susan Ames became a distant, melancholy, and sickly woman, and in August 1840, William woke one morning in an empty bed to discover that his wife had vanished from their home. An extensive search of the surrounding countryside was organized, but failed to turn up any evidence of her whereabouts or fate. There was a rumor that Susan had run away with a whisky salesman from Philadelphia, but Ames dismissed this story, insisting that he could hear his wife calling out to him at night. He reported that her plaintive cries were especially distinct near an old oak growing on the property, and a second, smaller search party was organized. Again, no trace of the woman was found, and despite her husband's persistant claims, no one else was able to hear her nightly wailing but William Ames.

According to an account of his death, "Horror from Moosup Valley," published in the Providence Journal, Ames also reported a "great wild beast, larger than any wolf or panther" roaming about his property, which left "scat and terrible marks from its talons" on his doors. The creature was seen more than once (but only by Ames) in the company of a woman he believed to be Susan Ames. Finally, less than a month after his wife's disappearance, the farmer and former mill owner's body was found beneath the same oak where he'd reported to his neighbors having so clearly heard Susan calling out to him for help. His corpse was mauled almost beyond recognition and had been partly eaten, and a subsequent hunt for his killer ended when a young timber wolf was shot just south of Ames' property. Its belly was opened, but the Providence Journal article fails to record if human remains were found therein, stating only that the locals were "satisfied" they'd found the culprit responsible for the deaths of both Ames and his wife."

Like I said, grim reading. And the more of it I read, the more my mind fills up with questions. For example, exactly how old *is* this house, did this Ames fellow actually build it, and if it was constructed on a preexisting foundation, then how old is *that* structure? And is the basement (including the muddy area north of the archway where I found the manuscript) part of the original foundation, or was it dug later by William Ames in the 1830s? I suspect that these are questions that can be easily answered by the librarians at the Tyler Free Library, which is where I shall direct them next time I'm up that way, when I drop by to have Harvey's ms. copied before handing it over to the folks at URI.

Looking back over what I said before typing out the two quotations, I can't believe that I actually said this business about a "red tree" on Blanchard's land has me considering whether or not I should be scouting for a new place to live. Pull yourself together, old woman. This is New England, and you can't swing a dead cat without smacking a ghost or a haint or whatever. Worry about paying next month's rent, not about pulling up stakes because the local folktales have you spooked.

July 2, 2008 (11:24 p.m.)

There was some sort of minor delay in the arrival of the Dreaded Attic Lodger, buying me an extra day or two of privacy before the invasion. But she's coming tomorrow, or so I have been informed by the ever so thoughtful Mr. Blanchard. Thursday afternoon, he said. And Squire Blanchard wanted to know if, by any chance, I'd be around, just in case she had questions or needed help with this or that or what the hell ever.

I told him, "I feel it's my solemn duty to inform you

I'm not much of a Welcome Wagon. In fact, I might be the opposite."

He laughed, even though I hadn't, and then there was a long, uncomfortable pause in our conversation. I really do think he's beginning to regret having rented this dump to me. Also, I was warned that he'd hired some Mexicans to clean out the attic (I can only assume that if the lodger *had* arrived on time, she'd have been greeted by the dust and clutter I encountered up there the day I found the measuring stick). As promised, the cleaning crew showed up this afternoon, two men and one woman, and near as I can tell, they spoke not one word of English between the three of them. What I've retained from my two years of high-school Spanish barely allows me to order a taco and ask directions to the toilet. Quisiera un taco, por favor. Dónde está el tocador? Dónde está lavabo? Yeah . . . well, my language skills, my one purported talent, have never strayed particularly toward any foreign tongue (of course, there are plenty enough readers and reviewers who would argue I'm not so hot with English, either).

Anyway, the men hauled toolboxes, sheets of plywood, and some huge-ass shop-vac contraption up there, and before long the noise from all that hammering and shouting and vacuuming was intolerable. So I cleared out, deciding it was as good a time as any to visit Dr. Harvey's apparently infamous tree. The manuscript places "the red oak" only seventy-five yards north of the house, just a few meters east of the low fieldstone wall that runs along much of the length of the creek flowing south out of Ramswool Pond.

And, reading that, I realized the tree is within easy view of the goddamn kitchen window, that I've been *staring* at the thing for two months now with no idea whatsoever that it was anything more significant than the Very Big Tree between the house and the pond. So, not much of an adventure, except there's a tiny wilderness of briars and poison ivy that begins just beyond the back stoop.

Do New Englander's *have* stoops?

It was sunny, not more than a wisp of cloud in sight, and there was a nice breeze, so it seemed like a good day for a walk. And almost anything would have been preferable to the deafening roar of the shop vac and the pounding hammers. I pulled on the leather boots I rarely wear, a long-sleeve T-shirt (despite the heat), a pair of jeans, and grabbed a bottle of water from the fridge. I spritzed myself with tick repellant and smeared some sunscreen on my face. Then I lingered a moment in the kitchen doorway, looking out across and through the undergrowth towards that huge tree, its upper boughs silhouetted against the blue sky, wondering how many times during the past two months I've seen it, how many times I'd sat staring directly at it, and I considered how Dr. Harvey's text had changed a tree into an object of . . . what word would be appropriate? There's a quote from Joseph Campbell that I've always loved, and it seems to apply here: "Draw a circle around a stone and thereafter the stone will become an incarnation of mystery." Or something to that effect. Clearly, to my mind, a circle had been drawn about that old tree, and no matter how many times I'd already seen it, no matter how ordinary a tree it might in fact be, the story of doomed William and Susan Ames and everything else I'd read in those pages had traced a circle about the oak (and I'm sure Campbell would have agreed that if it's true for a stone, it's true for a tree).

I had only a little more trouble reaching it than I'd expected. The poison ivy is fucking rampant, and though I've never been allergic to it, not to my knowledge, there's always a first time. Also, about halfway to the tree, the wall's collapsed, and the "path" is blocked by a deadfall of jagged pine branches that I wasn't about to try to go over or through. Instead, I crossed the shallow creek, skirting the jackstraw tangle of branches and tumbled stones. My feet got muddy, and then climbing back over the stone wall where it resumed north of the deadfall got me to speculating on what sorts of poisonous snakes lurk in those woods (turns out, thank you, internet, there's some confusion over whether or not there are any venomous snakes in Rhode Island; there might be copperheads and timber rattlers, but, then again, there might not). I spotted a couple of rabbits, a doe, and almost twisted my ankle two or three times. By the time I reached the tree, it was nearly four p.m., and I was mosquito bitten and drenched in sweat. There's a large slab of rock at the base of the tree, and I sat down on it to get my breath and wipe away some of the sweat stinging my eyes. It's harder to see the house from the tree than it is to see the tree from the house, and I assume this is the result of some vagary of topography and vegetation.

At any rate, all in all, the tree was a disappointment.

Not much of a mystery, no matter how many circles Harvey and the local yokels might have drawn around it. It's big, sure. Huge, really. But . . . that was that. A huge oak tree. I was underwhelmed—though, honestly, what had I expected? To hear the ghostly, disembodied voice of lost and presumably wolf-gnawed Susan Ames calling out to me across a hundred and sixty-eight years? I was too tired to even think of heading back right off, so I lay down on the wide slab of granite or whichever brand of igneous rock is exposed at the base of the tree, and just lay there a while, staring up into the branches. There were catbirds, and they fluttered about and scolded me for intruding upon whatever secret catbird affairs they conduct out there. Truthfully, despite the sweat and the scratches from greenbriers, despite the bug bites, it was nice being there beneath the tree. So what if it has a bit of a bad reputation. So do I. In fact, I suspect I could have fallen asleep there, if not for all the noise the catbirds were making. Certainly, Harvey's talk of cutting the tree down or burning it—his evident *fear* of it—seemed entirely absurd, lying there, sheltered from the sun by its broad, whispering leaves.

When I'd gotten my second wind, I sat up and examined the oak a little closer. The roots are genuinely impressive, enormous, like gnarled, arthritic fingers digging into the soil and ferns and detritus of the forest floor. It was impossible not to be reminded of Tolkien's ents, and, in particular, of Old Man Willow snaring Merry and Pippin in the crushing folds of its trunk, but even these thoughts, of that cunning, black-hearted tree in Bombadil's Old Forest, failed to elicit from me any actual dread of "the red oak." A little awe, maybe, that this great tree still stood after all these long decades, after centuries, seemingly impervious to the ravages of time. I walked about its periphery, and found a few places where people had carved initials and dates into the wood. I'll have to go back and write them down. The only one I recall offhand is "1888," which I assume was carved into the bark more than forty years after the whole Ames affair had supposedly occurred.

It's getting late. I should take my pills and go to bed. I have no idea what time that woman will actually show up tomorrow. I ought to get up early and head for Providence or Newport, stay gone a few days and let her wonder, let Blanchard worry about whatever questions she might have. But what I *ought* to do and what I *do* are very rarely ever one and the same.

CHAPTER THREE

July 4, 2008 (2:04 a.m.)

Constance Hopkins was born not far to the south of here, born and raised in some little slip of a once-was town called Greene that I might well have driven through two or three times now, but I'll be damned if I can recall the place. She says it was originally named Coffin Corner, until the paternal grandfather of H. P. Lovecraft, Whipple Phillips, bought pretty much the whole village back in the 1850s and renamed it after Nathaniel Greene, the Revolutionary War hero. In the Nineteenth Century, Greene was an important stopping point along the railroad, but then Henry Ford showed up and fixed that good and proper. Now I gather it's hardly even a town at all. I didn't ask her why the place had originally been named Coffin Corner, and she didn't volunteer the information, so maybe she doesn't know, either. Maybe it's one of those things that nobody remembers. Maybe it's a memory that's been entrusted to a crumbling bit of paper in a library book somewhere.

She showed up around two, driving a rented PT Cruiser, and the car was almost the same color as the summer sky. Almost that exact same shade of blue. I walked down to meet her at the footbridge that fords the creek from Ramswool Pond, and, I'll admit, at the time, I wasn't thinking about much more than how maybe I should at least make an effort not to be a bitch. Fake it. Affect a neighborly attitude, because it wouldn't kill me, and the last thing I need right now is Squire Blanchard deciding I'm more trouble than I'm worth. For all I know, this woman can actually pay her rent on time, and maybe she'll up and decide she wants to lease the whole damn house out from under me. So, yeah, stuff a cork in it and play nice.

She had a bunch of cardboard boxes and some mismatched suitcases, along with an assortment of stuff you'd expect the artist who's going to take up residence above your head to arrive with. Two huge wooden easels, for example. I introduced myself, and then helped her lug some of her things back to the house, things she didn't want sitting out in the hot car—paints and art supplies, several rolled canvases, a plastic milk crate of old LPs. I quickly showed her around the first floor, including the bathroom we will now be sharing, and ended up at the steep, narrow flight of stairs leading to the attic.

"Bet it's hot as fuck all up there," she said, squinting into the gloom gathered at the top of the staircase, the gloom and the heat crouched so thickly you could almost see it, and I think I just nodded.

"I don't suppose you've got beer?" she asked me. "A *cold* beer?"

"I think I probably can fix you up," I said, and we left her things at the foot of the stairs and backtracked to the kitchen. I'm trying to develop a taste for Narragansett, and there was a whole six-pack in the icebox and two bottles left over from another. I opened one for her, and a second bottle for myself, and pointed at the table and chairs by the window.

"Try to excuse the mess. Try hard," I said, and she laughed.

I don't exactly recall now what it was I'd expected from this woman, whatever preconceptions and images I might have formed of her in my mind's eye. But whatever it was, Constance Hopkins entirely defied and negated my expectations. I think I'd call her striking even if I *weren't* a lesbian. And I think I'd call her beautiful, too. Not the sort of beauty you see these days, touted in magazines and on television. That calculated, cookie-cutter glamour of the dull that so many people seem, increasingly, to gravitate towards. Hers is not the sort of face that would ever get lost in a crowd, and sitting here now, I'm not at all confident I can explain what it is about her that leaves me with this impression. Her eyes have some odd, drowsy quality about them—unfocused, distant—but it's nothing that suggests a lack of alertness. They're a very particular shade of reddish brown. Maybe I'd call it cinnamon. Or rust. I don't think I've ever seen eyes like hers before. That color, I mean. Her complexion is pale, but not at all pasty. Her hair is jet black and straight, and she was wearing it pulled back in a long ponytail. Sitting there, drinking beer with her, talking, I noticed there's a very small chip out of one of her upper incisors. I wanted to ask her how that had happened, but I didn't. Maybe later.

"You smoke?" she asked, and nodded at the ashtray on the table, near Dr. Harvey's typewriter. It was half-full of butts and ash, because I hadn't emptied it in a couple of days.

"Yeah, well . . . I *was* quit, you know, but now it seems like I'm not so quit anymore."

"So you don't mind if I smoke?"

"No, I don't mind in the least," I replied, and she fished a pack of Camels out of the bulging leather shoulder bag she carries for a purse. The Camels and a pink disposable Bic lighter, and she offered me one of the cigarettes, which I gladly accepted. She lit it for me, and then sat staring silently out the kitchen window for a minute or so. It was a silence that was beginning to grow uncomfortable, when she said, "I like your books. The novels. Your short stories are better written, though. But, I never would have guessed that you wrote *anything* on something like that," and, with her cigarette, she pointed at the antique typewriter. Suddenly, I was flustered, disarmed, whatever you want to call it, left feeling as though I ought be simultaneously thanking her for the compliment (as it happens, I like my short fiction better, too), apologizing for the old dreadnaught of a typewriter, *and* explaining that I normally work on a laptop. Instead, I just nodded and took another long drag on my own cigarette.

"We don't have to talk about it, Sarah, not if you would prefer not to," she said.

"Well, then," I replied. "In that case, I would prefer not to, thank you."

"I know how it goes," she told me, and sort of half smiled. "Or, how it doesn't *come,* as the case may be."

"So, you drove all the way from Los Angeles?" I asked, changing the subject, though I'd already asked her that same question outside, and she'd already answered it. And never mind that Blanchard had told me she was driving; it was something to say, words to fill in empty space, misdirection, and the only thing I could think of.

"I like to drive," she said. "I hate planes. Even before 9/11 and all this security crap, I hated planes. When I go somewhere, I want to *see* where it is I'm going, all the places I pass through on the way there. You know what I mean?"

I told her that I did, even though I suspected I actually didn't understand, at all. I've always despised long drives, ever since I was a kid and it was my father's idea of Sunday afternoon recreation. Just driving. Driving nowhere at all. Back before the oil crisis in '73, when gas was, what, thirty or forty cents a gallon. Constance Hopkins smoked her cigarette and watched the window, watched the bright, shimmering summer day *outside* the window, and I smoked mine and watched her, trying hard not to be too obvious about it. Trying not to stare. Trying hard. I asked her how it had gone, the drive from LA, and she shrugged and smoke leaked from her nostrils.

"Fine, except for the fucking breakdown in Gary."

"Indiana?" I asked, immediately wishing that I'd said nothing at all, becoming all too acutely aware that my questions and replies were suffering from my unexpected fascination with this woman whom I'd expected would be nothing but an inconvenience.

"Yeah, Indiana. Only Gary I've ever had the misfortune to be stuck in. Car blew a head gasket or cracked a cylinder or something of the sort, and there was a mix-up getting a replacement. Added an extra day, waiting around while they sorted it out."

"But otherwise?"

Constance looked away from the window, those drowsy red-brown eyes shifting towards me, and she nodded. "Fourteen states in less than a week. My second grand tour of Flyover Country. May I never, ever have to do it again." She crossed herself, then smiled and took another sip of her beer, before setting the bottle down on the table. And, turning back to the window, as though the unexpected had become the order of the day, she said the very last thing I was prepared to hear.

"So, I suppose you know all about that old tree out there?" and she smiled again and jabbed an index finger towards the kitchen window. I laughed out loud, a nervous, somewhat unsettled laugh, I suppose, and realized that my bottle was empty, and my mouth had gone very dry.

"Not like it's some sort of big secret," she said, sounding amused. "Just part of that whole local legend scene, the crap you know by heart 'cause you grew up hearing it all the time. Well, if you grew up around here, I mean," and she paused long enough to tap her cigarette against the edge of the ashtray. "Mercy Brown and the plague of consumptive vampires, all the phantoms, witches, ghost towns, shunned pastures, the haunted cemeteries, and whatnot. The usual New England spookfest. Hell, there's even supposed to be some sort of swamp monster lurking about in a bog up around Gloucester or Chepachet."

"Chepachet?" I asked, and she shrugged.

"Sure. Not all that far from here."

"Well, okay, but the tree was news to *me*. Want another beer?" I asked her, and she glanced at her bottle, still almost a third full, but gone warm, and she nodded. I stood and walked across the room to the icebox.

"Old man Blanchard didn't bother mentioning it, before you signed the lease?" she asked.

"No. Must have slipped his mind," I said, opening the bottles and returning to my seat, handing one to her. "I had no idea I'd rented a house on a haunted farm. Or that the last tenant here was writing a book about the tree, then went and hung himself from it."

"Ah, yeah. *That* would be Chuck Harvey," Constance said. "Took a couple of classes from him, when I was an undergrad at URI. Again, not exactly a big fucking secret. I always did think the dude was, you know, sort of out to lunch."

I let my eyes stray towards the window, towards the huge green canopy of that tree moving slowly in the afternoon breeze, recalling my walk the day before and how I'd found absolutely nothing the least bit out of the ordinary about the oak. How I'd almost dozed off on that big flat stone at its base.

"He was writing a book about it when he died," I said again.

"Really? I never heard that part of it. I don't think it made the news."

"So this happened before you moved out to LA?"

"Yep," she nodded. "I only went out there late last summer, near the end of August. No idea what I was thinking, really. I knew someone from college who wanted to split the cost of an apartment in Silver Lake, and there really wasn't anything here tying me down. But Jesus, Joseph, and Mary, I swear to fuck, Los Angeles is the *worst*. It's like someone decided to build a concentration camp for assholes or something, hoping the earthquakes and wildfires would clean up the gene pool."

I told her I'd never been very fond of the place myself, and she started in explaining to me about the friend from college, another painter, and how this girl had gotten mixed up with a heroin dealer, how it turned out the roommate was a junkie herself. After all manner of drug-related *Sturm und Drang,* Constance had decided it was time to get out, and so here she was, drinking Narragansett Beer with me at the kitchen table. "I think they're all probably in jail by now," she told me. "In jail or dead. I'm just glad to be away from there, clear and free of that bunch of jerk-offs and needle freaks. Maybe now I can get back to work."

And here she stopped and squinted at me through a gray veil of cigarette smoke. "So, he was writing a book, yeah? About the red tree? I wouldn't have guessed there was enough material there for a whole damn book."

I shrugged and pointed to the manuscript box. "Well, he seemed to think so. I found it in the basement. Rather, I found what there *is* of it. He died without finishing it."

She took a last puff from her Camel, then crushed the butt out in the ashtray. "No shit? I thought that was maybe something *you* were writing. It just got left here, after he died?"

"That would seem to be the case, though I've talked with someone at the university who's taking it off my hands next week. Someone who used to work with him, I think. He has a daughter, but she doesn't seem to want anything to do with him."

"Didn't know that, either," Constance said. "In school, we always assumed he was gay."

"Maybe he was. He was certainly divorced."

"Weird shit," she sighed, and sipped at her beer. "So, Sarah Crowe, tell me. Are you the sort who believes in ghosts and cursed trees and the like?" she asked. "Does it make you nervous, all these skeletons in the closet?"

"No, I do not believe in ghosts," I replied. "*Or* Rhode Island vampires, *or* swamp monsters. I'd be lying, though, if I said learning about Harvey's suicide didn't . . ." and I trailed off, searching for words that wouldn't be taken the wrong way, because suddenly I found myself caring about this stranger's opinion of me. "It was unsettling," I said. "And then, finding that manuscript, hidden away down in the basement . . ."

"You think Blanchard intentionally hid the manuscript?"

"Sorry, no," I said, shaking my head. "Just a figure of speech," and see there what I mean about being careful of the words I choose, because I hadn't meant that at all.

"Don't you wonder, though, why he didn't just toss it out, burn it or something?" Constance Hopkins asked, and now there was a faintly mischievous glint in her lazy eyes. "I mean, why *save* it? Why go to the trouble to stash it away in the basement?"

"You got me," I said. "I don't write mystery novels."

"No, that's right. You don't, do you?" And as quickly as it had appeared, the glint faded from her rusty eyes. She lit another cigarette, and offered another to me, but I declined.

"How about you?" I asked, and, with hindsight, I see that the question was not merely an act of reciprocal curiousity, but a response to what had felt like a challenge or taunt from a woman almost fifteen years my junior.

"What about me *what*?"

"Are *you*, Constance Hopkins, the sort who believes in ghosts . . . or cursed trees, for that matter? Are you the sort who goes in for all this Fortean nonsense?"

She peered back at me through a thick cloud of smoke, looking confused. "Fortean? You just lost me."

"You mean to say, you've never read Charles Fort, king of the cranks, archenemy of all that is rational, self-professed defender of so-called damned phenomena excluded by orthodox science? Rains of blood, fish and frogs falling from the sky, unexplained disappearances, mystery animals, and what have you?"

"Sorry," she said, shaking her head. "Not ringing any bells."

"No problem," I replied. "It's probably for the best. Anyway, you haven't answered my question."

"Do I believe in ghosts?" she smiled.

"Yes. That's the one."

She continued to smile, and I did my best not to stare at that chipped tooth while she seemed to gaze through me, at least through the *surface* of me. Finally she nodded, very slightly, her smile widening just a bit, and shrugged.

"It's complicated. Maybe we should come back to that question another time," she said. "I expect I ought to wander upstairs and see just what I've gotten myself into," and she looked at the ceiling.

"Sure," I replied. "No hurry," but there was an odd and unmistakable pang of disappointment, that she hadn't answered the question. For a moment, I thought she was going to leave the table, but then she started talking again, and the conversation turned to more mundane affairs—just how much she dreaded going up those stairs to the attic, because she knew what a dump it would be. How there was a sleeping bag and an air mattress out in the car that would have to do, as far as bedding was concerned. How she hoped we didn't both freeze to death when winter came around.

"I try not to think about the winter," I said, truthfully. "I've never lived anywhere cold in my whole life."

"Sometimes," she said, "it's not so bad. Though it tends to get colder here than it does nearer to the sea. Sometimes, we get mild winters."

"Other times?"

She winked, and then blew a series of perfect concentric smoke rings before replying. "Well, I was born during the Blizzard of 1978. It snowed for thirty-three hours straight, drifts fifteen feet high some places. Hurricane-force winds all across Rhode Island, Connecticut, and Massachusetts, but the worst of it was right here in Providence County. It was a hell of a mess, and a lot of people died. My mother used to say, 'You came in like a lion, Connie, riding on that wind.' " She laughed then, and I think I laughed, too. I know I was regretting not having accepted that second cigarette.

"People still call you Connie?" I asked, preferring not to contemplate all the many ways a person can die in a blizzard.

"Only once," she said and winked again. "And now, if you will excuse me, I really *should* get off my ass and meet my garret. I assume we share the kitchen?"

"Looks that way," I said, and then I offered to help with the stuff we'd left sitting at the foot of the attic stairs. She shook her head and told me it wasn't anything she couldn't handle on her own. She thanked me for the beer and promised to exchange the favor soon, then glanced down at the box containing Dr. Harvey's manuscript.

"Before you unload that thing, could I maybe have a look at it?" she asked.

"Sure, though I'm planning on having it photocopied at the library, so it's not like there's a rush."

She chewed at her lower lip a moment, then said,

"Sarah, if you don't mind, I'd sort of like to read the original. You know, the actual artifact. Reading a copy wouldn't be the same, somehow."

"Of course," I replied, because, after all, I haven't actually worked out when and where I'm supposed to meet the woman from URI to hand it over. "Truthfully, I've only read about half of it myself. But yeah, no problem. You can take it now, if you'd like."

"Later will be fine," she said, then thanked me again for the beer, and for helping her carry the stuff up from the car. After she left, I sat here, wondering how long it would take me to get used to the sound of footsteps overhead. And now it's almost four o'clock in the morning, and the birds are yelling their heads off, and it just occurred to me that the clack from these noisy goddamn typewriter keys might be keeping her awake.

July 4, 2008 (9:39 p.m.)

Not much to report, really. I thought of taking the car and driving somewhere there would be fireworks—Foster, or all the way down to Westerly or Watch Hill, maybe even Mystic—not so much because I give two hoots for Independence Day, but just to mark the passage of time, to stay oriented (or reorient myself) to some sort of calendar beyond my own reclusive rhythms and the inevitable progress of the summer towards autumn. I even went so far as to look online for potential destinations, places where fireworks displays were scheduled and so forth. But then Constance asked me to help her with the last few boxes from the rental car, and she started telling horror stories about traffic and drunken tourists and asshole college students, and I dropped the idea. Earlier, just after dark, I did hear some distant concussions, from the south, I think, so I'm afraid that's it for my Fourth of July this year.

It's really not so bad in the attic, aside from the heat, which was almost intolerable before we set up a little window-unit air conditioner that the Mexicans seem to have left behind. But it's clean up there, and roomier than I remembered, and Constance seems happy enough with the space. I sat with her a while, and we talked and drank more Narragansett beer while the attic cooled down around us. I don't think I could ever get used to that single, long V-shaped room, those steeply slanting walls meeting overhead like the hull of a capsized boat. Nothing very remarkable about the conversation, nothing worth putting down here, except that she claims she's bi, that she's had a couple of girlfriends, so maybe . . . well . . . I can't be blamed for wishful thinking. Sure, I was already thirteen when she was born, but what the hell.

Later, she wanted to take a nap, and so I found myself downstairs again, looking over Dr. Harvey's manuscript for the umpteenth time. Not so much reading it, as scanning what I'd read already. To be honest, the thing is a mess. There are chapters, but after the first, these divisions seem more or less arbitrary, and there's almost no effort at presenting any sort of chronological history of the origin and traditions surrounding "the Red Tree" (it would be too kind to call this writing "non-linear"). Also, often, the author veers off into subjects that are, at best, tangential. The nearest thing I can compare it with are the writings of Charles Fort—which, I should note, are mentioned on that page I discovered in the typewriter's carriage, and are also liberally cited in other portions of the manuscript. I haven't read Fort since college, but I recall his rambling, unfocused style gave me fits. Anyway, here's an example of what I mean—the tangents—from Chapter Two (ms. pg. 112). Right in the middle of a discussion of one of the better-documented episodes involving the tree, a series of murders dating from the 1920s, Harvey pauses to discuss an unrelated haunting:

Here I should like to mention the purported haunting at Portsmouth Abbey, which is said to have followed from the slaghter [sic] and mass burial of some thirty to sixty Hessian soldiers during the Revolutionary War. The largest land-based battle of the conflict occurred on August 29, 1778, at Portsmouth, Rhode Island, near a stream now known as Barker's Bloody Brook (or the Bloody Run), a stream that flows through the Portsmouth Abbey grounds. Indeed, the very name of the brook is tied to this battle, as the waters were said to have run red for days afterwards, polluted by blood, so great was the loss of life. The precise location of the Hessian burial is uncertain, though most do agree it was beneath the boughs of a large willow tree, long ago cut down. The dead soldiers are said to rise from a great depression marking the grave site, often referred to as the

"Hessian Hole" (again, reports vary on the location of this sunken area marking the grave). Spectral sightings are said to be especially likely on foggy nights. One wonders if director Tim Burton was aware of this tale when crafting his popular 1999 retelling of Washington Irving's "The Legend of Sleepy Hollow" (1820). It should be noted that there is no actual archaeological evidence that the mass grave is anything more than legend, and a recent survey of much of the battleground by Salve Regina University (Newport) failed to turn up any burial matching the description of the infamous "Hessian Hole."

I will assume Harvey felt justified in making this digression from his discussion of the murders of 1922–1925 because the Hessian Hole story involves a tree and a bloody brook, vaguely echoing some elements of the "Red Tree of Barbs Hill Road." Anyway, I realized that I wasn't really sure how far back the legends surrounding the tree extend—because of Harvey's haphazard attention to chronology—only that the oldest accounts predate the story of William Ames and his wife by more than a century. I sat down on the floor with the manuscript, and spread the pages out around me, trying not to think about Constance upstairs, napping beneath the air conditioner while I sweated below. Or the possibility that she might be napping in the nude. It would appear that the earliest account Harvey was able to locate regarding something amiss with a tree in the wilderness south of Moosup Valley dates to the years following the "West Quanaug purchase" of 1662 (and I confess that I am almost entirely ignorant of local history, so I'm taking Harvey's word on this stuff). He writes (Chapter One, ms. pg. 29):

It seems to have begun in the decades after the acquisition of roughly fifteen square miles of land from the Narragansett sachems Awashouse and Newecome, generally referred to as the West Quanaug purchase. "West Quanaug" (or, alternately, "Westconnaug" is an English corruption of the Narragansett "Wishquatnoqke"). Three men were instrumental in the purchase: William Vaughn of Newport, Robert Westcott of Warwick, and Zachariah Rhodes of Pawtuxet. The Westconnaug Company was organized in June 1678 to see to the tract's subsequent apportion. A surveyor was not appointed until 1707. The West Quanaug purchase may be seen as the second major acquisition in an expansion authorized in 1659 by the Colonial General Assembly, encouraging Providence settlers to "buy out and clear off" all Indians west of the Seven-Mile Line. Following the resolution of disputes over ownership between the aforementioned Providence Proprietors and the West Quanaug Company (October 28th, 1708), both were eager to place settlers on the new land, largely to help resolve a persistent boundary dispute with Connecticut.

Though the first deed issued by the West Quanaug Company, to John Potter of Warwick, dates from 1714, family tradition has it that Mr. Potter, in fact, took up residence in a small cave along the east bank of the Moosup River as early as 1704, where he then lived until the construction of a house. Though this story may be purely anecdotal, appealing to a romantic ideal of the pioneering spirit, a much later entry in John Potter's journal (Special Collections, Providence Athenaeum), dated May 15, 1715, makes reference to "the red indyen dread of an olde tree s'd haunted by the divel Hobbamock, an enimy to all good, who appeareth there by night." Potter then relates a story of the Narragansett's offerings of freshly killed game left at the base of the tree, as Hobbamock was "s'd by the heathens to be appeas'd above al else by the shadding of blood." In this entry, indulging his imagination, Potter even supposes that occasional human sacrifices may have been made to "the daemon, so great ware theire fear of this malevolent thinge."

In Part 1 of The Origin and Development of Religious Belief (1878), the prolific English scholar and folklorist Reverend Sabine Baring-Gould writes, "New Englanders supposed Hobbamock to be the arch-fiend of the Indians, because the myths told of him represented him as malevolent; but, in fact, he was their Supreme Oki, or God." So, regardless of Hobbamock's proper place in the pantheon of the Narragansett people (a redundancy, as "Narragansett" translates, literally, as "The People"), it is consistent with the contemporaneous impression of Native American mythology that John Potter would have regarded (and probably distorted) this being to conform to the popular impression of the time, that Hobbamock was an Indian devil. This same being was also known as Cheepie (chippe, meaning alone, separate, secluded, or apart).

It is also worth mentioning here that "Hobbamock" was a title bestowed upon high-ranking tribal members, such as the case of a Pokanoket sachem called Hobbamock who was sent, in the spring of 1621, to Plymouth Colony by Massasoit, chief of all the Wampanoag. Hobbamock and his family lived alongside the colonists until he died in 1641.

As we shall see, John Potter's life would, eventually, become inextricably and fatally linked with the Red Tree, which he first set eyes on, it appears, from a journal entry dated only as August 1716, little more than a year after his first mention of the Hobbamock story. At this time, he notes the presence of an enormous stone believed to have been placed at the base of the accursed oak by the Narragansett and used as an altar. He describes the rectilinear slab as marked by a shallow groove carved into its upper surface, forming a rough circle within which the offerings were placed. This groove, Potter writes, led to a "spout" or opening on the southern edge of the altar stone (which he believed served to drain blood from sacrifices that had collected in the groove).

However, though mentioning that the stone was covered with lichen, he fails to make any mention of bloodstains, which one assumes would have been inevitable, unless the Narragansett regularly scrubbed the stone (or Hobbamock's nocturnal feedings were sufficient to have wiped it clean).

Such "altar" stones are known from other sites in New England, including one from the Mystery Hill megalith site ("America's Stonehenge") near Salem, New Hampshire, and another displayed at the Hadley Farm Museum in western Massachusetts. The latter, which is almost identical to that located at the base of the tree, has been identified as a cider press. The Mystery Hill "altar" is suspected of having been carved in either the Eighteenth or Nineteenth Century by local farmers for use in the manufacture of lye soap. Other notable examples of stones quite closely matching that on the Blanchard property may be seen today at Groton, CT, and Leominster and Westport, MA. In each case, the stones are believed by archaeologists to be of relatively recent, non-Native American origin, and to have been used for production of lye, pine tar, or potash, and even the pressing of grapes. Nevertheless, these artifacts have long fired the popular imagination, and appear in such canonical works of pulp fiction as Lovecraft's "The Dunwich Horror" (1929) and Karl Edward Wagner's "Sticks" (1974).

In this same entry (see Appendix B for the relevant excerpts from John Potter's diary in full [A shame Harvey didn't live long enough to actually write the appendices!—S.C.]) the tree described, along with the "altar stone" perfectly match the tree now identified by locals as "the Red Tree," and I have little doubt that the two are one and the same. He states that "it has an evil feel about it" and that he has begun to consider cutting it down and having the stone broken up. Obviously, this never happened, and as we shall soon see, John Potter would live to regret not following through with his plan to destroy the tree. Despite his apparent loathing of the tree and his belief that the Narragansetts gathered at the spot to summon evil spirits, Potter built his home, in 1707, well within sight of the oak. Indeed, at the time, one can assume that, the land having been recently cleared by Potter for agriculture, the tree would have been more visible from the house than it is now. Records in the Tyler Free Library, the Foster Preservation Society, and the Providence Athenaeum indicate that Potter's original house burned in 1710, and that Potter rebuilt directly on the foundation stones he'd lain three years earlier. So, given this chance to relocate his house farther from the oak, he once again acted in a way that, at first glance, seems contrary to his notions and misgivings about the tree. However, I believe that, by studying Potter's diary, we can arrive at satisfactory explanations for these actions, and that in the beginning they amounted to little more than stubbornness and an unwillingness on his part to be perceived as having been in any way intimidated by native superstitions.

Yeah, okay, enough of this already. My eyes are giving out. Didn't I say I *wasn't* going to hand copy Harvey's damn manuscript, that I was going to have it Xeroxed? And here I've just transcribed about four pages of the damned thing! But, that said, the upshot is that people have been afraid of this old tree (hidden now, out there in the dark beyond my kitchen window) for almost three hundred years. And the stone I lay down on, and where I almost dozed off below those branches, has (or had) a reputation as an altar used by Indians in human sacrifices. I have to admit, reading back over that part gave me just a bit of a shiver, even if I'm most emphatically *not* the sort of woman who believes in ghosts and Rhode Island vampires and bog monsters.

Oh, speaking of Constance, she came down about five this afternoon, looking refreshed from her nap, and offered to fix dinner for the both of us. I never turn down a home-cooked meal, so long as someone else is doing the cooking. She scrounged about in the kitchen and somehow came up with the ingredients for a couple of cheddar-cheese omelets, with French fries on the side (I had a pack of Ore-Ida frozen shoestrings). While we were eating, she asked about the manuscript pages scattered all over the floor, and I told her about the "altar" at the base of the tree. I said that I wanted to make a second trip out to the tree, as I didn't recall seeing the groove and spout mentioned by Harvey, and she asked if I'd mind if she went along. Like I was going to say no, right? So, it's a date. We're planning to pack lunch and have a proper picnic on the stone, dubious past or no, bloodthirsty demons or what have you. Okay, so maybe it's *not* a date, strictly speaking, but at least it's not me sitting here on my ass, smoking too much and drinking lousy beer, moping about the novel that I'm not getting written while I obsess over Dr. Harvey's manuscript.

July 5, 2008 (10:27 p.m.)

The best-laid plans of mice and men and bored writers, as they say. Or as they *ought* to say. The heat was exceptional today, the sun like a searing hole punched into the sky leading straight up to Hell. By one this afternoon, the mercury had reached 93F, and Constance and I decided to put our plans for a picnic at the red tree off until another, cooler day. The meteorologists (whom I've noticed are even less reliable here than back in Atlanta) are promising cooler weather soon. I suppose the proximity to the sea complicates matters, adding a greater degree of uncertainty into that already dubious undertaking of predicting the future course of cold fronts, high- and low-pressure centers, the whims of the polar jet stream. But, the long and short of it, the day was dangerously hot, and, in lieu of our picnic, Constance invited me up into her garret to partake of the air-conditioning. The little window unit was hardly able to keep up, what with the hot air rising from below and the sun blasting down on the roof, but the attic was still a far sight better than being downstairs.

Earlier in the day, before the heat got so bad, I'd gone with her up to Foster, to return the rented PT Cruiser. On the way home, she talked, mostly, and mostly she talked about growing up around here. There were questions I'd wanted to ask, about her painting and California, and about what taking classes from Charles Harvey had been like, but I'd kept them to myself. Then, up in the attic, I saw that she hasn't yet begun painting, which I suppose is hardly surprising. She *has* begun stretching two canvases (the stretcher bars were Brazilian white pine, she informed me), and the place already smells like oil paints and linseed oil and gesso. She sat on her air mattress, me in a metal folding chair, and we smoked and drank Narragansett and listened to the window unit chug and wheeze and try to keep up with the heat. She has a little portable stereo, and something by Lisa Gerrard was playing on repeat. I can't now recall everything we talked about, and I won't try. The stuff two people from different parts of the country talk about. The things two artists working in completely different media talk about. But, there was one thing I wanted to get down here, and as I prepare to do so, I realize that I have developed a certain relationship with this typewriter and the journal I'm using it to keep (instead of writing my novel)—it would appear that I have taken it into my confidence, and I'm going to have to stop leaving these pages lying about where Constance could easily come across them and be tempted to read things I would really rather she didn't.

"You asked if I believed in ghosts," she said, and I think maybe we'd been talking about Henry James, for whatever reason, and so it didn't seem strange to me that she had returned to the unanswered question.

"And you said it was complicated," I replied, and sipped at my beer.

"I wasn't trying to be coy. It *is* complicated. The answer, I mean. But, if you're still interested, I'll try to explain."

"I'm still interested," I said, not adding that I strongly suspected she *was* being coy. "If you want to tell me, sure, I'm interested."

"Well, I *don't* believe in ghosts," she continued, wiping beads of condensation off her own bottle with a corner of the sheet. "At least, not in any traditional sense. I don't believe in the soul, or that the mind is capable of surviving death, so a logical consequence is that I can hardly believe in restless spirits and the like. See what I'm saying?" and she scooted a few inches across the air mattress and a little closer to my chair.

"Sure," I said. "It sounds like maybe it's not so different from my own reasons. The physicalist approach to monism and the so-called mind-body problem. Thought is merely a function of the brain—"

"—no soul," she said, cutting in, and I think that, in retrospect, I'm a little embarrassed at how I was trying to wow her with my knowledge of things that I really know very little about (I'm not much better with psychology than I am the weather). Constance tapped at her head with an index finger. "Just my brain, and my mind exists no more independently of my brain than my chewing exists independently of my teeth. Thought, mind, whatever . . . it's just what the brain *does*. The dichotomy between that which we call mental, or spiritual, and those things we call physical, is merely an illusion. It's *all* physical."

"No arguments here," I told her, hoping that the conversation was not about to step off into some hard-core philosophical waters much too deep for me to follow. I'd already pretty much used up my bag of jargon with *physicalism, monism,* and the *mind-body problem.*

"No soul," she said. "No spirit, so no ghosts, right? The brain dies and rots, taking its functions, including mind, with it. So, no ghosts."

"Bingo," I said, and she laughed.

"*Except*—and I know how freaky this is going to sound, so bear with me—maybe there's a sort of cosmic escape clause that allows for the existence of the set of phenomena that people tend to call ghosts and hauntings. And it's not that ghosts don't exist, it's just that most people are mistaken about what they are, or aren't."

I think I blinked and let the metal folding chair rock back on two legs. "Okay, now you've lost me," I admitted, and she laughed again.

"Oh, Sarah, you're plenty smart enough to keep up," she said. "Just give me a second. See, maybe it's not about souls or spirits at all. Maybe it's actually something that has a lot more to do with physics and how the universe operates. We know that matter distorts space and time, right? Well, what if there are other ways that space and time can be distorted by matter, perhaps not only by the gravity generated by an object's mass, but by the behavior or experiences or . . ." and here she paused, searching for some word.

"It's an old idea," I said, letting the chair bump back down to the attic floor. "Events so traumatic that they warp time and space and create what parapsychologists and other crackpots call residual hauntings, I believe. Nonconscious hauntings that work sort of like a loop of videotape."

I realized that Constance had stopped smiling, and now she was just sitting there, staring at the walls.

"Crackpots," she said, and took a drink of beer.

I sighed and fought the sudden urge to punch myself in the mouth. "I'm sorry I interrupted you," I said, instead, but she just shrugged and leaned over the side of the air mattress, setting her bottle on the floor.

"You *said* that you were still interested, or I never would have started in on this. I *know* how it sounds."

I apologized again and told her to please continue, to finish whatever it was she had been about to tell me. And then she said she blamed the heat, that if the day weren't so hot, we'd have gone out to the tree as we'd planned, and this conversation would not have happened, and I wouldn't think she was a crackpot.

"I never said I think you're a crackpot," I protested.

She stared at me a few moments, then shrugged and said, "It was fairly implicit, don't you think?"

I closed my eyes tightly, seeing yellow-white afterimages of sunlight and restraining myself from blurting some smart-ass quip or another—"Do we have to have our first lovers' spat *before* I get to fuck you?" Something equally self-destructive.

Instead, I told her, "I'm sorry, Constance. I honestly

didn't mean it that way. I think maybe I'm a little drunk," and I probably was. I opened my eyes, and she was still staring at me. "No, *really,*" I said. "I was *not* calling you a crackpot. You're just gonna have to take my word on that, okay?"

And she smiled at me and lay down on the air mattress, and I was glad for the smile, whatever it might mean, and glad that those cinnamon eyes were now trained on the sloping attic ceiling and not on me. "Do you want to hear it or not?" Constance asked.

"I do," I replied, and she furrowed her brow, making what A. A. Milne might have called a thoughtful face. Only, it was obvious this was a sort of *mock*-thoughtful face, and I knew this expression was some part of my punishment for having implied she was a crackpot.

"You have to swear that you won't just use it as an excuse to make fun of me again."

"I *wasn't* making fun of you."

She squeezed her eyes shut tightly and pointed straight at me with her left index finger. "You have to fucking *swear,* Sarah Crowe. Otherwise, you're never gonna hear it."

"And that would ruin my day," I muttered, and her brow grew more furrowed, the thoughtful face edging towards an impatient face.

"Fine. I fucking swear," I said, before she could withdraw the stipulation and any chance I might have of hearing whatever it was she was trying to decide whether or not I should hear.

"Scout's honor?"

"Sure. Cross my heart and hope to die."

"Yeah, that's better," she said, smiling again, and the creases wrinkling her forehead began to relax. But she didn't open her eyes. In fact, she didn't open her eyes again until she was almost finished telling me her ghost story, as though she needed to try and shut out the sunlight filling up the little attic in order to recall the events in question. I sat in my metal folding chair, smoking, and she lay there on her makeshift bed, while the window unit droned and gurgled wetly to itself. I'll freely admit, I've never been a very good listener, and yet, there was something in the way she stacked the words . . . and I seemed to hang on every one, every syllable, every pregnant pause. Then again, maybe it was only lust and a peevish libido keeping me focused.

"Back when I was in high school, just after I got my license, I used to drive out to the Cliffwalk in Newport whenever I could. Usually, I went alone. In the summers, I'd try to find the days when the tourists weren't so bad, but it's Newport, and so that's always a crapshoot."

I exhaled smoke and cleared my throat. "Constance," I said. "I know I'm interrupting you again, but . . . I've never been to Newport, and I have no idea what this Cliffwalk thing is. Keep in mind I'm just a dumb redneck from Georgia and this will go better."

She sighed very loudly and shook her head in disgust or disbelief. "The Cliffwalk," she said, speaking very slowly now, the way one might talk to a small child with attention issues, "is a trail leading along the cliffs, over on the east side of Newport Island, behind Salve Regina College and all those great fucking mansions that people like the Vanderbilts put up back in the 1890s. You *have* heard of the Gilded Age, right? The fallout of the Second Industrial Revolution? John D. Rockefeller, Silas Desvernine, Andrew Carnegie, J. P. Morgan, all those guys?"

"I think maybe I heard of it once," I said, not bothering to smile because her eyes were shut. I took another drag on my cigarette.

"So, *behind* the mansions," she continued, "there's a pathway. It was just a dirt trail back when, a long time ago, kept clear by the Indians and the colonials and then the Victorians and whatnot. It runs on for miles, and in some places the drop to the sea is seventy feet or more. But over the years, hurricanes took their toll on the path, and finally, I think, the Army Corps of Engineers came in sometime in the seventies and paved it and repaired all the storm damage, fixed the walk up all nice again. Better than new, I'm sure."

"Our tax dollars at work," I said.

"It's nice," Constance said. "Maybe I'll take you sometime. Anyway, so I used to drive out there, back when I was sixteen, seventeen, hoping there wouldn't be crowds of sightseers. And one day it was foggy and sort of cold for summer, so there was hardly anyone, and I pretty much had the place to myself. July 21, 1995, so that's what . . . thirteen years ago?"

"Almost," I told her, counting on my fingers. "Sixteen days from now, it'll have been thirteen years."

"Fine, so twelve years, eleven months, and spare change.

And there I was, alone at the Forty Steps, down at the end of Narragansett Avenue—"

"What are the Forty Steps?" I asked, and she shook her head again, so I added, "A Georgia redneck, remember?"

Constance made an exasperated sound, and somehow managed to roll her eyes without opening them. "At the east end of Narragansett Avenue, on the Cliffwalk, there's a granite staircase leading down to a sort of balcony above the sea. Used to be, the steps were wooden, and back in the Gilded Age, the Irish servants from the mansions would gather there for dances and socials and whatever the Irish immigrants called such things. There's a Gaelic word for it. . . ."

"Céilí," I volunteered, and she nodded.

"Ten points to the ignorant redneck dyke from Georgia," she laughed. "Yeah. Well, so they had their parties at the Forty Steps, to blow off steam, back in the 1880s and 1890s and so on. Nowadays, though, the old wooden steps are gone, and there's a sturdy red granite staircase enclosed by walls made from blocks of limestone and mortar, so it's a lot safer. It was still new, in 1995. There's a name engraved on each step, the name of the person who ponied up the dough to pay for that particular step. It cost something like three thousand dollars a step. And then, from the little balcony—which is probably two-thirds of the way down the cliff—it's, I don't know exactly, but I'd guess another twenty or thirty feet down to the rocks and the sea. Far enough you wouldn't want to fall."

"Or jump?" I asked. And Constance frowned, and I thought for a second she might even open her eyes.

"Or fucking *jump*," she said. "Far enough that if you didn't die outright, you'd be pretty busted up. I used to sit there on the limestone wall of the balcony, because it's a good view, and there are lots of fossils in the limestone. That rock didn't come from anywhere around here, but I don't know where it did come from. Also, there's a sea cave, below the south side of the balcony, and it's great to just sit there and watch the water rushing in and out again. But that day in July 1995, I was just coming down the stairs, and I looked up, off towards Purgatory on the other side of the harbor, and for a second I didn't see her, just the sea and the far shore—"

"Didn't see who?" I asked.

"I am absolutely sure that she wasn't there when I first looked up," Constance went on, ignoring my question. "And then she was. Like someone throwing a light switch, like a magic trick. She just . . . appeared."

"Or you simply didn't notice her for a second or two."

"I've tried hard to believe that, over the years, Sarah, but it's not the truth. The *truth* is, I looked down those granite steps at the balcony, and one second she wasn't there, and then, the next, she was. That's the truth, whether you *believe* me or not. That's what I saw."

"But . . . you *know* . . . whatever you saw is not necessarily what happened. Optical illusions—"

"I won't finish this story if you're not interested," she said. "I mean, if you'd rather argue, we can do that."

"I'm not trying to start an argument."

"Then just shut up for a few minutes and listen. It wasn't an optical illusion, or a mirage, or whatever. Yeah, there was some fog, but I know what I saw. She looked a little older than me, no more than twenty, say. She was wearing a dress and boots, and my first thought was this was one of those Society of Creative Anachronism types, or some sort of goth or something, because the clothes were tailored and the boots. . . . It was like seeing a postcard or an old photograph from the Nineteenth Century. And she had this antique-looking pistol gripped in her right hand, and the barrel was set against her temple. She was looking out to sea, and so her back was turned to me."

And at this point, I have to admit, Constance had my attention, and I just sat there listening, staring at the smoldering tip of my Camel.

"I stopped where I was, there on the steps, and for a minute or two, I just stood there, watching her. Her finger was on the trigger, and I could hear that she was crying. Well, sort of sobbing, softly. I almost couldn't hear it over the breakers. And then I took another step or two towards her, though she hadn't seemed to notice I was there, and I said, 'The fall will probably kill you. The gun . . . I really don't think it's necessary.' Something to that effect. And she turned around, turned and looked straight at me, and her face . . ." Here Constance trailed off and was silent for a while.

Finally, I said, "You can tell me the rest some other time, if you'd rather."

Her eyes still tightly closed, she shook her head and took a deep breath, as if summoning some necessary courage, as if filling her lungs with the requisite will to finish her story. She breathed out slowly, and, sitting there, I thought of Lamaze classes and childbirth and of taking a very deep breath before a dive into cold saltwater.

"I'm fine," she said. "So, anyway, she turns and looks at me, this woman with her revolver and her dress that looks like she just stepped out of a Merchant-Ivory film. And the look on her face, Sarah, I knew, then and there, that expression was exactly what people mean when they say someone looks like she's just seen a ghost. The woman lowered the revolver, letting her arm go limp at her side, and very slowly, very carefully, without ever saying a word, she climbed down off the wall onto the balcony. And vanished."

"Vanished . . ." I said, not meaning to sound skeptical, but sounding it anyway.

"Just gone, Sarah. The whole thing couldn't have lasted more than a minute. Two minutes, at the most."

"And there were no other witnesses?" I asked.

"No, no one. I walked over to the wall, and stood there a long time, staring down at the sea sloshing against the boulders. It's all charcoal-colored shale there, and the sea foam looks so white against it, and the sea is so many shades of green and blue, and I remember seeing strands of kelp in the surf that day, down there below the Forty Steps. There was no one else, just me and a few cormorants and gulls."

She paused again, but this time I didn't say anything. Just sat listening to the wheezy AC and the birds outside the old house far from the sea, but maybe not far enough. When she started talking again, Constance opened her eyes, but she didn't look at me. She lay there, very still, staring at the ceiling.

"A few days later, I went back to Newport, to the public library, and found this book there on local ghosts. I don't remember the title. Oh, wait . . . yes, I do—*The Hauntings of Newport*—written by a history professor up at Harvard. Right near the end of the book, there was a story—not really a ghost story, not exactly—about a woman in 1901 who went down the Forty Steps to kill herself. She'd found out that her husband was sleeping around on her, getting it on with the maid or some such, and she'd brought his gun with her. She planned to shoot herself and fall over the edge, let the current carry her body away so that no one would ever know she was a suicide, and she'd never have to face the shame of her husband's infidelity. Maybe people would just think she slipped on the steps and fell, whatever. But she *didn't* shoot herself, Sarah, and she *didn't* jump, either. Decades later, when she was an old woman, when her husband was dead, she told all this to a newspaper reporter. She said that she heard someone, right as she was about to pull the trigger, and turned to find this strangely dressed girl watching her, and the strangely dressed girl told her that the gun was unnecessary, that the fall alone would do the job. And then the girl just . . . wasn't there anymore. That's precisely how she described it. 'Then the girl wasn't there anymore.' The woman's name was Anna Turner."

There was another silence here, and I stubbed out the butt of my cigarette and set my empty beer bottle on the floor, waiting, because I wasn't sure if she was finished, and, really, what do you say to something like this? She rolled over on her side, towards me, and the air mattress complained with a rubbery, scrunching noise.

"I promise, I'm not making any of this up," she said, and I either nodded or shrugged, I can't remember which. Constance furrowed her eyebrows again, like someone trying to solve a trigonometry problem, and licked nervously at her lips. "I imagine the book's still in the Newport library, if you ever wanted to look it up yourself."

"Did I say I don't believe you? I don't think I did."

"No, you didn't," and she sat up, reaching for her unfinished beer. She took a swallow, then returned the bottle to the wet ring of condensation it had left on the unfinished hardwood. "What I *really* think, Sarah," and here she lowered her voice as if someone might overhear. "About ghosts, I mean—is that there are weak spots in the universe, or thin places in time. In the fabric of time or the quantum foam, whatever physicists are calling it these days. And where these weak spots exist, they essentially act as windows, connecting two moments that otherwise would be separated by months or years or even by centuries. Maybe they only last for an instant or two, maybe a few minutes, then wink out of existence. Maybe, sometimes, they recur at the same place and time repeatedly. It explains what I saw that day, and what I found in the book later on. It explains what Anna Turner saw, and why she didn't kill herself. You stop and think about it, well, it explains a lot of things that people call ghosts."

"It does," I agreed, lighting another Camel and blowing smoke towards the ceiling.

"But you don't buy it?"

"Well, come on. You *have* to admit, it does seem rather too convenient, or fortuitous, whatever, that a randomly occurring flaw in spacetime would just happen to manifest at a point that would have allowed you to save this woman's life that day, the two of you ninety-four years apart." I took another puff, exhaled, and squinted at her through the smoke.

"I never said I believe that it's necessarily a random event. Maybe, somehow, human consciousness plays a role in the process. Perhaps, Sarah, consciousness, like mass, can distort space and time. So, traumatic emotions can act as a catalyst, if certain conditions are just exactly right. Or, maybe, there's some greater mind—maybe Jung's collective unconscious, let's say—that determines when and where these thin spots appear."

"Or God, maybe? A beneficent, intervening cosmic intelligence . . ."

"I thought you said you're an atheist," she said, scowling slightly.

"Oh, I am. Through and through. But I also don't believe in the collective unconscious, so, for me, if you're looking for potential causal agents for this hypothesis of yours, one's just as good as the other. Anyway, it would make for a pretty fickle fucking god, don't you think, since your thin spots seem picky about who they show up to save? Well, unless *that's* the random part."

Constance laughed then, and that was good, just knowing that my skepticism hadn't pissed her off. She lay down again, and the talk moved on to other things. Nothing else was said about ghosts or Jung or holes in time, and that was good, too. Because, sooner or later, I might have done something stupid like tell her I *do* think it's a crackpot idea. Or, I might have pointed out that her having discovered the account of this Anna Turner woman in a library book only works as evidence in favor of her proposal *if* I accept that she's not lying about having found it *after* the supposed ghostly sighting, instead of having come across it first and then fabricated the story of that day at the Forty Steps to match what she'd read. If I had to bet green folding money, well, I fear that's where I'd place my wager.

But, I will admit, hearing her "ghost story," I couldn't help but be reminded of what I thought I saw in a chert quarry in the sweltering summer of 1977.

Sitting here now, pecking at the typewriter of the late Dr. Charles Harvey and watching the clock hung above the kitchen sink, I've just remembered something Isak Dinesen wrote. Well, I'm sure I'm not recalling it exactly, so this is a paraphrase—*God made the world round, so we wouldn't ever be able to look too far ahead.* Something like that. And I'm thinking, maybe it isn't nearly round enough, and what would be the point of limiting how far ahead we can see, when we can see so far back the way we've come? It's too late at night for thoughts like these, and the pads of my fingers are feeling tender. Sometimes, these days, that's the only way I know that it's time to give up and go to bed, when my fingertips get sore from slamming at these keys. Anyway, Constance and I have rescheduled our picnic at the "Red Tree" for tomorrow, assuming the weathermen are right and the day's really going to be cooler, like they're predicting. I hope so. I need to get out of this house for a few hours.

CHAPTER FOUR

July 6, 2008 (7:54 a.m.)

No coffee yet, and only one cigarette, and it only half smoked. If I were any less awake, sitting upright wouldn't be an option. There was a very minor absence seizure last night, late; Constance had come downstairs to bum a cigarette, and she had not yet gone back upstairs when it happened. No big deal. I faded out for a few seconds, but she made a huge fuss over it. Can't wait until she's unlucky enough to be around for one of the big ones, if that's how she's going to react to the *petit mal* episodes. She brewed a pot of tea, and kept asking if she could look at my pupils, and if maybe I smelled oranges—stuff like that—and sat with me a while, though, of course, it was entirely unnecessary. I *told* her it was unnecessary, but she insisted. It must have been almost four in the morning before she climbed back up into her garret and left me alone to try and sleep. And I really didn't do much *better* than try. My head filled itself with all the sorts of unease that comes on nights like that, the unanswerable questions, the heavy thoughts to needle me and keep me awake. My health, the book, money, and also the story that Constance had told me about her ghost, the "ghost" she claims to have witnessed in Newport years ago. So, even though it's probably not fair, I'm going to blame her for the nightmares that came when I finally *did* doze off. It was almost five a.m., and the sky was going gray. I'm still not accustomed to how early the sun rises here, compared to Atlanta, and I really hate when it catches me off my guard like that. But I was sleeping before genuine daylight came along, thank fuck, or I wouldn't have gotten even the lousy couple of hours that I managed.

The house is so goddamn quiet. Mist over Ramswool Pond. Birds singing. Little sounds I can't identify. And these noisy fucking typewriter keys. Constance said not to worry about it, that, after her time in LA, she could sleep through an earthquake (and, in fact, she has, she tells me), but I still find myself trying to strike the keys with less force, endeavoring to somehow muffle that clack-clack-fuckity-clack of die-cast iron consonants and vowels against the paper and the machine's carriage. *The intractable guilt of the insomniac typist*—sounds a bit like a stray line Ezra Pound might have wisely persuaded Eliot to cut from *The Waste Land*.

But the reason that I'm sitting here at the kitchen table (if I need a reason), painfully uncaffeinated, squinting at Dr. Harvey's accursed typewriter by the wan light of eight ayem, are those nightmares I've already blamed Constance for summoning. Just another set of bad dreams, sure, in a parade that's never going to end until I'm dead and buried (and, oh, what a happy thought, that death may come with nightmares all its own: unending, possibly, an afterlife of perpetual nightmares). But I can't shake the feeling that there was something new there, and I want to try and put down some of what I recall before I lose it. It's *already* fading so goddamn fast, so quit stalling and get to it, woman!

I was walking by the sea, maybe one of the nearby stretches of Rhode Island coastline that I've visited—so, it's no great stretch to understand why I'm blaming the tale of the "ghost" of the Forty Steps. I assume the tide was rising. It *seemed* to be rising, but I have spent far too little of my life by the sea to be sure. The surf was rough, the waves coming in and crashing against a beach that was more cobbles and pebbles than sand. The air was filled with spray. My feet kept getting wet. Well, I mean my shoes, as I wasn't barefoot. My *shoes* kept getting wet, and my socks, because the foamy water was rushing so far up the beach towards the line of low dunes that stretched away behind me. The sky was the most amazing thing, though, and maybe if I weren't so asleep I could find the language to do my memories of it justice. Maybe. Then again, maybe the demeanor of that sky is forever beyond my abilities to wordsmith. I know a storm was approaching, but no usual sort of storm. Something terrible, something magnificent rolling like a cumulus demon of wind and rain and lightning over the whitecaps, sweeping towards the land, and no power in the cosmos could have waylaid or detoured that storm.

At the library in Moosup, a while back, I read part of a book about the Great Hurricane of 1938, the fabled Long Island Express, and maybe *that's* what was in back of my sleeping conjuration of this advancing line of towering thunderheads. The colors, they're still so clear in my head, a range of blue and blacks, violets and sickly greens bleeding into even sicklier yellows, and that does not even begin to convey those clouds. This was an angry, bludgeoned sky. A bruised sky. A sky bearing the contusions of some unseen atmospheric cataclysm.

I stood there, the polished stones slipping about beneath my wet feet as though they were imbued with a life all their own (and I wish I could recollect that line from Machen about the horror of blossoming pebbles, but I can't, and won't do it a disservice by trying). The wind and the spray swirled about me, plastering my clothes and hair flat, filling my nostrils and mouth with all the salty, living flavors and aromas of a wrathful sea. And as the gusts blown out before that storm howled in my ears, I realized that I was not alone, that Constance had followed me down to the shore. She was saying something about her former roommates, the Silver Lake junkies, but I couldn't make out most of it. I told her to speak up, and, instead, she grew silent, and, for a time, I thought I was alone again.

The sea before me was filled with dark and indescribable shapes, all moving constantly about just below the waves, not far offshore at all, and occasionally something slick and black—like the ridged back of an enormous leviathan or the bow of an upturned boat—would break the surface for a scant few seconds. Smooth, scaleless flesh scabbed white-brown with barnacles and whale lice, or there would be a glimpse of writhing serpentine coils, or of tentacles, perhaps . . . there would be something festooned with poisonous spines as tall and broken as the masts of a sunken whaler cast up from the depths after a hundred and fifty years lying lost in the silt and slime.

And I felt myself leaning into the wind, and I felt the wind bearing my weight, the resistance of that stinging gale force pushing against my body. I could only wonder that it did not lift me like a kite or a dead leaf and toss me high, tumbling ass over tits, into the air.

Behind me, Constance remained taciturn, and as the storm's voice grew ever greater in magnitude, ever more insistent, seeming intent upon devouring all *other* sound, her silence began to wear at my nerves. For whatever reason, her not speaking had become more corrosive than the salt and the lashing blow. As the storm chewed at the shoreline, so her refusal to speak ate at my nerves. And I turned to her, then, and she was standing naked, only a foot or so behind me, her clothing ripped away by the hurricane (if it *was* a hurricane). Jesus, I need to get laid, because—despite the horrors of the dream—I woke horny from this vision of her, and writing it down, I'm getting horny again. Amanda always said I was easy. I never really argued with her on that point. But, anyway, there's Constance standing buck-naked on this pebbly, shifting beach while the battered, choleric heavens assailed her pale and unprotected flesh. In that moment, I wanted only to throw her down on the sand and fuck her. I can admit that. Let the tempest take us both, but at least I could go with a goddamn smile on my face. In that moment, or those moments, I wanted to feel my lips against her lips, wanted the heat of her body pressed against my own, wanted to explore every seen and unseen inch of her with my hands and tongue and—yeah, it's obvious enough to see where *that* was headed.

But then she did speak, after all, and her voice—though she spoke so, *so* softly—had no trouble whatsoever reaching my ears over the din of the storm.

"You went to Greece," she said, "and what you remember most is a dead turtle?"

And in *that* moment, all my lust was transmuted to mere anger by the alchemy of human emotion. She was not Amanda, and I had never told her my Grecian sea turtle lie. This was a far greater intrusion than her arrival at the farm or her showing up uninvited in my dreams. This was some manner of mnemonic rape, I think, or so it seemed to me then.

"I never told you about the turtle," I replied, struggling to stay calm, doing a lousy job of it.

"You went all the way to Greece," she continued, staring past me, staring out to sea. "And then you wrote a book about it. But you left out that thing that made the greatest impression upon you?"

"There never was a fucking turtle," I told her. "That was just a lie, because . . ." and I trailed off, as the *whys* of my old lie were really none of her business. "I just made it up.

And I've never told you about that night, about Amanda and the turtle and *The Ark of Poseidon*."

She wiped saltwater from her flushed cheeks and smiled a sad, broken sort of smile. "Lady, you wear your past right out in the open, where anyone can see, if they only bother to look. So, don't blame me for seeing what *you've* put on exhibit."

Behind me, the bludgeoned sky was suddenly lit by a flash of lightning so brilliant, so blinding, that it seemed to sear our shadows into the beach, like those photos you see taken after the bombing of Nagasaki and Hiroshima. *The sand will melt and turn to glass,* I thought, waiting and bracing myself for that seven-thousand-degree fireball. But it didn't come—no atomic pressure wave, no flames, no air superheated by X-rays to instantly vaporize the fragile shells of me and her. Only a thunderclap rattled the world, and then, as the rumble echoed across the land, Constance leaned forward and gently kissed me on the cheek.

"When I was a kid, Sarah, I always wanted a Lite-Brite," she whispered in my ear, and not one single syllable was lost to the jealous, wailing storm, "but it never happened."

"You are a thief," I replied, not whispering. "You are a thief of memories that were never yours," and she laughed at me. There was nothing cruel in the laugh, nothing spiteful. It was more the way you might laugh to lighten a tense mood, to put someone at ease, to make a moron feel less like a moron because she or he is so goddamn dense they can't see whatever obvious truth is staring them in the face.

And it only just this second occurred to me—presumably waking me—that it did *not* occur to the dreaming me that Constance could have learned these things simply by reading the journal I've been keeping on Dr. Harvey's typewriter. So, is this the subconscious expression of some unsuspected paranoia on my part? Is my sleeping mind fretting that I've never made any attempt to hide these pages where no one else can see them, or over my having written all this down in the first place?

"Two billion trees died in that storm," she said. "Think about it a moment. Two *billion* trees." Before I could ask her which storm she was talking about, if maybe she meant the blizzard that brought her into this world like a lion, I saw that she was crying. Only, she wasn't crying tears, but, rather, diluted streaks of oil or acrylic paints bled from the corners of her eyes, paint in all the shades of that awful storm, as though it had somehow gotten into her and now was leaking out again.

She wiped at her face, smearing the paint across her cheekbones and the bridge of her nose. Then Constance was not speaking, but singing to me, and while the music was a mystery, I knew the words at once—" 'What matters it how far we go?' his scaly friend replied. 'There is another shore, you know, upon the other side.' "

And because this is a dream, and because dreams appear even less fond of resolution than waking life, I woke. I woke horny and covered in sweat and gasping, nauseous and my chest aching, any number of panicked thoughts rushing through my mind—a heart attack? Another seizure? Maybe the seizure to come along and end all my fits once and for all. And too, I had not yet passed so completely beyond the borders of the dream that I did not still fear that hurricane bearing down upon me, bearing down to scrub away the shingle and me and Constance and two billion fucking trees. But, no need to worry, right? Because there is another shore, you know, upon the other side.

I've got to end this and get up off my fat ass and make some coffee. It's almost nine, and I think I hear Constance thumping around upstairs. The typewriter probably woke her, regardless of what she's been saying. Hopefully, we'll get our postponed walk in today, out to "the red tree," if the weather is not too hot and we're not both too delirious from sleep deprivation.

July 6, 2008 (10:27 p.m.)

I'm admittedly at a loss how to write all this down—the events of the past twelve or thirteen hours—but I'm also determined that I *will* write it down. Some part of me is genuinely frightened, reluctant to put the experience into words, and, still, I find myself driven to compose some account of it. Are we back to writing as an act of exorcism? Wait, don't answer that question. In fact, no more questions requiring answers, no more questions, just what I am left to believe occurred this afternoon when we tried to visit the tree. We talked about what happened over dinner, which Constance fixed because all I could do was sit here and smoke and stare out the kitchen window at twilight dimming the sky. We talked, but it was an indirect, guarded conversation punctuated with lengthy, uncomfortable silences. I asked her if she'd ever read Shirley Jackson's *The Haunting of Hill House,* specifically the scene where Eleanor and Theodora get lost just outside the house and stumble upon a ghostly picnic. She hasn't, and asked if I've read Borges' "The Garden of Forking Paths." I have. Of course, I have. We ended up talking about *The Blair Witch Project,* though that seemed to come uncomfortably near the bald *facts* of the matter, and so I brought up Joseph Payne Brennan's short story "Canavan's Back Yard," precisely *because* I had a feeling Constance hadn't read it. Inevitably, by fits and starts, we came to Joan Lindsay's *Picnic at Hanging Rock,* both the novel and Peter Weir's film, to Miss McCraw and Mrs. Appleyard and her charges, Irma, Miranda, Edith, and Marion.

Constance said, "The girl who wasn't allowed to go on the picnic, because she hadn't memorized the assigned poem. The one who had a crush on Miranda? Wasn't *her* name Sara?"

I didn't answer the question, and, thankfully, she didn't ask it again.

Yes, I know it's sort of twisted that we had to resort to fictional metaphors and parallels because we were both too goddamned scared to talk about the thing straight on. But I suppose that's what I'm trying to do now, talk about the thing straight on. Just write it down. Make it only words. Sticks and stones can break my bones, but . . . I'm starting to think maybe our dear departed Dr. Harvey figured out that words can do more harm than we generally give them credit. You're *stalling,* Sarah.

Yes, I am.

We didn't get out of the house until almost noon, and I'm not writing all that. Neither of us had slept very much, and we kept finding little chores that needed doing, little distractions. Hindsight can create all manner of illusions, and here, hindsight might suggest some prescience. You know, the man who misses his flight because he needs new shoelaces or Starbucks takes too long with his frappuccino or what the hell ever, and then he finds out the plane crashed, so surely some extrasensory force or guardian spirit was at work? That sort of thing. But the *truth* is we were bleary and distracted by exhaustion, and neither of us was really up to it. She didn't get much more sleep than I did.

And she was still worried about me, because of last night's seizure, and that kept coming up, and whether I was actually well enough for the walk. But the day was much, much cooler than yesterday, and the humidity quite decent, and I assured her that I would be fine. She pointed out that I couldn't possibly know that, and I reluctantly conceded and told her that I'd learned I couldn't let this condition turn me into a shut-in. I have no means of predicting these episodes, but I have to live my life, regardless. What I *didn't* say was, Constance, please mind your own goddamn business, although, by then, that's what I was thinking. She'd asked me twice about my medication, had I taken it, should we carry it with us, what sort of side effects do I experience from it, do I tire easily, shit like that.

"We're not even going a hundred yards from the back

door," I told her. And *there's* the single most damning fact of this thing, right there, the undeniable that I wish I could find some way to deny. *We were not going even a hundred yards from the back door.*

"Sarah, it's just that I need to know what to do, if something happens," she said, packing a canvas tote bag with bottled water and a couple of apples and the sandwiches she'd made. "And I *don't*. I don't know what's myth, and what's for real."

"You saw what happened last night," I replied. "What else is there you need to know?"

"Yeah, but that was only a little one, you said. Right? So what if there's a really *bad* seizure? What then? I don't know what I'm supposed to do to help you. I mean, should I take along a spoon or something, to keep you from swallowing your tongue?"

I laughed at her, which didn't help the situation, and said, "Only if you want to watch me break the few good teeth I have left."

"It's not fucking funny," she growled and stuffed a whole handful of granola bars into her bag, enough granola to keep a troop of Boy Scouts hale and hearty and regular for a couple of days.

"No," I said. "It's not funny at all, which is probably why I make jokes about it."

"Well, it's not funny, and the jokes won't help, if something happens."

And so I told her what she could do, which really isn't very much—that she should try to make sure I don't hit my head on anything hard or sharp, and that she should roll me over into the recovery position, if possible, so I don't strangle on saliva or anything. It seemed to help, just telling her that stuff, and at least she didn't cram any more granola bars into the bag. I guess I'd taken the edge off the sense of helplessness she was left feeling after last night.

"How would I know if it's bad enough to call an ambulance?" she asked.

"Constance, do I look like I could afford whatever it would cost to get an ambulance and paramedics all the way out here?"

"Jesus," she sighed. "*I'd* fucking pay for it, alright? I would pay for it before I'd let you lie there and die in the woods."

I lit a cigarette and stared out the screen door towards that huge red oak, silhouetted against the cloudless northern sky. "If it ever lasts more than five minutes," I said. "Now, are we going to do this, or stand here talking about my fits all day?"

"I'm ready when you are," she replied. And that's what was said before we left, as best I can now recall. There wasn't much else said until fifteen or twenty minutes later, when we realized that we were lost. Or, rather, when we began to admit aloud to one another that we were lost. At first, I think it was more embarrassment than anything, embarrassment and confusion, and I'm sure we both thought that whatever had gone awry would right itself after only another minute or two. We'd simply gotten turned around somehow, that's all. People don't like to admit when they're lost, not only from a fear of looking like a horse's ass, but also because the admission entails an acceptance that one is in some degree of trouble. And, in this case, I spent half my childhood and teenage years in the woods back in Alabama and know well enough how to walk less than a hundred fucking straight yards from Point A to Point B, plus I'd already visited the tree once. Constance is a local and, despite her time misspent in Los Angeles, is also no stranger to walks in the woods. So, we were both fairly, and not unreasonably, reluctant to admit, even to ourselves, that something was wrong.

Near as I can tell, it started when we reached the break in the fieldstone wall and the deadfall of pine branches and had to leave the path to cross the stream running out of the pond in order to make our way around that impenetrable snarl of rotting wood, poison ivy, and greenbriers. We were both sweating by this time, and I paused at the stream to wet the bright yellow paisley bandanna I'd brought along before tying it once again about my throat. Constance crossed before me, and stood there staring in the direction of the red tree and Ramswool, talking about catching salamanders and turtles when she was a kid. I made some joke about tomboys, and then followed her across, noting how very dark the water was. I didn't remember this from before—the somber, stained water—but it made sense, thinking about it. All that rotting vegetation surely produces a lot of tannin, which leaches directly into the stream. Where the water was moving, it was the translucent amber of weak tea, and where is wasn't, here and there in deeper, stagnant pools, it was the rich, almost black brown of a strong cup of coffee. I associate this sort of "blackwater" with bayous and with the Southern coastal plain, and it seemed oddly out of place here on Squire Blanchard's farm. Also, it brought to mind Dr. Harvey's mention of the Bloody Run in Newport, that stream supposedly painted red with the blood of so many slain Hessian conscripts during the Revolutionary War.

She suggested we follow the west bank a little farther, as there was considerably less in the way of briars and underbrush on that side of the creek. And since we could still plainly see the upper boughs of the red tree from the broad gully the stream had carved, it made sense to me. The ground was a little muddy, and maybe the gnats and mosquitoes were worse, but the air was cooler down there in the leafy shadows of that hollow. We could always cross back over, scale the steep bank, and then the stone wall, when we were even with the tree. And now, typing this, another (rather obvious) literary parallel occurs to me, "Little Red Riding Hood" and the mother's instructions that her daughter not dare stray from the path leading safely to her grandmother's house. The Brothers Grimm, and Charles Perrault's *"Le Petit Chaperon Rouge,"* and also, of course, Angela Carter's retellings in *The Bloody Chamber*. Constance and I had strayed from the path, like mannish Miss McCraw and the four doomed students who followed her up Hanging Rock, or . . . digression, digression, fucking digression. Tell the story, Sarah, or *don't* tell the story, but stop this infernal beating around the bush (and no, I shall *not* here initiate yet another digression regarding that unfortunate choice of words).

I think we'd walked for about ten minutes, when Constance noted how odd it was that the tree did not seem to be getting any closer. Or rather, that we didn't appear to be getting any nearer to it. I laughed it off, said something about optical illusions or mirages, and we kept going, slogging more or less northwards towards the tree, which was still clearly visible. Fifteen or twenty minutes later, there was no longer any denying the fact that, somehow, the red tree had become a fixed point, there to the northeast of us, and that we should have already long since passed it and reached the edge of the pond. By then, it should have become necessary to turn 180° and look south to see the tree, but it remained more or less precisely where it had been, relative to our position, when we'd climbed down from the path to the nameless little stream.

"This is sort of fucked-up," Constance said, not exactly whispering, but speaking very softly, as though she might be afraid someone would overhear.

"No," I replied. "This is bullshit," and I turned right, sloshing back across the tannin-stained water, getting wet to my knees and hardly caring. I scrambled up the bank, and over the fieldstone wall, and there was the path, and there was the far side of the deadfall, standing between me and the house, even though the pile of branches is, at most, only ten feet wide, and we would have passed it *immediately*, as soon as we began following the stream towards the tree. I stood there, out of breath, a stitch in my side, tasting my own sweat, and I shouted for Constance to get her ass up there.

After she'd seen it for herself, she shook her head and said, "It's a different one, that's all." But the uncertainty in her eyes didn't even begin to match the intended conviction of her words.

"Constance, I was here less than a *week* ago. Trust me. There was only one deadfall."

"Well, then this one's new," she said, her voice taking on a frustrated, insistent edge. "*These* limbs fell later, *after* you came through here, okay?"

I took the bandanna from around my neck and watched her while I wiped at my face with it. The stream water had long since evaporated, and the only moisture on the yellow cotton was my own perspiration.

"Fine," I said, because I could see she was scared, and I know I was getting scared, and nothing was going to be accomplished by arguing about the hurdle of vines and rotting white pine blocking our route back to the house. "But how long have we been walking, Constance? How long have we been following that creek, with the tree not getting any closer?"

She looked at her wristwatch, and then looked towards the oak, and then looked back to me.

"I'm guessing at least half an hour, right?" I said, and, before she could reply, I continued, because I really did not need or want to hear the answer to my question. "And even if you take into account the time needed for us to climb down to the stream and back up here again, and the few minutes we spent by the water, talking about salamanders and tadpoles and shit, even if you take *all* that into account, why aren't we at the tree? How the hell does it take half an hour to walk three quarters the length of a football field?"

"We'll clear it up later, I'm sure," Constance said, turning away from the deadfall and towards the tree. But the *way* she said it, I was left with little doubt that she'd prefer I never even *mention* the matter again, much less try, at that safely unspecified, but *later,* point in time, to puzzle out what we'd just experienced.

She started walking along the narrow path, and because I had no idea what else to do, I followed her. All around us, the trees were alive with fussing birds and maybe a chattering squirrel or two. I still have a lot of trouble telling angry birds and angry squirrels apart. There was a warm breeze, and, overhead, the branches rustled and the leaves whispered among themselves. Constance walked fast, and so I had to move fast to keep pace. Before long, she was almost sprinting, her footfalls seeming oddly loud against the bare, packed earth of the trail.

Five or ten minutes later I was breathless and sweating like a pig, and I shouted for her to please stop before I had a goddamn coronary. And she *did* stop, but when she looked back at me, there was an angry, desperate cast in those brick-red eyes of hers. Those irises not unlike the tannin-colored water of the stream.

"*Look* at it," I gasped, leaning forward, hands on knees, gasping for air and hoping to hell I could get through the next couple of minutes without being sick. "Jesus Christ, Constance, just stop and fucking *look* at it."

And she did. She stood there in the muttering woods, while I struggled to catch my breath, while my sweat dripped and spattered the dirt. She stared at the red tree, and then she asked, "Why doesn't it want me to reach it? It let you, but it won't even allow me to get near." I am moderately sure these were her precise words, and I managed a strangled sort of laugh and spat on the ground.

"Let's go back," I said, doing my best to conceal my own confusion and fear. "Like you said, I'm sure it will all make sense later. But I don't think either of us is in any shape to keep this up."

"What if it's me, Sarah?" she asked. "What if doesn't want me getting close?"

I stood up, my back popping loudly, painfully, and I took her arm. "Let's go back," I said again. "It's just a tree. It doesn't want anything, Constance. We're hot and confused and scared, that's all."

She nodded slowly, and didn't argue. I held her arm and softly urged her back the way we'd come. She took a bottle of water from the canvas tote bag, twisted the cap off, and when she was finished, passed it to me. The water was warm and tasted like plastic, but it made me feel just a little better. I remembered the sandwiches and apples and all the damned granola bars she'd packed; if we *were* lost, at least we wouldn't starve right away.

"Come on," she said, returning the water bottle to the

tote. "I don't want to be out here anymore. I need to be home now."

"That makes two of us. But, please, do me a favor, and let's not try to make a footrace of it, alright?"

"Fine. You go first," she replied, and the tone of her voice, her voice and the circumstances combined, there was no way I could not think of some adolescent dare. An abandoned house, maybe, a door left ajar, hanging loose on rusted hinges, opening onto musty shadows and half light. *You go first. I dare you. No, I double-dog dare you.* I was always a sucker for dares.

"If you keep your head, when everyone about you is busy losing theirs," I said, and began walking south again, following the trail back to the house.

"Who said that?" she asked, and pulled her arm free.

"I'm paraphrasing," I replied.

"So *who* are you paraphrasing?"

"Rudyard Kipling," I told her, though, at the time I was only half sure it *was* Kipling and not Disraeli.

"The same guy that wrote *The Jungle Book*?" she asked, and I knew Constance was talking merely to hear her own voice, to keep *me* talking, that she was busy trying to occupy her mind with anything mundane. "Mowgli and Baloo and Bagheera, right?"

"Yeah," I answered. "But my favorite was always 'Rikki-Tikki-Tavi.' My favorite story by Kipling, I mean. You know, the one about the mongoose and the two cobras—"

"I never read it," she said. "But I saw the Disney movie when I was a kid. I don't remember a mongoose."

"Rikki-Tikki-Tavi wasn't in the Disney film."

"I never read it," she said again.

And the conversation went on like that for a while, I don't know exactly how long. Kipling and Disney and what the hell ever, until she stopped and checked her watch, and I stopped and waited on her.

"So, where's the deadfall?" she asked, and laughed a brittle, skittish laugh, looking up from her wrist and staring down the trail winding on ahead of us. "We should be back to it by now."

I didn't answer her, and I also didn't *ask* how long it had been since we'd turned back towards the house. I didn't need to ask to know that we should have already reached the deadfall. I glanced off to my left, and the fieldstone wall was exactly where it ought to be, sagging in upon itself with the weight of all the centuries that had passed unnoticed since its construction, the long decades since the last time this land was farmed and anyone had bothered with the wall's maintenance. I could hear the little stream mumbling coolly somewhere beyond it.

"Well, we're going the right way," I said, peering up through the dappled light, checking the afternoon sun to be sure we were still walking south.

"Maybe the trail forked somewhere back there, and we were talking and not paying attention, and we went the wrong way," she said hopefully, and I nodded, because it was a better story than whatever was running through my head. "Maybe," she said, "we went left when we should have gone right, or something like that."

I looked again at the stone wall, those moss- and lichen-scabbed granite and gneiss boulders, and I could feel her eyes following mine.

"So maybe there are two streams," she said, and now the brittleness in her voice was edging towards panic. "And those goddamn stone walls are everywhere out here. That doesn't mean anything, Sarah."

"I didn't say it did," I told her, knowing perfectly goddamn well it was the same wall, and that I was hearing the same stream. "I didn't say anything."

"You're *thinking* it, though," she said. "Don't lie to me, because you're standing there thinking it."

"You never told me you were fucking clairvoyant," I said. "Why is that, that you never bothered to say you could read my mind?" the words hard and mean and out before I could think better of it. And probably, at that juncture, I was somewhere past caring, anyway. I had my own apprehensions to worry about, and I was tired of coddling her.

"We're lost," she said. "We're lost out here, and you *know* we're lost."

"Seventy-five yards," I reminded her. "Constance, *no one* gets lost walking seventy-five yards from their back door to a goddamn tree, walking in a *straight line,* when you never even lose sight of where it is you're headed." And it occurred to me, then, and for the first time, that I couldn't see the farmhouse, even though I'd been able to keep track of it almost the whole way the *first* time I'd gone to the tree. Even though, as I believe I mentioned in an earlier entry, a quirk of the landscape had, admittedly, made it harder to keep the house in view than the red tree. I walked a little farther down the trail—another ten or twenty yards—and Constance followed me silently; I was grateful that she didn't ask what I was doing or what I was thinking. But I still couldn't see any sign of the house. I stopped (and she did likewise, close behind me), checking the sky again to be absolutely certain I'd not lost my bearings, that we were, in fact, still moving roughly due south.

"Next time, just to be on the safe side, how about we bring along a compass," I said, trying once more to make a joke from something that wasn't funny, something that might *become* funny—tomorrow maybe, or next week—when we were safely out of these woods. When the inevitably obvious rational explanation had finally, mercifully, *become* obvious. Predictably, Constance seemed to find no more humor in the compass remark than in my earlier failed attempt to get her to loosen up and laugh about the seizures. She glared at me, a spiteful, how-*dare*-you glare, and then let the canvas tote bag slip from her arm and fall with a thump to the ground between us.

"I'm tired of carrying it," she said, though I had not asked. "My shoulder's sore."

I simply nodded, not taking the bait, if, indeed, she was baiting me. Instead, I stared back towards the red tree, and for the first time since finding Dr. Charles Harvey's manuscript, hidden away in the basement, it seemed to me *more* than a tree. It seemed, in that moment, to have sloughed off whatever guise or glamour usually permitted it to pass for only a very old, very large oak. Suddenly, I felt, with sickening conviction, I was gazing through or around a mask, that I was being *allowed* to do so that I might at last be made privy to this grand charade. I saw wickedness. I could not then, and cannot now, think of any better word. I saw wickedness dressed up like a tree, and I had very little doubt that it saw *me*, as well. Here was William Burroughs' *Naked Lunch*—the frozen moment when I clearly perceived what lay at the end of my fork—and the perfect Dadaist inversion of expectation, something, possibly, akin to that enlightened state that Zen Buddhists might describe as *kensho*. The epiphanic realizations of Stephen Dedalus, only, instead of Modernist revelations I was presented with this vision of primeval wickedness. And I knew, if I did not look away, and look away quickly, that what I saw would sear me, and I'd never find my way back to the house. I thought of Harvey, then, and I thought of William and Susan Ames, and John Potter's fears of Narragansett demons.

"Listen," Constance whispered, and her voice pulled me back to myself, and I was only standing on a path in the woods again, staring at her sweat-streaked face, the dread and terror shimmering brightly in her eyes. "Did you hear that, Sarah?"

"We're going to be fine," I told her, not acknowledging the question I'd only half heard. "We have to stay calm, that's all."

And she held an index finger to her lips, then, shushing me. Speaking so quietly that the words were almost lost in the background murmurs of the forest, she said, "I heard voices. I heard . . ."

But then she trailed off, and I could have been sitting at the kitchen window, watching one of the deer, its every muscle tensed and ears pricked. I could have been sitting at the table, waiting for the deer to bolt at whatever I could not hear.

And I realized that Constance was holding my left arm, her hand gripping me tightly just above the elbow.

"I don't hear *anything*," I whispered back to her, despite her silencing finger, despite my head so filled with the view of that awful, dizzying wickedness sprouting from the stony soil.

But then I *did*, though it was not voices or anything that could be mistaken for voices. From our right, past the fieldstone wall, came the undisputable commotion of something large splashing through the stream. And despite the prickling hairs at the nape of my neck, despite the gooseflesh on my arms and the rush of adrenaline, I opened my mouth to tell her it was only a deer, only a deer or a dog—a wild dog at the very worst. But she had already released my arm, was already *off the path* and running, and helpless to do anything else, I followed. I cannot say how long I chased her through those woods, the greenbriers ripping at my exposed face and arms, branches whipping past, my feet tangling in the wild grapes so that it is only by some miracle I didn't fall and break my neck. As we ran, I was gradually overcome with the conviction that I was not so much trying to catch up with her, as fleeing some unspeakable expression of the wickedness I had seen manifest in the red tree. All I had to do was look over my shoulder to see it. But I did not look back. Like Constance, like the frightened does and fauns, I ran.

And then we were through the last clinging wall of vines, the last bulwark of poison ivy and ferns, dashing wildly across the weedy yard surrounding Blanchard's farmhouse. I was shouting for her to stop, that we were safe now, that it was over, because that sense of being pursued had vanished, abruptly and completely. She *did* stop, so suddenly that I almost ran into her, though I know now it wasn't because of anything I'd said. Constance stood a few feet away, drenched in sweat, wheezing so loudly I might have taken her for an asthmatic. There were tears in her eyes, and blood from what the briars had done to her face, and she was laughing uncontrollably. She pointed at the house, and at first I didn't see what was wrong with it, what it was that she *wanted* me to see, what she *needed* me to see. For a time, I saw only the house, and the house meant only that the ordeal was over and we were safe, and neither of us would ever be so foolish as to go wandering off towards that wicked, wicked tree again. But the relief washed away, rolling easily out from under me, like pebbles on a beach before the towering clouds and indifferent winds of an advancing hurricane.

We were standing on the *south* side of the house, not far from the *front* door, despite the fact that we'd been walking, and then *running*, south, bound for the *back* door. And sure, later we would tell ourselves that, obviously (there's that word again), in our panicked flight and having forsaken the path, we'd wandered in a half circle, passing east of the house, and then doubling back again without having realized we'd done so. Never mind the questions left unanswered, the inexplicable events that had led to that pell-mell dash.

And now I look at the clock on the wall and see I've been sitting here the better part of three hours. My eyes hurt, I have a headache, and I feel like every bone in my body has been pummeled using a sock filled with pennies. No more of this tonight. I've set down the broad strokes, and I probably shouldn't have done even that much. I'm going to have another beer, a handful of ibuprofen, and go the hell to bed.

July 7, 2008 (8:33 p.m.)

I sat down after dinner and read back over what I'd typed out last night. I even read a few bits of it aloud to Constance, which was, all things considered, rather ballsy of me, I think. She listened, but didn't offer much beyond the occasional frown or shrug. Since yesterday, her mood has seemed to grow increasingly sour, and tonight she is distant, uncommunicative. I can't be sure if she's angry at me, or angry because she's embarrassed, or just plain angry. Maybe some combination of the three, and understandably freaked out, in the bargain. Anyway, after I read the pages, I considered trying to make a more detailed and more coherent account of the experience. But, on the one hand, I don't think I'm up to it, and on the other, what I wrote last night—for all its considerable faults—is likely far more honest and interesting in its immediacy than any carefully considered, reasoned version of our "lost picnic" (Constance's phrase, and I take it as a reference to Lindsay's novel) than I would produce tonight, more than twenty-four hours after the fact. I've had too much time to think about something that seems pretty much impervious to explanation. I mean, to any explanation that does not assume or require a violation of the laws of physics or recourse to the supernatural. And I think our stroll through the woods has taught me how deeply committed I am to a materialist interpretation of the universe, even when the universe deigns to suggest otherwise.

I woke this morning to find Constance sitting on the porch, smoking and staring into the trees and undergrowth at the edge of the front yard. There was a sketchbook lying open in her lap, and an old coffee mug of charcoal pencils on the porch rail. But the paper was blank. Near as I could tell, she'd drawn nothing. She didn't seem to notice me until I said her name, and repeated it a second time; even then, when she turned and looked at me, there was something about her eyes, something about her expression, that made me wonder if she understood I was addressing *her*.

"How about some breakfast?" I asked, yawning and scraping together half a smile or so.

Constance blinked at me, like maybe she was having to work to remember my name. After a few seconds, there was a faint glimmer of recognition, and she turned away again. She took another drag from her cigarette and looked back towards the yard and the woods beyond.

"Sarah, I don't feel like cooking for you today," she said.

"That's not what I meant," I replied, caught slightly off guard and determined not to begin the day with an argument. "How about I cook something for the both of us. I think there are still a few eggs in the fridge."

"I'm really not hungry," she said.

I started to go back inside and leave her alone with her thoughts, whatever they might be. I'm sure that's what I *should* have done. There was nothing I had to say that she wanted to hear, and I'm not quite so dense that I couldn't see that. But, just as our inexplicably failed bid to reach Dr. Harvey's red tree seems to have caused Constance to withdraw, so it has left me somewhat less content with my own company than usual.

"So how about I make you a cup of joe?" I asked. "Or tea? Or, hey, fuck it, what about a beer? A cold Narragansett wouldn't be such a bad way to start things after yesterday."

"I'm *fine,*" she said, grinding that last syllable and sounding anything but, and she stubbed out her cigarette in a ginger Altoids tin she's taken to carrying around with her. She popped the butt inside and snapped the tin shut.

"Constance, you know, some things, no matter how long you sit and stare at them, they just stay weird. You don't always find a library book—"

"Don't you patronize me," she said, and, looking back, it was probably for the best that she interrupted me when she did. I just wish I'd have had the presence of mind to keep my mouth shut to start with. Constance glared at her Altoids tin, clutched tightly in her right hand, and I was beginning to think she was going to turn around and throw it at me. I suppose I'd have had it coming.

"Don't you fucking *dare,*" she continued, slipping the tin into a pocket of one of the black smocks she wears when she paints. "And don't try to tell me there's no point obsessing over it, because I know you're doing the same goddamn thing."

"I won't," I said. "I wasn't trying to."

"You know what I think?" she asked, and then told me before I could reply. "I think you could go inside and pack yourself another picnic lunch right now and head back to the tree alone. I think you could do that, Sarah Crowe, and you wouldn't have any trouble whatsoever finding it, or finding your way back here again, afterwards."

I shrugged, wishing I hadn't left my own cigarettes inside, but not about to ask Constance for one.

"You know," I replied, getting a bit pissed, but doing my best not to let it show. "Me not patronizing you, that would have to include my telling you how crazy that sounds, right?"

"Yeah? So why don't you try it, Sarah? If it's crazy, what have you got to lose?"

"Look, I'm going to make a pot of coffee, and maybe when I've had three or four cups, when I can see straight, maybe then we'll continue this conversation."

And I was already stepping across the threshold, back into the house, already pulling the door closed, when she said, "You won't do it, and you won't do it because you're scared. But I wish you would, Sarah. I wish you'd try going back without me."

"Okay. So, maybe I will," I said, knowing full well I wasn't about to do any such thing. "But first, I'm making coffee, and getting something to eat. And you are more than welcome to join me, if you should happen to get tired of sitting out here not drawing whatever it is you're staring at so intently." And I shut the door, quickly, before she could get another jab in or possibly raise the stakes of her silly little dare. *Hey, old lady, I'll even screw you if you'll just try to find the tree again without me. Sure, give it another shot, and, if you make it back, I'll throw a pity fuck your way.* I went to the kitchen and wrestled with the temperamental old percolator that came with the place, and I listened to NPR and had a bowl of stale Wheat Chex without milk, because the carton of "Rhody Fresh" had gone over. Constance didn't join me, though halfway through my second cup of coffee, I heard the front door slam, heard her stomping upstairs to her garret. When I was done, I tried valiantly to occupy my mind by doing a half-assed job of cleaning the kitchen and the bathroom. Both badly needed it, though the work did little, if anything, to distract me. I kept stopping to stare up at the ceiling, wondering what Constance was doing overhead in the air-conditioned sanctuary of her attic, if she was painting or sketching or just lying on the futon beneath the chugging window unit, worrying at her memories. Or I'd find myself sweat-soaked and gazing at a sink filled with dirty dishes and sudsy water, or at the toilet brush, and realize that I'd spent the last five minutes standing there, thinking about the tree, playing back over the events of the day before. No less guilty than my housemate of trying to see past what *had* happened to anything else that would make more sense and not leave that cold, hard knot in my guts.

When Constance finally *did* reappear, it was late afternoon, and I was lying on the sofa in the den, intermittently dozing and trying to concentrate on Alice Morse Earle's unutterably dry *Customs and Fashions of Old New England* (1893), which I'd brought home from the library in Moosup a few days before. She slipped into the room without a word and sat down on the floor not far from me. There were a few fresh-looking smears of paint on her smock, and she was accompanied by the pine-sap smell of turpentine. There were motley stains on her hands and fingers, too, several shades of blue and green and red.

After a moment, she cleared her throat, so I closed my book and dropped it to the floor beside the sofa.

"We still on speaking terms?" she asked.

I rubbed at my eyes, and watched her a moment or two before answering. "It would be damned inconvenient if we aren't," I said.

"Good," she smiled, guarded relief creeping over her face. "I shouldn't have said those things. I know I shouldn't have."

"Yeah, well, we both saw some seriously freaky shit. Not exactly the sort of thing you tend to forget overnight. And, besides, I really should have had enough smarts to leave you alone this morning."

She picked up *Customs and Fashions of Old New England* and stared at the spine. "You were actually reading this?" she asked.

"No," I told her. "Not actually."

Constance set the book back on the floor between us and, with her left index finger, traced invisible circles and figure-eights on the black cover.

"I'm never at my best when I'm afraid," she said.

"Not many people are," I replied. But it sounded trite, maybe even condescending, and I sighed and shut my tired eyes. Orange and yellow ghost images floated about in the incomplete darkness, a swirling, leftover smutch of four-thirty sunlight generated by my confused retinas.

"What I said about you going back out there alone, I know I wasn't making a lot of sense."

"It's okay, Constance. Really. Don't worry about it."

"But I want to try to explain," she said, and I opened my eyes. "I don't like people thinking that I'm scared, but it's worse when they think I'm crazy."

"I don't think you're crazy," I said, and she lifted her finger off the cover of the library book and glared up at me, looking more confused than anything else. "You *know* what I meant," I said, and there was undoubtedly more exasperation in my voice than I'd intended there to be.

"I know what you said."

"I *say* too much. You'd think anyone lives this long, she'd have figured that out by now. Regardless, you don't need to explain anything to me. I *don't* think you're crazy. I was half asleep and just mouthing off."

"I never should have come back here," she said. "I should have stayed in Los Angeles." And this time I didn't reply. I lay there on the sofa, rubbing my eyes and waiting for whatever it was that she would or wouldn't say next. There was a noise outside, the wind or an animal poking about, but nothing unusual. Still, Constance turned her head away, turning towards the direction from which the noise seemed to have come. It wasn't repeated, and after a while, she asked, "Have you read the whole thing? All of it?"

"Lord no," I said, assuming she meant the library book. "I've hardly started it. Frankly, I don't know why the hell I brought it home. *Good Housekeeping* in the age of Cotton Mather."

"I wasn't talking about *this,*" she said impatiently, and tapped the cover of the library book with her knuckles. "I mean Chuck Harvey's manuscript. Have you finished reading *it*?"

"He didn't even finish *writing* it," I replied.

"Yeah, I *know* that, but have you read everything he did write?"

"No," I told her, sitting up, and wondering if she'd be up for a drive to the beach, thinking it would do us both good to get out of the woods and away from this house for a little bit. Hell, I even thought about volunteering to spring for a room in Stonington or Mystic (because, after all, that's what credit cards are for). "I haven't. I've read, I don't know, maybe half of it."

"But you do *intend* to finish it before you take it to that woman at URI, right?"

"Maybe it would be better if I didn't," I sighed, not sure where she was headed, but already pretty certain she'd say no to a night away from the house.

Constance had gone back to drawing her invisible curlicues on the cover of the library book. "Well," she said, "that's up to you. But I need you to promise that you won't get rid of it before you let me read it all."

"You think your answers are waiting in there somewhere?" I asked, trying to remember if we had anything for dinner or if I'd have to drive into town.

"Just promise me that, alright?"

"Sure. No problem. I promise, cross my heart and hope to die," and after that, she seemed to relax a bit.

"Scout's honor?" she asked.

"Not fucking likely," I laughed and had a go at combing my hair with my fingers.

"Oh, I was a Girl Scout," Constance said. "Troop 850. I had my first taste of weed on one of the camping trips."

"No shit? The Girl Scouts have a marijuana merit badge?"

She laughed, but we didn't talk very long, and after a while she vanished into her garret again, saying that she wanted to get back to work. She came down for dinner (Velveeta grilled cheeses and Campbell's Soup; at least I didn't have to go to the store), but didn't stick around long afterwards. Maybe I'll do the beach thing by myself tomorrow, and hope that the tourists aren't as bad on Mondays, that their numbers have declined since the Fourth.

July 8, 2008 (2:24 p.m.)

Earlier today, I was going through one of the boxes of books I brought up here with me from Atlanta, one of the few that didn't go directly from the old apartment into storage. Comfort books, I call them, a hodgepodge of familiar volumes that I've read again and again and again, some of them since childhood. My personal take on Linus van Pelt's blue security blanket, I suppose; the bookworm's dog-eared solace. So, I was sorting through the box, only half remembering having packed most of what was in there, and at the very bottom was a big hardback, *The Annotated Alice,* with all Martin Gardner's marginalia and John Tenniel's illustrations. It was a Christmas gift when I was only eight years old, and I guess that would have been 1972. Yeah, '72. I didn't *own* many books as a child, and certainly not hardbacks. My father, a high-school dropout, said it was a waste of good money, paying for books when there was a library right there in Mayberry (though I suspect he himself never set foot in it). Anyway, my mother found a used copy of *The Annotated Alice* at a yard sale sometime in the autumn, and then gave it to me for Christmas that year. You can still see where $1.25 was penciled in on the upper-right-hand corner of the title page, and she tried unsuccessfully to erase it. The book was printed in 1960, so it was already, what, twelve years old when she gave it to me. And Jesus, how I loved that book. There are long passages that I committed to memory, that I can still recite.

Today, I lifted the book out of the box, and it fell open to pages 184–85, a little more than halfway through, just past the beginning of *Through the Looking Glass and What Alice Found There*. On page 184, the Tenniel woodcut shows Alice entering the mirror above the fireplace, and on the opposite page, she's emerging from that *other* mirror in the reversed world of the Looking-glass House. Hidden in between these two pages—and Alice's act of passing from one universe into its left-handed counterpart—was a folded sheet of wax paper, and pressed between the two halves of the wax paper were five dried four-leaf clovers, and also a tiny violet. I removed the wax paper and closed the book, setting it aside. Seeing the pressed clovers and the single faded violet, there was such an immediate flood of memories. I don't know how long I sat there holding those souvenirs and crying. Yeah, crying.

Amanda and I used to joke that it was her superpower, finding four-leaf clovers. I've never been any good at it myself, but she could stand over any given patch of clover, and, within only a minute or two, without fucking fail, spot at least two or three. And here were five from some spring or summer afternoon that I could not recall, only that *she* had found them for me. I picked the violet. I can't even remember now what led to the preservation of these *particular* clovers. I mean, if I'd saved every four-leaf clover Amanda ever found and gave to me, I'd have hundreds of the things. I didn't even put them in the book, so I can only assume that Amanda did. For some reason lost to me, or never known to me, *these* were special. Maybe if Amanda were still alive, she'd know why. I could have picked up the phone and called her, and she would have laughed and told me, would have described that morning or evening, the circumstances that made these matter so much more than all the others.

I've spent so much energy casting Amanda as the villain, even though I know perfectly well that's bullshit. It's easier to recall the constant bickering, the minute wounds we inflicted upon each other, her low blows and my cheap shots, and incidents like her taunting me outside the Morewell Tunnel, than to tell the truth. The truth is so much more inconveniently complicated. But here were these five clovers and the violet stashed inside this book I've cherished since I was a kid, undeniable evidence that it wasn't all hurtful, no matter how "toxic" her therapist might have deemed our relationship. Here was proof that a moment had existed when she loved me enough to put these tokens of good luck, which came so easily to her, but always eluded me, where she *knew* I would always have them.

I sat on the living room floor, and held the wax paper, and cried until my sinuses ached and there was nothing in me left to cry. I was terrified that Constance would come downstairs, and I'd have to try to explain, but she didn't. And then I put Amanda's keepsake back between pages 184 and 185, closed the book, and returned it to the bottom of the cardboard box.

July 9, 2008 (5:33 p.m.)

In Chapter Five of Harvey's manuscript, he relates an apparently well-documented incident from 1957 that bears an unnerving similarity to what happened to Constance and me on Sunday afternoon. An unnerving similarity, or a remarkable similarity, or both. This is new territory for me, and so I'm not entirely certain what adjectives are most appropriate. In all honesty, I'd pretty much resolved to stop reading the manuscript. I'd decided, before Sunday, to let Constance read it and satisfy whatever morbid curiosity motivates her, then deliver it to the sociologist in Kingston. The thing has begun to make me nervous, and before Sunday, I would have said it makes me nervous in no way that I can lay my finger on. Now, I can lay my finger on page 242, and point to the precise source of my unease—or one of the sources, as I am beginning to see that it all fits together somehow, even if I cannot yet fully articulate the extent of the nature of this interconnectedness.

On page 242, Harvey writes:

The odd case of Olivia Burgess bears discussing in detail, in part because it was reported in numerous newspapers, not only in Rhode Island and New England, but all across the country. Here we do not have to rely upon the frail pages of antique diaries or local folklore or turn to urban legends where the only sources that can be cited are the inevitable FOAFs. In my files, I have forty-seven separate newspaper and magazine accounts of the Burgess incident, all of them printed between October 17, 1957, and May 2, 1974, including a number of interviews with Ms. Burgess. Though a few of the periodicals in question may rightfully be considered suspect (the December 1963 issue of _Fate_, for example, and a particularly sensationalized piece in the September '71 issue of _Argosy_), most of the reporting is straightforward and often outwardly skeptical of Ms. Burgess' claims (many of the later accounts appear as "seasonal" Halloween-related pieces, neither taking the story seriously nor bothering to get the facts straight).

On the morning of Thursday, October 10, Olivia Burgess, a widowed 45-year-old native of Hartford, Connecticut, was visiting the Wight Farm as part of research for a book on the history of agricultural practices in pre-Revolutionary War New England. Having been told that there were remains of an old cider press located within easy walking distance of the house, at the base of a large tree somewhere near Ramswool Pond, Ms. Burgess set out on foot, alone, to see if she could confirm or deny the report. By all accounts, in the fall of 1957, the land between the farmhouse and the flooded quarry was still being kept clear, and the walk would surely have seemed a simple enough detour. However, the story she would eventually tell a friend back in Hartford, who urged her to repeat it to a local reporter, was anything but simple.

According to Ms. Burgess, she found the large stone situated at the base of the old red oak, just as it had been described to her by the landowner's wife. She reported photographing the stone from several angles using a Brownie Bull's-Eye camera. It was only when she'd finished and had headed back towards the house that her visit to the Wight place took a macabre turn. Olivia Burgess claimed to have become immediately disoriented, though she was certain from the position of the sun and the fact that the tree was visible behind her, that she had to be heading in the right direction. Also, she noted, she soon lost sight of the farmhouse, though it should have lain directly ahead of her, to her south.

"The longer I walked, the farther away from me the house appeared to get. It literally grew smaller as I approached, as though I were experiencing an inversion of parallax or stereopsis. The effect was not only frightening, but I soon became nauseated, almost to the point of vomiting." Finally, the house vanished from sight completely and Burgess grew "very afraid, because I could still see the tree quite well whenever I looked back towards the pond." After almost half an hour of trying to reach the house, she retraced her steps to the tree and tried once again to reach the farmhouse, with identical results.

"It was getting late," she told The Hartford Courant, "and twilight was coming on. I became terrified that I would be unable to get back to the house before nightfall, even though it lay less than a hundred yards away."

After a third failed attempt to walk back to the house, Ms. Burgess had the presence of mind to try a different tack. Though it was growing dark, she crossed the stone wall west of the tree and walked in that direction until she managed to reach a farm on Barbs Hill Road. She then caught a ride into Moosup Valley, and did not return for her car until the next morning, and then only with the company of a male acquaintance from Foster, as well as an off-duty fireman, the landowner, and another local (unnamed) farmer. She is quoted in the original Hartford Courant article as having said, "I know perfectly well that all four of them thought I was certifiable, and I told them a lot less than I'm telling you. But I wouldn't go back out to that tree for a million dollars."

When the film in her Brownie was processed by a photo lab a few days later, all the prints were returned black, devoid of any image whatsoever, as though the film had never been exposed.

There's quite a bit more of this. In fact, Harvey devotes the majority of Chapter Five to the episode, to various interviews with Olivia Burgess (*née* Adams) and to numerous secondhand sources. He claims (and it does appear, from his account) that Burgess stuck to her story, as first reported, until her death in 1987 at age seventy-five. Some of the later versions of the tale, notably those appearing in *Fate* and *Argosy* magazines, took considerable liberties and embellished the story, as though it weren't bizarre enough to start with. The *Argosy* article states that Burgess found fresh bloodstains on the stone and around the base of the old oak, and the *Fate* article not only claims that she was pursued by a "large black wolflike animal" during her ordeal, but tries to link the episode to both UFOs *and* the nuclear accident in Windscale, Cumbria, which happened to occur that same day (and was considered the world's worst reactor mishap until Three Mile Island).

While certainly not identical to the apparent distortions of space and time that Constance and I experienced on our "lost picnic," the parallels are unequivocal. I have packed the unfinished manuscript back into its box and left it at the foot of the attic stairs for her to read. I think I've had enough. Enough of those pages and enough of this place, enough of that wicked tree that I have to see every time I forget not to look out the kitchen window. Enough, period. If someone had told me Olivia Burgess' story a week ago, I'd have called them a crank or a liar. Now, I'm wondering if it's possible to sue that bastard Blanchard for neglecting to mention that he was renting me a house built on Hell's doorstep?

CHAPTER FIVE

July 14, 2008 (11:43 p.m.)

I thought perhaps I'd made the last entry to this journal, if you can even call this a proper journal. Dr. Harvey's typewriter has sat here on the kitchen table, neglected, untouched (at least by my hands), for the past four days. So, I was hoping I'd kicked the habit. No such luck. Clack, clack, clack. And I'm not entirely sure what has brought me back to these clangorous keys, whether it is today's events or merely force of habit. If I claim the former, I can feel as though I am compelled, and so what I am saying has some importance. If I plead the latter, well, then this is really no different than the nicotine, and perhaps nothing happened today that was any more remarkable than the nothing that happened yesterday, and the nothing from the day before that. But, because I need a fix—the motion of my fingers, the syllables spilling from my mind, the "sound" of my own goddamn droning voice talking to myself—I'm willing to inflate the significance of the afternoon to give me an excuse to write.

For the most part, Constance has kept to her attic, and, for the most part, I've passed the time downstairs reading and watching old movies. Mostly, I suspect we've both been trying not to think about whatever happened when we tried to reach the tree last Sunday. I have avoided the manuscript, and I have also avoided glancing out the kitchen window. I know she's been painting, because she tells me so when I bother to ask. And the variegated stains on her hands and the smocks she wears change from day to day. The smells of linseed oil and turpentine leak down to me. Before today, we weren't talking very much, mostly only when we happened to share a meal, which has been less frequent than before. She's either got some food squirreled away up there, or Constance has simply been skipping meals. I would guess the latter. I can tell she hasn't been sleeping well. Her eyes are bloodshot and the flesh beneath them looks bruised.

But she came down to breakfast this morning, seeming a bit more like her old self; that is, seeming a bit more like she did before our "lost picnic." She made eggs and bacon, and while we were eating I suggested we take a drive. I was surprised when she agreed.

"Have you seen Beavertail?" she asked, and I told her that sounded like a pickup line from a dyke bar. At least I made her smile for a moment.

"It's over on Conanicut Island," she continued, the tines of her fork rearranging what was left of her scrambled eggs. "On the way to Newport. There's a lighthouse, and the tourists usually aren't too bad there. No real beaches. Just rocks."

"Sounds good to me," I told her. "I'm sick to death of this place."

"You're not writing," she said. It wasn't a question, but I answered like it was.

"No, I'm not."

Constance frowned and stopped picking at her eggs.

"Have you talked to your agent?"

"No, I haven't. Honestly, I think she's about ready to give up on me. The woman has the patience of a saint, but even saints have their limits."

"I really don't know much about Catholicism," she said, and when I laughed, she just sort of stared at me.

"Jesus, girl. I think maybe you need to get out of this dump even more than I do." And then I told her to get dressed while I saw to the dirty dishes. So, she went back upstairs to change clothes while I washed the plates and coffee cups, the greasy skillet and utensils. Half an hour or so later, a little before noon, we were headed south on Barbs Hill Road. Constance talked quietly while I drove, and as we got farther from the Wight place, her mood seemed to lighten a little, her features becoming gradually, but noticeably, less weary. She told me stories about visiting the lighthouse on Conanicut Island, pausing now and then to give me directions, because I had no map and no idea which roads to take. Her stories were entirely unremarkable, and I was glad for that. No "ghost of the Forty Steps" here, just the sorts of anecdotes that tend to accumulate when someone has gone back to a particular place very many times over the course of a life. The sorts of stories that make a place familiar and comforting. I don't have a lot of those sorts of places myself, for many different reasons.

As we headed out across the span of the Jamestown Verrazano Bridge, leaving the mainland behind and crossing the west passage of Narragansett Bay, she pointed to the ruins of an older, smaller bridge on our right. It ended abruptly a few hundred yards from the shore.

"That's the *old* Jamestown Bridge," she informed me. "They demolished it a few years back. Shaped charges, TNT, you know, the whole controlled-demolition thing. I don't know why they left that part standing. Used to scare the hell out of me, crossing the old bridge, 'cause there were just the two undivided lanes, and the grade was so steep sometimes cars stalled, but there really wasn't anywhere to pull over and get out of the way. And out there is Beavertail," she said, pointing past the bridge to a low green bit of land a couple of miles to the south of us. The day was clear and hot, hardly a scrap of cloud to be seen anywhere, and the color of the bay wasn't all that different from the color of the sky.

"It was even worse in the winter," she added. "The bridge, I mean." And then Constance didn't say anything else until we were almost off the bridge, and I asked her about the exit.

I still haven't quite gotten used to how close together everything seems in New England, compared to the careless sprawl of the South. We stopped at a grocery store in Jamestown, because Constance said she needed to pee and this was our last chance, and when I checked my watch, I saw that it had only been about forty-five minutes since we'd left the house. I'd just assumed the drive would take a lot longer, that it would be late in the day before we reached our destination. But no, here we were, almost there, and less than an hour had gone by. The air smelled like saltwater, and the woods and fields of Moosup Valley seemed much farther away than the thirty or so miles we'd driven. This landscape of picturesque cottages, salt marshes, and sailboats hardly seemed to belong in the same state as Squire Blanchard's peculiar tract of land.

I followed Constance inside, because my own bladder's seen better days, and I was getting hungry, and needed a fresh pack of cigarettes. Inside, it was cool, and there was a mix of what Shirley Jackson might have called "summer people" and year-round residents. In the checkout aisle, Constance (who was buying a Hostess lemon pie and a Dr Pepper) turned to me and said, speaking softly enough that no one else would hear, "You never talk about her."

And, no lie, for a second or two I had no idea who she meant.

"Why is that, Sarah, that you never talk about Amanda?" she asked, smiling for the cashier, who asked if it would be cash or debit. Constance told her cash, and then fished a couple of crumpled bills from her jeans pocket.

"We've talked about Amanda," I replied, thinking I was surely telling the truth, that she *must* have come up at some point since Constance had returned from LA and taken up residence in the attic.

"Nope," she said. "Not even once. I've never even heard you say her name."

The cashier took Constance's money, but looked at the crumpled one-dollar bills like she didn't see such unsightly things very often.

Constance turned her head and looked at me. "If you need to talk about her, Sarah, I don't mind listening. I'm actually pretty good at listening."

"I've never mentioned her to you?" I asked. "Not even once?" and Constance shook her head.

"Not even once," she replied.

"Then how did you know to ask about her?" and I realized that the cashier was staring at me, as though she, too, was curious why I'd never spoken to Constance about my dead girlfriend.

"I've been reading your new story," Constance said. "It's dedicated to her, right?"

"I don't *have* a new story," I said, and the cashier was watching me now.

"You're a writer?" she asked, smiling a blandly eager sort of smile. "Wow. That's so interesting. You know, I've always wanted to be a writer."

I glared at her a second or two, then turned back to Constance, who was screwing the cap off her bottle of Dr Pepper. "That's utterly fucking fascinating," I said, "because, you know, I've always wanted to be a checkout girl."

Constance laughed, and the girl at the register muttered something angry and offended. I'm not sure *what* she muttered, because I was already on my way out the door, whatever I'd intended to buy forgotten, my hunger forgotten, the need for cigarettes forgotten, too. Behind me, I could still hear Constance laughing, and all I could figure was that she must have been sneaking downstairs while I was asleep and reading this journal, that she'd begun reading it before I had finally decided to start hiding the pages.

"Sarah, you are totally overreacting to this," she said, emerging from the market. "I wasn't trying to pry. I only asked you a question."

"A pretty goddamn personal question."

"I wasn't trying to upset you."

"Just get in the car," I told her, turning the key and unlocking the driver's-side door. "This isn't a conversation I want to have in a parking lot."

"Well, don't you think you were kind of harsh back there?" she asked, nodding towards the store. "I mean, sure, I get that stupid shit, too. Everyone seems to think it must be completely marvelous to be a painter—or a writer—because they've never had to try to make a living doing it. But, still—"

"I *asked* you to please get in the car," I said, interrupting her, and Constance sighed and rolled her eyes and smirked back at me across the roof.

"No, Sarah, in point of fact, you *ordered* me to. But I will, just as soon as *you* unlock my door," and now her voice had affected an almost singsong rhythm, and that forced and utterly self-satisfied excuse for a smile remained painted on her pretty face.

When we were in the car again, she switched on the radio and tuned it to some noisy college-rock station broadcasting from Providence, then stared out the windshield while I drove. There were plenty of road signs, so at least I didn't need to ask her for directions. I followed the narrow, curving rind of asphalt laid between Mackerel and Sheffield coves. There was a cobble-strewn beach on my left, Mackerel Cove Beach, speckled with fat sunbathers and fatter children. Through my open window, I could smell the heady sewage stink of low tide, the stench of stranded seaweed baking beneath the July sun, and I was dimly amazed that people were actually swimming in that. Farther out, I could see bobbing plastic buoys marking the positions of sunken lobster pots, and a couple of large rocks jutted up from the steely blue water. And then the coves were behind us, and on either side of the road there was farmland again, fields of hay and tall, rustling corn marked off by low stone walls. We passed a few horses, and the houses of people who could afford to live by the sea.

"I wasn't trying to piss you off," Constance whispered, and I only just caught her words above the radio.

"Sure could have fooled me," I said.

"Sometimes things just come out the wrong way, that's all. Yeah, I suppose maybe it wasn't the most appropriate place to ask that question. But why in the world would I have wanted to start a fight with you in public?"

There were about a dozen things I wanted to say to her then, all of them vicious, all of them the scathing sorts of things you can't take back once they've been spoken. But, instead, I only said, "Amanda killed herself, back in February. That's why I never talk about her. I came up here to try and forget about Amanda."

Neither of us said anything else then for a while, and there was only the radio, the tires humming against the road, the wind whipping in through my open window. Before much longer, we came to a sign that informed me we'd reached Beavertail State Park, and Constance lit a cigarette and turned the radio off.

"I'm sorry," she said. "I didn't know. I honestly had no idea."

I shrugged, catching a glimpse of the sea through a break in the trees. "How could you have known, Constance? You're the first person in all Rhode Island that I've told. Just don't fucking apologize, okay?"

The road led all the way down to the point and to the tall whitewashed lighthouse. Land's end, literally, there where the Atlantic had spent however many million years chewing away at the southern tip of the island, and the woods and underbrush and grassy open spaces suddenly gave way to a steep line of cliffs leading down to the sea. It was a breathtaking sight, even through the obscuring haze of my confusion and anger, and I felt like I'd driven out of the world and into a picture postcard.

"That's the new lighthouse," Constance said, though it didn't look very new to me. "It was built sometime in the mid–Nineteenth Century, after the old lighthouse burned down. There's been a lighthouse at Beavertail since 1753."

"Burned down?" I asked her, glancing from the sea cliffs back to the stone tower, which, to my eyes, seemed fairly impervious to fire.

"Well, the first one was wood," she said. "Actually, I think there might have been *two* wooden lighthouses, before they finally built this one. Anyway, Sarah, you can't stop here," and she pointed ahead of us, where the road curved north again. "There's a parking lot right up there."

And so nothing else was said about Amanda or the scene at the market or the nonexistent "new story" she claimed I'd let her read. I parked in a paved lot a couple hundred yards northeast of the lighthouse, and for the next couple of hours or so, I followed Constance across the rocks. Turns out, she's a veritable font of information about the place, and I listened while she rambled on about naval history, shipwrecks, the local geology, how you could find trilobites farther up the coast if you know where to look, and the whale carcass that had washed ashore here when she was a teenager.

The air was filled with the cries of gulls and with cormorants and smaller seabirds that I didn't recognize. The waves seemed tremendous, rushing in and slamming against the tilted, metamorphosed strata, breaking apart and rushing out again. There was a brisk, cool wind coming off the sea, but I was glad I'd thought to wear sunscreen, because I burn at the drop of a fucking hat. We were not entirely alone, but close enough for comfort. There were a few fishermen here and there, casting their lines into the waves, and they paid us no mind. Finally, winded and sweating, I found a place to sit, a high flat boulder safely out of reach of the salty spray and not too covered with the white splashes of gull shit that dappled almost everything above the high-tide line. Constance sat down next to me. She gave me a cigarette and we sat together smoking (though, later, I learned it's now illegal to smoke at Rhode Island beaches, beginning this year) and watching the waves.

"I never knew anyone who committed suicide," she said. "I can't imagine what it must be like. I really can't."

I stared down at my tennis shoes dangling over the edge of the boulder, guessing it was at least twenty feet down to the water.

"And I couldn't tell you," I replied. "All these goddamn months later, I still can't put it into words."

"Was she sick?"

I laughed and asked her to define "sick." Instead, she stubbed her cigarette out on the rock and took her ginger Altoids tin from a pocket, depositing the butt inside.

"She wasn't sick," I said. "I think she just didn't want to be here anymore. Half the time, I think I know exactly how she felt. I just don't have the requisite nerve to act on my convictions."

"You don't mean that," she said, looking at her Altoids tin and not at me.

"Don't tell me what I do and do not mean, Constance."

"You're still mourning, that's all."

"Yeah, sure," I said. "That's all," and I took a long, last drag, then flicked the half-smoked cigarette at the waves.

"You really shouldn't do that," she said, scowling, slipping the tin back into her pocket. "Cigarette butts are poisonous to birds and fish. And the cellulose acetate they're made from isn't biodegradable. I read somewhere, people throw out four and a half trillion cigarette butts a year. Four and a half *trillion*."

"We should head back soon," I said.

Constance looked over her shoulder, back towards the trail leading through a thicket of beach roses, bayberry, Queen Anne's lace, and poison ivy and back up to the parking lot. "What's the hurry?" she asked. "What's there to get back to?"

"I'm just tired," I told her. "Tired and on edge."

"So, sit here and listen to the sea. It's good for you, Sarah. Even better than Valium," and she laughed as a giggling gray gull sailed by low overhead. I'm not exactly sure what happened next. I remember the shadow cast by the low-flying gull, and her laughing, and then she was kissing me. And Jesus, it was a fucking good kiss. I don't know how long it lasted, only that it wasn't long enough. Still, I'm the one who pulled away, the one who ended it. Then we sat there on the rocks, just staring at each other, and I didn't even realize that I was crying until she started wiping at my face.

"It's okay," she said, and her red-brown eyes sparkled in the sunlight like polished agate, and she said it again, "It's okay." I think I hate her for that.

I don't want to write any more about this shit, not now, not tomorrow, not ever. I want to burn what I *have* written and then never write any more. It doesn't matter how much there is left to be said, all the things that happened next. If you keep going, there's *always* something that happens next. Always something more, if you lack the courage to type THE END at the bottom of the page. I want to take up Dr. Harvey's goddamn 1941 Royal typewriter and fling it out the back door into the darkness. Let the grasshoppers and skunks and deer have it. Let it rust away to nothing. But I'm a coward, and I'm no more capable of getting rid of this typewriter than I am of taking my own life.

July 15, 2008 (1:27 p.m.)

Constance has borrowed my car to drive into Foster for groceries and some things she needed, art supplies, and so I have a little time alone to try to set this down before she returns. I don't believe that I could ever manage to write it with her here in the house with me. Hell, I'm not sure that I can write it with her *out* of the house.

It was almost two a.m. before I was finished at the typewriter last night—this morning—and so much has happened since then that I suspect I'm never going to get back around to writing about that part of yesterday after the kiss on the rocks. Maybe it all follows from that kiss, or maybe these events were set in motion the day we got lost trying to find the tree, or the day she arrived here. Maybe it all began with Amanda's death. It's a losing proposition, a futile game of infinite regression, trying to guess at the particulars of cause and effect that led to my waking up this morning in the attic on Constance Hopkins' futon.

And, of course, there's the problem of the "new story" I am supposed to have written, the one that she brought up yesterday in the market in Jamestown. It's lying here on the table, right next to the box with Dr. Harvey's unfinished manuscript. Seventeen typed, double-spaced pages, apparently composed on this machine, using the same onionskin paper I've been using for these journal entries. It is titled simply "Pony." I've read all the way through the thing five or six times now, and if it *wasn't* written by me, then someone's done a damn fine job of forgery. There are numerous corrections on the pages in what I cannot possibly deny is my own hand. That is, I cannot deny these things, unless I am willing to suggest the perpetration by Constance of an elaborate hoax or practical joke, and unless I am also to assume that she possesses the skills required to actually pull the hoax off successfully. That she could perfectly ape my voice *and* forge my handwriting, *and* that she could have managed it on this noisy fucking typewriter *without* my knowledge, when I hardly ever leave the house. And *then,* with these assumptions in mind, I must try to conceive some motive for the hoax, what she might possibly have to *gain* by gaslighting me. Of course, here I may be falling prey to the assumption that she *needed* anything like a rational motive. And, somehow, I've already gotten ahead of myself. I'll clip the seventeen pages of the story to the end of this entry, though it's another thing I know I'd be better off simply destroying.

Last night, after I made the entry, and immediately after I'd put those pages with all the others, in that hiding place I will not name here, I went to check the front door before brushing my teeth and getting ready for bed. I found it open, the porch light burning and swathed in a swooping, fluttering halo of moths and nocturnal beetles. And Constance was standing just a few yards from the steps, dressed only in a T-shirt and her panties, staring up at the night sky.

"What are you doing out there?" I asked, and she didn't answer right away. In fact, a couple of minutes probably went by, and so I asked, "Constance, are you okay? Is something wrong?"

She turned around then, and she was smiling. "I'm fine," she said. "I just wanted to look at the stars, that's all. Sometimes, I need to look at the stars. To get my bearings, to remember where I am."

I squinted at the lightbulb again, at all those bugs, a few of which had managed to get inside, what with me standing there holding the front door open.

"Well," I told her, swatting at a beetle, "I'm going to bed now. I'm exhausted. I think I got much too much sun today."

She nodded, turning away from me again, looking back to the sky. "But it was good for you," she said. "It was good for both of us, to be away from here. To be there, at the sea. To talk."

There was an instant pang, then. Disappointment, mostly, that there had only been the *one* kiss, and perhaps embarrassment that there had been any kiss at all. But she was right, it *had* been good, as had the conversation that followed. And we both knew, and had openly acknowledged, that we never would have been able to talk as freely as we did, to find that level of intimacy, if there had not first been the kiss. It had broken down something inside us both. Or so it seemed. Unless, of course, it was only another part of the hoax. Right now, I don't know what's true and what's a lie. This morning, I awoke in the cool of Constance's attic, in her arms, thinking that, just maybe, I'd stumbled ass-backwards into a goddamn glimmer of hope, that maybe I was finding *my* bearings. I'm getting ahead of myself again.

"I saw a shooting star," she said. "Just before you opened the door," and she pointed at the sky.

"Only one?" I asked.

"Only one," she answered. "I've never been very good at spotting them, even during meteor showers."

"Maybe you just try too hard," I said, and she shrugged and lowered her arm to her side again. "Did you make a wish?" I asked.

"I saw a comet once," she said, as if she had either not heard my question or had chosen to ignore it. "Back in 1997. I was nineteen, I think. Eighteen or nineteen. But that's not at all like seeing a falling star."

I batted away a huge brown moth, then asked her what the difference was, between seeing a falling star and seeing a comet. She looked at me again, and I had the impression that it was only with considerable reluctance that she took her eyes off the eastern sky.

"Comets have often been considered harbingers of doom," she said. "But you'd know that, I suspect." And while I continued my struggle to keep Mothra and all her flitting companions out of the house, Constance slowly walked back to the porch. Her bare feet were damp from the heavy dew, and a few blades of grass stuck to her skin.

"1997," I said. "So, that would have been Comet Hale-Bopp. Yeah, I saw that one myself. Lots of people did. Probably anyone in the Northern Hemisphere who bothered to look."

"See?" Constance laughed, picking some of the grass out from between her toes. "Nothing special."

"No, I didn't mean it like that," I sighed, and Mothra flapped triumphantly past me and vanished into the house. "Constance, I'm letting bugs in. Really *big* bugs."

"I'm not afraid of bugs," she said. "Well, except for centipedes. I was stung by a centipede once. Hurt like fuck. Do spiders count as bugs?"

"Bugs are insects. Spiders are arachnids. Anyway, centipedes aren't spiders."

And it went on like that for a time, five or ten more minutes—the comfortable, meandering talk of comets and bugs. She mentioned the Heaven's Gate Cult suicides, their connection to the comet she'd seen, and I told her that I'd also seen Comet West, way back in 1976, two years before she was born. Then Constance finally came inside, and I shut off the porch light and locked the door behind her. She asked if I wanted a cup of chamomile tea. I didn't, but I lied and said that I did. She filled the kettle and put it on the stove, then took a couple of tea bags from a green box of Sleepy Time. And fuck it, at this rate, she's going to be back from Foster long before I get to the point, supposing there is a point to *any* of this, that any fraction of it's more or less important than any other.

She made us tea. And then she asked me if I'd like to fuck her. And there it is, no more beating about the bush (ha-ha fucking ha, ba-da-pa-pa), and she really wasn't much more subtle than that. She sat down at the table with the two steaming mugs of tea, and asked, "Sarah, how long's it been since you've had sex?"

"Jesus," I said, and I must have forced a nervous laugh or twiddled my thumbs or done something equally inane. "You do have a delicate way with words."

"Do you want to sleep with me tonight?" she asked, sipping at her tea, and watching me intently over the rim of the mug. "No strings attached," she added. "Right now, I think we're both pretty lonely people. I think it might do us both good. Like the sea."

"Sort of like that kiss at the beach," I said, staring at my own cup of tea.

"Sort of," she replied. "I don't know about you, but I've been working too much. It's never good for me, when I get that far into my work. Anyway, I won't be insulted if you say no. I'm a lot better at taking rejection than I am at finding four-leaf clovers."

And I noticed then that the big moth from the front porch was circling about the light hanging above the table, and I let my eyes stray to the kitchen window, and sat there staring into the night decently hiding the red tree from my sight.

"You feel it, too?" she asked, and before I could reply, she said, "I try not to think about it, but I never stop feeling it, squatting out there, watching me."

"It's only a tree," I said, unconvincingly, and Mothra beat her fragile wings against the thin shell of glass standing between her and the deadly heat of the 60-watt incandescent bulb.

"No strings attached," Constance said again.

"Oh, there are always strings," I replied. "Whether we *put* them there or not."

"Yes or no?" she asked, and there was only a hint of impatience in her voice. Of course I said yes. She nodded and took my hand, and led me out of the kitchen, our twin mugs of chamomile tea abandoned on the table. I followed her down the narrow hall and up the narrower stairs to her garret. There, surrounded by her canvases, all of them hidden beneath drop cloths, she undressed me, and then I sat naked on the mattress and watched while she undressed herself. She's thinner than I'd thought, almost bony, and there's a tattoo perfectly centered in the small of her back. Two symbols placed side by side, somewhat reminiscent of a child's stick figures, only there were no circles to indicate the heads, and the vertical lines that would form the torsos and necks extended downwards between the "legs," like a tail. They also looked a bit like a pair of stylized arrows pointing upwards, the tips of each crossed by a horizontal stroke. The tattoo had been inked in shades of gray, and was no more than five or six inches across. It, or perhaps they, looked like this (drawing these in with a pen):

"What is that?" I asked, as she tugged her T-shirt off over her head, revealing breasts just beginning to lose the enviable firmness of their youth. Her nipples were darker than I expected, my expectations based on her generally pale complexion. They were, I saw, almost the same terra cotta as her irises, and for a moment I actually considered the possibility that she rouged them to *match* her eyes. "The symbol tattooed over your ass, what does it mean?"

She dropped the T-shirt to the floor at her feet and stood staring down at me, her forehead creased very slightly, as though the answer to my question escaped her.

"The *tattoo,*" I prompted. "I don't know that symbol."

"Oh," she said. "That. I had that done at a parlor in Silver Lake. I was pretty drunk at the time. It wasn't even my idea."

I lay down, admiring her breasts, her flat belly, her hips, and trying not to be ashamed of my own body, which bears all the scars and blemishes and imperfections earned by the chronic inactivity that generally accompanies the life of a professional writer.

"It's a *kanji,* a Chinese character."

"I know what a *kanji* is," I said, probably sounding more defensive than I'd meant to. "What does it mean?"

"What difference does it make what it means?" she asked, slipping out of her panties, letting them fall to the floor on top of her T-shirt. Her pubic hair was the same jet-black as the hair on her head. "Maybe I was so drunk I don't even remember what it means."

"You really don't remember?"

"Are you *trying* to spoil the mood?" she countered. "Do you want to discuss my tattoos or do you want to fuck me?"

"I wasn't aware the one necessarily precluded the possibility of the other," and then she frowned and told me to shut the hell up, and shut up I did. She climbed on top, and pretty much stayed there the whole time, which was just fine by me. She's the first person I'd been with since Amanda. I didn't *tell* her that, but I'm going to assume she knows it. I didn't sit down here to write some silly erotic confessional, and it's all a blur anyway—her fingers and her tongue, her attentive lips and those odd clay-colored eyes of hers. I'm not sure how many times I came, and I have no idea how many times she came. Afterwards, she switched off the lamp by the futon, and we lay together in the darkness, hardly talking, listening to the night outside the farmhouse.

"Forest," she said to me. "It's the *kanji* for 'forest.' At least, that's what the tattoo guy told me."

"And why did you have the *kanji* for forest tattooed on your back?" I asked. "Unless it's a secret, I mean."

"I swear to fuck," she sighed, "I honestly *can't* remember that. I wasn't kidding about being drunk. We'd been doing shots of Jägermeister with Bud all night."

"We?"

"Nobody important," she said, and I didn't press the matter. She laid her head on my left shoulder, and told me that she could hear my heart beating.

"That's usually a good sign," I said. She laughed very softly, and sometime after that, I drifted off to sleep. If there were dreams, I can't remember them.

I woke to the angry caw of a crow, which seemed loud even over the chug of the AC unit.

I made coffee while Constance made breakfast, and while we were eating, she mentioned the short story again. I'd forgotten all about it, and would have been very happy to let things stay that way.

"I'm not sure about the title, but it's actually pretty good," she said, and, deciding maybe it was easiest not to argue, I asked if the manuscript was still upstairs.

"Yeah," she replied. "But I'll bring it back down right after I finish my coffee," which she did.

Seventeen onionskin pages, held together with a plastic paper clip, and most of them bearing corrections and proofreader's marks in red pencil. My handwriting. And so now I've come full circle, and if there's anything I'm forgetting, anything that matters, it's going to have to wait until later, because I think I hear the car.

PONY

FOR AMANDA

I. The Window (April)

Helen opens a window, props it open with a brick, and in a moment I can smell the Chinese wisteria out in the garden. The first genuinely warm breezes of spring spilling across the sill, filled with the smell of drooping white blossoms and a hundred other growing things. The sun is so warm on my face, and I lie on the floor and watch the only cloud I can see floating alone in a sky so blue it might still be winter out there. She was reading her poetry to me. I've been drinking cheap red wine from a chipped coffee cup with an Edward Gorey drawing printed on one side, and she's been reading me her poetry and pausing to talk about the field. At that moment, I still think that neither of us has been back to the field in years, and it's surprisingly easy to fool myself into believing that my memories are only some silly ghost story

Helen's been slipping in between the stanzas. Not the vulgar sort of spook story that people write these days. More like something an Arthur Machen might have written, or an Algernon Blackwood, something more mood and suggestion than anything else, and I congratulate myself on feeling so removed from that night in the field and take another sip of the bitter wine. Helen's been drinking water, only bottled water from a ruby-stemmed wineglass, because she says wine makes her slur.

I open my bathrobe, and the sun feels clean and good across my breasts and belly. I'm very proud of my belly, that it's still flat and hard this far past thirty. Helen stops reading her poem again and squeezes my left nipple until I tell her to quit it. She pretends to pout until I tell her to stop that, too.

"I went back," she says, and I keep my eyes on that one cloud, way up there where words and bad memories can't ever reach it. Helen's quiet for almost a full minute, and then she says, "Nothing happened. I just walked around for a little while, that's all. I just wanted to see."

"That last line seemed a bit forced," I say. "Maybe you should read it to me again," and I shut my eyes, but I don't have to see her face to know the sudden change in her expression or to feel the chill hiding just underneath the warm breeze getting in through the window. It must have been there all along, the chill, but I was too busy with the sun and my one cloud and the smell of Chinese wisteria to notice. I watch a scatter of orange afterimages floating in the darkness behind my eyelids and wait for Helen to bite back.

"I need a cigarette," she says, and I start to apologize,

but it would be a lie, and I figure I've probably done enough damage for one afternoon. I listen to her bare feet on the hardwood as she crosses the room to the little table near her side of the bed. The table with her typewriter. I hear her strike a match and smell the sulfur.

"Nothing happened," she says again. "You don't have to be such a cunt about it."

"If nothing happened," I reply, "then there's no need for this conversation, is there?" And I open my eyes again. My cloud has moved along an inch or so towards the right side of the window frame, which would be east, and I can hear a mockingbird singing.

"Someone fixed the lock on the gate," she says. "I had to climb over. They put up a sign, too. No trespassing."

"But you climbed over anyway?"

"No one saw me."

"I don't care. It was still illegal."

"I went all the way up the hill," she tells me. "I went all the way to the stone wall."

"How many times do I have to tell you I don't want to talk about this," I say and roll over on my left side, rolling towards her, rolling away from the window and the cloud, the wisteria smell and the chattering mockingbird, and my elbow hits the Edward Gorey cup and it tips over. The wine almost looks like blood as it flows across the floor and the handwritten pages Helen's left lying there. The burgundy undoes her words, her delicate fountain-pen cursive, and the ink runs and mixes with the wine.

"Fuck you," she says and leaves me alone in the room,

only a ragged, fading smoke ghost to mark the space she occupied a few seconds before. I pick up the empty cup, cursing myself, my carelessness and the things I've said because I'm scared and too drunk not to show it, and somewhere in the house a door slams. Later on, I think, Helen will believe it was only an accident, and I'm not so drunk or scared or stupid to know I'm better off not going after her. Outside, the mockingbird's stopped singing, and when I look back at the window, I can't find the white cloud anywhere.

2. The Field (October)

This is not the night. This is only a *dream* of the night, only my incomplete, unreliable memories of a dream, which is as close as I can come on paper. The dream I've had more times now than I can recall, and it's never precisely the truth of things, and it's never the same twice. I have even tried putting it down on canvas, again and again, but I can hardly stand the sight of them, those damned absurd paintings. I used to keep them hidden behind the old chifforobe where I store my paints and brushes and jars of pigment, kept them there until Helen finally found them. Sometimes, I still think about burning them.

The gate with the broken padlock, the gate halfway between Exeter and Nooseneck, and I follow you down the dirt road that winds steeply up the hill through the old apple orchard, past trees planted and grown before our parents were born, trees planted when our grandparents were still young. And the moon's so full and bright I can see everything—the ground-fall fruit rotting in the grass, your eyes, a fat spider hanging in her web. I can see the place ahead of us where the road turns sharply away from the orchard towards a field no one's bothered to plow in half a century or more, and you stop and hold a hand cupped to your right ear.

"No," I reply, when you tell me that you can hear music and ask if I can hear it, too. I'm not lying. I can't hear much of anything but the wind in the limbs of the apple trees and a dog barking somewhere far away.

"Well, I can. I can hear it clear as anything," you say, and then you leave the dirt road and head off through the trees.

Sometimes I yell for you to wait, because I don't want to be left there on the road by myself, and sometimes I follow you, and sometimes I just stand there in the moonlight and branch shadows listening to the night, trying to hear whatever it is you think you've heard. The air smells sweet and faintly vinegary, and I wonder if it's the apples going soft and brown all around me. Sometimes you stop and call for me to hurry.

A thousand variations on a single moment. It doesn't matter which one's for real, or at least it doesn't matter to me. I'm not even sure that I can remember any more, not for certain. They've all bled together through days and nights and repetition, like sepia ink and cheap wine, and by the time I've finally caught up with you (because I always catch up with you, sooner or later), you're standing at the low stone wall dividing the orchard from the field. You're leaning forward against the wall, one leg up and your knee pressed to the granite and slate as if you were about to climb over it but then forgot what you were doing. The field is wide, and I think it might go on forever, that the wall might be here to keep apart more than an old orchard and a fallow plot of land.

"Tell me that you can see her," you say, and I start to say that I don't see anything at all, that I don't know what you're talking about and we really ought to go back to the car. Sometimes, I try to remember why I let you talk me into pulling off the road and parking in the weeds and wandering off into the trees.

We cannot comprehend even the edges of the abyss.
So we don't try.
We walk together on warm silver nights
And there is cider in the air and
Someone has turned the ponies out again.

It's easier to steal your thoughts than make my own.

"Please, tell me you can see her."

And I can, but I don't tell you that. I have never yet told you that. Not in so many words. But I can see her standing there in the wide field, the tall, tall girl and the moon washing white across her wide shoulders and full breasts and Palomino hips, and then she sees us and turns quickly away. There are no clouds, and the moon's so bright that there's no mistaking the way her black hair continues straight down the center of her back like a horse's mane or the long tail that swats nervously from one side of her ass to the other as she begins to run. Sometimes, I take your arm and hold you tight and stop you from going over the stone wall after her. Sometimes you stand very still and only watch. Sometimes you call out for her to please come back to you, that there's nothing to be afraid of because we'd never hurt her. Sometimes there are tears in your eyes, and you call me names and beg me to please, please let you run with her.

The cold iron flash from her hooves,
And that's my heart lost in the night.
I know all the lies. I know all the lies.
I know the ugly faces the moon makes when it thinks
No one is watching.

And we stand there a very long time, until there's nothing more to see or say that we haven't seen. You're the first to head back down the hill towards the car, and sometimes we get lost and seem to wander for hours and hours through the orchard, through tangles of creeper vines and wild grapes that weren't there before. And other times, it seems to take no time at all.

3. The Pantomime (January–February)

This is almost five months later, five months after that night at the edge of the field halfway between Exeter and Nooseneck. We never really talked about it. Helen would bring it up, and I would always, always immediately change the subject. I didn't tell her about the dreams I'd started having, living it over and over again in my sleep. And then one night we were fucking—not having sex, not making love—*fucking*, hammering our bodies one against the other, fucking so hard we'd both be bruised and sore the next day, as if this were actually some argument we lacked the courage to ever have aloud, fucking instead of screaming at one another. And she began to whisper, details of what we'd seen or only thought we'd seen, what we'd seen reimagined and embellished and become some sick fantasy of Helen's. I pushed her away from me, disgusted, angry, and so I pushed too hard, harder than I'd meant to push her. She slipped off the side of the bed and struck her chin against the floor. She bit her tongue, and there was blood on her lips and her chin, and then she *was* screaming at me, telling me I was a coward, telling me I was a bitch and a coward and a liar, and I lay still and stared at the ceiling and didn't say a single word. Most of what she said was true or very nearly true, but hearing it like that couldn't change anything. A few minutes later she was crying and went off to the bathroom to wipe the blood off her face, and I took my pillow and a blanket from the closet and spent the night downstairs on the sofa.

And this is another month after that, so late in February that it was almost March. I'd done nothing worth the price of the canvas it was painted on in months. Helen's been away in the city, a writer's workshop, and I take long walks late in the day, trying to clear my head with the cold air and the smell of woodsmoke. Sometimes I only walk as far as the garden, and sometimes I walk all the way down to the marshy place where our property ends and the woods begin. And I come back from an especially long walk one night, and Helen's car is in the garage. I have an owl skull I found lying among the roots of a hemlock, and I'm thinking it's the missing piece of the painting I haven't been able to finish. In through the kitchen, and I call her name, call her name three times, but no one answers me. I hear voices, Helen's voice and another woman's, and I climb the stairs and stop outside the bedroom door, which has been left open just wide enough that it's almost shut but I can still see what's going on. And I understand that I'm *meant* to see this. Helen isn't trying to hide anything. She'd have stayed an extra night or two or three in the city, and I never would have asked why. This is being done for me almost as much as it's being done for her.

I sit down in the hallway, the owl skull cradled in my hands, and I watch them. I wonder how long Helen's been home, how long I must have lingered at the marshy place and the hemlock. I wonder what would have happened if I'd come back sooner or if I'd never gone out at all.

The other woman is pretty—prettier than me, I think—and her blonde hair's pulled back into a tight bun. She's dressed in a dark green riding jacket, white jodhpurs, and tall black boots with neat little spurs on them. Helen's naked, or nearly so. She's wearing a bridle, an elaborate thing of black leather straps and stainless steel. She has a curb bit clenched tightly between her teeth, and her legs have been laced into tall leather boots that come up past her knees and end in shaggy fetlocks and broad wooden hooves. No heels, just the hooves, so she's balanced somehow on the balls of her feet. The pretty blond woman whispers something in her ear and smiles. Helen nods once and then bends over the edge of the bed, leaning on her elbows now as the woman smears her right hand with KY and works her fingers slowly into Helen's ass.

And I'm watching this, all of it. I'm watching this because I know that I'm meant to see it, that it's a performance, and I can at least not be such a goddamn, ungrateful coward that I refuse to simply see. I watch this because I know I have it coming. This is Helen pushing me off the bed. This is Helen making me bite my tongue. This is me forced to share my dreams.

The blonde woman is holding something like a severed horse's tail, glossy chestnut strands hanging all the way down to the floor and attached to a thick rubber plug, which has also been smeared with KY. She eases the rubber plug deep into Helen, who doesn't flinch or try to pull away, who doesn't make any sound at all, who remains perfectly still and perfectly quiet until the tail is firmly in place. The blonde woman is wiping her hands clean on a white bath towel, and then she takes Helen's reins and gives them a firm tug. Helen stands up straight again, not wobbling in those boots, not seeming even the least bit unsteady on her wooden hooves.

"You know what comes next?" the woman asks her, and Helen nods. "That's because you're a good girl," the pretty blonde woman tells her. "You're such a good, good pony."

And Helen leans across the bed again. But this time she

raises her left leg and rests her knee on the mattress, and I can't help but be reminded of the way she leaned against the stone wall at the edge of the orchard.

The cold iron flash from her hooves,
And that's my heart lost in the night.

I watch from my spot on the floor while the woman uses a small ball-peen hammer to nail shiny new horseshoes onto Helen's hooves, first the left and then the right. And I watch almost everything that comes afterwards. I look away just once and then only for a few seconds, because I thought I might have heard someone else in the hall with me, someone walking towards me, someone who isn't there, and that's when I realize that the owl skull's gone. So I tell myself I must have only thought I brought it upstairs, that I must have absentmindedly set it down somewhere in the kitchen or on the table at the foot of the stairs. And then I go back to watching Helen and the pretty blonde woman in riding clothes. . . .

4. The Paintings (May)

And this last part, this is only a week ago.

I wake up from a dream of that night, a dream of wild things running on two legs, wild things in moonlit pastures that seem to stretch away forever. I wake up sweating and breathless and alone. *She's gone to take a piss, that's all,* I think, blinking at the clock on the dresser. It's almost three in the morning, and for a while I lie there, listening to the secret, settling noises the house makes at three a.m., the noises no one's supposed to hear. I'm lying there listening and trying too hard not to remember the dream when I hear Helen crying, and I get up and follow the sound down the hall to the spare bedroom that I've taken for my studio.

Helen's found the canvases I hid behind the old chifforobe and pulled them all out into the light. She's lined them up, indecently, these things no one else was ever meant to see, lined them up along two of the walls, pushing other things aside to make space for them. I stand there in the doorway, knowing I should be angry and knowing, too, that I have no *right* to be angry. Knowing that somehow all my lies to her about that night at the edge of the field have forfeited my right to feel violated. Some lies are that profound, that cruel, and I understand this. I do, and so I stand there, silently wondering what she's going to say when she realizes I'm watching her.

Helen glances at me over her shoulder, her eyes red and swollen and her face streaked with snot and tears. "You saw what I saw," she says, the same way she might have said she was leaving me. And then she looks back at the paintings, each one only slightly different from the others, and shakes her head.

"You asshole," she says. "You fucking cunt. I thought I was losing my mind. Did you even know that? Did you know I thought that I was going crazy?"

"No," I lie. "I didn't know."

"How long have you been painting these?" she asks me, and I tell her the truth, that I painted the first one only a week after the night we walked through the orchard.

"I ought to have them framed and put them on the walls," she says and wipes at her eyes. "I ought to hang them all through the fucking house, so you have to see them wherever you go. That's what I ought to do. Would you like that?"

I tell her that I wouldn't, and she laughs and sits down on the floor with her back to me.

"Go to bed," she says.

"I wasn't trying to hurt you," I tell her. "I wasn't ever trying to hurt you."

"No. Don't you *dare* fucking say anything else to me. Go back to bed and leave me alone."

"I promise I'll get rid of them," I tell her, and Helen laughs again.

"No, you won't," she says, almost whispering. "These are mine now. I need them, and you're not ever going to get rid of any of them. Not tonight and not ever."

"I was scared, Helen."

"I told you to go back to bed," she says again, and I ask her to come with me.

"I'll come when I'm ready. I'll come when I'm done here."

"There's nothing else to see," I say, but then she looks at me again, her eyes filled with resentment and fury and bitterness, and I don't say anything else. I leave her alone with the paintings and walk back to the bedroom. Maybe, I think, she'll change her mind and destroy them. Maybe she'll take a knife to the paintings or burn them, the way I should have done months ago. I sit down on the edge of the bed, wishing I had a drink, thinking about going downstairs for a glass of whiskey or a brandy, or maybe going to the medicine cabinet for a couple of Helen's Valium. And that's when I see the owl skull, sitting atop the stack of books beside her typewriter. Bone bleached white by sun and weather, rain and snow and frost, those great empty, unseeing eye sockets, the yellow-brown sheath still covering that hooked beak. I looked for it after that night in February, three months ago, the night Helen brought the blonde woman home, but I never found it. So maybe, I told myself, maybe that was just some other part of the dreams. I lie down and do my best not to think about Helen, all alone in my studio with those terrible paintings of the thing from the field. And I try not to think about the owl skull; too, too many pieces to a puzzle I never want to solve. And before Helen comes back to bed, as the sky outside the window begins to go dusky shades of gray and purple with the deceits of false dawn, I drift back down to the orchard and the stone wall and someone has turned the ponies out again.

16 July 2008 (1:43 a.m.)

I am so sick of this typewriter, and right now, sitting here pecking at these fucking black keys is the very last thing I want to be doing. And yet, I will not even try to deny that I *need* this, the outlet of writing, the words, the pages, the goddamn typewriter. As surely as I need the Tegretol and Klonopin and sleep, as surely as I need to stop drinking again and stop smoking so much and write another book, and while I'm making this little wish list, as surely as I need to take an ax to that goddamn wicked tree out there. As surely as I need all those things, so, too, do I need to reduce the day to mere nouns and verbs and adjectives. It has been entirely too strange and frustrating, this day, and that's *after* fucking Constance and after the inexplicable fact of "Pony." I mean, it seems now, somehow, that the worst of it began after Constance returned from Foster, though, truthfully, very little has happened since she got back to the farmhouse.

Whether I'm actually talking in circles or not, I *feel* as though I'm talking in circles. Reading back over that last paragraph, it seems like nothing so much to me as the Ouroboros of my consciousness struggling futilely to consume itself *in toto*. Maybe in the hope that the act of consumption, of self-annihilation, would lead, finally, to peace and an end to this fear and confusion. I've never really thought much of (or on) the whole writing-as-therapy line of reasoning—James Pennebaker and the curative virtues of self-disclosure. I say *that,* and yet I need *this*. Right now, I think my ability to "write it out" might be the only thing holding me together. Well, that and the pills and the beer I shouldn't be drinking.

I'm not sure what I expected from Constance this afternoon, only that I expected something. I know that last night she said, "No strings attached." In fact, I'm pretty sure that she said it twice. And when she said it, it was no doubt exactly what I wanted to hear, the little push necessary if I was to follow her up those stairs, the promise that we could share this thing without commitment or emotional baggage or whatever. Just sex. Just the physical release and the comfort of having another woman's body against mine for the first time since Amanda's death. Looking back, I *know* that was all she offered and all I agreed to, all I thought I wanted or needed. But . . . she's acting like it never *happened*.

And what? What the fuck am I whining about? I'm upset because she meant what she said? Did some desperate recess of my mind allow itself to believe that, regardless of what we said and what we thought we meant, last night would be the beginning of something more? That Constance Hopkins would be the end of my mourning for Amanda, and the floodgates would open wide, and I'd be free to shit out the book that Dorry and my editor are waiting for, and we'd all live happily ever after? Is *that* what this is all about?

She came back from Foster and, almost immediately, retreated to the sanctuary of her attic, and I've hardly seen her since. She's come down a couple of times to use the toilet, once to get something from the fridge. She's been perfectly pleasant with me, and I'd be lying to say that she's behaving differently towards me (and isn't that the problem, Sarah, that she *isn't*?). There was the usual small talk, but no suggestion that tonight would see an encore of last night's tryst. I'm forty-four years old, and I've had more one-night stands than I can even recollect. I'm not supposed to act like this. I am ashamed that I feel so rejected or betrayed or ignored simply because Constance meant "no strings" when she said "no strings." I am more than ashamed that I can't stop thinking maybe I just didn't do it for her last night, that I was invited into her bed and found wanting.

And maybe what's eating at me isn't even so much Constance's inattention as the mystery posed by the "new story," which, try as I may, I can't stop suspecting is somehow her doing. And that's not to say that I think she wrote the thing. Having been over it so many times now, there is genuinely no way left for me to attribute the authorship of "Pony" to anyone but myself. It's my voice, my handwriting, me exploring my own very personal concerns, and, most damning of all, a set of line edits that includes several proofreader's marks that, so far as I know, are entirely of my own invention.

Even if I were to go so far as to imagine that Constance could have mimicked my style, forged my handwriting, and had these sorts of insights into what happened between Amanda and me—and all those things are at least not beyond the realm of *possibility*—I still cannot account for thc proofreading marks. I brought no finished or unfinished manuscripts with me from Atlanta that she might have cadged them from. All that shit's locked up in a storage unit back in Georgia. So, when I stare at those pages and see there six or seven of the "operational signs" of my own invention, I'm left to conclude that either an elaborate conspiracy exists between Constance Hopkins and one of the handful of people familiar with my peculiar editing tics (my lit agent, my editors and copy editors past and present, and a couple of exes), or she's clairvoyant, or I wrote the story myself and subsequently blocked having done so from my mind (purposefully or unintentionally, consciously or unconsciously). And I find that even when faced with so unsavory a proposition as my own insanity, I cannot simply abandon *lex parsimoniae*. That the simplest explanation here is also the most unsettling is irrelevant, if I am to at least remain honest with myself.

I wrote the story, and I must admit that I wrote it. I just don't *remember* having written it. All evidence would indicate that I composed it sometime between July 8th and July 13th, the span of time during which I produced no journal entries. Four days, and the story comes to about 3,850 words, which is about (actually just under) what I would normally be able to produce in four days. I have spent a great deal of the afternoon and evening trying to distract myself from thoughts of Constance by trying to clearly recall everything I did over the course of those four days. My memory is decent, despite the drugs, and I've not come up with any apparent "missing time" or blackouts. I know my memory's seen better days, but everything appears to be in order. There is one last avenue of investigation open to me that I have not yet pursued, and that is simply to ask Constance if she heard me at the typewriter on those days, or if she ever actually saw me working on the story, or if I talked about it with her while I was working on it. I just haven't found the courage to do that yet. I've promised myself that I will do it tomorrow, and then I'll call my doctor in Atlanta and see what she thinks.

About the only aspect of the story that might argue against my having written it is that I am rarely so transparently autobiographical. Especially when it comes to details. For example, the chipped Edward Gorey coffee mug. I've had that mug for years (but it's also in storage, so there's no way that Constance could have seen it), but it's the sort of thing I almost never borrow from my own life and insert into my fiction. Doing so has just always sort of given me the creeps. But, it's hardly legitimate grounds for dismissing myself as the story's creator. Oh, and the ruby-stemmed wineglasses. Amanda bought those somewhere, and I got rid of them after she died.

It's late, and I just want to go to bed. My eyes are beginning to water, and the words are starting to swim about on the page. But I did want to mention one other thing, lest, looking back on this entry, however many years from now, I allow myself the luxury of believing that I was, on this night, being haunted by nothing more than the specter of free love and a story I can't recall having written. Lest Dr. Harvey's typescript and the red tree begin to feel neglected. Any other day, this final item might have struck me as so strange and portentous as to have formed the matter of an entire entry. But tonight, it seems somewhat inconsequential by comparison. I went into my bedroom this evening, after dinner (alone), and found three leaves lying on the floor at the foot of my bed. They were quite fresh and not the least bit wilted, so I think they could not have been lying there very long before I discovered them. I knew, without a doubt, what they were as soon as I saw them, but, still, I carried one to my laptop and looked it up online. It (and the other two) are dead ringers for *Quercus rubra,* the Northern Red Oak. I could pretend to pretend to find comfort in the precise language of botany. Doesn't science always scare away the monsters? I have these notes I made: upper surfaces of fully developed leaves are smooth and glossy dark green, contrasting with yellow green undersides, with either smooth or hairy axils. Stout, frequently reddish petioles measuring one to two inches long; stipules caducous. Mature leaves usually possess seven to nine lobes (oblong to oblong-ovate) tapering from a broad base and measure five to ten inches in length, four to six inches wide; leaf margins repandly denticulate; conspicuous midrib and primary veins; second pair of lobes from leaf apex largest. There. I copied that word for word from my handwritten notes, putting it down like a prayer or incantation. There are only a few words whose meanings escape me ("caducous," "petioles," axils," etc.), and I'll look them up later. But no, I do not feel all better now. I do not feel any different at all.

I threw two out and kept the third, pressing it between the pages of Harvey's manuscript.

CHAPTER SIX

16 July 2008 (10:45 p.m.)

The sky was already beginning to turn the purplish gray shades of dawn before I finally managed to get to sleep "last night." Though in my last entry I made much less of the three oak leaves I found on the bedroom floor than I made of "Pony" and the whole mess with Constance, as soon as I'd shut off the light and was lying there, waiting for the Ambien to kick in and send me tumbling away to whatever nightmare was waiting, I could hardly think about anything else. What I'd first accepted as just another—and rather humdrum—consequence of living here, next door to that tree and old Hobbamock's sacrificial stomping grounds, seemed suddenly a threat, an insult, a gibe.

What the hell am I trying to say? The words are not coming to me easily tonight. I'm exhausted, and it's been a long damn day. What I'm trying to say is that I began to seriously consider the possibility that Constance placed the leaves there, that there was nothing the least bit preternatural about their appearance.

And, so, I was suddenly back at the gaslighting scenario. I got angry, and I lay in bed, sweating, trying to find some way to absolve her, but kept coming back around to the things I'd written about parsimony and the provenance of "Pony." I began to mull over the implications, that Constance might have visited the tree to get the leaves (though I can hardly rule out her having acquired them from a different red oak, possibly one she encountered on her recent trip into Foster, and that's probably much more realistic). It was all I could do to stay in bed. I *wanted* to get dressed and march up those attic stairs and pound on her fucking door. I wanted to see the *look* on her face when I confronted her and called her on pulling such a sick fucking joke at my expense.

I thought worse things, too. Furious, vengeful ruminations I'm not going to put down here.

The last time I remember looking at the digital clock beside my bed, it was sometime after five. And when I finally slept, there were the dreams. I might have written those down if I'd gotten to this entry before sunset, but I didn't, and so I'll either save them for next time or just let them go. Let them fade, and be forgotten.

As for Constance, I hardly saw her again today, and when I did, I mostly kept my mouth shut. She seems completely consumed in whatever it is she's painting up there. Maybe meaningless sex with older women is her muse. I made no accusations, and she did nothing the least bit suspicious. I did ask her about her work, how it was going, on one of her trips down to the toilet. I was sitting on the living room sofa, trying to make my way through a story on snow leopards in the June issue of *National Geographic*. Her hands looked as though she'd given up on brushes; indeed, there was paint, mostly shades of green and blue, halfway to her elbows. There were also smears on her face.

"Do you know anything much about painting, Sarah?" she wanted to know, not a trace of condescension in her voice, and I admitted that I knew very little. She watched me a moment, then stared past me, and I couldn't decide if she was trying to think what to say next, or if, maybe, she'd forgotten we were talking. That unfocused quality to her eyes, which I believe I noted after first meeting her, seemed more pronounced than usual. Her gaze seemed fixed on something far away, well beyond the walls of the house.

"You're not familiar with František Kupka?" she asked, at last, and once more I admitted my ignorance. I asked her to please write the name down for me, so I could look it up online, so we could talk about the painter later. She seemed skeptical, and in a hurry to get back to work, but did as I asked.

"I don't know," she said. "It's not really so much like Kupka, now that I think about it. He's just the first thing came to mind."

"Kupka. Is that Czech?"

"Yeah," she replied. "Well, it was still eastern Bohemia when Kupka was born. Later, though, he went to Vienna, and eventually to France, of course. You might recognize some of his work, when you see it." And she named a few of his paintings then, though the only one I can remember is "The Black Idol."

"Do you ever miss having other writers to talk to?"

"No, not really," I said. "Truthfully, I've never much cared for the company of other writers. I usually just get into arguments I don't want to get into. Why? Do you miss having other painters around?"

"Sometimes," she said. "Excuse me, Sarah. I really should get back," and Constance pointed at the ceiling.

"Of course," I replied. "I don't mean to keep you," and without another word, she turned and disappeared down the hall again. I sat there listening to her footfalls, to the opening and closing of the attic door. I sat staring at the name she'd scribbled on an index card, and the aquamarine smudges her hands had left on the paper. Suddenly, it seemed utterly absurd, that I'd lain awake all night, entertaining notions that Constance was sneaking about trying to freak me out by putting oak leaves on my bedroom floor. Or, for that matter, that she'd written "Pony."

Later, sometime after a bland lunch of tuna fish and saltines and beer, I went back to Dr. Harvey's typescript, skipping ahead, only half conscious of what I was looking for there until I'd found it. Beginning on page 262, Harvey documents a number of instances in which those who have had encounters with "the red tree" have been visited afterwards by the appearance of its leaves:

Does the oak perhaps leave calling cards, meant to remind those who have visited it that they have been marked in some way? The pun was unintentional, but I shall let it stand. Does the oak leave calling cards. I have discovered a number of accounts that seem to indicate that at least some of those who've gone to the tree have later experienced the spontaneous manifestation of Quercus rubra leaves. The earliest such account goes all the way back to John Potter, fittingly, who in October 1710 wrote of the repeated appearance of "stupendous quantities" of such leaves, "gone red as blood and flame with autumn, and acorns, too," appearing inside the house he'd built two years before. He recorded his wife's alarm at the coming of the leaves, and also her consternation at having to repeatedly sweep them out of her home. Then, again, in the summer of 1712, Potter found his rooftop blanketed with "a heavy falling" of red oak leaves, though he claims he was unable to find even a single such leaf lying on the ground anywhere around the house. "The wind seemed unable to dislodge them, and they lay still." I have even seen one of the leaves from the October '10 manifestation preserved between the pages of his journal, where, I assume, he himself must have placed it. Potter also mentions an acquaintance from "Satuit" (Scituate) who, following a call on the Potters, found red oak leaves beneath both his bed and writing desk on several different occasions.

This is the earliest example of the leaves appearing a considerable distance from the tree, though it is hardly the last. I have so many newspaper accounts of such episodes that it would be tiresome for me to recount them all here (see Appendix B). Instead, I would call attention to two rather disturbing and exceptional cases.

Enter this under things I should have begun to wonder about long before now, but . . . here's Harvey's unfinished manuscript, yet there's no sign anywhere of all these clippings and notes and such that he repeatedly mentions in the text. How is it, then, that the manuscript was saved, but the files on which the manuscript are based apparently were not? Did he destroy them before his suicide? Were they discarded or destroyed by someone else after his death, even though the manuscript itself was stashed away in the basement? Or are they still here in the house somewhere, so well hidden that I simply have not come across them? Admittedly, I have not *searched* for them, but I have, since coming here, had occasion to casually peer into almost every nook or cranny where they might have been sequestered. Then again, maybe I have been anything but thorough, and my bored rummaging has been too haphazard. Regardless, I'd love to see some of his sources, if only to confirm that they exist, and to discover to what degree Harvey might be selectively reporting these incidents, thereby distorting them, to suit his needs. But, as he was saying:

The first concerns British Anglican occultist, poet, and novelist Evelyn Underhill (1875-1941), who,

I will note, was briefly a member of the Hermetic Order of the Golden Dawn (along with such Edwardian luminaries as William Butler Yeats, Florence Farr, and Maud Gonne). Shortly after the publication of her third, and final, novel The Column of Dust (Methuen; London, 1909) and while at work on Mysticism: A Study of the Nature and Development of Man's Spiritual Consciousness (Methuen; London, 1911—possibly the most renowned work in a very prolific life), Underhill received a long letter from Margaret Cropper, a close acquaintance who was traveling in New England. Cropper had heard tales of "the fearsome blood oak somewhere south of Foster, in Rhode Island," and had even visited the tree for herself. The letter in question, which has been printed in the Collected Papers of Evelyn Underhill (Longmans, Green and Co.; London, 1946, edited by Lucy Menzies), recounts a visit to the "old White [sic] farm," and includes fairly accurate descriptions of the house, the tree, and the supposed altar stone. When the letter reached Underhill, the envelope also contained a single dried leaf, which she identified as having come from a red oak. However, only a few months later, Cropper returned to England, and Underhill notes that her friend had no memory of having sent one of the leaves to her friend. "Indeed, she found the strange tree most wholly repellent and wished to take nothing physical away from her encounter with it," Underhill writes (ibid). The mystery was compounded when red oak leaves began to appear in Evelyn Underhill's home with increasing regularity, and she writes of having found more than *fifty* of them, between the years 1909 (when the letter from Cropper arrived) and 1914, when the peculiar manifestations abruptly ceased. The leaves turned up throughout her home—beneath her bed, in a steamer trunk, in a box of correspondence that had gone *unopened* since June 1903, inside shoes and coat pockets, and, most bizarrely, once inside a can of plum pudding. Underhill describes the affair as "a botanical haunting, and a most unnerving, if ultimately harmless, affair." The leaves were usually green and unwilted, though several of them ". . . wore the gaudy colours of autumn." The case of Underhill's "haunting" is also mentioned briefly in both Sir Arthur Conan Doyle's *The History of Spiritualism* (Vol. II, G. H. Doran; New York, 1926) and Slater Brown's *The Heyday of Spiritualism* (Hawthorn Books; New York, 1970).

The last instance of leafy manifestations which I will here discuss is surely one of the most grisly episodes associated with the red tree. And yet it is also one of the most obscure episodes in this mystery, and my only records of it, beyond the memory of locals I have interviewed, is recorded in a pair of short articles in the always dubious pages of the Fortean magazine *Fate* (which has, over the decades, noted the odd goings-on associated with the tree in a number of articles)—"The Vampire Tree" (January 1982) and "Rhode Island's Killer Oak!" (October 1983)—both penned by the same author, Patrick Baumgartner (about whom I can learn nothing, and he may have never been more than a pseudonym employed by the magazine's editors and/or staff writers).

To summarize, according to these two articles, on January 17, 1981, a man from nearby Rice City (just south of here), a goat farmer and cheesemaker named in Fate as George Farrell, went to the Blanchard farm on business. He knew of the tree's strange reputation, and at some point on that day, he visited it in the company of one of the landowner's sons (the son is, by the way, the current owner of the property, though he professes no recollection of Farrell or the events described in Fate). Farrell was reportedly disappointed by what seemed a perfectly ordinary oak, and to show his contempt for the local tall tales, used a pocketknife to carve his initials into the bark, above the altar stone. Three weeks later, so both articles report, Farrell's goats began to give extremely bitter milk. In the weeks to follow, three of the animals began to waste and finally died. Both pieces (which differ very little, and almost amount to reprints of the same article twenty-two months apart) state that the animals were summarily autopsied by a veterinarian from Coventry, who discovered that the they were each missing a "considerable quantity of blood" and that "their udders were distended, and, when opened, it was discovered that they were filled with a dark viscous material that stank of rotting vegetable matter, but, more remarkably, with the undigested acorns and leaves of a Northern Red Oak (Quercus rubra)." The January '82 article states, "The acorns of this species of oak are notoriously bitter and astringent, though they are still eaten by deer and other wildlife. The bitter flavor of the acorns is the result of high levels of the polyphenol tannin." The veterinarian in question is never named (not even a gender is provided), and I have been unable to find anyone in the area who can tell me who he or she might have been.

The articles state that Farrell was so "angry and disturbed" by the unexplainable deaths of his goats, that he visited the Blanchards again, this time with a hatchet and three cans of gasoline, ". . . prepared to put an end to the demonic oak." Fortunately, less hysterical heads prevailed, however, and he was discouraged from seeking his revenge upon the tree. However, Baumgartner's articles state that, in his efforts to calm the man, Blanchard agreed to remove the section of bark that the goat farmer had carved his initials into, and it was reportedly then delivered to Farrell, who is said to have had it blessed (!) by a Catholic priest before he burned it to ash (in a twist reminiscent of the infamous Rhode Island vampire "epidemic"). The ashes he then buried in a sealed tin box in consecrated earth, possibly in the Greenwood Cemetery in nearby Coventry. The articles both claim that the lid of the tin box was engraved with a cross. In my interviews with locals, I have heard several variants of the story of the poisoned goats, however, in true urban-legend fashion, the details never match, and it is always attributed to the ubiquitous "friend of a friend." Moreover, I can find no record of a goat farmer and cheesemaker named "George Farrell," though it is possible that his name was changed by the editors of Fate (who, so far, have not replied to my inquiries for more details on the case, assuming, of course, that their files contain any additional information).

Having transcribed all that, one thing that sort of leaps out at me is the surname of the possibly pseudonymous *Fate* "journalist"—*Baumgartner*. Anyone with even a smattering of German will see what I mean, that *Baumgartner* translates to "tree gardener." Odd that Harvey missed that; it certainly would have bolstered his assertion that the name was merely a *nom de plume*. Or, I don't know, maybe he did catch it, but appreciated the wordplay too much to spoil it for those among his readers who'd get it on their own. Also, I wonder if I ask Blanchard about this George Farrell fellow, if he'd be any more forthcoming with me than he was with Dr. Harvey. That is, assuming that there's something here to be forthcoming about. It all smacks of "witch trial" histrionics to me, and if not for mine and Constance's lost picnic, that damning firsthand experience with the tree, I wouldn't be disposed to believe a word of this, giving the tales in the typescript no more credence than I've given the stock-in-trade of supermarket tabloids—Elvis sightings, Nostradamus, Bible prophecies, women who claim to have been impregnated by Bigfoot, UFOs communicating via crop circles, astrology, the Bermuda Triangle, and so forth.

Oh, there's quite a bit more here about all the attempts over the years to burn and cut down the tree, I just don't feel like copying it. But there have been *many* unsuccessful and aborted attacks upon the oak, it would seem. It strikes me as just shy of miraculous that the thing is still standing more than three centuries after the first word of it reached the ears of white men. You'd have thought, if nothing else, some bunch of teenagers would have cut it down and or something as a prank. Maybe I should not be so awed at the tree's apparent wickedness as by its resilience. Then again, maybe they're one and the same.

Bedtime, old lady. Put the spooks to rest.

`July 18, 2008 (2:16 a.m.)`

Have I mentioned the heat? I don't generally whine about weather. I've never much seen the point, but Jesus fuck. I'm about a hairbreadth from breaking down and getting a little window unit AC of my own, stick it on the damn credit cards, and worry about it later, after I *haven't* died of heat prostration. The meteorologists say there are cooler days ahead, and I do hope they're not just fucking with us.

Constance came down from the icy *sanctum sanctorum* of her garret this afternoon, as paint-stained as ever, but somewhat more talkative. I must admit, it was something of a relief, at least at first. My own company wears so goddamn thin. Even that of a flaky, temperamental artist is preferable, at this point. However, one of the first things she did was comment on the heat downstairs, and I briefly contemplated murdering her and hiding the body in the basement. Or taking it to the red oak, in hopes that Hobbamock the Narragansett demon might be pleased, take pity upon me, and grant a boon of cooler weather.

"You should come upstairs," she said, and "You should ask me," I replied.

Constance laughed, but did not proceed to invite me back to the attic. We sat on the living room floor for a while, talking and sweating, before moving to the kitchen table, which was even more cluttered than usual. She looked over a few pages of Dr. Harvey's manuscript, offering no comment. We drank cold beer and nibbled at Spanish olives, whole-wheat crackers, and slices of Swiss cheese, because, lunchtime or no, we were both too hot for an actual meal.

"You know what it makes me think of?" she asked, and nodded at the window, nodding towards the tree. This was fifteen or twenty minutes after she'd returned the pages to the manuscript box, and it took me a moment to realize what she meant.

"No," I replied and took another sip of my beer.

"It's like something from Violet Venable's awful garden in New Orleans. You know, in *Suddenly, Last Summer*."

I forced myself to stare out the window, north towards the tree and the steely shimmer of Ramswool Pond, for a moment before answering her. "I think, technically, it was Sebastian's garden. Mrs. Venable had merely become its caretaker after her son's death."

"Is *that* what you think?" and now, suddenly, there was a trace of derisiveness in her voice, something verging on contempt. I looked at the tree again, at the high blue sky suspended above it, not a cloud in sight. The sun seemed to have robbed the entire world beyond the window of shadows, or even the potential for shadow. Given the topic at hand, it was impossible for me not to be reminded of Catherine Holly's fevered description of the sun on the day of her cousin's murder—a gigantic white bone that had caught fire in the Mediterranean sky.

"Is it?" Constance prodded.

"It's too hot to argue with you about Tennessee Williams," I told her.

"I didn't know we were arguing, Sarah. I only thought we were having a conversation. I thought you might be getting lonely, down here all alone. I thought maybe you would appreciate someone to talk with."

"Sebastian planted the garden," I said. "It was Sebastian's garden," and she laughed and lit a cigarette.

"The garden, it's a womb," she said. "The green and, in the end, barren hell of Violet's own womb, guarded by carnivorous plants. I mean, really, those pitcher plants and the Venus flytrap and whatever the hell else Violet was keeping in that miniature greenhouse, that garden within the garden, those plants she hand-fed—if that's not the *vagina dentata*, I don't know what would be."

I turned away from the window and stared at Constance a moment or two before saying anything more. The smoke rising from her cigarette curled into a sort of spiral above her head.

"I tend to avoid conversations about vaginas with teeth," I said, finally, and she laughed again and tapped ash into an empty saucer.

"So not a big fan of Freud?" she asked.

And, by this point, I was growing angry, what with the heat and the sunlight and the fact that Constance was clearly, for reasons known only to her, trying to pick a fight with me. Thinking back on what I said next, I'd like to believe it was something more than me being a cunt, that she had the embarrassment coming, whether or not it's the truth of the matter.

"The *vagina dentata* isn't a Freudian concept," I replied. "I'm not sure Freud ever even addressed it, as that image runs counter to the whole Oedipal thing. Freud said that little boys are afraid that their mothers have been castrated, *not* that their mothers' vaginas have teeth."

Check.

Constance glared at me and narrowed her hazy red-brown eyes, taking a long drag on her cigarette and then letting the smoke ooze slowly from her nostrils. I could tell that she was choosing the words that would form her retort with exquisite care. I glanced back to the window.

"What about our friend out there?" she asked. "You believe that old tree has teeth?"

Checkmate.

"You'd think it would fucking rain," I said, and I suppose that can stand as a white flag of surrender, my refusal to acknowledge her question.

"Screw it," Constance muttered, and I didn't look at her, but I could hear her standing, could hear the legs of her chair scraping loudly across the floor as she pushed back from the table. "There are better ways than this to waste my time." And when she'd gone, and the attic door had slammed shut, I sat alone and watched the red oak, pretending that I didn't feel like *it* was watching me.

July 18, 2008 (9:15 p.m.)

Home again, home again . . .

Home. Does that word, and the concept behind the term, retain any meaning whatsoever for me at this point? If not, how long since it has? Did Amanda and I ever have a home? Any of the women I lived with before Amanda, did *we* have homes? Was that shitty little house I shared with my parents, back in the dim, primeval wilds of Mayberry, was *that* home? I can hardly look at this old farmhouse of Squire Blanchard's and see it as anything more than a place where I am presently sleeping, eating, writing this idiot journal, hiding from New York and the ruins of my career, and so forth.

The house I share with Ms. Constance Hopkins. A few nights ago I fucked her, and briefly thought I'd found some sort of fulfillment or satiety or surfeit, whatever. This morning, I came very goddamn near to murdering her. I don't know *what* she's doing up there, in the chilly seclusion of her ivory garret. But unless she has contrived some daring new oil-painting technique that involves hammers, power tools, and stomping about as loudly as possible, I'm left to conclude she's just trying to get on my nerves.

Late this morning, after washing my breakfast dishes, I was trying to read, nothing important, nothing of any consequence, nothing I was really even interested in reading, but still, I *was* trying to read. In this house where I also live, and for which I also pay rent, whether it is or is not a "home." Finally, I got the broom and banged the handle sharply against the ceiling several times. She responded with about fifteen minutes of complete and utter silence, after which, the noise resumed anew, with the addition of Very Loud Music (it might have been the Pogues, but I'm really not sure, as I could only clearly make out the bass lines). Maybe the right thing to do would have been to knock on her door and politely ask her to hold it down. But, I know myself well enough to know that what I would have done, instead, is *pound* on her door and *order* her to lay the hell off before I strangled her. A fight would have ensued.

So, I got in the car and drove up the road to the Tyler library in Moosup. I'm not sure what effect my retreat might have had on Constance. Did she see it as a victory, having chased me from the house? Or, if her objective was to bedevil me, did I rob her of the satisfaction? I don't *care*, not really. I'm only thinking out loud. I realize that, either way, the trip to the library merely delayed some inevitable confrontation. If she's spoiling for a showdown, I cannot hope to avoid it indefinitely. Sooner or later, tomorrow or the next day, I'll find the proverbial end of my proverbial short fuse and tell her to lay the hell off or die. Jesus, how many times *have* I, directly or indirectly, threatened the bitch's life in this entry? When they find her rotting corpse in the basement, this will be the document that sends me to the chair. Or to the room where the lethal injections are administered. Does Rhode Island have the death penalty? I should hope so. I'd hate to actually serve a life sentence for the death of Constance Hopkins.

Really, Judge. Honest injun. The noisy little clit-tease had it coming.

So, yeah. The library. The woman at the front desk commented that she hadn't seen me in a while and wanted to know if maybe I'd been working on a new book. Out of the frying pan and into the fire, right? I said something inoffensive, I can't recall what, found an anthology of New England writing (essays, scary Puritan sermons, short stories, etc.) and did my best to hide among the shelves. At least the place is air-conditioned, so it was an escape from the heat, which shows no signs of letting up, regardless of what the weathermen are telling us. I found a reasonably comfortable armchair, and proceeded to read an excerpt from Thoreau's *The Maine Woods* (1864). I've never read much Thoreau, beyond *Walden,* of course, which I think I "had" to read for some college lit class or another. Anyway, this excerpt from *The Maine Woods* sort of sucked me in, and I sat there for more than an hour, reading. At one point, I got up and photocopied a page, to get a passage that had struck a chord. I think I'm going to include part of it here, though I'd not planned to do so when I sat down and started typing. Reading the following lines by Thoreau, I could not help but see them in light of Dr. Harvey's manuscript and the red tree:

> . . . Nature was here something savage and awful, though beautiful. I looked with awe at the ground I trod on, to see what the Powers had made there, the form and fashion and material of their work. This was that Earth of which we have heard, made out of Chaos and Old Night. Here was no man's garden, but the unhandselled globe. It was not lawn, nor pasture, nor mead, nor woodland, nor lea, nor arable, nor waste-land. It was the fresh and natural surface of the planet Earth, as it was made for ever and ever,—to be the dwelling of man, we say,—so Nature made it, and man may use it if he can. Man was not to be associated with it. It was Matter, vast, terrific,—not his Mother Earth that we have heard of, not for him to tread on, or be buried in,—no, it were being too familiar even to let his bones lie there,—the home, this, of Necessity and Fate. There was there felt the presence of a force not bound to be kind to man. It was a place for heathenism and superstitious rites,—to be inhabited by men nearer of kin to the rocks and to wild animals than we. We walked over it with a certain awe, stopping, from time to time,

to pick the blueberries which grew there, and had a smart and spicy taste. Perchance where *our* wild pines stand, and leaves lie on their forest floor, in Concord, there were once reapers, and husbandmen planted grain; but here not even the surface had been scarred by man, but it was a specimen of what God saw fit to make this world. What is it to be admitted to a museum, to see a myriad of particular things, compared with being shown some star's surface, some hard matter in its home! I stand in awe of my body, this matter to which I am bound has become so strange to me. I fear not spirits, ghosts, of which I am one,—*that* my body might,—but I fear bodies, I tremble to meet them. What is this Titan that has possession of me? Talk of mysteries!—Think of our life in nature,—daily to be shown matter, to come in contact with it,—rocks, trees, wind on our cheeks! The solid earth! the *actual* world! the *common sense! Contact! Contact! Who* are *we? where are we?*

Is this a fraction of the tree's apparent mystery, that it exists, essentially, out of time, and so, in some sense, out of sync with the world that surrounds it? Having been spared (or successfully having resisted) the tripartite ravages of deforestation, agriculture, and human population that so quickly reshaped the geography of New England, has the red oak become—I don't know—an embittered survivor? Does it hold within it resentful memories of an earlier state of this land, Thoreau's elder ". . . Earth of which we have heard, made out of Chaos and Old Night." I am well enough aware what shaky ground I am on, seeming to ascribe the potential for acrimony to a *plant,* to something that, even now, I could not believe is in any way sentient.

And yet, have I not previously, and with all fucking sincerity, called the red tree wicked? Am I trying to have my cake, and eat it, too?

This afternoon, sitting there in the AC and the reasonably comfortable armchair, reading Thoreau, I was interrupted by the librarian who'd seen me come in. She's the sort of woman who puts me in mind of egrets and herons—tall and thin and frail, the skeleton beneath her skin seeming hardly more substantial than the hollow bones of wading birds. Maybe ten years my senior, and, admirably, she's made no attempt to hide the gray in her hair, which, unfortunately, had been molded into some do that would have been out of style when I was still in high school. She was standing over me, holding the only book of mine anywhere on the library's shelves (and I was surprised, back in May, to see even that one), a ten-year-old hardback of *Silent Riots*. The paper dust jacket was protected behind one of those crinkly, clear cellophane covers they put on library books. Both were somewhat tattered and had yellowed with time.

"I'm sorry to bother you, Miss Crowe," she said, "but would you please sign this for us?" And she held the book out to me, and a ballpoint pen, making it clear that telling her no really wasn't an option.

"Have you read it?" I asked, and she nodded.

"I have, indeed. Right after the first time you came in, I guess, I remembered seeing it. And I read it then."

I took the book from her, and the pen, and opened *Silent Riots* to the title page. I signed my name, trying to remember the last time I'd signed one of my books, trying hard to recall how long it had been.

"Not the sort of thing I usually read," she admitted, "I mean, it is rather explicit. A bit grim for my tastes. But, even so, I thought it was quite well written. Poetic, even."

I gave the pen back to her, but kept the book, flipping past the dedication and indicia pages and the table of contents to the first story, "The Ammonite Violin."

"If a few more reviewers had agreed with you," I said, forcing a smile, "maybe it would still be in print. Then again, maybe not."

"Is that very important to you, what critics say, or what readers think?"

"I won't lie," I replied. "Audiences are nice. So are royalty checks."

She stared at me then, mired in that uncomfortable sort of silence that often follows the receipt of unexpectedly candid answers. Finally, she nodded and said something about how nice it must be to have the "cottage" all to myself, how conducive to writing the solitude must be. To my meager credit, I didn't laugh at her. But I did explain that I was no longer alone, and I mentioned Constance by name and added that she was a painter.

"Oh," the librarian said, her face brightening at once.

"Oh, well, now that's wonderful, isn't it? I mean, a writer *and* a painter, under the same roof. Why, you almost have your very own artists' colony, don't you?"

"Almost," I replied.

"Please ask her to stop by here sometime. I'd love to meet her."

I told her that I would, knowing that I wouldn't do anything of the sort. Then I asked the birdlike librarian if she'd mind me holding on to the book a while, and she said certainly not, because, after all, I'd written it, hadn't I? So, she left me by myself again, and I laid the anthology of New England writing on the floor beside my chair and spent the next couple of hours reading those stories I'd written more than a decade ago. Some of them hold up well enough. Some of them *almost* do. And others make me cringe, and leave me thankful that *Silent Riots* vanished after the hardback and then only one paperback printing.

It was almost six o'clock when I finally closed the book and allowed myself to think about heading back to the sweltering house and temperamental Constance. The library's open until eight on Wednesdays, and I seriously considered hanging around until they shooed me out the door. But poring over all those old stories had a peculiar effect on me—I never read my own stuff after it's published. Well, practically never. I wasn't exactly depressed, at least no more than usual, no more than when I'd come in. But I found myself wanting to be back in the house, because even if it *isn't* home, it's the sorry substitute that has to suffice for the foreseeable future, and at least there are enough of my things there to foster the illusion that it's where I belong. I wanted a beer, and I desperately needed a cigarette, and to lie in my "own" rented bed for a while. Maybe, I thought, while I was gone, Constance had succumbed to an attack of ennui and hung herself. Or maybe she'd had a nasty accident with a nail gun.

No such luck.

I found her sitting in the hallway, not far from the foot of the attic stairs. Just sitting there, sobbing, her legs pulled up close to her chest, her arms wrapped tightly about them. The hall light was off, and the shadows had grown almost as thick as the heat and the incongruent reek of sweat and turpentine coming off her. I stood staring at her, wondering what the hell I was supposed to do or say, and then she let me off the hook by speaking first.

"I think I owe you an apology, Sarah."

"Yes," I agreed, squatting down next to her. "I think you do."

"I'm never at my best when I'm afraid," she said, and I recalled her telling me the exact same thing the day she'd dared me to go back to the tree alone and we'd argued (And how long ago was that? A week? Ten days?). She wiped roughly at her snotty nose with a paint-stained hand, then, leaving a dark smear of indigo across her upper lip and the end of her nose.

"Constance, have you entirely given up washing your hands? Or is that part of your process?" I asked, and she smiled and almost laughed.

"They just get dirty again," she replied. "Well, no. Not dirty. It's not dirt, is it? But you know what I mean."

"The sacred grime of creation," I said, affecting as professorial a tone as I was able. I stopped squatting, because it was making my hips ache, my hips and my kidneys, and I sat down on the floor.

"Anyway, I wanted you to know, I am sorry."

"You should be," I told her.

She didn't respond immediately, but stared at her hands a while, staring into all those competing, intermingled hues of blue and green smudged across her palms and knuckles, the flecks of red and orange and yellow on her fingers. Her hands made me think of autumn leaves tumbling in a rough surf. In the waves before a storm, perhaps.

"You know, last time," she said, "you were a lot more gracious."

"Last time was the *first* time. And last time, we'd not made love."

Constance smirked and shrugged her shoulders. She'd stopped sobbing. "Is *that* what we did, Sarah? Did we make love? I thought it was just sex."

I sighed and dug my cigarettes and lighter out of my shirt pocket. I offered her one and she accepted, and then I lit it for her before lighting my own. I breathed the smoke in, and breathed the smoke out, hurrying the nicotine into my bloodstream.

"Yeah, it was just sex," I admitted. "Poor choice of words. I'm not feeling at all perspicuous at the moment."

"I'm not saying it wasn't good."

"I didn't take it that way," I told her, and watched our

cigarette smoke rising, commingling, curling and slowly dissipating in the muggy air.

"It *was* good," she said. "At least, it was good for me. And it helped clear a lot of negative shit out of my head. It just didn't *stay* cleared out."

I blew a smoke ring, and said, "I'm always available for repeat performances." Which is about the best I'm capable of, when it comes to flirting.

She laughed and stopped looking at her hands long enough to wink at me.

"Then I'll keep you posted," she said. And, changing the subject, "I think there's a coyote hanging around the house."

"So there *are* coyotes up here."

"Oh, yeah. There are," she replied. "Lots of them. But this might only be a fox. I'm not sure."

"No *wolves,* though, right?" I asked her, and looked about for something within reach that could serve as an ashtray.

"Not likely. Not anymore. Though, back in March, a farmer shot a wolf somewhere up in western Massachusetts. It was in the newspapers. It was even on television." She took the now-familiar ginger Altoids tin from her smock and opened it, tapping ash into it, then passing it to me. "It was killing livestock," she continued. "Still, the first wolf anyone's seen in Massachusetts in something like a hundred and sixty years, and this Swamp-Yankee fucker up and shoots the poor thing for eating his goddamn sheep."

And I very nearly asked Constance how she knew

what had been in the local papers and on the local news, given she was in Los Angeles back in March. But there are always phone calls to, and from, relatives and friends back east, right? There's always the internet. I kept the question to myself.

"You saw a coyote?" I asked, instead.

"No. Well, maybe. I've seen something a couple of times now, skulking around by the garbage cans. It might only be a fox, but it seemed big for a fox. And the wrong color."

"Should we tell Blanchard?"

"What for?" she asked. "So he can murder the poor thing." That was the word she used—*murder*.

And then we were talking about bears, specifically about the black bear that was spotted around South County in May. It had displayed a fondness for bird feeders. But I wasn't thinking about bears or birdseed. I was thinking about Harvey's manuscript and the account of Susan and William Ames. Back in 1840, not so long before the last wolves were exterminated from the forests of New England, didn't the doomed Mr. Ames claim to have repeatedly seen his missing wife in the company of a very large wolf? That's what I remember, though I haven't looked back through the manuscript to see if my memory is mistaken.

Time to end this meandering mess of an entry and go to bed. If I'm lucky, I won't dream about wolves and the wayward wife of William Ames. If I'm really lucky, I won't dream about Amanda, either, or Constance Hopkins, for that matter. Somehow, in only the space of half an hour, while we were sitting there in the hallway talking about wildlife, I went from furious to horny. I think I prefer furious; it's quite a bit less distracting.

July 19, 2008 (4:34 p.m.)

So far, I've hardly seen Constance today. She came down for breakfast. And she walked with me to the mailbox. But that's pretty much it. Whatever she's doing in the attic, at least she's returned to doing it more or less quietly. On the way back to the house, I brought up her "coyote" sightings again, though I didn't tell her I'd had a nightmare because of them. Unlike yesterday, she seemed oddly reluctant to talk about the matter, almost as if, in the interim, she'd thought better of having mentioned it at all.

"If there are coyotes around, doesn't it seem odd that we never hear them?" I asked. "I've always gotten the impression they're pretty noisy animals."

Constance shrugged and sorted through the day's junk mail. "It might have only been a stray dog," she said. "There must be lots of feral dogs about. Maybe a stray German shepherd or something like that."

"Maybe," I said, and didn't press the issue, as it does seem perfectly reasonable that someone could mistake a feral German shepherd for a coyote.

As for the nightmare, I might just as well blame Harvey's manuscript as Constance's coyote. I didn't go to bed last night when I was done at the typewriter. I sat in the living room a while, trying to concentrate on a DVD—Deborah Kerr and Jean Simmons in *Black Narcissus* (1947). It's one of my favorites, has been for ages, but

I couldn't stop thinking about Harvey's manuscript in its cardboard box. So I ended up in the kitchen again, flipping through the pages in search of the account of William and Susan Ames (if only the thing had an index). Turns out, it was way back in the first chapter, right there in the first few pages. But Harvey returns to the subject later, and on page 173 proceeds from numerous retellings and embellishments of the Ames legend to the subject of ghostly dogs and purported cases of lycanthropy in Rhode Island and Massachusetts. His writing here is somewhat less focused than usual, and I'm assuming that, like most of the book, he must have meant this only as a rough first draft:

Traditions of spectral canines of the sort best known from the British Isles are, as it happens, not alien to the States. Indeed, I have assembled numerous examples from various parts of New England. Though hardly as well known as the Barghest of Yorkshire or dreadful Black Shuck of East Anglia, there is, for instance, central Connecticut's "Black Dog of West Peak." Like many of its ilk, the appearance of this "black dog" is said to be an omen. Indeed, there is even a folk rhyme devoted to the animal's seeming ability to bestow good luck or ill upon those who happen to catch of glimpse of it: "If a man shall meet the Black Dog once, it shall be for joy; and if twice, it shall be for sorrow; and the third time, he shall die."

Though often sighted, the dog that haunts the steep volcanic Hanging Hills south of Meriden is said to leave no tracks and to utter a silent howl. The most oft-recounted tale associated with this apparition concerns the fate of one W. H. C. Pynchon, a geologist from Manhattan who frequently made excursions to the area to study its igneous rock formations. The April-June 1898 issue of The Connecticut Quarterly includes the definitive account of Pynchon's three encounters with the beast, which, as the rhyme dictates, ends with his death (though, in actuality, the geologist did not perish in the Hanging Hills at the end of the Nineteenth Century, but died peacefully on Long Island in 1910).

Closer to home, there is Rhode Island's own "phantom dog of Fort Wetherill" in Jamestown. Less renowned, perhaps, than its cousin to the west, sightings of this dog are also reputed to portend doom. In Tiverton, there are reports of a "pitch-black dog" that has been seen to transform itself into the figure of a woman, who then proceeds to play a violin before vanishing. Similarly, though less musically inclined, is the shape-shifting black dog of Newport, which also transforms itself into a woman who is given to peering in through windows.

That last detail is reminiscent of the famous Bête du Gévaudan, an unidentified wolflike animal that terrorized the peasantry of France's Margeride Mountains from 1764 until at least 1767, slaughtering as many as one hundred and thirteen people. La bête was also alleged to have possessed shape-shifting abilities, and some of the reports indicate that, like the Newport lycanthrope, it was fond of gazing in through windows. Similarly, there are reports of a huge animal, suspected of being a werewolf, that is said to have wrecked a coach and laid waste to a farm east of Gresford in northern Wales in 1791, and to have stood up on its hind legs "like a human being" to gaze in through the windows of the farmhouse. The creature was said to have had blue eyes.

Yeah, I know. Precisely the sort of shit I needed to be reading before bed. Anyway, Harvey eventually finds his way back to the red oak and the strange happenings here at the "old Wight place":

We see an element of the lycanthropic associated with the property, beginning with the death of Mr. and Mrs. Ames. The latter, you will recall, was said by her distraught husband to have been witnessed walking in the company of "a great wild beast," though he also seems to have been of the opinion that it was nothing so mundane as either a wolf or panther. I will assume he also ruled out bears. A contemporary account of the affair, from the Providence Journal ("Horror from Moosup Valley," October 2, 1840), even mentions that Ames had repeatedly looked up to find the face of Susan watching him from one of the windows, and that, on one occasion, William saw both the woman and her bestial attendant staring in at him.

During my research, I have assembled more than a dozen additional tales from the Moosup Valley/Coventry region featuring wolflike creatures, and often *were*wolflike creatures. Many of these encounters are reputed to have taken place on the farm, usually within sight of the red oak, though a fair number come from what is now the George B. Parker Woodland Wildlife Refuge in Coventry. I will begin this catalog of lupine oddities with those sightings from the Parker Woodland.

This 860-acre tract of land is located along the northern side of Maple Valley Road, about 250 yards east of the intersection of Route 102 (Victoria Highway), about ten miles from Providence. The tract has something of a reputation as a "ghost town," as the woods are dotted with evidence of Colonial-era agriculture, including a multitude of fieldstone walls, foundations, wells, rock-wall pens that once held livestock, and the stone foundations of numerous buildings. In 1760, a dam was built on Turkey Meadow Creek, north of Maple Valley Road, and two abandoned stone quarries likely date from roughly the same period. Remains of a sawmill (ca 1760–1785) can be seen at the brook. The lion's share of this land was part of the Shawomet Purchase (1642), and was then obtained by the Waterman family in 1672. After almost a century, the Watermans sold the land to Caleb Vaughn in 1760. Probably, the most celebrated structure here is the meager remnants of the Isaac Bowen House, a center chimney that was added to the National Register of Historic Places in 1980. Much has been made of the low stone cairns that are situated between Turkey Meadow Brook and Biscuit Hill Road (to the north), and the usual bevy of wild assertions have been made as to their possible origin, everything from Phoenician to Celtic settlers (and stranger things, as we'll soon see). In truth, they are likely only the remains of furnaces used in the Eighteenth and Nineteenth centuries to produce large quantities of charcoal, and rock piles made by Colonial settlers and the Narragansett Indians before them. One marvels at the constant invocation of Celts, Vikings, and other European races as an explanation for the creation of such cairns, as though Native Americans lacked the know-how to simply stack stones.

However, the most colorful interpretation of the Parker Woodland cairns—and the most relevant here—is to be found in the writings of the Hungarian-born orientalist Arminius Vámbéry (who, by the way, was an acquaintance of Bram Stoker's; Vámbéry makes a cameo appearance in Chapter 23 of Dracula, when Van Helsing refers to "my friend Arminius, of Buda-Pesth University"). The "Coventry Center stones" are briefly mentioned in Vámbéry's Werewolvery in Europe and Rituals of Corporeal Transformation (London, 1897), a digression from his study of supposed episodes of werewolvery in Ireland during the spring of 1874. In the book, the author tries to link a string of Gévaudan-like attacks in County Limerick to "a tradition among the people . . . of 'raths' or 'hollow hills' leading down into the chthonic realm of the Gælic Daoine Sidhe.

He pauses in his examination of the "Black Beast of Limerick" to note that the "mysterious cairns in Rhode Island, while having no known link to fairy lore or even the mythology of the Red Indians, were, in the year 1843, the scene of an attack that appears to fit the pattern herein suggested." Vámbéry proceeds to discuss the death of a mill worker, named as John Shattuck, who ". . . is said by newspaper accounts to have been slain by an enormous wolf. Some witnesses, however, dispute the identification of the killer, agreeing that it was a beast, but that the creature walked upright, yet was no bear . . .

I can't say that I've ever been much for stories of wolf-men (or man-wolves), but, reading this section of the ms., I *was* struck by the prevalence of such stories in legends, superstition, religion, and folktales. Cynophobia on a cultural (or even species) level, something that almost seems hardwired into human consciousness.

Wolves (along with jackals, foxes, wild dogs, etc.) are a sort of all-purpose boogeyman, from the Christian bible to the *Qu'ran,* from the *Aesopica* to the Brothers Grimm, the "Big Bad Wolf" to Lon Chaney, Jr. Wolves, like snakes, have played the fall guys and villains in mythologies since almost forever.

In fact, I can even cite an example from my own childhood. When I was a kid, my maternal grandparents lived out in the wooded mountains maybe five or six miles south of town. And ever since I was very small, they both regaled me and my sister with stories about something they called the "wolfeener" (I never saw the word written out, so that spelling is admittedly one of my own invention). They both claimed not only to have *heard* this creature's peculiar, high-pitched howl, but, on one occasion, to have seen it with their own eyes. They insisted that, though wolflike, it was no wolf—that it was larger, fiercer, and, well, just *different*. My grandfather, who was a brick mason by trade, could reproduce what he said was the creature's call, and that sound never failed to scare the bejesus out of us. Even my mother claimed to have repeatedly heard the animal. I recall my grandmother once coming across a photograph of a hyena in a book, and telling me that when she'd seen the wolfeener, it had looked a lot like that; she had been adamant on this point.

I have often thought that this word they used—*wolfeener*—might have originated somehow from *wolverine,* though the wolverine has been extinct in the southern

Appalachians since the end of the Pleistocene, some ten or eleven thousand years ago. For that matter, to my knowledge, red wolves (*Canis rufus*) were extirpated from Alabama by the early 1920s, when my grandparents were still small children. And coyotes (*Canis latrans*) didn't reenter the state until after the 1960s, so neither red wolves nor coyotes seem likely suspects for the actual identity of the "wolfeener." Of course, one wonders what stories *their* parents and grandparents told *them*, about a much wilder land. Okay, enough of this crap. Back to Harvey:

". . . Local folklore attributes the ancient stone mounds south of the mill where Shattuck was employed to Native devil worship, and also consider it a site frequenty chosen for the sabbats of witches. The mounds were, therefore, feared by locals and generally avoided. A witness to the attack upon Shattuck claimed that the beast emerged from one of the mounds and, afterwards, retreated back into the earth, by way of the same cairn from which it had arisen."

Vámbéry then proceeds to recount a second, earlier incident involving the George B. Parker Woodland cairns, this time dating from 1828 and involving a young woman named Sally Waite, said to have been the youngest daughter of a farmer ". . . who worked a plot of land not very far distant." According to Vámbéry, the Waite girl suffered a series of "nightmares and waking visions" in which she witnessed elaborate "ceremonies conducted by demonic entities dwelling below the mounds, involving the blood sacrifice of both farm animals and human infants." She ". . . repeatedly claimed that these beings were calling out to her, wishing for her to join them in their unholy fellowship and subterrestrial depredations." She is reputed to have said, "The night has teeth. The night has claws, and I have found them. Walking through these woods, I have faced it." After talking so openly of her dreams, Sally's parents began to worry about both her sanity and her soul, and are said to have consulted a local Presbyterian minister. Then, on a snowy night in January, the girl slipped out of her family's house (shades here of Susan Ames) and was found dead, two days later, her frozen and mutilated body spread out across one of the cairns. "Much of the corpse had been devoured, and tracks discovered in the mantle of new-fallen snow were queer, recalling no animal familiar to the people of the countryside. They seemed to vanish at the periphery of one of the mounds. Though there was much panic and talk of tearing open the stone heaps to find and destroy whatever lay inside, I can find no record that any such action was taken."

Unfortunately, Vámbéry fails to cite his sources, and I have personally been unable to find any newspaper or periodical account of either incident, nor have any of the locals I've interviewed known of them. However, I have succeeded in uncovering an intriguing pair of sightings dating from the mid-1950s, recounted in an article in <u>Argosy</u> (April, 1962) by Don Valigursky, "A New England Wolfman?" In this short and somewhat lurid article, two sightings of a "hairy beast that walked upright" were made along Maple Valley Road. One might, at first, relegate these to Bigfoot lore (not unknown to the state), except that the witnesses both emphasized that the "loping monsters" they saw exit the woods and cross the road in front of their car's headlights (both sightings were at night) had long, dog- or wolflike muzzles. In one of the two sightings, the driver—named as Mrs. Joann Laycock of Foster—reported that "I hit the brakes when I saw it come out of the trees, because at first I thought it was a deer. I'm used to seeing deer on the road at night, and you don't want to hit one. But I soon saw it wasn't a deer, and it rose up on its hind legs and stared directly at me, looking through the windshield. Its eyes were red in the headlights, and I'd swear before a court of law that the thing smiled at me before crossing the road and vanishing into the forest again. I saw its teeth, and they looked like a dog's teeth." Again, local newspapers do not back up these stories, nor have I found any evidence that the two witnesses named in the article ever lived in the area, or even existed (though both names may certainly have been changed for publication). Don Valigursky, I will note, also wrote a number of articles in the 1970s on the "pigman" of

Northfield, Vermont, and one on Sasquatch sightings in Massachusetts and New Hampshire.

But now, let us return to a number of similar occurrences here at the Wight Farm, some of which are clearly linked to the "red tree."

Jesus, it's got to be some kind of neurotic me sitting here transcribing this outlandish manuscript, a suicide's obsession. Has it become my *own* obsession? In touching and reading these pages, in my trip to the tree and my exploration of the vast basement below the house, have I become infected by this same *idée fixe*? Has Constance's "coyote" only exacerbated it? Did Harvey see coyotes of his own? I wonder. I need to stop and cook dinner, for myself, and for Constance, if she will come downstairs long enough to eat. But first, my dream from last night.

It's nothing much, and anyone can see that it was plainly inspired by what Constance said, and what I later read in Harvey's typescript.

I was outside, out back behind the house, not far from the steps. There was an amazing moon in the sky, the sort I always think of as a harvest moon—low and huge and a luminescent yellow orange, rising over Ramswool Pond and the red oak and everything else. I smelled smoke, and wondered if there was a forest fire, and I remember hearing a raucous chorus of birds—catbirds, robins, mockingbirds, jays—and thinking it was strange to hear so many songbirds at night. The air was cold, and my breath fogged. I turned to go back inside, and that's when I spotted the pale figure of a woman crouched in the weeds at the edge of the yard. There was a very large dog with her. I won't call it a coyote or a wolf. It just struck me as a very large dog. It licked her face, and, in return, she licked at its muzzle, and I realized then that the two of them—this woman and the dog—were lovers, and I felt suddenly ashamed, as though I'd been caught spying on some especially private moment.

The woman stood up, and though I think she'd been clothed when I first saw her, she was now entirely naked. The dog sniffed at the space between her thighs, and she stroked the top of its shaggy head. I started to say something, but then I saw the way her eyes shone red in the night. She was watching me now, and I realized that she looked a great deal like Amanda, but also a lot like Constance. Her face was the perfect amalgamation of their two faces.

She spoke, finally, and it surprised me, because I think perhaps I had assumed she was feral and so probably had never learned to talk. At least, not any language of men. The hound stopped snuffling her crotch and pricked its ears, listening as she spoke.

"There is another shore, you know," she said, "upon the other side." And in my dream, I recalled that earlier dream, me and Constance on the beach with the tempest at my back, and that she'd said those very same words.

The woman with the dog smiled then, and the teeth that filled her mouth were inhuman things. Then she turned and disappeared into the woods, though her companion peered at me a while longer before it also turned away and followed her. I woke sweating and disoriented, and I knew that I'd been crying in my sleep.

What she said, what Constance said in the earlier dream, I knew it was familiar. I googled it this morning. It's Lewis Carroll, from *Alice's Adventures in Wonderland,* a line from the "Lobster Quadrille":

> *"What matters it how far we go?" his scaly*
> *friend replied.*
> *"There is another shore, you know, upon the*
> *other side."*

CHAPTER SEVEN

July 21, 2008 (8:47 p.m.)

Excerpt from ms. pages 108–14, *The Red Tree* by Dr. Charles L. Harvey:

Some authorities on the subject of criminology, in general, and, in particular, serial killers, consider there to be only two well-documented cases of "authentic" mass murderers dating from the 1920s. Earle Leonard Nelson, popularly dubbed "the Gorilla Killer" and "the Dark Strangler," was a necrophile who killed more than twenty people (including an infant) between early 1926 and June of 1927. The notorious cannibal and pedophile Albert Hamilton Fish (also known, variously, as "the werewolf of Wysteria," the "Gray Man," and "the Brooklyn Vampire") may have been far more prolific, if one trusts Fish's own outrageous claims, which would place the number of children he murdered and/or sexually assaulted near four hundred by the time he was arrested in September 1930.

However, I have found no book on the phenomenon of serial killers that records the events at the Wight Farm between 1922 and 1925, even though they were reported at the time in local papers and are easy enough to verify by recourse to police and court records. And yet there seems to be a sort of cultural amnesia at work regarding the affair, and I have been unable to locate printed references to the bizarre murders committed by Joseph Fearing Olney (1888-1926) published any later than April 1927. The final accounts concern his suicide by hanging while awaiting trial for the killings, and the general consensus seems to have been that by taking his own life, Olney, in effect, confessed to the crimes and proved his guilt beyond any reasonable doubt. What follows here is merely an overview of the case, and the reader is referred to Appendix C for a much more complete account. [Of course, keep in mind Harvey never got around to writing those appendices.—SC]

Born in Peace Dale, RI, to the recently widowed wife of a Presbyterian minister, it is difficult to learn much about Joseph Olney's life prior to his arrest by police in Foster on December 12, 1925. However, we do know that he was an exemplary student hoping to pursue a career in medicine, and that he briefly attended college in Boston before he was forced to leave school for financial reasons. Afterwards, Olney returned home to Peace Dale, where he worked in the same mill that had employed his paternal grandfather, and he remained with his mother until her death in 1918. Olney received only a very modest inheritance, primarily his parents' small house on High Street.

In the winter of 1919, at the age of thirty-one, Joseph Olney sold the house and took a train west, first to Denver, then on to San Francisco, and then south to Los Angeles, living in cheap boardinghouses and occasionally working at odd jobs. An examination of his personal effects shortly after his arrest indicated that he'd spent part of this time attempting to write an obviously autobiographical novel about the life of a bright young man condemned by circumstance to follow in his father's unremarkable footsteps. It is unclear whether any portion of this manuscript survived at the time of Olney's arrest, and the title is not known. But he did manage to finish and sell two short stories during his years in California, both crime tales placed with the successful pulp magazine Black Mask ("Midnight in Salinas," March 1920; "The Gun in the Drawer," August 1920). He'd written several other stories in this vein, none of which were to see publication.

During his time in Los Angeles, Olney had what was apparently his first and only romantic relationship.

His frequent letters to family members back east report his having met a twenty-four-year-old stenographer and would-be painter named Bettina Hirsch, whom he described as "a beautiful, talented, and educated woman who, like me, finds herself at odds with the world." There was even talk of marriage, before Hirsch apparently took her own life on Christmas day in 1920. Her body was discovered by a roommate, after she used a straight razor to open both her wrists. The degree to which Olney was affected by his girlfriend's death is evident in a number of surviving poems and letters he wrote at this time, and in the fact that it abruptly ended his infatuation with California.

There's a handwritten notation in the right margin here, beside the above paragraph. I'm pausing to mention this if only because, all in all, Harvey's typescript is surprisingly clean and generally free of such marks. The note reads, simply, "No death certificate on file w/LA Co. Office of Coroner." I assume this means that Harvey made an inquiry himself, though I suppose it's possible he learned of the missing death certificate from another sourcc. At any rate, he continues:

He [Olney] returned to New England in 1921, having, with the help of a maternal aunt, managed to find employment as an office clerk for the Ocean State Stone and Monument Company, then operating the granite quarry which would, decades later, flood and become known as Ramswool Pond. And it is at this point that his involvement with the "Red Tree" begins. Joseph Olney was living in a rooming house in Moosup Valley when he heard tales of the locally infamous tree from coworkers. He appears to have first visited it himself just after Easter in '21, and, thereafter, returned to the site almost weekly; he also began collecting and writing down the history and folklore associated with the tree and the strange occurrences on the Wight Farm. Many of his papers are deposited in the collection of the Foster Preservation Society, and I have had the opportunity to read most of them. To his credit, Olney carefully interviewed dozens of residents of Moosup Valley, Coventry, Vaughn Hollow, et al., regarding the oak, using techniques not dissimilar from those now employed by professional anthropologists and folklorists. He speaks, in his journal, of desiring to write a book detailing the history of the tree, and, here, his mood seems generally upbeat, despite the fact that he must still have been mourning the loss of Bettina Hirsch. There is evidence that he may even have written query letters to publishers in Manhattan, gauging the potential interest in such a volume.

Then, during the summer of 1921, his disposition suddenly changes, and his writings on the tree become darker and less organized. This period seems to have been triggered by a series of nightmares wherein he encountered the "ghost of my dear lost Bettina" at the tree and "in which she led me beneath the rind of the earth, into a fantastic and moldering rat's maze of catacombs accessed by a secret doorway below the Indian altar stone." Olney wrote of witnessing "grisly, unspeakable acts performed underground by demonic beings, and, somehow, Bettina was a willing party to it all, and she wished nothing so much as to initiate me into that ghoulish clique." Still, he continued his research, and his visits to the tree, though it was noted that his work had begun to suffer, and his supervisors complained that he "seemed always distracted, his mind rarely on the job." Fortunately, most of Olney's research and writings on the tree are extant (having been seized as evidence for the prosecution).

Though I will not here detour into the grisly details of each murder that Joseph Fearing Olney is alleged to have committed beginning in May of 1922, I will provide a brief summation, as the case has received so little attention. It is important to note that less than one month before the date of the first murder, Olney purchased a used 1915 Model T Ford from a farmer on Cucumber Hill Road, having borrowed $175 from a relative. The automobile would allow him the freedom of movement needed (so the State would argue) to seek his victims from towns a safe distance from his room in Moosup Valley. Olney, it seems, killed by the maxim "Don't shit where you eat."

On Saturday, May 14th, a seventeen-year-old girl named Ellen Whitford vanished from her home in Tuckertown, west of Peace Dale. Four days later, fishermen discovered her mutilated and decapitated body floating in the Saugatucket River. A scar allowed the girl's parents to identify the nude body. The next headless corpse was also found in the Saugatucket, only two weeks later, on May 29th, however this one remained unidentified for several months, until the woman was determined to have been a mill worker from Peace Dale. A third body was found on Saturday, June 17th, caught in a logjam on a bend of the Chipuxet River, east of Kingston Station, just north of the Great Swamp. By this time, newspapers as far away as Boston and New York were carrying stories of "the Rhode Island headhunter," and after the discovery of the fourth victim—Siobhan Mary Dunlevy, also a Peace Dale mill worker, also found in the Chipuxet River—the killings (or at least the discovery of corpses) halted until the fifth body turned up in September. The badly decomposed remains of twenty-three-year-old Mary Wojtowicz, the daughter of Polish immigrants, was discovered in the weeds at the northern end of Saugatucket Pond. Identification was facilitated by a birthmark on the woman's left ankle.

For almost a year no additional bodies were discovered, and we know from Olney's journals, that he killed no one else until the next spring, when "the South County ripper" resumed his activities on the anniversary of the death of Ellen Whitford. Between May and August, six bodies were found, all decapitated and having suffered other mutilations, all of the victims women between the ages of nineteen and twenty-one, and all but one of them mill workers. In each instance, the bodies had been dumped into a river or pond after the murder, and none were found nearer to the rooming house in Moosup Valley where Olney was still living than that of Joanne Leslie Smith, recovered from the Wood River near Barberville, a good fifteen miles to the southeast. At summer's end, the waterways of southern Rhode Island once more stopped yielding these gruesome revelations.

I will pause here in my catalog of Olney's victims to discuss his journals, which more than his suicide, surely stand as undeniable proof of his guilt. The man was exacting in his description of every one of the murders he perpetrated, describing such details as the time of day each girl was killed, the weather, the clothes she was wearing, and the place where he disposed of the body. Every victim's name was provided, which, in many cases, allowed identifications that might otherwise have been impossible, given advanced decay and/or mutilation. In most cases, Joseph Olney even recorded snippets of his conversations with the victims, and graphic particulars of each death. However, what is most interesting to the problem of the "red tree" are the passages he wrote seeking to explain, to himself, his motives in these crimes, and what psychologists would now refer to as his "delusional architecture."

The nightmares that he had begun to suffer after his first visit to the tree grew more intense, and, in his writings, Olney claims that it was in the dreams, during his sleeping reunions with Bettina Hirsch in a cavern he believed to exist beneath the oak, that he was instructed by "dire beings" to commit the murders. He writes, on November 5th, 1922, following the first series of slayings:

"I cannot say what they are, these bestial men and women I have glimpsed in that hole. I cannot be sure, even, if they are beast or human beings, but suspect an unholy amalgam of the two. At times, I think they look like dogs born of human mothers, and at others, the human offspring of wolves. Below a high ceiling formed of earth and stone and the knotted, dangling roots of that evil tree, these crossbreed demons caper and howl and dance about bonfires, singing songs in infernal tongues unknown to me. Their eyes burn like embers drawn from those same fires, and she [Hirsch] insists that I watch it all, in order to see and fully comprehend the horrors of her captivity. They have their turns at her, both the male and female horrors, raping her, slicing her flesh with their sharp teeth, torturing her in ways I cannot bring myself to write down even by the light of day. And she tells me, again and again, that her freedom may be gained in only one way, by my making certain sacrifices of flesh and blood to these monsters. In exchange for the fruits of my sins, in time they will release her, and we can walk together beneath the sun. They require only the heads and, occasionally, other organs of the poor wretches I am driven to slaughter. As I have said already, I do not deliver these foul offerings during the dreams, of course, but in my waking hours. All must be buried about the circumference of the great oak, at a depth of not more than three feet. From these shallow graves, the demons retrieve their prizes, and then, during the nightmares, I have watched what they do with my gifts. Bettina says I must not waver in my determination, that I must remain strong, if she is to be given back to the surface, like Persephone after her abduction to the underworld by Hades. I understand. I do understand. I tell her this always. But I can see the fear in her face, and I can see, too, that she is becoming like her jailors, that she *is slowly taking on aspects of their terrible form*. She says this is because they force her to join in their feasts, and so she has become a cannibal. I tell her I am doing their awful work as quickly as I dare, but that I must be cautious, lest I am found out. If I am caught, she will never be freed."

Indeed, it is difficult, when reading Olney's journals, not to feel great sympathy for this man, driven to commit murder dozens of times over by these nocturnal visions of his beloved's torment and imprisonment. To pick up on his allusion to Greek mythology, this madman has become a latter-day Orpheus charged with freeing his Eurydice, though by means incalculably more horrendous than those set forth by Virgil and Plato. In his fractured mind, Joseph Olney was left to choose between, on the one hand, becoming a monster himself and, on the other, allowing the monstrosities from his deliriums to slowly transform his dead lover into one of their own. Albert Fish might have claimed that he was charged by God to kill children, but in Fish's claims there is not this conviction that another's damnation hangs in the balance. I am, obviously, not here arguing that Olney's crimes (or those of any such killer) can be justified, only that, if these "confessions" are genuine, that I cannot view him as an unfeeling fiend. He writes, repeatedly, of the almost unendurable remorse he feels after each kill, and on two separate occasions, he went so far as to write out letters of confession that he'd intended to mail to newspapers, and another he considered sending to a Roman Catholic bishop, in which he asked that someone "well trained in the dark arts required when combating evil spirits" be sent to intercede on his and Hirsch's behalves. At no point does Olney seem to derive any sort of gratification from his activities. . . .

There's what seems to me a fairly glaring contradiction in all this. First, we have Bettina Hirsch described as "a willing party to it all," intent upon her former lover's induction into this bacchanalia of the damned. But, *then* we have her beseeching Olney to commit multiple murders because ". . . her *freedom* may be gained in only one way . . . certain sacrifices of flesh and blood to these monsters. In exchange for the fruits of my sins, in time they will release her. . . ." (Though, Harvey *also* says that Olney wrote he was told to murder by the "dire beings" he imagined lived below the tree.) I have no idea whether Harvey recognized these contradictions or not, and I have even *less* idea why I'm worrying over it all.

July 23, 2008 (11:32 a.m.)

The last two days, Monday and Tuesday. I don't even see how I can *hope* to write coherently about the last two days. They have come and gone, and they have changed everything, utterly, and yet, I understand, it is not a change of *kind*, but merely one of *degree*. Constance and I should have run. We should be far away from this place, but we're not. We are here. I did try to get her to go. I tried even after she went back upstairs and locked herself in tight behind that attic door. But I'm getting ahead of myself, and, besides, maybe Constance knows something I'm too damn thick to fathom. It may be that it's too late to leave, and it may be that it was too late weeks ago. Possibly, it was too late before I ever laid eyes on this house and the tree and Constance Hopkins, or even before Amanda's death.

I find myself saying and writing things I would have found laughable only a few days ago. Maybe Constance knows all this stuff, already. She's at the head of the class, the bright pupil, perhaps, and I'm sitting in the corner with my pointy hat, my nose pressed to a circle drawn upon the wall.

I am alone down here, in the stifling, insufferable heat (though a thunderstorm is brewing to the west, I think, and maybe there will be some relief there), and she's upstairs. I am alone, but for my shabby, disordered thoughts and whatever mean comfort I can wring from the confidences I divulge to this typewriter, to the onionskin pages trapped in its carriage.

Thunder, just now. But I didn't see any lightning.

What I'm going to write, this is how I remember it. This is thc bcst I can do. It is, by nccessity, a fictionalized recalling of the events. Of course, it's been that way through this entire journal (and I must surely have said *that* already, at least once or twice or a hundred times). I cannot possibly remember even a third of the actual words, what was said and by whom and when, every single thing that was done and cannot now be undone. But that's okay. That's fine and dandy. I just have to get the point across, the broad strokes—the essential *truth* of it—putting some semblance of these things down here, so that they are held somewhere besides my mind (and, presumably, Constance's mind, as well). My excuse for an "entry" yesterday, the long excerpt copied from Harvey's manuscript, that was me avoiding *this,* sitting down to do the deed and then losing my nerve. But still needing, desperately, to type *something,* almost anything, even if it was something terrible that only made it that much more impossible to "look away" from what is happening here. At least, it forced me to not look away, all that shit I retyped about lunatic Joseph Olney and the women's heads and limbs and livers and all that he buried around the oak. Looking back, it seems remarkably masochistic, but, then again, Amanda did always insist I am the sort who takes a grand, perverse pleasure in causing herself discomfort.

Start *here*. It's as good a place as any.

Early Monday afternoon, day before yesterday.

I was reading a book I'd brought back from the library. My agent had called, an hour or so earlier, with the usual questions, which I'd avoided answering. But it had put me in a mood, because I've been trying so hard not to think about the fact that the novel isn't getting written. I was sitting in the living room, on the sofa, sweating and drinking beer and reading *A Treasury of New England Folklore*. I was reading, in particular, about something called the "Moodus Noises" in East Haddam, Connecticut. Strange sounds and earth tremors dating all the way back to the Indians, who had given the place where this was all supposedly happening a name *meaning* "place of bad noises." Anyway, I was reading about the Moodus noises when Constance came downstairs.

I'd not seen her since our walk to the mailbox together, and that was on Saturday. So, here it was Monday, and I'd not seen her in almost two days. She'd stopped coming down for meals, or even to use the bathroom, unless it was while I was sleeping. And, probably, that's exactly what she was doing, sneaking downstairs while I was asleep. Well, no, not sneaking. I should not say sneaking. Merely deliberately choosing to avoid contact. But she finally showed her face, paint-stained, as it always is now, and smiled, and she pretended there was nothing the least bit odd in shutting herself away like that since Saturday afternoon.

She looked like hell, truth be told. Her cinnamon-colored eyes were bloodshot, and she squinted like the sunlight hurt them. It was obvious—whatever else she's doing up there—she'd not been sleeping. She had a strip of cloth in her hands, a rag, and she was wiping her hands with it, over and over, obsessively, but the rag was so thoroughly impregnated with paint I can't imagine it was doing any good. She asked me for a cigarette, and I gave her one, lit it for her, and then Constance sat down on the floor, not far away from me. She took the Altoids tin from a pocket of her smock and set it on the edge of the coffee table, opened the lid and tapped ash into it. She asked what I was reading, and I think I showed her the cover of the library book. She might have nodded. I didn't tell her about the Moodus noises.

I don't remember the small talk, only that there were ten or fifteen minutes of nothing in particular being said. Nothing of substance or of consequence. And then, suddenly, she laughed, stubbed out her Camel, and snapped the lid of her ginger Altoids tin shut again.

"That day in Jamestown, on the way to Beavertail, when we stopped at McQuade's because I had to pee," she said and wiped at her paint-stained nose. "You acted like you didn't remember having written that story. Why would you do that, Sarah? Why would you lie about something like that?" And it actually took me the better part of a minute to realize that she was talking about "Pony."

"I wasn't lying," I said, finally, and she laughed again and shrugged.

"So . . . it was like some sort of a blackout? Like alcoholics have? You're saying you did that, but you don't remember doing that, so it was like a blackout."

"I didn't say that, either."

"I know, later on, when I gave the story back to you, you pretended like you'd never said there wasn't a new story. When I gave it back to you, in the kitchen."

I took a deep breath, and lit a cigarette of my own. She stared at the floor instead of watching me. And it was so hot, on Monday afternoon. The mercury was somewhere in the nineties, and before she came downstairs, I'd been thinking about Constance in her garret, painting, and about an old *Twilight Zone* in which the Earth's orbit had changed, bringing it nearer to the sun. There was a girl in that episode who was a painter, trapped in a deserted, doomed city that I think was meant to be New York, and, at the end of the episode, her paintings of the huge devouring sun were all melting, and someone—another woman—was screaming at her to please stop painting the sun. That's what I'd been thinking about before Constance emerged from her garret; well, besides the mysterious underground noises in Connecticut. Oh, those were blamed on Ol' Hobbamock, too, by the way. Sometimes, the book said, they'd been felt as far away as Boston and Manhattan. Then, in the 1980s, a seismologist explained it all away. Micro-earthquakes. Something like that. Constance, where is *our* scientist-errant on his white steed, microscope and slide rule in hand to combat the darkness pressing in about us?

"I don't remember writing it," I admitted.

"And so you thought *I* wrote it, like maybe I was trying to make you think you were losing your mind."

I set my book down, then, wanting so very badly to remain calm, but knowing full fucking well that there was only so long I could keep the anger at bay, only so long I could push down the things I *wanted* to say to her. It was so close to the surface, and had been since she'd first mentioned the story, that day out on Conanicut Island.

"Why would I do something like that to you?" she asked, sounding hurt, and I told her I had no idea, but pointed out that I'd never actually accused her of writing the story.

"No, but you *thought* it."

"You don't know what I thought."

"Even if I could write, that doesn't mean that I could write just like you," she said, and tapped a fingernail against the lid of the Altoids tin.

"I know that," I replied, straining to keep my voice level, calm. I probably gritted my teeth. "Constance, no matter what I may have *thought,* I never *said* that you wrote the story. I don't *think* you wrote the story. Clearly, *I* did. That's pretty inescapable. I just can't *remember* having done it."

"So, you're telling me you wrote a whole story during blackouts. Or is this missing time, like those people who say they've been abducted by space aliens talk about?"

"I don't know *what* this is," I said, truthfully. "But I *don't* remember writing the story, and I *have* tried. I've tried hard, believe me."

"Usually, I'm the crazy one," she said, and pocketed her Altoids tin. "Maybe you should see a doctor, Sarah."

"I don't have the money to see a doctor. I don't have insurance. Anyway, when all this started—my fits, I mean—I saw doctors then, and I spent a fortune doing it, and, in the end, they couldn't tell me shit."

She nodded, but it was a skeptical nod.

"I keep meaning to read the stuff Chuck Harvey wrote about the tree," she said, changing the subject. "I suppose I'd better hurry, before you give it to that person at URI."

And it occurred to me then that I'd forgotten all about the professor in Kingston who'd agreed to take the typescript off my hands. She'd never called back after the Fourth, and I'd never contacted her again. Maybe she was glad. Maybe she'd never wanted anything to do with it, and was only trying to be polite.

"No hurry," I told Constance. "I don't think I'll be turning it over anytime soon. That woman never got back to me, and I never called her, either."

"You found it in the basement?" Constance asked, even though I'd already told her that I had.

"Yes," I said. "I probably mentioned that when we first talked about it."

"People forget things," she said, and there was no way for me to miss the fact that those three words were meant to cut me. Meant to leave a mark.

"Yes," I replied. "Yes. People forget things." Maybe I sounded as cool as a fucking cucumber, and maybe she could hear that I was losing the battle with my anger. I don't know. The way things turned out, it hardly matters.

"I've been thinking about that," she said. "The basement. I've been thinking about it a lot. I mean, you haven't been back down there since the day you found Harvey's book, right? And me, I've *never* been down those stairs. Isn't that odd, Sarah, that I've been living here for almost a month, and I've never gone into the basement?"

"No," I replied. "I don't think it's all that odd." The anger was changing over to panic, now, and I found myself gripped by an urgent, almost overwhelming need to keep Constance from going down to the basement of the farmhouse. I'd started sweating, and my heart was racing. "There's nothing down there. Just a lot of junk. Junk and dirt and spiders."

"If I went, would you go with me, Sarah?"

"I'd rather not," I said, and forced out a laugh.

"Why?" she asked. "Are you afraid? Are you afraid of the basement?"

I sat up, and here it was, the anger bubbling to the surface at last. I heard it in my voice. I felt it leaking from me, felt the release of letting out even the smallest fraction of it. "This isn't grammar school, Sarah. This isn't grade school, and we're not on the fucking playground, making dares."

"You're scared," she said with an awful sort of certainty, and her eyes were still on the floor. Only, I knew then that it wasn't the floor she was staring at. It was the basement *beneath* the floor that she was trying to see through the boards.

"Fine. I'm scared."

Constance picked up the rag (she'd lain it beside her) and started wiping at her hands again.

"I've been thinking a lot about *this,* too," she said. "That's where it all began, down there," and she stopped wiping her palms long enough to jab an index finger towards that enormous unseen vacuity below us. "That's where it started, in the cellar. With you finding the typewriter, and then going back—"

"It's not even half that simple," I said, cutting her off, and she looked up, glaring at me. Her eyes were different, intent, *focused,* and they reminded me of something that I am reluctant to put down here. Something, I suppose, I am loath to acknowledge having seen in her face, or in any woman's face. Many years ago, I was at the zoo in Birmingham, and there was this area devoted to local wildlife. The cages were all out of doors, but they were *still* cages. Raccoons, foxes, bobcats, owls, possums, a black bear, and so forth. The animals native to northern Alabama. And almost all of them were pacing back in forth in their small enclosures, pacing restlessly, frantically even. Maybe it was nervous energy, or maybe they were stuck in a sort of instinctual loop, looking for an escape route that must surely exist, somewhere, if only they kept looking. But there was this cougar, just lying in her cage, *not* pacing, but lying perfectly still. I stared in at her, and she stared back out at me. And I swear to fuck, if animals *can* hate, I saw hatred in her eyes. As if she understood the situation through and through—the iron bars, the futility of trying to find an exit, her captors, that I was of the same species as her captors, even that I was part of the conspiracy that had made her a prisoner. It gave me a shiver, that day, though it was a hot summer afternoon, gazing into the reddish eyes of that cat, knowing that the only thing in the world keeping the panther from tearing me apart were the bars.

There was the exact same malice in Constance's eyes. I mean, *exactly* the same. It didn't help, either, realizing that her irises were so similar in color to the cat's. She glared up from her place on the floor, and there were no iron bars in between us, restraining her, protecting me. But then it passed, the expression, that clarity of purpose or whatever, almost before I could be certain what I'd seen. Her eyes were only *her* eyes again, sort of distant, distracted, far away, and she glanced back down and shook her head.

"Now, I've made you angry at me," she said. "I wasn't trying to. I promise I wasn't."

"I'm sorry, but I would rather not go back down there," I said, deciding it was best not to get into whether or not I thought Constance was trying to get a rise out of me. Better not to question her sincerity, so I simply chose to ignore what she'd said, that and the passing, unfamiliar glint in her eyes.

"Then I'll go by myself. It's no big deal. I just want

to have a look around. It bothers me, not knowing what's down there, underneath us."

I took a deep drag on my cigarette and peered at her through the smoke I exhaled. "Why didn't it bother you before? Why all of a sudden?"

"I don't know," she answered. "Maybe it *did* bother me. Or maybe I just never stopped to think about it."

"There's *nothing* down there," I told her again, more emphatically than before. "Just junk. A whole lot of junk, sitting around in the dark, gathering dust."

"Then I'll see it for myself, and I can stop wondering about it. I can start thinking about my painting again, and get back to work."

"You won't just take my word for it? My word isn't good enough for you?"

"Sarah, that's not what I mean. Don't make this into something it isn't," and she sighed and ran the long fingers of her right hand through her tangled hair. It wasn't pulled back in her usual ponytail, and was dirty enough I could believe she'd not washed it in weeks. "I won't be long. I'll go down and see whatever there is to see, and I'll come right back up. Are there lights down there?"

"No," I replied. "There are no lights in the cellar."

"But we have a flashlight, right?"

I nodded, then pointed towards the kitchen with my cigarette. "Yeah. A couple of them. In the drawer beside the sink. The drawer on the right of the sink."

"You won't be mad at me?" she asked. "If I go, you won't be mad at me?"

"No, Constance. I *won't* be mad at you," I lied, an *easy* lie, given how pissed I was with her already. "I just fail to see the point."

"So, what was the point when *you* went, Sarah?"

And I wanted to say I'd only gone into the cellar back in June because I was hot as hell and looking for someplace to get away from the heat, someplace cool to read. But then she would have asked why I did *more* than read, why I ever went poking about, and then, having found the typewriter, why it was I returned to search for the rest of the manuscript. I knew I had no answer that would satisfy her or convince her not to go down there. So, I didn't bother. The answer, in both instances, was that I was curious, and my curiosity was no more valid than whatever was eating at her.

I think I was a cunt not to have tried harder to stop her from going into the basement. I *know* I was a cunt for letting her go alone.

I didn't tell her about the slate threshold with its array of chiseled symbols, or about the archway dividing the basement. I didn't mention all that space *beyond* the arch and the threshold that I'd not had the nerve to explore. I certainly did not mention the nightmare I'd had about finding Amanda down there in a Vernean landscape of giant mushrooms.

My fingers hurt, and I've got to take a break. Get something to eat, maybe. Go upstairs and see if I can get Constance to talk to me. I know I can't, but I need to try, anyway.

July 23, 2008 (continued; 1:57 p.m.)

She didn't open the door for me, but she says that she's alright. The way things stand, I don't suppose I have any choice but to believe her. Believe her or break down the damn door and be done with it. But I think I'm finished with heroics for the time being. I have to wait until she's ready to open the door and come out on her own.

Anyway, yeah, I showed Constance where the flashlights were, and I pretended not to hear the cellar door creaking open. I sat there on the sofa, pretending to read *A Treasury of New England Folklore*. I stared at the pages, reading the same paragraphs over and over again; something about a sea serpent flap in Gloucester Harbor, back about 1817 or so. An assortment of "tall tales"—ghost ships and the ghosts of drowned sailors, Ocean-Born Mary and Caldera Dick and crazy, bloodthirsty Cotton Mathers. *Wonders of the Invisible World.* But, in truth, I *know* now that I was sitting there *listening,* waiting, though I probably could not have said for what. For some sound or sign from below, and when I heard it, I would know. Still, I tried to reassure myself, because I knew there really *wasn't* anything beneath Blanchard's old farmhouse but all the refuse that had accumulated down there over the years—over the centuries, no doubt. Constance would dig about in the mess until she grew bored, and then she'd come back upstairs, and I could say I'd told her so. I could bask in smug vindication, and she'd skulk away to her garret again in a cloud of turpentine fumes. All would be as right with the world as I could reasonably expect.

Only, that's not the way it went, not at all.

About an hour and a half passed, me sitting there trying to read, and the day seeming to grow hotter, my T-shirt sticking to me. We were out of beer, but I wasn't about to drive into town to get more, not with spelunker Constance prowling around in the cellar. I was just about to give up on the book and look for something else to read when I heard what I'd been listening for.

It was the smallest sound. Any smaller, and I'm sure I wouldn't have heard it.

It might have been my name. It might have been something else, the particular words, I mean. It hardly matters, these specifics, because it was plainly a cry for help. It was alarm, and it was dismay, and it was fear. I called out to her, once or twice, fairly certain that there would be no answer, and there wasn't. I waited until the sound came again, and it wasn't a long wait. I went to the kitchen, to get the second flashlight from the drawer to the right of the sink. I switched it on and off, checking to be sure the batteries hadn't gone dead. The casing is blue plastic; the one that Constance took with her is green. She'd left the cellar door standing open, as I've said, and I lingered a moment before that low entryway, shining my flashlight across the ten wooden steps leading to the hard-packed dirt below. They seemed steeper than I recalled, the stairs, and the air rising up from that pit was cool and smelled much too stale, too sour, to ever describe as simply "musty."

Constance's paint-stained rag was lying on the topmost step, and I picked it up. I shouted for her again, and, again, there was no answer. It occurred to me that a draft might cause the door to swing shut, and I took the time to wad the rag and wedge it firmly into the space between the bottom edge of the door and the floorboards. Also, I went back for my cell phone, which I'd left on top of the television after Dorry called that morning. I'm not very fond of cell phones, and I've often threatened to get rid of mine. But suddenly I saw it as a lifeline—a second source of light, a clock, and a means of reaching the outside world (assuming I could get reception down there). I slipped it into my front jeans pocket and went back to the cellar door; that's when I heard Constance yelling again, and, this time, it was clearly my name.

And I said something then like, "If it turns out you're just fucking with me, if it turns out this is a joke, you're a dead woman, Constance Hopkins." I said it loudly enough that she *should* have heard me, but there was no response. The old stairs complained softly beneath my feet, and I went down them quickly. In only a few more seconds, I was looking *up,* at the dingy yellow-white rectangle leading back into the hallway and the house and the sweltering summer world above. That's when I almost lost my nerve, and thought maybe it would be best if I called Blanchard and let *him* deal with this, whatever *this* was. But what the hell would I tell him? That his attic lodger was lost in the basement, and I was too chickenshit to go looking for her? An absurdity compounded with an absurdity. And if you put it like *that,* pride wins out. The fear of lasting embarrassment trumps the fear of things that go bump in the cellar, so I turned away from the stairs, playing the flashlight slowly over all those sagging shelves and cardboard boxes, the broken furniture, the rotting bundles of newspapers dating back to god knows when.

There was no sign of Constance anywhere, and my mind went to the fieldstone-and-mortar archway waiting somewhere up ahead, and the slate threshold and the odd marks or glyphs carved deeply into it. I thought about how far away her voice had *seemed* to be. Now, the basement around me was, as they say, silent as a tomb.

"Constance!" I screamed into the darkness. The darkness made no reply whatsoever. "I'm coming!" I screamed. "Just stay where you are and wait for me to find you!"

Moving quickly as I dared along one of the crooked aisles between the shelves, it didn't take me too long to reach the arch marking the northern edge of the house. And there was the upside-down horseshoe, just like I remembered, all its luck spilled out long ago. There was the threshold, scarred with occult gibberish, and I shone the flashlight into the gloom packed in ahead of me. I spotted the shelf weighted down with its load of elderly Mason jars and spoiled bread-and-butter pickles. Then I saw the cast-off chifforobe where I'd found Harvey's manuscript more than a month earlier (only it feels like it's been three times that long, at least). I took a deep breath, a *very* deep breath, and stepped across the threshold, passing beneath the inverted horseshoe, and into air so cold and damp and heavy I might well have slipped beneath the surface of some unclean winter-bound pond.

The muddy ground sucked at the soles of my tennis shoes, but I pushed on, leaving the drawerless chifforobe and the jars of pickles behind me, calling out for Constance and still getting no answer. This far in, the junk and litter abruptly ended, and now there was only a broad, more or less flat expanse of muck and rock, broken by an occasional shallow puddle. The ground here had begun to slope gradually downwards, an incline of only a few degrees, at the most, just enough that I was aware of it. There was no sign of a wall anywhere, in front of me or to either side, and the thought crossed my mind that, maybe, when John Potter excavated for the original foundation, more than three hundred years before I'd ever had the misfortune to set eyes on the house off Barbs Hill Road, maybe he'd stumbled across some sort of cavern. And having thought *that*, there was really no way not to let my mind wander back to Joseph Olney's mad visions or the tales of the Parker Woodland cairns. I know enough geology to know that solutional caves *can* form in granite and gneiss bedrock, as well as in limestone, so it certainly wasn't impossible. But if that *were* the case, there was no knowing how far or in what directions this underground space might lead. Besides, if the house was built atop a cave system, wouldn't Blanchard have at least fucking mentioned it? Wouldn't he surely have cautioned us not to go prowling around beneath the house?

I stopped and looked back over my shoulder, back the way I'd come, aiming the flashlight towards the brick archway and the chifforobe. But the beam revealed nothing behind me now except the otherwise featureless plain of mud and stones and pools of stagnant water. I'll admit, it isn't much of a flashlight, but I *knew* I couldn't possibly have gone more than twenty or thirty yards past the slate threshold. Thirty yards at the most. And that was the last straw, I suppose, not being able to see the archway, and the panic I'd managed to keep at bay since descending the stairs started closing in on me.

I dug the cell phone out of my jeans and flipped it open. It chirped at me, just the silly little tone it makes when opened or closed, but, in the darkness, the sound was loud and unexpecteded, and it startled me. I almost dropped the flashlight. The phone's colorful display screen glowed cheerfully in my hand, informing me that it was 2:23 p.m., and I cursed myself for not having noted the time before entering the cellar. The phone was showing two bars, so I figured I could at least get a call out, if it came to that. I saw the battery was low, so I closed the phone and put it back into my pocket, then pointed the flashlight north again. The mud and darkness seemed to go on that way forever, sloping very gradually, almost imperceptibly, in the direction of the red tree and Ramswool Pond.

For the first time, I shone the flashlight up, sweeping the beam along the ceiling of the chamber, the space, the cavern—whatever I should call it. The word *abscess* comes to mind, with all its various connotations. At any rate, the ceiling was maybe fifteen feet above me, and, near as I could tell, appeared to be composed mostly of stone, though I noted that, in places, the roots of trees and smaller plants had broken through. Which got me to thinking—if I *had* found a cavern exposed when the foundation was dug back in the 1700s, such a broad hollow at such a shallow depth, what the fuck was keeping it from simply collapsing in upon itself and creating a huge sinkhole behind the farmhouse? I shone the light to my left and right, but still saw no evidence of a wall to either my west or east, respectively. It seemed impossible to me, and still seems so now, that the ceiling could have supported its own weight (not even taking into account the trees and such). I tried not to dwell on it. At least, I thought, I could easily follow my muddy footprints back to the archway and the cellar proper, and took all the solace in that thought that I could scrounge.

Belatedly, I began to count off my steps, and, probably, it was more to have something to occupy my mind than anything else. I kept walking north, towards the place where the pond and the red tree waited, shining the flashlight ahead of me, occasionally calling out to Constance. I'd not heard her since entering the cellar. My shouts echoed down there, the way voices echo in empty buildings, or large enclosed spaces. The way voices echo inside abandoned warehouses, or in cathedrals, for example.

When I'd counted thirty or so steps—counting silently to myself to avoid that unnerving echo—I stopped again, and, again, I shouted for Constance. The gradient was becoming steeper, and another odor had been added to the dank stink of the place, the smell not of rotting plants and not of mildew, but of rotting flesh. I suppose it might well have been nothing more than my imagination grinding away in the darkness. As it was, I was trying hard not to consider the possibility that the same bizarre violation of physics that had plagued our "lost picnic" was now at work, belowground, the same warping of distance and time that Olivia Burgess claimed to have experienced when she visited the tree in October 1957. That possibility was plenty enough morbid without adding to it the faint reek of death. And the air was growing noticeably colder. My breath had begun to fog. Of course, it was so awfully humid down there—the dew point would have been so high—it would not have had to have been *that* cold in order to see my breath. Unless I'm misremembering the science about relative humidity and dew point and the condensation of moisture, which is always a distinct possibility.

Regardless, for whatever reason, I found this is where I was unwilling to go any farther. Thirty or so paces past where I'd begun counting my footsteps. I'm not even sure it was any sort of conscious decision; I simply could not bring myself to go any deeper into that place. I stopped and shouted for Constance, and my voice sounded enormous. But, when I once again shone the flashlight to my left and right, I found rough granite walls only ten or fifteen feet away on either side of me, and when I pointed the beam at the ceiling, it was near enough that I could have reached out and touched it, despite my strong impression that the northward slope here was, if anything, a few degrees *more* acute than when I'd first noticed it. I stared at the walls a moment, and then at that ceiling. The stone did not look like the stone of a natural cavern, but appeared to have been hewn with picks and chisels. Quite some time ago, by the look of it, as the marks left on the granite by iron tools were faint, faded by time and erosion. But they were unmistakable. Someone *made* that passageway.

That's when I heard something behind me, and I'm not ashamed to admit that I almost screamed. I turned quickly around, expecting anything at all, but there was only Constance, standing a scant few yards away. She was naked, though almost every inch of her bare skin was smeared with the ocher mud, a yellowish shade of ocher leached, I guess, from the minerals in the gneiss or granite. Her long hair was matted with mud, tangled with it, and, by the flashlight—if only for an instant—her eyes seemed to glimmer iridescently, the sort of predatory eye shine I would have seen, say, from that cougar at the Birmingham Zoo, or from a coyote or feral dog prowling about our garbage cans. She said something then, though I honestly have no idea what. It was barely more than a whisper.

I said something, as well, but it wasn't a reply. I think it was only her name. I must have sounded relieved, and perhaps surprised, as well. I must have sounded breathless. I remember realizing that I was sweating, despite the chilly air.

"I got lost," she said, speaking louder now, but only slightly louder. I am sure that is what she said, but the next part was, I am equally sure, not in English. At the time, it sounded to me like German or Dutch, or even a mix of the two. She said it twice, seeming to take special care to enunciate unfamiliar syllables. Later, trying to recall the details before I sat down to write this, I became convinced it *was* German that she'd spoken to me, and that what she'd said was something close to *"Irgendwo in dieser bodenlosen Nacht gibt es ein Licht."* Or, if it was Dutch, instead—*"Ergens in deze bodemloze nacht is er een licht."* Both would translate the same—"Somewhere in this bottomless [or unending] night there is a light."

Constance has since told me that she neither speaks nor understands German (or Dutch). Moreover, she has no memory of my having found her down there, much less anything she may have said. She tells me she remembers going down the stairs, and that she remembers finding the fieldstone archway and the chifforobe, before she became disoriented.

Anyway, I think I said something about the cold, then, that she must be freezing, that we had to get her back upstairs, something of the sort. I won't even pretend to know precisely. I expect I said the sort of thing one says after finding a lost friend underground. And Constance shook her head and frowned, like there was something she needed me to understand, and I wasn't listening. Or I was too thick to grasp her meaning. And that's when she raised both her arms, which had been hanging limply at her sides. And I saw the leaves she was clutching. They were green, and not the least bit wilted. She might have picked them from the boughs of the red oak only moments before.

"Sarah, do you *see*?" she asked, and there was more than a hint of urgency in her voice. "Do you see it *now*?"

"Where did you find those?"

"You're not listening to me," she sighed.

"We *have* to *go,*" I said, unable to take my eyes off those fresh green leaves. "Where are you're clothes? We have to get you out of hear."

"My clothes?" she replied, as if she hadn't quite understood the question.

"Yes. You're clothes. Your *naked,* Constance. Where are you're clothes?"

And I am *absolutely* certain off what she next to me. Letting the oak leaves slip from her fingers and settle about her feet, sunk in too the sticky mud too her ankles, Constance Hopkins said, "The *men* took them, Sarah. The men with the hammers, they took them away."

I open my mouth to ask, I think, what she meant, what the fuck she was talking about, and that when I haerd another sound behind me. From the chance inn her expresssionn I coulll

July 25, 2008 (5:17 p.m.)

Constance found me after the seizure that interrupted the last entry. The thing couldn't have lasted more than two or three minutes, but there's no way to know for sure. It's all pretty much guesswork, figuring out what happened. I struck my chin hard against something, and bit my lip. There's actually a spot of blood on the page that was in the carriage at the time. I also hit my forehead, possibly on the edge of the table, but I might have hit it against the floor. That's where Constance found me, on the kitchen floor. Then I spent most of yesterday lying in bed, headachy and feeling hungover, thinking through a fine yellow haze (to employ an old simile I invented while trying to explain the postseizure disorientation and grogginess to Amanda). Anyway, if this wasn't the worst of the fits I've experienced so far, it was surely a close second or third. I *should* have seen it coming—the stress and lack of sleep, all the crazy shit from the cellar, then sitting here for hours on Wednesday, trying to make some coherent record out of my disjointed memories.

Constance keeps trying to blame herself.

She looks at the bruise on my forehead, or the one on my chin, or the cut on my lip, and she says, "I shouldn't have left you alone." Or "If I hadn't gone into the basement, and then you hadn't had to come after me." Or "I should have made you rest." That sort of thing. Whether she's right or wrong, it's a pointless, stupid game, and, right now, I haven't the stomach for this sort of futility and hindsight.

Looking back over the paragraphs I typed immediately before the seizure, I can see evidence of the mild aphasia that sometimes prefaces the attacks, in the particular pattern of misspellings and typos and so forth. I've seen that before, so it's nothing new.

My head still hurts like hell, and now Constance is talking to me, telling me to "give it a rest," and I think I will. More later.

July 26, 2008 (4:48 p.m.)

"You should try to get some sleep," Constance said, gently pressing her left index finger to the ugly plum-colored mark centered between my eyebrows.

"But I'm not sleepy," I replied. "I feel like I slept all day yesterday. I'm not sleepy. I'm bored."

She sighed loudly and moved her finger to the bruise on my chin, which looks quite a bit worse than the one on my forehead.

"Does it hurt?" she asked.

"Yeah, but not so much."

"It looks like you were in a fight."

"Well, does it look like I won, or does it look like I lost?" and so she told me she couldn't say for sure, that she'd need to see the other woman. She brushed a strand of hair from my eyes, and I marveled that her hands were nearly clean, most of the oil paint scrubbed away.

That was late yesterday afternoon, after she had shooed me away from Dr. Harvey's typewriter and talked me into lying down again. Constance sat on the bed next to me, and whenever I'd open my eyes, the room was filled with the most brilliant buttery light. The bedroom has two windows, one facing south and one facing west, so it gets the afternoon sun (Constance says that'll help keep it warm in the winter). I'd open my eyes, and she'd be sitting there, worrying over me, scowling like she does, and there would be the dressing table and the chest of drawers and the ivory walls and all that butter-yellow light washing over everything. There's a framed Currier and Ives print on the bedroom wall, "The Return from the Woods." Like the furniture, it came with the place. In that light, I could imagine no other picture hanging on the bedroom wall.

In that light, her eyes were only a dark shade of brown.

She was reading to me. It had been her idea. I don't think I've had anyone read to me like that since I was a girl. But, like the light, and like the simpler brown it made of her eyes, it was comforting, and I listened while she read from an old Ray Bradbury paperback I'd brought with me from Atlanta, *A Medicine for Melancholy*. She has a good, strong reading voice. She was halfway through "The Day It Rained Forever," and I broke in and told her so.

"It's hard to find people with even halfway good reading voices," I told her, "and most times, when you do, they come off like they've been practicing for some sort of slam-poetry thing."

"Thank you," she said, then went right back to reading to me about Mr. Terle and Mr. Fremley, Mr. Smith and Miss Hillgood in that hotel in the desert. The light coming in the west-facing window seemed perfectly suited to the story, and, mostly, I lay still and listened, concentrating on her voice more than the words, watching dust motes caught in that sunlight, rising and falling at the whim of whatever forces govern the movement of dust motes.

Later, though, when the sun had set, and after I'd eaten the dinner of ramen noodles and wasabi-flavored rice crackers Constance had made us, I began to grow antsy. I told her I needed to do *something*, that I was probably as rested as I was going to get. She asked me if I meant I needed to write, and I think I laughed.

"Are you going to finish it, the stuff you were writing about what happened down there?" She glanced at the floor, as though I needed any clarification.

"Do you think I should?" I asked her, and Constance didn't answer right off. When she finally did, she turned her head away, towards the Currier and Ives print and the west window. I could still see her face reflected in the dressing table mirror. She closed her eyes while she spoke.

"I know you didn't have to come after me," she said, and there was more, but it wasn't anything she hadn't already said—Constance thanking me again for finding her and getting her back upstairs, thanking me for bathing her and washing the mud from her hair, for getting a Valium and some hot soup into her, and so on.

"You didn't answer my question," I said, at the risk of seeming less than gracious. She opened her eyes, and I saw that she saw me watching her through the looking glass.

"No," she said. "I didn't, did I?"

"Do you *want* me to write the rest of it?"

"Part of me does," she said. "I think it's the same part of me that's glad you never got rid of the manuscript. And the same part of me that wanted to reach the tree and that was angry when we couldn't."

"The part of you that had to see the cellar?"

"Yeah, more than likely," and she turned towards me again, though I kept my eyes on the mirror, which now showed me only the back of her head, her black hair pulled tightly into a high ponytail.

"And what about the other part of you?" I asked. "What does it want?"

"It wants to go back to my paintings," she said. "It wants me in the attic, working like a fiend. I suspect it really doesn't care what you write and what you don't write."

"Well, then, maybe that's the part you should be listening to," and I asked her for a cigarette.

"We smoke too much," Constance said. "Both of us. We're both gonna die of emphysema or lung cancer or something if we keep it up."

I laughed, and she told me she was serious, but then she laughed, too.

"Personally, I don't think I need to write the rest of it down," I said. "I know that I certainly don't *want* to. So, perhaps it's best if we keep it between us."

"But we're not talking about it."

"We're talking about it right now, Constance," and she scowled again. She told me not to be an ass, that I knew damn well what she meant.

"I don't have answers," I said. "If that's what you mean, I don't have any more answers than you do." And, frankly, I was thinking that maybe I had quite a few less. There were questions that I wanted to put to Constance, questions about what she'd seen down there, below the floorboards, about the things she'd said to me, and where those oak leaves had come from, for starters. But, the few questions I *had* dared to ask, she'd been unable, or unwilling, to answer.

"Do you think we should stay?" she asked.

"I can't afford to leave," I replied. "I simply don't have the money. But if *you* do, I would understand if you found another place, Constance."

"I wouldn't leave you here alone," she said, and I think maybe she said it a little too quickly, too eagerly, as though she'd practiced the line beforehand. I wished that the sun were still up, the room still bathed in that buttery late-July sun that the twilight had stolen. By the lamp beside the bed, Constance's eyes had taken on their old reddish tint.

As for today, well, it was almost as if the whole thing never occurred. She's gone back up to her garret, and I've hardly seen her since breakfast. I've gone back to my reading and the television and this typewriter. Earlier, I sat here and just stared out the kitchen window at the red tree for the better part of an hour. Maybe I'll try to reach the woman at URI again. Maybe I'll talk to Blanchard. I dreamed of Amanda last night, and it was not a pleasant dream. She's something else that Constance wanted to talk about, but I told her I thought we had plenty enough ghosts to deal with, thank you very much.

"Besides," I added, "Amanda is my own *private* haunting. She's nothing I want to share. And she's nothing you need to hear about." And Constance nodded, but it was more of a if-you-say-so sort of nod than anything else.

I'm thinking of getting a combination lock for the cellar door, next time I go into town.

CHAPTER EIGHT

August 2, 2008 (9:12 p.m.)

I honestly believed I was finished with this journal. Over the past six days, I *allowed* myself to start believing that. Certainly, I've wanted nothing more to do with it, or with Harvey's manuscript, or that goddamn tree. And those six unrecorded days were remarkable only in their consistent, unwavering sameness. I read, watched television, and took a couple of long drives, one as far as Providence. Constance stayed in the attic, appearing only rarely, once more distant, and taciturn, and stained always with paint. I began to imagine this is how the remainder of the summer would proceed. And possibly the autumn, as well. Just yesterday, I sat here and thought how July seemed like some long, thoroughly ridiculous nightmare, but that now it was finally over. Two days ago, I packed Charles Harvey's unfinished book back into its cardboard box and put it at the bottom of the hall cupboard, under some spare blankets. I had planned to do the same with his typewriter, but, for whatever reason, had not yet gotten around to it.

And then, late this morning, I opened the back door, the kitchen door (I can't recall why), and found neon green fishing line tied about the porch railing near the bottom step. It was drawn taut, suspended maybe a foot above the ground, and led away into the briars and goldenrod and poison ivy, north, towards the red tree. I stared at it for a few minutes, I think. It seems now it took me a moment to fully process *what* the fishing line signified. I was startled that it was so very green, and couldn't recall ever having seen that sort of fishing line before. And then I was shouting for Constance, and when she didn't answer, I went back into the house. I went directly to the attic stairs. I knocked and asked her to please open the door. Then I tried the knob and discovered that it was locked. I banged on the door again, hard enough to hurt my knuckles. But no response came from the attic, and the door remained closed.

I very briefly considered breaking it down. I'm pretty sure that I *could* have, but then I admitted to myself that Constance was not behind the door. That she was not in the attic, or, for that matter, anywhere else in the house. Standing there on the narrow landing at the top of the stairs, in the darkness and the heat, I admitted to myself that the only place I would find her was at the other end of the length of green fishing line tied to the back porch. For a minute or two, I permitted myself the luxury of pretending that there was no way on earth I was going after her. It was only seventy-five yards, after all, from the house to the tree, and she'd taken precautions, done her little Hansel-and-Gretel trick with the nylon line. If she'd wanted me along, she would have asked me. Constance Hopkins is a grown woman, and she can damn well look after herself. I thought each of these things, in turn, and then I retraced my steps and stared at the fishing line stretching away into the weeds and underbrush. I called her name a few more times, shouting loudly enough that people probably heard me all the way up in Moosup. And then, suddenly, the whole thing felt absurdly like a replay of the episode in the basement, and I stopped calling for her.

It was cloudy, and we haven't had much of that this summer. Even so, the air was very still, oppressive, and I could tell the day was only going to get hotter. Even if it rains, I thought, the heat will only get worse.

I hesitated, lingering there on the porch, and then I took what I prefer to think was, realistically, the only course of action left open to me. I could hardly have called Blanchard or the police, could I? Even now, I don't know what else I could have done, except maybe go inside and wait to see if she eventually found her way home. And I *couldn't* do that, even though that's what I *wanted* to do. I've known Constance less than a month now, but, in that time, we've shared a bed, and we've shared the experience of living in this house on this godforsaken plot of land. I'd gone into the basement and brought her back. I'd washed the filth from her skin and hair, and she'd played nursemaid after my last fit and read Bradbury to me. More importantly, perhaps, we'd tried *together* to reach the tree, and *together* we'd become lost, when getting lost was all but impossible. All this went through my head, I know, in only a matter of seconds, and then I left the porch and followed the trail of fishing line leading away from the house. I didn't call her name again, and I didn't look at the tree first. I just went.

I walked fast, and it took me hardly any time at all to reach the deadfall marking the halfway point between the house and the red oak. I discovered that the fishing line had been looped several times around one of the sturdier of the fallen pine branches, one that's not so rotten. From there, it turned west, towards the fieldstone wall and the creek, just as I'd expected it to do. I stopped only long enough to catch my breath and wipe some of the sweat from my face. There was a tick crawling on my pants leg, and I flicked it away. Somewhere nearby, a catbird mewled and warbled, its voice sounding hoarse and angry. I looked up and spotted it, perched fairly high in the limbs of a small maple, and it occurred to me that from that vantage, the bird would likely be able to see both me and Constance. So, it could be fussing at either one of us, or both.

I followed the line through the wide breach in the stone wall, and then down the bank to the creek. Here, the nylon had been looped securely round and round the base of yet another tree, before continuing north again, following the stream a little ways. I disturbed a huge bullfrog hiding in a patch of ferns and skunk cabbages at the edge of the stream, and it jumped high into the air and landed with a splash, darting away into the tea-colored water. The ground is pretty soft down there, quite muddy in places, and my shoes left very distinct prints in the mossy soil. But mine were the only prints I saw. The only human prints (I think I also saw a raccoon's). Somehow, Constance had walked over the very same ground as me and managed to leave none at all. Sure, she might weigh a few pounds less, but not enough that she wouldn't have left behind footprints. Anyway, I soon found the next tree that had been used to anchor the fishing line; it turned east, heading straight back up the steep bank on the far side of the deadfall. I decided that I'd find Constance first; she had to be close now. I could worry about the missing tracks later on.

The bank was more difficult to climb than I remembered it being, or I was more careless, and twice I slipped and almost tumbled backwards into the stream below. The second time, I scraped my left elbow pretty badly. In the confusion, I briefly lost sight of the fishing line, but immediately spotted it again at the top of the bank. It had been wound about the base of another white pine, and now resumed its path north, leading me directly to the red tree.

Whatever distorting force or trick of distance had prevented Constance and me from reaching it on the sixth of July did not repeat itself. Other than my growing sense of dread, and the fact that I couldn't find her footprints at the creek, there was nothing even the least bit disquieting or out of the ordinary about the walk from the back porch to the oak. And I suspect maybe I was beginning to let my guard down. I found the end of Constance's lifeline tied to a sapling maybe ten feet away from the red tree. The plastic spool that had held the fishing line was lying nearby, and I picked it up. It's lying here on the kitchen table as I type this. McCoy "Mean Green" Super Spectra Braid, thirty-pound test, eight-pound monofilament diameter, 150 yards. I suppose she picked it up on one of her trips into Moosup or Coventry or Foster. It hardly matters. The label on the spool reads, "Soft as Silk, Strong as Steel." Part of the price tag has been pulled away, but I can still see that the spool cost $14.95.

These details mean nothing, I know. I *know* that. I am only trying to put off what came next. That is, I'm only putting off writing it down. Consecrating it in words. But it is *so* simple. I'd bent over to retrieve the spool, and that was when I saw the spatters of blood dappling the dead leaves, and also dappling the living leaves of creeper vines and ferns and whatever else grows so near the base of the oak. The blood was thick and dark, and had clearly begun to coagulate, but was not yet dry. And what still seems very strange to me—seeing it, I didn't get hysterical. I didn't freak out. In fact, I felt as though some weight had been lifted from my mind, a weight I'd carried for a long, long while. Maybe, it was only relief, relief that, seeing the blood, I no longer had to wonder *if* something was amiss. I can't say. But I looked up, towards the gnarled, knotted roots of the enormous tree, its bole so big around that three large men could embrace the trunk and still have trouble touching fingertips. And spread out above me, its heavy, whispering boughs, raised against the cloudy sky. And, even though I'd seen it up close once before, and dozed in ignorance beneath its limbs, I looked upon it now as though I was seeing the red oak for the first time. And I wondered how I ever could have mistaken it for anything so uncomplicated and inconsequential as a mere *tree*.

There's a passage from Joseph Conrad that says what I felt in that moment far better than I can possibly hope to articulate on my own. Maybe it's cheating, cadging the words of another author because I find myself wanting, inadequate to the task at hand. I just don't care anymore. *We could not understand, because we were too far and could not remember, because we were traveling in the night of first ages, of those ages that are gone, leaving hardly a sign—and no memories.* Or, again, Thoreau's "Earth of which we have heard, made out of Chaos and Old Night." Or, finally, in my own faltering language, here, before me, was all time given substance, given form, and the face of a god, or at least a face that men, being only men, would mistake for the countenance of a god.

There was a great deal more blood. And something broken lying on the stone slab at the foot of the tree. I made myself look at it. It would have been cowardice to turn away, and I hope I can at least say I am not a coward. The rabbit's throat had been cut, and its belly torn open. The wet, meaty lumps of organs and entrails decorated old Hobbamock's altar, and there were also a few smears of blood on the rough, reddish-gray bark of the tree itself. My legs felt weak then, and though I don't actually recall having sat, I remember standing up again sometime later. I cannot say how long I rested beneath the tree, gazing into those gigantic branches, making my eyes return again and again to Constance's sacrifice. It may have been as long as an hour. It may have been only half that. By the time I left, the dead rabbit had begun to attract a cloud of buzzing flies, and I understood that the insects, and the maggots they heralded, were also there to serve the tree, in a cycle of life and death and rebirth that I could only dimly comprehend.

Whatever drove Joseph Fearing Olney to murder all those women and then bury choice bits of them beneath the oak, and whatever had finally driven John Potter insane centuries before—whatever it was that had taken Susan Ames and then her husband, and whatever malignancy had at last left Charles Harvey with no choice but to end his own life, I sat there before it, clutching the empty plastic spool that had recently held 150 yards of fishing line. I was sure that the tree would not allow me to leave. Or that, having seen it stripped of any pretense at being merely a tree, I would find myself incapable of walking away. Here was my burning bush, or the Gorgon's face. Here was epiphany and revelation and, if I so desired, the end of self. So many had been undone before me, and I knew that secret history, and now I also knew the *why* of the thing.

But I did find the requisite will to leave the tree. Or it allowed me to leave. I'll likely never know which, and, likely, it makes no difference.

By the time I got back to the house, it was a quarter past two in the afternoon. I could hear Constance moving about upstairs. I considered trying, again, to get her to open the attic door, and I wondered if we'd passed one another somewhere in the woods. If she'd been headed back, following some alternate route to the one she'd marked with the fishing line, as I was picking my way towards the tree. I wondered where she'd gotten the rabbit. And then I went to the bathroom, undressed, searched my skin and hair for deer ticks (there were none), and took a hot shower.

I still have not seen Constance. I have not heard her come down the stairs. But I was in bed early last night, utterly exhausted, and then I slept late. She might have come down then. She might have stood in the doorway of my bedroom, watching me dream and trying to decide what is to become of the both of us, and by whose hand. She did a messy job on the rabbit.

August 3, 2008 (3:29 a.m.)

Three things.

First, about half an hour ago I reached into the front right pocket of my jeans and discovered there a section of jawbone, maybe two and half inches long, sporting two molars. That the jaw is human is undeniable. One of the teeth even has a gold filling. The bone is stained a dark brown, and there is clay and soil packed tightly into various cracks and into both the severed ends, partially clogging the porous interior. I held it awhile, as the initial shock faded, turning the fragment over and over in my hands, straining in vain to remember having picked it up and put it into my pocket. Then I stopped trying, and set it on the kitchen table next to the typewriter. I *assume,* in the absence of any other viable explanation, or any evidence to the contrary, that I must have discovered this scrap of jaw while sitting beneath the tree yesterday. That I must have picked it up (and maybe, when I found it, the bone was even still half buried in the ground), dusted it off, and then slipped it into my pocket. The fact that I remember doing none of these things does not strike *me* as having any bearing, any relevance, on whether or not this is actually what transpired.

Sitting, staring at that dirty timeworn piece of bone and the two dingy teeth still plugged tightly into their sockets, I thought about going to the closet and retrieving Harvey's manuscript, so I could read back over the circumstances of the Olney killings. But I didn't. I put those pages away, and I mean them to *stay* put away. Regardless, I recall the peculiarities surrounding the recovery of the decapitated heads and other skeletal remains that, between 1922 and 1925, the murderer had buried around the base of the red tree. Chiefly, that not all of the heads could be located, despite the fact that Olney had, in his journal, gone so far as to draw a map of the area around the oak, indicating each spot where he'd deposited bits of his victims. And, also, that all the heads that *were* recovered, even those of the most recent victims, impressed the medical examiner handling the case as having been in the ground much longer than Olney claimed. No trace of flesh or hair was left, and Harvey writes that the coroner commented that the bone looked more like what one would expect from the excavation of an Indian grave, hundreds of years old, than from a recent burial. There was some speculation, at the time, that the earth below the tree might have been unusually acidic, or more amenable to some sort of grub or insect that may have picked the bones clean. We call this clutching at straws. And now I'm *typing* these words, these sentences, these paragraphs, stating it all plainly in black and white, and it looks more absurd than just about anything else I've written down since coming to Rhode Island and first laying eyes on the tree.

And, as long as we're talking absurdities, the more I stare at the chunk of jawbone from my pocket, the more I think about tales of fairy gifts. Or, rather, the perils of accepting any manner of food or drink or gift while within the perimeter of a fairy circle. The base of the tree is round, and so many people have drawn circles about it, repeatedly making of it a mystery (to once again paraphrase Joseph Campbell), or merely underscoring the mystery it has always been. Olney swore that these hills were hollow.

Constance made her offering yesterday, and, shortly afterwards, I sat beneath the heavy green boughs, marveling at the "face" of gods laid bare. And now I find that I came away with a grisly souvenir that I cannot recollect having found, much less having decided it would be a good idea to bring *back* with me.

And here's the second thing.

Reading my last entry, I see that twice now, since I began keeping this journal, I have written of experiencing epiphany in the presence of the red tree. Indeed, the second instance seems like little more than a revision, a better-worded second draft, of the first instance (July 6,

2008 [10:27 p.m.]). In its own way, I find this repetition as inexplicable and jarring as the jawbone from my jeans pocket. Or "Pony." Back in July, when we tried to reach the tree and failed, I *first* saw the tree for what I now believe it to be. I wrote, ". . . it seemed to me *more* than a tree. . . . I saw wickedness dressed up like a tree." But, then, in an entry I made only a few hours ago, writing of my latest trip to the oak, I wrote, "I looked upon it now as though I was seeing the red oak for the first time. And I wondered how I ever could have mistaken it for anything so uncomplicated and inconsequential as a mere *tree*." Also, in both cases, I attempt to illustrate or elaborate on my revelation with a string of metaphors and similes.

Now, if the first "epiphany" were genuine, it would preclude the occurrence of a second, would it not? And if my narrative is to be trusted—if my goddamn *memories* are something upon which I can continue to *rely*—then I must find some way to account for and reconcile this redundancy. And it *is* a redundancy. I don't see how mere forgetfulness could ever possibly account for this repetition.

Finally, a thought has occurred to me, and maybe it's not the sort of thought I should write down. But I probably shouldn't be writing *any* of this down, so, fuck it. I have begun to question my assumption that Constance used the fishing line so she'd be able to find her way back. Sure, I know how rattled she was by our having gotten lost, trying to reach the tree in July. And then her misadventures in the cellar. But she clearly did *not* use the line to get back to the house. She took some other route. So, possibly it was put there not as a lifeline, but as a means of leading *me* to the oak. A carrot on a stick. A trail of breadcrumbs left for a hungry animal to lap up. I'm moving the typewriter into my bedroom, away from the kitchen window. I'd rather not sit here now.

August 3, 2008 (4:57 p.m.)

It's raining today, a hard, steady rain, and there's wind and thunder and lightning. It's coming at us from Connecticut, I think, and before that this storm must have seen New York, and Canada, perhaps. Maybe it was born in the Arctic, and has spent weeks looking for the sea. Upon reaching the Great Lakes and realizing they were landlocked, perhaps it felt cheated. If a tree can be wicked, surely a storm can feel betrayed. Anyway, I've spent most of the day shut away in my room (leaving only to go to the toilet), reading and trying hard not to think my own thoughts, trying only to lose myself in what others have thought before me. But somehow, as though escape from morbid rumination has now been forbidden, I ended up with Poe's *Tales of Mystery and Imagination*. I'd meant to read something harmless, something new, the sort of throwaway paperback that commuters buy at airport newsstands, intended only to amuse or distract them for the duration of any given flight. Instead, I reread "The Fall of the House of Usher," "The Gold Bug," "The Murders in the Rue Morgue," and "MS. Found in a Bottle." There are two passages from the latter I wanted to write down, because they seem to speak not only to what I experienced yesterday, upon reaching the end of Constance's tether and finding myself at the red tree, but also because they say something, I believe, about my present state of mind:

> *A feeling for which I have no name, has taken possession of my soul—a sensation which will admit of no analysis, to which the lessons of by-gone times are inadequate, and for which I fear futurity itself will offer me no key. To a mind constituted like my own, the latter consideration is an evil. I shall never—I know that I shall never—be satisfied with regard to the nature of my conceptions. Yet it is not wonderful that these conceptions are indefinite, since they have their origin in sources so utterly novel. A new sense—a new entity added to my soul.*

Of course, Poe's narrator, marooned on that ghostly black galleon as it sails the south polar seas, is a man bereft of the capacity for fancy and imagination. As he says, ". . . a deficiency of imagination has been imputed to me as a crime . . ." And here *I* am, a woman afflicted since childhood with far too *great* a proclivity for fancy. At least, this is the judgment that was passed upon me at a very early age. All those elementary schoolteachers and aunts and my parents and whoever the hell else, those wise adults in Mayberry who fretted about and tsk-tsked at my "overactive imagination." But I suppose that I've shown them. Well, then again, considering the lousy sales of my books, maybe they get the last laugh, after all. And maybe it is just those sorts of minds, closed as they are to the corrosive perils of fantasy, that are most suited to encounters with the uncanny. I can only say that Poe's words ring true. Here is another passage from the same story:

> *To conceive the horrors of my sensations is, I presume, utterly impossible; yet a curiosity to penetrate the mysteries of these awful regions, predominates even over my despair, and will reconcile me to the most hideous aspect of death. It is evident that we are hurrying onwards to some exciting knowledge—some never-to-be-imparted secret, whose attainment is destruction.*

August 3, 2008 (8:28 p.m.)

Not long after I made that last entry, as I was beginning "The Cask of Amontillado," Constance knocked at my bedroom door. I said that I was busy, that I didn't wish to be disturbed. It was a lie, on both accounts, but, still, those are the words that came out of my mouth.

"I heard the typewriter," she said, her voice only slightly muted by the wood through which it had to pass to reach my ears. "So, I was surprised when I came downstairs, and saw you weren't in the kitchen. I was surprised that the typewriter wasn't on the table. Are you okay, Sarah? Is something wrong?"

I almost asked if she'd noticed the plastic spool lying near where the typewriter used to sit, the empty 150-yard spool of McCoy "Mean Green" Super Spectra Braid. But I didn't. If I *was* meant to find that line and follow it to the oak, then we are playing a game now, the sort where one does not show her hand. And if I was *not,* it would have been an odious thing to say. There's the worst of this, right there. Not knowing if I am consciously being led down these abominable and numinous roads. Or if we are both adrift on the same black galleon, in the same icy sea. Are we now damned together, or might I be the oblation that will set her free? Has she struck a deal with the tree, her life in exchange for something more substantial than a gutted rabbit? And if *that's* the truth of it, was the fishing line an attempt to warn me?

"I'm worried about you," she said.

The door wasn't locked, and I told her she could open it, if she wanted. She opened it partway, and peered in.

"There's no need to be worried," I replied. "I'm fine."

I was sitting on the floor at the foot of the bed, and she was standing in the doorway. I was wearing only my bathrobe and a T-shirt and panties underneath it. She was wearing black jeans and one of her black smocks, and her hands and arms and face were a smudged riot of yellows and browns, crimson and gold, orange and amber and a vacant, hungry shade of blue, as though she'd begun, prematurely, to bleed autumn. Dr. Harvey's antique Royal was (and still is) parked on the dressing table.

"Sarah," she said, "has something happened? After the seizure, or because of it? Something I should know about? Or maybe when we were in the basement—"

"Do you remember it now, the basement?" I asked, and she stared at me a while before answering.

"Nothing I haven't told you already."

"Irgendwo in dieser bodenlosen Nacht gibt es ein Licht," I said, not meeting her eyes. "Has that part come back to you?"

"Sarah, I don't even remember what that means, what you *told* me it means." And she took a step or two into the room, though I'd only given her permission to open the door, not enter.

I shut my eyes and listened to the rain peppering the windowpanes, the one in front of me and the one on my right, south and west, respectively. I wished that she would leave, and I was afraid that's exactly what she was about to do. I could hardly bear the thought of being alone, so near to the oak, but her company had become almost intolerable. So, there's me between a rock and a hard place. Scylla and Charybdis. The devil and the deep blue sea. The fire and the frying pan.

"If you need to talk, I can listen," Constance said.

"But you're so busy," I told her, and if I'd had my eyes open, I think I would have seen her flinch. "So much canvas, and so little time, right? That muse of yours, she must be a goddamn slave driver."

"Sarah, are you pissed at me? Have I done something wrong?"

"Not that I'm aware of," I answered. "Is there something I might have missed?" I opened my eyes, then, and I smiled at her. I wanted to shut the fuck up and not say another single word, and I wanted to take back what had been said already. I was sitting there—detached, dissociative—

watching Constance, listening to the madwoman who'd hijacked my voice. In that fleeting instant, it seemed so perfectly crystal clear that I'd entirely lost my mind. But then the comforting certainty dissolved, and I could *not* dismiss the possibility that the madwoman—despite, or because of, her madness—might be wholly justified in her apprehensions.

"Not that *I'm* aware of," Consytance replied. Her voice had become wary, and she glanced over her shoulder, back towards the hallway and the kitchen. And the cellar door, of course, which lies in between the two. When she turned to face me again, the corners of her mouth were bent downwards in the subtlest of frowns.

"You must miss Amanda terribly," she said. There was not even a hint of anything mocking or facetious in her voice. There was no sarcasm. But, still, there was that wariness.

"Didn't I already tell you that Amanda is none of your concern?" I asked her. Or what I asked was very similar. Typing this, I am once more forced to admit that much of these recollections are approximations. Necessary fiction. My memory does not hold word-for-word, blow-by-blow transcripts. Very few minds are capable of such a feat, and mine doesn't number among them. To again quote Poe (from *The Narrative of Arthur Gordon Pym of Nantucket*):

> *One consideration which deterred me was, that, having kept no journal during a greater portion of the time in which I was absent, I feared I should not be*

> *able to write, from mere memory, a statement so minute and connected as to have the* appearance *of that truth it would really possess, barring only the natural and unavoidable exaggeration to which all of us are prone when detailing events which have had powerful influence in exciting the imaginative faculties.*

I've had more than one heated "discussion" with readers and other writers regarding the use of unreliable narrators. I've seen people get absolutely apoplectic on the subject, at the suggestion that a book (or its author) is not to be faulted for employing an unreliable narrator. The truth, of course, is that *all* first-person narrations are, by definition, unreliable, as all memories are unreliable. We could quibble over varying degrees of reliability, but, in the end, unless the person telling the tale has been blessed with total recall (which, as some psychologists have proposed, may be a myth, anyway), readers must accept this inherent fallibility and move the fuck on. Have I already mentioned the crack someone at the *New York Times Book Review* made about my apparent fondness for digression? Consider the preceding a case in point.

Whatever specific words I might have used, I made it plain to Constance I did not wish to discuss Amanda.

"She was a painter, too," Constance said, as though she hadn't heard me. And it wasn't a question, but presented as a statement of fact.

"Not exactly," I said, wishing like hell that I had a cigarette, but I was out, and I wasn't about to bum one off Constance.

"How do you mean?" she asked, and took another step into the room. The paranoid woman sitting at the foot of my bed noted both the physical incursion being made and Constance's refusal to drop the obviously prickly matter of Amanda. "She didn't paint?"

"Not with brushes," I said. "Not with tubes of paint. At least, not usually. She used computers."

"Graphic design?"

"She called it photo-montage," I told Constance, who nodded and glanced at the typewriter on the dressing table. "She created composite images from photographs."

"Oh," Constance said. "Photoshopping," and whether or not she'd meant to attach any sort of derisory connotation, that's how the paranoid woman at the foot of the bed received the comment. And it triggered in me something that had not been triggered for quite some time, and I found myself needing to defend Amanda.

"It was amazing, what she did," I said, sitting up straighter, keeping my eyes on Constance. "She made photographs of things that couldn't *be* photographed."

"Right," Constance nodded, looking at me again. There was no trace of malice in her distant sangría eyes. "I had a course on photo manipulation in college. But I'm not a photographer, I'm a painter."

"I think Amanda might have told you she was both."

"Do you have any of her work here?" Constance asked, and I shook my head. I don't. Everything of Amanda's that I still own (including her artwork) is back in Atlanta, in the storage unit there. I almost brought a scrapbook with me, printouts of fifty or sixty of her favorite pieces. She referred to them as "giclées"—what she sold to her clients and from her website.

"There's still some stuff online, I think," I said. "Unless her agent or someone else has had it taken down."

"That seems unlikely," Constance said very softly.

"Does it?"

She didn't reply, but sat, uninvited, on the floor a few feet away from me. She offered me a cigarette, and, having one offered, that's not the same as bumming. She also offered me a light, but I had a book of matches in the pocket of my robe. I smoked and stared at the rain streaking the south-facing window.

"I'm scared," I said, and the paranoid woman curled up inside my skin cringed, and cursed, and called me a traitor.

"We're *both* scared," Constance said. "I'm not ashamed to admit that. I only work the way that I've been working when I'm hiding from something, Sarah."

"So, you've been hiding from something since you arrived," I said, and laughed. Thinking back, I wish that I hadn't, but it slipped out, like the smoke slipping across my lips and out of my nostrils. And it pleased the paranoid woman. Maybe she's the one who laughed, and it wasn't me, at all.

"Haven't we both been hiding?" Constance countered. "You think the only baggage I brought back from LA was the crap you helped me carry in? Fucking shitstorm out there," she said. "I've been trying to forget about it, just live my life and forget things *best* forgotten."

"I never said that Amanda was something best forgotten," the paranoid woman muttered, all but whispering, and kept her eyes on the window. Constance sighed loudly, and apologized. It made me want to hit her; I'd not asked for an apology, and I didn't expect one.

"That's really not what I meant," she said. "It just came out wrong. I know there's not a one-to-one correspondence going on here, Sarah. We both got bad shit in our immediate pasts, that's all I mean. And then we come here, and what do we get? Chuck Harvey's pet fucking obsession. That goddamn tree. . . ." And I'll say she trailed off here, because I got the distinct impression that there was something else she *wanted* to say, but didn't.

And now the paranoid woman was yammering from someplace inside my head, intimations of seduction and guile, insincerity and head games. I silently told her to shut the hell up and leave me alone, but, I admit, I also hung on every word she said. Constance wanted something. Probably, Constance had wanted something all along, and I was getting tired of waiting to find out what it might be.

"I know that I shouldn't be shutting myself away up there," she said and pointed a finger towards the bedroom ceiling and the attic. "But it wasn't so bad . . . I mean, maybe I didn't quite realize what I was doing, until *you* shut yourself up in here."

"Not room enough in one house for two reclusive madwomen?" I asked, and she didn't laugh.

"Is that what you think, Sarah? That we're insane?"

"Don't you? I mean, isn't it preferable to the alternative?" And I stopped staring at the window, then, and stared at her, instead. "Oh, wait. You're the one who opened a wormhole to 1901 and reached through space and time to stop that woman from shooting herself. I nearly forgot that part. So, for you, I guess *this* isn't so strange at all, is it?"

Constance stared back at me for a second or two, then let her eyes stray to the floorboards. She laid both her paint-stained hands palms down on the varnished wood and took a very deep breath. The paranoid woman smiled with my mouth, no doubt quite entirely pleased with herself.

"We can be cunts about this," Constance said, and it sounded as though she were choosing her words now with great deliberation. "If it's what you want, we can each retreat to our respective corners of the cage, and cower there in our own private misery and fear. We can be alone while we wait to see what happens next, if that's how you think it ought to be. But it's not what I want, and you need to know that."

"What do you want?" I asked, crushing my cigarette out on the floor. "What do you *expect* me to do? I've already told you I don't have the money to leave this place, to find somewhere else to live. So, will it really be so much better if we cower in the same corner? Is that what you want, Constance, someone to hold your hand while we wait for whatever came for Charles Harvey, and all those other people, to come for us? Or is it just the sex? Is the fear starting to make you horny?"

Constance shook her head very slowly and licked anxiously at her lips, which I noticed were very raw, chapped, like she'd been gnawing at them.

"You won't even try to listen," she said. "I can leave here, Sarah. If I'm willing to leave you alone with that . . ." and she glanced towards the north wall, but I understood that she was really glancing towards the red tree. "All I have to do is pack my shit and make a phone call or two, and I *could* be somewhere else."

"Then that's what you should do," I told her, and used an index finger to wipe at the ashy gray-black smear I'd left on the floor. "In fact, that would probably be for the best, don't you think?" And I said those things. I know perfectly well I said those things, or something similar. There seemed no possibility of reaching all the way down to the solid bottom of my anger, the bedrock bottom of the well of spite and bitterness and resignation that's opened up in me after my last visit to the oak. It just goes on and on, that great invisible wound, like the cavern below this house goes on and on. It didn't matter one iota that what I *wanted* was to put my arms around Constance, to beg her not to leave, to tell her how much it terrified me even to *think* of being alone. The paranoid woman spoke from the wound the tree has left in me, and I simply could not summon the will to silence her and deny her and permit the day to take some other, less self-destructive, route.

"Yes, you should go," I said.

"Sarah, I've told you already that I'd never leave you here. I couldn't do that. I won't." I glanced at Constance from the corners of my eyes, and she looked like she was about to start crying. Seeing that pleased the paranoid woman no end, and the wound in me grew wider by some terrible, immeasurable increment.

"Don't you *dare* start crying," I sneered. I could say "the paranoid woman" sneered, but I'm not letting myself off the hook so easily. *I* sneered, and I balled one hand tightly into a fist. "It makes me sick to my fucking stomach, the sound of a woman crying."

"Is this how you talked to Amanda?" Constance asked, covering the lower half of her face and turning away from me. "When she needed you, is this the way you treated her?"

"We're not talking about Amanda," I said, and clenched my hand so tightly that my short nails dug bloody half-moon grooves into the flesh of my hand.

"No," Constance replied. "No, I don't guess we are."

"It's *only* a tree," I said through gritted teeth, full in the knowledge that I'd never told so great a lie in all my life, and would never find one to top it. "And if you think differently, I believe there's an ax in the basement. Or Blanchard would probably loan you a chain saw, if you think you're up to it."

Constance wiped at her nose, and quickly stood up. It wasn't hard to see that I'd frightened her, or, to be more precise, that I'd added another dimension to her fear. At the time, it seemed like I'd only evened the score.

"I'll be in the attic," she said, and left me in the bedroom, easing the door shut behind her. When the lock clicked, I went back to staring at the window, at the rainy day outside, and tried not to think about the tree. Later, though, I took the piece of human jawbone I found in my jeans pocket yesterday and tossed it out the back door, into the high grass and weeds.

I'm going to stop typing now. I don't think I can bring myself to say anything more.

`August 4, 2008 (9:17 a.m.)`

> "The images produced in dreams are much more picturesque and vivid than the concepts and experiences of their waking counterparts. One of the reasons for this is that, in a dream, such concepts can express their unconscious meaning. In our conscious thoughts, we restrain ourselves within the limits of rational statements—statements that are much less colorful because we have stripped them of most of their psychic associations."
>
> Carl G. Jung, *Man and His Symbols* (1964)

`August 4, 2008 (10:01 a.m.)`

The house is so awfully quiet this morning. Maybe Constance took my advice and left in the night. I would almost believe this, the house is so quiet. There is no sound of her footsteps from upstairs. I am dressed, but have spent most of the last hour sitting on my bed, watching the south-facing window, and the trees, and the sky. Occasionally, I have heard a bird or an insect, but these noises seem to be reaching me from someplace far, far away, and are muffled by distance. I am unaccustomed to there being such a profound silence in this house. You can always hear the birds, the cicadas, the wind, the creaking of venerable timbers still settling after hundreds of years, whatever. This is a new sort of quiet.

So, yes, I *would* think that Constance Hopkins has gone, and I am alone; that she left in the night, only I hardly slept. My body seems to have found some way around the meds. The Ambien has ceased to work. I don't know. But I *was* awake, save maybe half an hour between three and four, and then an hour (at most) between about seven-thirty and eight-thirty. Both these intervals are plainly far too brief to have accommodated her departure. I feel certain of this. She couldn't have gotten out of here that quickly. Constance wouldn't have dared to go on foot, not after her talk of coyotes or wild dogs on the property, and a car or truck would surely have awakened me.

Am I alone? It should be a simple enough question to resolve. Leave my room, and learn whether or not I am alone in the house. I did leave once already, but only long enough to go to the bathroom. I didn't try to find Constance, because, honestly, the possibility that she's gone had not yet occurred to me. The profundity of this silence had not yet occurred to me. I figured she was sleeping, and then I realized that I couldn't hear her window unit chugging away up there. That's not so unusual, early in the day, but it started me thinking, I suppose. It would serve me right, after what I said to her yesterday. I am well enough aware of that. It's nothing I wouldn't have coming.

I'll go looking for her when I finish this entry. I'll go upstairs and knock on the door to her garret, and she'll tell me to get lost, or we'll make nice, or she'll ignore me, but there will be some minute sound to betray her presence. I'll press my lips to the keyhole and whisper apologies, and assure her that I wasn't myself yesterday. I wasn't. But I think that I'm getting better now.

There was a dream this morning, and I want to write it down, all of it that I can recall. I know it was the honesty that comes in sleep, that it was me trying to get through to me. I started to write it earlier, but didn't get any farther than that quote from Jung. I suppose I intended it as some sort of an abstract or preface, a deep breath before diving headlong into icy waters. Then, as I was typing the last few words of the excerpt, there was a sudden rustling in the bushes below my window (the west window), and I had to stop and try to see what it was. But I couldn't *see* anything out there, nothing that could have caused the commotion, and I'm going to assume it was only a rabbit, or a bird, or an errant breeze.

I have never been comfortable writing out my dreams. That used to mystify Amanda. Or she claimed that it did. I know that I've included only a handful of dreams since I began keeping this journal, back in May. I had a therapist, years ago, who insisted that I keep a dream journal as part of our work together. I reluctantly acquiesced, but made at least half of it up. She never knew the difference, and reading back over it, later, I discovered that I had a great deal of trouble distinguishing between the real dreams and the counterfeits. That bothered me at the time. What more intimate lie can a person possibly tell herself? I would suppose forgetting which was which was me getting some sort of cosmic comeuppance, if I believed the universe worked that way. My forty-four years have yet to reveal any consistent, compelling evidence of justice woven into the fabric of this world.

I'm digressing. I'm stalling.

In the dream, Amanda and I were on the road in the same sky-blue PT Cruiser that brought Constance here from Gary, Indiana. Amanda was driving, and I was sitting in the backseat. At first, I didn't know where we were. I'd been listening to her talk, watching as we passed an unremarkable procession of woods, pastures, houses, farms, roadside convenience stores, and gas stations. Then I remembered Amanda's funeral, and I assumed the whole thing—her death—had been some sort of misunderstanding. I didn't bring it up, but there was an indescribable sense of relief, that we'd all clearly been mistaken in thinking that she'd died of the overdose, or of anything else. I know that these sorts of dreams are not uncommon, encountering a loved one who has died and "realizing," in the dream, that the person never actually died. But, to my knowledge, this is the first time I've had such a dream about Amanda.

She was talking about a difficult client, a bisexual

woman with a thing for horses and centaurs and Kentaurides and so forth. The client wanted some elaborate set of photographs done, but hated the idea of photo manipulation and was insisting that as much be done with makeup and prosthetics as possible, because she wanted pictures of "something real, not fake." In the dream, this was the last client that Amanda had before she killed herself. Or, rather, the last one before I'd only *thought* that she killed herself. In the dream, this was the woman she slept with, and then lied to me about having slept with. And, in the dream, I clearly remembered having written "Pony," in our apartment in Candler Park though, now, awake, I recognize that those memories were false. Also, the woman that Amanda was fooling around with wasn't a client. She owned a sushi restaurant in Buckhead.

"It's *all* fake," Amanda said. "I *told* her that. Either way, it's all pretend. But that only seemed to make her more determined to have her way."

And then we were walking together along a narrow wooded path, though I don't recall our having stopped and gotten out of the car. It was very hot, and the air was filled with mosquitoes and gnats. I remember shooing away a huge bluebottle fly that had lighted on my arm. The path was familiar, even though it was someplace I'd not been since I was a teenager. It was the trail leading down to the flooded quarry in Mayberry where I used to collect trilobites, where I discovered *Griffithides croweii* in 1977. I was very excitedly explaining all this to

Amanda, and I said that maybe we'd get lucky and find another one of the trilobites before we had to leave. I was talking about crinoids and brachiopods, horn corals and blastoids, all the sorts of sea animals preserved in the hard yellow-brown beds of cherty limestone. There was a tropical ocean here then, I told her, three hundred and fifty million years ago, aeons before the coming of the dinosaurs, in an age when hardly anything ventured onto the land.

"Dear, you're not paying attention," she said.

And I realized then that we *weren't* approaching the nameless chert quarry in Alabama, but the granite quarry that is now Ramswool Pond. Soon, we were standing at the edge, staring down into what looked a lot more like molten asphalt than water. It was that quality of black, *pitch* black, and seemed to my eyes to have the same consistency as hot tar. When I picked up a stone and threw it in, it didn't vanish immediately, but lay on the surface for a moment before slowly sinking into the substance. There were no ripples. There was no splash, either. The surface of that pool was perfectly, absolutely smooth.

"I don't think we should be here," I told Amanda, but she sat down on a boulder and pointed into the morass spread out before us.

"Well, it wasn't exactly my idea," she said. "Isn't this where you saw that girl drown herself?"

That's something I never told Amanda about, the naked girl I'd seen (or thought I'd seen) that summer afternoon thirty-one years earlier. The beautiful girl whose hair I recall being as black as tar.

"Wasn't her name Bettina?" Amanda asked. "The girl you saw drown, I mean. Didn't it come out, that her name was Bettina. Wasn't she *also* some sort of an artist?"

And then I saw something lying in a clump of weeds not far from us. Clearly, it had crawled out of the pool. It was still alive, but seemed to be in a great deal of pain, its skin entirely coated in the black goop from Ramswool Pond. Amanda said something, but I can't remember what. I couldn't take my eyes off the writhing thing on the shore. It had been a woman once. I could see that now—a female form discernible through the glistening, tarry ooze—but any finer features were obscured. She was dying as I watched, because the black stuff was very slowly eating her alive. It was corrosive, I think, like digestive fluids, and an oily steam rose from the body and lingered in the air.

"You don't want to see this," I told Amanda.

"My name is not Amanda," she protested.

"No, but it's what I call you when I write about you. You wouldn't want me to use your real name, would you?"

"You use *hers,*" she replied, and pointed at the writhing mass in the cattails and reeds. "What the fuck's the difference, Sarah?"

And then the thing in the weeds began to scream—a scream that gave voice to both pain *and* fear—as the black water ate deeper into its flesh. I took Amanda's hand and tried to pull her to her feet. "We're not supposed to be here," I said.

She looked up at me, surprised, a guarded hint of a smile on her lips. And she said, "Turn not pale, beloved snail, but come and join the dance." And before I could reply, the sun had gone down, and risen again, and set a *second* time. We were no longer at the edge of Ramswool Pond, but standing at Hobbamock's altar stone with the red tree towering above us. And the moon was so full and bright I could see everything, and, too, there was a roaring bonfire somewhere nearby.

I know the ugly faces the moon makes when it thinks
No one is watching.

I could smell the woodsmoke, and I could hear the hungry crackling of the flames. And all about the tree, but farther out from it than the place where Amanda and I stood, there was a ring of wildly capering figures. She told me not to look at them, just as I'd told her not to look at the dying thing from the pool, but I stole a glance. *Just* a glance, but it was enough to see that they weren't exactly human. In the firelight, their hunched silhouettes were vaguely canine, and I said something to Amanda about the coyotes that Constance thought she'd been seeing hanging around the garbage cans. Then Amanda was reciting Edgar Allan Poe, and her voice was as fervent, as *fevered,* as the swirling, whooping, careening dancers:

And the people—ah, the people—
They that dwell up in the steeple,

All alone,
And who, tolling, tolling, tolling,
In that muffled monotone,
Feel a glory in so rolling
On the human heart a stone—
They are neither man nor woman—
They are neither brute nor human—
They are Ghouls:—
And their king it is who tolls:—
And he rolls, rolls, rolls,
Rolls
A paean from the bells!

And if I'm to believe anything that Charles Harvey wrote in his unfinished book, the serial killer Joseph Fearing Olney became obsessed with these same lines, writing them over and over in his journals and on the walls of his jail cell. He even wrote them on slips of paper that he would place inside the mouths, beneath the tongues, of the decapitated heads he buried at the base of the red tree. Beneath the tongues he had forever silenced.

In my dream, there was no wind. The air was as stagnant as whatever vile black vitriol had seeped up from the earth and filled in Ramswool Pond. But, even so, the branches of the ancient, wicked oak moved, swaying, creaking, scraping against one another, leaves rattling like dragon scales, as though a hurricane were bearing down upon the land.

"Two billion trees died in that storm," Amanda said. "Think about it a moment, Sarah. Two *billion* trees."

"Not *this* one," I replied, gazing up into those restless boughs. "This one seems to have ridden out the tempest just fine."

"Yes," she said and smiled. "But don't think that was all luck, Sarah. It took a lot of blood and sweat to keep her safe when that storm came tearing through. It has always taken a lot of blood and sweat, keeping her safe. Like all doors, she tends to swing open, and so care must be taken to mind the hinges and the latch."

And I think I asked, "We *are* talking about the oak?"

And I think that Amanda replied, "If that's how you see her, yes, we're talking about the oak."

I forced myself to make notes in pencil, not long after I awoke, or I'd have lost almost all of this. But even so, I'm having trouble making sense of much of what I scribbled down, half asleep. Partly, that's because most of the handwriting is illegible, and, partly, because a good deal of what I can read still refuses to yield anything like meaning. I know that I'm filling in some of the gaps. Making some of this up. Approximating. That therapist who wanted me to keep the dream journal, I told her I could not possibly remember my dreams verbatim, and being a writer, it was inevitable that I might invent things as I wrote them out. But she said not to worry. So, right now, I'm trying hard not to worry.

I stood with Amanda, at the altar beneath the red tree, and the dancers howled and skipped around us. Sparkling embers rose into the sky to meet a grotesquely swollen full moon. The moon was still low on the horizon, and only half visible above the tree. I would call the scene *hellish,* only, at the time, I don't believe it struck me that way at all. Only my waking mind would render it hellish in retrospect, measured against my waking values and fears and preconceptions. Dreaming, I *wanted* to accept Amanda's invitation and "join the dance," that perverse "ring around the rosie" and whatever it might entail. I wanted to be initiated into the mysteries of the tree, or into the mysteries that the tree merely represented.

"What have you brought for her?" Amanda asked, and I felt entirely inadequate, standing there beneath the single glaring white eye of the moon. At first, I was certain that I'd brought nothing at all, no offering to lay upon the slab that I now understood must have been placed at the foot of this tree long before John Potter, long before the Narragansetts. Watching those giant branches moving against the backdrop of the moon and stars and the indigo nothingness of space, I didn't need Amanda or Harvey or anyone else to explain to me that this ground was consecrated long ages before the Europeans came in their sailing ships, before tribes of nomads wandered across an icy spit of land connecting two continents. Before *any* man stood here, and before any tree was rooted in this soil, the land was touched and claimed and set aside.

In the dream, I was wearing the ratty wool coat that Amanda finally gave to Goodwill so she wouldn't have to see it anymore, so that I'd have to buy a new one. I reached into the coat and retrieved from an inner pocket several pages of Charles Harvey's manuscript, rolled into a tight bundle and tied off with a piece of green fishing line. I held the pages out so that Amanda could see them.

"Well," she said, still smiling, "that's a start."

"I would have brought more, but he never finished writing it."

"He *couldn't* finish," she said. "You cannot ever conclude what has no end. It's like walking the circumference of a circle. You can only get tired and find some arbitrary place to stop."

"Do you know how tired I am?" I asked her, and she said that she did, and then she took the rolled-up pages of typescript from my hands. I was glad to be rid of them. I remember, distinctly, being extremely glad that they were no longer my responsibility. And that was the sense I had, that they'd been a responsibility I'd shouldered for a very long time.

"Stop looking at the sky," Amanda said. "You'll go blind, if you don't look away."

And so, instead, I looked down at the altar stone, seeing clearly for the first time all the sacrifices painstakingly laid out upon or near the stone, or set in amongst the roots of the tree, or tucked into knotholes (I have always called these "Boo holes," after Boo Radley in *To Kill A Mockingbird*). There were bloodier things than murdered rabbits, but I do not think it will serve this narrative to describe them in detail. Even that monster Joseph Fearing Olney would have felt himself inadequate before that banquet. And I knew it *was* a banquet, that there would soon be a feast, of one sort or another.

"Hercules did not slay the child of Typhon and Echidna," Amanda said, speaking very softly. She bent down and lifted a white votive candle from the altar stone. "In severing that immortal head, he only set the Hydra free, so that she could take her rightful place in the Heavens."

"Echidna," I said, and the word brought to mind nothing but those spiny little egg-laying mammals from New Guinea. Amanda nodded, and with the candle, she set the pages I'd given her on fire. Some of the ashes settled across the altar, while others rose upwards, like the embers of the bonfire, becoming lost in the swaying branches of the red tree.

And Amanda said to me, "And again she bore a third, the evil-minded Hydra of Lerna, whom the goddess, white-armed Hera, nourished, being angry beyond measure. . . ." Then she paused, the flame having burned down very near to her fingertips, and she dropped the smoldering remains of my offering onto the stone with everything else. "Only, Mother Hydra was *not* evil-minded, though I well imagine Hera *was* angry," Amanda said, but did not bother to elaborate.

And around me, the dream moved like the tumbling colored beads or shards trapped inside a kaleidoscope's tube, and I tumbled with them. The night passed away, and Amanda was replaced by Constance, and the scene at the tree by the attic of Blanchard's farmhouse. The din of the dancing creatures was replaced by the commotion from the air conditioner, which was making much more noise than usual. Constance was sitting on her inflatable mattress, and I was sitting nearby in a chair. She said that she was pretty sure the AC was on its last leg, that it was about to blow the fan or an evaporator coil or something of the sort.

"I sounded like that the time I caught pneumonia," I said, and she laughed.

"I thought you'd be at the tree," she said, and jabbed a thumb in the direction of the oak. Bright moonlight shone in through the attic windows, and the same sort of votive candles that had burned at the altar were scattered about Constance's garret. "I thought they'd have you out there for the festivities. Way *I* had it figured, Ms. Crowe, you'd be the guest of honor, or the main course."

"Is it that sort of feast?" I asked, and she shrugged.

"Wasn't that how it went, when those boys caught up with Sebastian Venable beneath the blazing bone sky? Wasn't he finally devoured for his sins by vengeful Mediterranean urchins, while poor Catherine watched on?"

"That's not how it ever seemed to me," I said. "To me, it always seemed that Sebastian merely consummated his desires. He'd looked upon the face of god, when he and Violet took their cruise to the Galapagos Islands—"

"The part of the play with the predatory birds and the baby sea turtles," Constance said, and I nodded.

"Sebastian was only seeking after release, having seen too much, and that day the boys at *Cabeza de Lobo* were only providing that release."

"It means 'head of the wolf,'" she said. *"Cabeza de Lobo,"* and I told her that I already knew that.

"Well, you're a smart cookie. Not everyone would," she replied, and then added, "But yes, I think it's exactly that sort of a feast."

"They never proved that Olney was a cannibal," I said. "Not like old man Potter. They had no real evidence that he ate from any of the women he killed. And he denied it."

This conversation, there was so much of it. It went on and on while the air conditioner wheezed and choked and sputtered. And at some point I realized that, while I was still wearing my old wool coat, Constance was completely naked. I hoped she would invite me into her bed again. She sat there like some heathen idol, some Venus made not of marble but living, breathing tissue. Her legs were open, revealing the wet portal of her sex, and she didn't seem to mind that I stared, but, like Amanda, she warned that I could go blind, if I looked too long or too closely.

"I thought that only worked with masturbation and the sun," I protested.

"Moonlight is merely reflected sunshine," she said, "and every star is another sun." Then, as I watched, her skin changed, or I noticed for the first time that it had been meticulously painted with a pattern of overlapping oak leaves. And, before my eyes, the painted leaves turned from summer greens to rich shades of red and brown. And they began to fall, slipping off her body and settling onto the mattress all around her. I remembered the kanji tattooed above her buttocks:

and for a while, I could only watch the spectacle of the leaves drifting down from Constance's shoulders and breasts and face. It was too beautiful to turn away from, and like Harvey's *Quercus rubra,* somehow too sublime, too terrible. I realized that the air in the attic had lost all its characteristic odors—turpentine, oils and acrylics, linseed oil, gesso, stale cigarette smoke. Now there were only the faintly spicy smells of autumn.

"Did you do that all by yourself?" I asked, meaning the elaborate painting on her skin.

"Oh, hardly," she laughed. "Too many spots I could never reach on my own. I had help. But, I don't think you're paying very close attention."

"That's what everyone keeps telling me," I said.

"Maybe, Sarah, it happens that you can't see the forest for the trees." And we both laughed then, because it was such a corny thing for her to have said, even in the interminable, rambling dream of mine.

"All two billion?" I asked.

"At least," she said. The leaves were still falling from her painted body, and I marveled that she could shed so many and not be diminished. I thought how each one must be like a dead skin cell, sloughed off to make room for its successor.

And then Constance took a piece of powder blue chalk from a fold in the sheets and held it up for me to see.

"You may need this," she said.

"Colored chalk?" I asked.

"No, Sarah. Not colored chalk. *This*," and now she leaned forward, her body rustling like a blustery day in October, and she used the stick of chalk to draw something on the floor between us.

"I'm never going to be able to remember all that," I said, and, indeed, whatever she wrote or drew, I'd forgotten it completely by the time the dream ended and I awoke.

Constance scowled, the way she does. "I can hardly do everything for you," she said and then pointed at what she'd written on the attic floor. "I can hardly make it any more perfectly straightforward than that."

"My memory isn't what it used to be, that's all."

Constance shrugged, dislodging a few more leaves. She sat up straight again, and she closed her legs, so I could no longer see her vagina.

"Is it a cipher?" I asked.

"It's a *door*, Sarah. And like all doors, it tends to swing open, and so care must be taken to mind the hinges and the latch. It must be kept locked, and someone has to keep the keys. But I imagine you know that already. Amanda would have told you that."

"Her name isn't Amanda."

"No, but that's what you call her, when you write about her. You call her Amanda. Or Helen."

I was no longer in the attic, then, but sitting at the

kitchen table, my fingertips resting on the typewriter's brass keys. I was looking out into the August night towards the red tree, and there was that bloated moon. And there, below the moon, was the flickering glow of the bonfire. I began typing, trying to recollect what Constance had drawn with her blue chalk.

This is my dream. What I remember of it, and for what it might be worth. I have to leave this room now, and find out whether or not I am alone in the house.

CHAPTER NINE

August 4, 2008 (4:28 p.m.)

She's gone.

Or maybe all that I can say with certainty is that Constance Hopkins is no longer *here*.

Or, perhaps, simply that I am unable to find her.

Which is not to say that, upon entering the attic, I found nothing.

I'm sitting at the dressing table, staring at one of the sheets of onionskin paper held fast in the typewriter's carriage, and my fingers move hesitantly across the keys. My head is filled to bursting with images, and with the implications and consequences of what I have seen, what I *still* see, sleeping and awake. But I seem never to have learned the language that I require to describe what is happening to me. If that language even exists.

I can't say what's made me sit down at the typewriter again, unless it's merely force of habit, or a sense that I am helpless to do anything else, or a delusion that this is better than talking to myself. I almost called someone. Who, though? That's the catch. Well, the first catch. Who would I have possibly fucking called? Who would have begun to understand the things that need to be said? My agent? My editor? Squire Blanchard? An ex? One of those various people I haven't heard from since I left Atlanta? A "writer friend" in New York or Boston or Providence or LA or San Francisco? Some family member I've not seen in twenty years? I sat on the sofa and held the cell phone for a time, and I opened it twice, but every number I might have "dialed" seemed equally irrelevant.

I found my car keys, and I considered the undeniable wisdom of driving away, driving anywhere that isn't here, and never looking back. I suspect that I could probably torch the house without getting much more than a stern "thank you" letter from Blanchard. Isn't that how these haunted-house stories usually end, with a purification by fire? Isn't that the handy old cliché?

I didn't telephone anyone. I didn't drive away. I'm not going to burn the house down and sow the charred ground with salt. And I'm not going after the tree with a chain saw or a hatchet or a can of gasoline. The worst I am capable of is following Virginia Woolf's example and filling my pockets with stones before walking into the local equivalent of the River Ouse.

I have gone to the attic, and Constance isn't there, but I still do not know if I am alone in the house.

I seem to have been afflicted with some unprecedented calm, something that settled over me while I was upstairs and which shows no signs of abating. Again, I know we're running counter to the received wisdom, in which our heroine, having glimpsed some unthinkable atrocity, parts ways with her sanity (at least for a time) and runs screaming into the night. Perhaps it's only that those sorts of books and movies are, too often, made by people who have never, themselves, stood at this threshold. Even Catherine ran screaming, that sunstroke day at *Cabeza de Lobo.* Couldn't I at least be as weak as poor Catherine?

No.

Fine. Then I'll write it down.

I went to the attic, immediately after finishing the entry this morning. Twice, I called out for Constance, and twice, no one answered me. I knocked, to no avail, and so I knocked again, and harder. There was a moment of serious *déjà vu,* a moment when it might still have been Saturday morning, after I discovered the fishing line leading away from the back porch, but before I followed it to the red tree. Then I tried the knob, and found that it turned easily in my hand, and the spell was broken. The door was not locked against me, and I couldn't help but recall what both Amanda and Constance had told me in the dream—*Like all doors, it tends to swing open, and so care must be taken to mind the hinges and the latch.*

A door, a tree, a hole for a white rabbit and a middle-aged novelist. Six of one, half dozen of the other.

> *In a another moment down went Alice after it, never once considering how in the world she was to get out again.*

The rabbit hole went straight on like a tunnel for some way, and then dipped suddenly down, so suddenly that Alice had not a moment to think about stopping herself before she found herself falling down what seemed to be a very deep well.

We speak in whimsy, or to children, and it all appears so uncomplicated, no matter how outlandish or monstrous a given scene may be. Me, I can't even seem to manage the tongue of madness without constant recourse to the perspective of reason, though I know it's long since ceased to be pertinent to my situation and circumstances.

I turned the knob, and the attic door swung open wide. And the cool air that I am so used to greeting me when Constance opens her door *wasn't* there to greet me. And instead of the smell of painting, there was a dank, shut-away odor, and, beneath that, the heady stink of decaying vegetation. I covered my mouth with my hand, with my right hand, and stepped into the attic. I left the door standing open.

The rabbit hole went straight on like a tunnel for some way, and then dipped suddenly down, so suddenly that Alice had not a moment to think about stopping herself before she found herself falling down a very deep well.

The attic was not dark, but, as usual for so early in the day, brightly lit by the sun shining in through the small, high windows. Constance told me more than once that the morning light was one reason she was happy with her garret. So, I can't dismiss what I saw there as a trick of shadow, an illusion created by a chiaroscuro conspiracy of half-light and poor eyesight. I cannot dismiss it at all, unless I am able (I am perfectly *willing*) to decide that it was an hallucination. I will not say "only" an hallucination, because I am *not* so naïve as to believe that what was seen would be any less important or consequential if it were the product of a broken mind and not an accurate perception of an objective, external reality. But yes, the attic was very well lit. Indeed, after the gloom of the stairwell, I found Constance's room painfully *bright*, and I squinted and had to wait a second or two for my eyes to adjust.

There was no one in the attic, no one but me, and the floor, and every other horizontal surface, was hidden beneath a thick blanket of green oak leaves. They were identical to the three I found in my room in July, and identical to those that grow on the tree near Ramswool Pond. They were not the least bit brittle or wilted. They appeared to have come freshly from the tree, or from some other tree of the same species. I didn't scream. I didn't even gasp. I think that I was expecting *something*, even if I could not have said what form that something might assume. I bent down and picked up one of the leaves, as though I needed to touch it, to *hold* it, to inspect the fine network of veins embedded within the pith, in order to verify that the leaves were real. But I must have known they were. I must have known that on some intuitive level as soon as I saw them, even if it took a bit for my conscious, doubting mind to catch up. The sunlight shone through the leaf, making it appear to glow.

So far as I can tell, none of Constance's belongings had been removed. The leaves covered over everything—her bed, the floor, her portable stereo, the books, clothes that had been left lying on the floor, the few pieces of furniture that Blanchard had supplied, everything.

Words fail. I've been sitting here staring at the typewriter, and at my reflection in the dressing table mirror, for the last fifteen minutes, trying to compose the next sentence in my head. Trying to find the words. Outside, birds are singing as though this were any other day. I can pick out the songs of catbirds, cardinals, jays, wrens, a crow or two farther away. And, of course, this *is* any other day.

First, I saw the leaves.

And then I saw the canvases. There were seven of them, arranged about the attic on seven wooden easels. They were not particularly large canvases, measuring maybe two feet by a foot and a half. All seven were blank, except for a single strip of paper that had been pinned near the center of each one with a thumbtack. The paper was newsprint, yellowed slightly with age. I began with the easel nearest to the door, reading the newsprint, then proceeded to the next.

> *She took down a jar from one of the shelves as she passed; it was labeled "ORANGE MARMALADE," but to her great disappointment it was empty: she did*

not like to drop the jar for fear of killing somebody, so managed to put it into one of the cupboards as she fell past it.

The first strip of paper read simply, "By Evil, I mean that which makes us useful."

I admit that I stared very closely at that first canvas, unable to accept its blankness as genuine blankness. I could not stop thinking of Constance's hands and arms and face and her black smocks, always smeared with paint. But no matter how carefully I inspected the canvas, it was completely empty, save the newspaper clipping. The coarse fabric had not even been given a primer coat that it might eventually receive and hold paint.

The next canvas was the same, only the clipping read, "Places with white frogs in them."

And on the third easel, standing very close to Constance's leaf-covered air mattress, was a blank canvas and a clipping that read, "Good in our experience is continuous with, or is only another aspect of evil."

I am *not,* by the way, recounting these lines from memory. I would never have remembered a third of them. There was (too conveniently, I thought) a stenographer's pad lying open on one of the windowsills, and a sharpened No. 2 pencil. Both were partly hidden beneath the oak leaves, but when I happened to spot them—halfway through the canvases—I backtracked and copied the text into the notepad. It's lying here on the dressing table beside the typewriter.

The strip of paper affixed to the third canvas read, "Angels. Hordes upon hordes of them."

I lingered, reading that line aloud several times, not wanting to proceed to the fourth, and my mind drew connections that were or were not there to be drawn.

> *There were doors all round the hall, but they were all locked; and when Alice had been all the way down one side and up the other, trying every door, she walked sadly down the middle, wondering how she was ever to get out again.*

At the fourth easel, which was set up in front of the south-facing dormer, was a scrap of newsprint reading, "Or the loves of the worlds. The call they feel for one another. They try to move closer and howl when they get there." The fifth canvas was placed so that it faced the wall, and I had to turn the easel about myself to read what had been tacked to it: "I have seen two of the carcasses, myself, and can say definitely that it is impossible for it to be the work of a dog. Dogs are not vampires, and do not suck the blood of a sheep, and leave the flesh almost untouched." Among the bits of paper on the canvases, this one is conspicuous, not only for being the most wordy, but also because someone had bothered to note its source. Written in sepia-colored ink in a spidery hand, I read, "*London Daily Mail,* Nov. 1, 1905."

Five down.

The birds are still singing, and I find their voices an odd comfort. But, right now, I'd give four fingers off my right hand for a cigarette and a cold beer. Sweat keeps running into my eyes. It must be at least eighty-five in this room. Eight-five or ninety, easy. I am waiting for a careless spark, and the oxygen in the air will instantly combust, and everything in the bedroom will mercifully be scorched to a cinder.

The sixth easel was on the far side of the air mattress, near a tiny dresser holding most of Constance's clothes. I checked the drawers; her T-shirts and underwear and sweaters and socks were all still there, though the drawers were also stuffed with oak leaves. The sixth strip of newsprint read, "I can draw no line between imposture and self-deception."

Which brings us to the end of this taut length of green fishing line, or to the point where Alice finally reached the bottom of her deep well. Seven. The final easel was standing a foot or two from the north dormer window. Before reading the piece of newspaper tacked to it, I glanced back towards the attic door, and was relieved to see that it had not swung shut. The seventh clipping read simply, "Out in open places there have been flows of a red liquid." So, there.

And if that were all—these seven canvases and their cryptic commentaries—I would suggest the following: Constance brought the leaves in herself, and placed them all about the room, to frame what she'd conceived of as some bizarre minimalist installation. I hadn't noticed, but so the hell what. I also hadn't noticed her leaving the farm, leaving me alone here, but, again, so what. I miss a lot, and the past few days, I expect I might have missed more than usual. If this is where it all ended, I *could* be satisfied with such an explanation, and I'd not bother with the handful of unanswered questions. But it *didn't* end here. I'm not certain, now, that it will ever end.

First, I saw the oak leaves. And then I inspected the seven canvases, each one bearing a single snippet taken from an old book or newspaper. Otherwise, the canvases were naked. And then they weren't anymore.

Glancing towards the attic door again, and preparing to leave and go back downstairs, I saw that the change had occurred. I didn't see it happen. That is, I did not catch the canvases in the act of metamorphosing, assuming that's what they did. I'm trying, hard, to make no assumptions about process, or cause and effect, as I write this out. But assumptions are inevitable. And again, the shock to my senses that I would have expected to accompany such an event failed to take hold of me. I wasn't horrified. I was not appalled. I didn't become perceptibly more frightened than I had been before the seven paintings "appeared."

I'm not even going to try describe all seven of the paintings. I saw them, and, for the most part, that's sufficient. They were garish, grotesque things. I remember telling Constance that I know very little about paintings and painters, and that's true. But these brought to mind the works of Francis Bacon, with whom I am familiar because Amanda was somewhat obsessed with him. But I'm certainly not knowledgeable enough to attempt to describe the style. I did look at the Wikipedia article on Bacon before I began writing this (I also checked my email, but there was nothing new there), and the images it included served to confirm my initial impression that the paintings in the attic are reminiscent of his style, especially *Three Studies for Figures at the Base of a Crucifixion* (1944), *Head* (1948), and *Study After Velázquez's Portrait of Pope Innocent X* (1953)—more notes from the steno pad, by the way. I cannot say that I committed those titles to memory. The Wikipedia article states that Bacon's ". . . artwork is known for its bold, austere, and often grotesque or nightmarish imagery."

I examined only one of the seven paintings from the attic closely. The last one that I'd come to (though it was blank when I reached it), the one propped on the easel near the north dormer window. The one that had, only moments before, held a strip of paper printed with a single sentence: "Out in open places there have been flows of a red liquid."

The first thing I looked for was the artist's signature, expecting to find Constance's. Instead, in minute white brushstrokes I read "B. Hirsch '19." I think that I said her name aloud, then—Bettina Hirsch—the painter that Joseph Olney had fallen in love with during his time in Los Angeles, but who'd hung herself on Christmas Day 1920. The woman that had formed the focus of his mania regarding the red tree. The woman he'd done murder for, an unknown number of times, because he believed that she was being held captive by demons who lived beneath the tree.

As for the subject of the painting, near as I could tell it depicted the mutilated body of a woman, and at the time I thought she was meant to have been attacked and mauled by some sort of animal. I don't know if that was the intention of the artist. The figure was rendered in shades of yellow, orange, and deep red, and she had been placed against a background that was primarily a dark brownish shade of purple. Eggplant, I suppose, or aubergine. Both the woman's legs and both her arms were missing, and there were only what I took to be bloody stumps. Her jaw was hanging open, as though frozen in the act of screaming. The paint had been applied very thickly to the canvas, almost caked on in places. In fact, I had the impression that there might have been another, older painting hidden beneath the one I was seeing.

And still, I didn't feel the chill up my spine or the possum across my grave or death breathing down my neck or whatever it is we are taught people are meant to experience under such conditions. I didn't scream at the sight of a murdered rabbit. Perhaps, by this time, I was in shock, and maybe I still am. However, I did feel a distinct sense of revulsion. There was no fear to it, no dread. One does not feel afraid looking at crime-scene photos, or roadkill, or something left too long at the back of the refrigerator. Seeing it, I felt the need to wash my hands (though I didn't touch the painting), more than I felt anything.

. . . suddenly, thump! thump! down she came upon a heap of sticks and dry leaves, and the fall was over.

On my way out of the attic, I paused long enough to inspect another of the canvases, the one nearest to the door.

It bore the same signature, but was dated 1917. I cannot say for sure what the artist had in mind, but I was reminded of an immense tree, crowned in crimson leaves, and watched over by a moon (or sun) the color of oatmeal. Bettina Hirsch *might* have placed a series of dancing figures about the base of the tree, or I might have only been seeing a few errant brushstrokes, or something intended as understory, bushes, weeds. But I didn't look at any of the others. I left the attic and pulled the door shut behind me. I wanted to lock it, but I don't have the key. I quickly descended the stairs, and for an hour or so I sat on the front porch, half expecting to see Constance emerge from the woods, or come walking across the little bridge over the stream that runs out of Ramswool Pond. I watched for her on the dirt road leading out to Barbs Hill Road.

And now, I think maybe I've had a change of heart. I think I do mean to leave this house. I can go to Providence, and it may be that, from a distance, I can begin to sort this out. Or forget it, if that's possible. Either way, I don't want to be here anymore.

4 August 2008 [*Time of entry not noted.—Ed.*]

I've just read back over my account of the dream of Amanda and Constance, Monday morning's dream. And I see that Sarah is up to her old tricks again. Which is to say, I can't begin to fathom why I bothered to add so much embellishment to what little I could truly remember. Half of it—at *least* half—is simply made up. I understand why I once fabricated dreams for an insistent therapist, but why bother here? I can't even say that I was lying to myself. I knew full well what I was doing when I did it. My best excuse would be to claim that it was some sort of defense mechanism kicking in, that I was falling back on the old habit of storytelling as a means of keeping myself calm or giving voice to fear, something of the sort. And having lied, it doesn't mean that I was necessarily dishonest, any more than "Pony" is dishonest. I am usually at my most brutally forthright when making shit up. That's the paradox of me. Regardless, seeing it now, all the parts of the dream I *didn't* genuinely dream, I find it annoying. Hell, I find this entry complaining about it annoying.

It's very quiet outside. A skunk passed by the window a little earlier. I didn't see it, of course, but smelled it. And there was some sort of owl hooting out there for a bit, but, otherwise, the house and the woods around it are quiet and still. I might almost believe that I have been taken away from the world and placed somewhere else. I've left all the lights downstairs burning, and the porch lights are on, too, so here I am, a little puddle of brilliance in the inky void. I brought my laptop into the bedroom a while ago, and tried playing a couple of CDs to dilute the silence—Bob Dylan's *Street Legal,* and then *Fables of the Reconstruction* by R.E.M. But the music only seemed to make me more jumpy. It masks the noiselessness of the night, but in so doing, it *also* masks the noises that I cannot stop listening for. I found myself straining to hear through the music, even if I can't say what I was listening for. Constance's coyotes, maybe. Or Constance herself. Or maybe the red tree, after it pulls itself free of the ground and begins an ent-like march towards the house. So, I turned the music off halfway through "Maps and Legends," and now the stillness is broken only by the *clack-clack-clack* of the typewriter's keys, the clack of the keys striking the paper.

This doesn't seem like the time for confession. Sitting here, swaddled in the dark, and the silence pressing in on my bright electric bubble. Though, on the other hand, the tree and this house don't seem shy about revealing *their* atrocities by the stark light of midday, so why should I balk at divulging my confidences by night?

When I discovered Amanda was fucking the owner of the Buckhead sushi restaurant, I confronted her. It was a very cold day, and it was raining, on and off. A misty, ugly sort of rain for a misty, ugly sort of day. It was late afternoon, and there was fog over everything, heavy fog like you don't often see in Atlanta. She was sitting on the chaise, reading, and I'd been pretending to edit something, the page proofs for a short story. There were pages in my lap and on the coffee table, marked in red. STET written in the margins again and again and again, which is usually the way I react to the ministrations of copy editors, whether they happen to be right or wrong. I write STET, and, half the time, I know I'm just being an asshole, but I do it anyway. They are my mistakes. Let *me* make them.

I can't remember what Amanda was reading. A novel. She'd taken the day off. And I said that I knew what she'd done. She laid down her book and stared at it for a time, and then she stared at me.

"So," she said, finally, "what happens now?"

"I don't know what happens now," I replied, and my voice seemed flat, betraying almost nothing of the rage that had been seething inside me for days.

"Who told you?" she asked.

"What difference does it make, who told me?"

She sighed and glanced out the windows at the fog.

"It's true?" I asked.

"Yeah, it's true. But you know it's true, without asking. You always know what's true, don't you, Sarah?"

She was baiting me, like I needed provocation, and I let the jab go. Or I tried to let it go. Every word that passed between us eliminated the possibility and served to set the future in stone.

At some point, she asked if I wanted her to leave, and I told her no. But I knew that what she was really asking for was *permission* to leave, that it's what she wanted, and I had no intention of making it easy. If she wanted to move in with the purveyor of eel and tuna, she could damn well screw up her nerve and *do* it on her own, without my complicity. And that's when *she* got angry, when I withheld a simple release from her predicament. She said things I have tried hard to forget, threw accusations the way some women might have thrown dishes or knickknacks or stones. And, mostly, I sat there with my pages and my red pen, listening, wishing I knew some magical incantation that might yet undo the whole mess. Wishing impossible, silly things, the way a child wishes, the way people pray to their gods. That I could have been the woman that Amanda needed, assuming that such a woman was ever born. That there were still words to set things right, words to facilitate salvage, and that I could find them. That she would just *stop*, and tell me she was sorry, and that it was over. That it wouldn't happen again. And that, hearing this, I would believe it, and go back to my copyediting, and she would go back to reading her book.

"Most of the time," she said (and I remember this; I will always remember this part), "I do not even know who you are, Sarah. You write, but you hate writing. And then you blame everything and everyone around you because writing is all you have. And now, these seizures of yours. How much more am I supposed to be able to deal with?"

"You're sitting there telling me that you fucked this woman because I hate writing, and because I'm having seizures?" I asked. For a second, I think I might have been more flabbergasted than angry.

"Yes," she shot back, suddenly standing up and letting the book fall to the floor at her feet. "Yes, Sarah, that's *exactly* what I'm saying. Because, goddamn it, you never let a day go by that you don't remind me and the whole damn world how utterly miserable you are, and how you expect us all to be miserable right along with you."

A lot of other things were said, but that's the upshot and the part I remember clearly. And later she told me that she was going out. I asked if she was meeting the owner of the sushi restaurant, and Amanda said who she might be meeting was her own business and none of mine. And that's the last time I saw her alive. Most of this, I told the police. Most of it.

I told them about the affair, and that we'd argued. I suppose I should be grateful that she killed herself in another woman's apartment. At least it spared me the embarrassment and inconvenience of being suspected of foul play. At least, the sort of foul play you can be arrested and brought to trial for. And I didn't have to worry about cleaning up the mess.

If I wrote "Pony"—and I must surely have—the rest of my confession is there, in that story, however turned around backwards and veiled it might be, however fictionalized and prettied up with metaphor. What Amanda wanted, I couldn't give.

The bridle chafed, I suppose.

That day, just before Amanda left, I told her I loved her, and she laughed and said, "Just because you feel it, doesn't mean it's there."

I'm finally running out of ribbon, I think, and I don't have another to replace this one with. Maybe I should conserve whatever is left. Isn't that a little like the miner trapped after a cave-in, waiting for rescue and trying to make his oxygen or flashlight batteries last as long as possible? Only, I know that no one is coming for me. No one is left who might bother.

I'm going to wait a while longer for Constance. The car keys are here on the dressing table next to the typewriter. I'm only going to wait until morning.

[*Date and time of entry not noted.–Ed.*]
I will add this.

Because this is true also. And because you go so far,

and it hardly seems to matter whether or not you let yourself go just a *little* farther.

I was falling-down drunk the night Amanda died (that is not meant as a caveat). I was drunk, and fell asleep on the sofa, because I could not stand to look at our bed, even though it had once been only *my* bed. Something woke me, very late, and I'd fallen asleep with the television on. Old black-and-white movies on TCM, and for a while I lay there, half awake at best, blinking and staring at the screen, bathed in that comforting silvery wash of light.

On the TV, a young woman stared out a window. She was watching another woman who seemed about the same age as herself and who was sitting in a tire swing hung from a very large tree. It was almost exactly like the swing my grandfather put up for me and my sister when I was a kid. Just an old tire and a length of rope suspended from a low, sturdy branch. From the angle of the shot, it was clear that the window looking out on the tree was also looking down. I mean, that it must have been a second-story window. Or an attic window. The woman in the tire wasn't swinging. She was just sitting there. There was no dialog, and no musical score, either. There was nothing but the sound of wind blowing. The woman watching from the window leaned forward, resting her forehead against the glass. With an index finger, she traced the shape of a heart on the windowpane. And then I realized that there was something approaching the tree. It came very slowly, and by turns I thought I was seeing a bear, a wolf, a dog, and a man crawling forward on his hands and knees. Whatever it was, the woman in the swing didn't see it, but I had the distinct impression that the woman watching from the window did. After a bit, she turned away, stepping out of frame, so that there was only the window, the tree, the woman in the swing, and the whatever it might have been slowly coming up behind her.

And I must have fallen back to sleep then, because that's all I can recall of the film. My cell woke me sometime after dawn, and there was a Buster Keaton movie playing on the television. I answered my phone, and the call was from the hospital, from a mutual friend who'd gotten the news before me. Amanda had been dead about two hours.

I have no idea what the film was, and possibly it was nothing but a dream. The night my grandfather died, my grandmother told us she was awakened by a very small bird, like a sparrow, beating its wings against the window. She'd been at the hospital for days, but she'd been convinced to go home and get some rest, because everyone thought my granddad was out of the woods. It was the dead of winter, and my grandmother knew the bird must be freezing, but she couldn't remember how to open the window and let it in out of the cold. She swore she wasn't dreaming, though my mother suspected that she was. A few hours later, the phone woke her with the news that Granddad had died in the night.

Grandmamma said that the little bird was a psychopomp, and that she should have understood.

I've been awake maybe an hour. I woke to find a very large dog standing at the foot of my bed, watching me. But when I sat up, startled, it was gone. I saw it very clearly. Its eyes were the same reddish brown as Constance's eyes, and it had a mottled tongue, gray and pink. Its fur was dark, but not quite black. Not quite.

It could have been the same dog that John Potter shot that summer day in 1724, shortly before both his daughters died. Charles Harvey described the dog very clearly, quoting from Potter's journal. I don't remember all of the story now, but it was broad daylight, and Potter had been sitting alone near a window, reading the Bible. He heard a noise and looked up to find this dog staring in the window at him. He said that it was standing on its hind legs, its forepaws propped against the sill. He called for his wife, and it ran. The dog ran. He said it had eyes the color of chestnuts. He said a lot of things, John Potter did, and I don't know if any of the stuff that Harvey put in that manuscript is true.

I never learned the name of the film, or the year that it was made, or who the actresses playing the woman at the window and the woman in the swing might have been. But then I never tried very hard. I've never mentioned it to anyone. My grandmother once told me she wished she'd never told anyone about seeing the sparrow.

I have to leave this place today. I can't stay any longer. She's not coming back.

[Date and time of entry not noted.—Ed.]

"Oh, I've had such a curious dream!" said Alice, and she told her sister, as well as she could remember them, all these strange Adventures of hers that you

have just been reading about; and when she had finished, her sister kissed her, and said, "It was a curious dream, dear, certainly: but now run in to your tea; it's getting late." So Alice got up and ran off, thinking while she ran, as well she might, what a wonderful dream it had been.

[*Date and time of entry not noted.—Ed.*]

I went up to the attic again, to get the paintings, Bettina Hirsch's paintings, and to bring them down. I meant to burn them all, because I could not bear the thought of them, of leaving them there to be discovered by someone else. So, I went up the stairs, and the door was still unlocked.

There are no oak leaves carpeting the floor, and there are not seven paintings arranged on seven easels. Everything that Constance brought here with her is gone.

No. Just this once, stop lying. It's worse than that.

The attic is the same as it was the first time I set eyes on it, that day I went looking for a yardstick. There are boxes and a few pieces of furniture, and everything is covered with a thick coating of cobwebs and dust. My handprints are still clearly visible on the lid of the old steamer trunk in which I found the yardstick. Otherwise, there's no sign whatsoever that the dust has been disturbed for a very long time. No one's been in the attic since I was up there in June. I stood there for almost half an hour, waiting to see through the illusion, desperate to find that it *was* an illusion. Like the blank canvases had been, before they became paintings. But no matter how hard I stared, or how many times I looked away, or shut my eyes, nothing changed. If I were to call Blanchard and ask him about his attic lodger, I think I know what he'd tell me.

I'm very tired, Amanda, and I need to rest.

I shouldn't be this tired when I try to find my way back to the tree. I'll rest for a while, and I'll drift back down to the orchard, and the stone wall. I'll lie in my bed and wait. Someone has turned the ponies out again.

EDITOR'S POSTSCRIPT

Excerpt from *A Long Way To Morning* (Sarah Crowe; HarperCollins, 1994):

Andrea lay very still, staring up at the ceiling, what she could see of it by the flickering candlelight. She lay staring at the high ceiling of the whore's bedroom, warmed by the afterglow of sex, and by the woman's naked body, so near to Andrea's own. It occurred to her that Michelle's sheets smelled like apple cider, which made her think of autumn. And it also occurred to her that it had been a long time since she'd felt this content.

"You promised you'd tell me the story," Michelle whispered. "After we fucked."

"You won't like it," Andrea replied, wishing silently that she could go back to the quiet, undemanding moment before.

"Isn't that for me to decide?" the whore asked.

"It'll only leave you with more questions than answers," Andrea said. "And just when you think it's one thing, this story, it'll go and become something else entirely. It's fickle. It's a fickle story."

"The whole wide world is fickle, and you promised," Michelle insisted.

"It's not even a real story," Andrea continued. "And it's populated with fairly reprehensible people."

"So is life," replied the whore.

"It really doesn't make a great deal of sense, this story. It's filled with loose ends, and has no shortage of contradictions. It shows no regard whatsoever for anyone's need of resolution."

"Just like life," the whore added, and she laughed softly and nipped lightly at Andrea's left earlobe.

"I doubt I'll be able to finish the whole thing before sunrise," Andrea said. "In fact, I'm almost certain I won't be able to."

"Fine," said Michelle. "Then I will have to call you Scheherazade, and you will have to think of me as the king. I will be forced to grant you a stay of execution until you're able to tell me all of it."

Andrea didn't respond immediately. She kept her eyes on the ceiling, and tried not to think about the antique straight razor in the pocket of her coat, draped over the back of a chair on the far side of the bedroom.

"How the hell did I wind up with such a literate whore?" she asked, and Michelle laughed again. "Anyway," Andrea continued, "you'd make a better Dinazade."

"That's dirty," the whore snickered, then added, "Vice is nice, but incest is best."

"Sure. Besides, the king has lots of other concubines to keep him occupied."

"Odalisque," Michelle said. "It's a prettier word."

"Fine, then. Odalisque. Regardless, you've been warned. This story, it has a *lot* going for it, as long as you can live with the questions it raises and never answers, and with a certain lingering inexplicability."

"I pays my money, and I takes my chances," said the whore, whom Andrea was unable to think of as either a concubine or an odalisque. Michelle was just a whore, and Andrea was just a trick, and the razor was just a razor.

"You don't get to whine about it afterwards, or ask for your dollar back."

"I never would," Michelle assured her.

"Very well," Andrea sighed, closing her eyes. "But only because Scheherazade always did carry a torch for her sister. Whenever she was getting banged by that fat old bastard Shahryar, she would shut her eyes tightly and think of Dinazade, instead."

"Well, there you go," said the whore.

There was a long moment then when neither of them said anything; there was no sound but a few cars down on the street, and a police siren somewhere in the distance. Then Andrea opened her eyes, and she took a deep breath, breathing in the cider sheets. And then she began.

"Not long ago, there was a very talented painter named Albert Perrault, but, before he could finish what would have been his greatest painting, he died in a motorcycle accident in Paris."

"Wasn't he wearing a helmet?" the whore asked.

"I have no idea," Andrea replied, sounding slightly annoyed. "And do not interrupt me again, not if you want to hear this. As I was saying, this unfinished painting, it *would* have been his masterpiece. . . ."

THE END

AUTHOR'S NOTE

In August of 2006, while walking in the woods near Exeter, Rhode Island, I happened upon an enormous oak tree. There were a number of peculiar objects set all about its base—dismembered doll parts, empty wine bottles, a copy of the New Testament missing its fake leather cover, faded plastic flowers, and other things I can't now recall. For no reason I could put my finger on, I found the sight unnerving, and didn't linger there. Perhaps it was only the tree's relative proximity to the Exeter Grange Hall and Chestnut Hill Baptist Church. The state's most famous "vampire," Mercy Brown (1873–1892), is buried in the church's cemetery. Or perhaps my disquiet arose from the simple, unsolvable mystery of those random objects scattered about the base of the tree. Regardless, like everything else that I see and hear, the oak tree was filed away as potential story fodder. And, two years later, from it grew the novel that became *The Red Tree.*

There are a great number of other sources of inspiration that I feel I should acknowledge, some of which have been quoted and/or alluded to in the text of the novel. These include: Michael E. Bell's *Food for the Dead: On the Trail of New England's Vampires* (2001); Jorge Luis Borges' "The Garden of Forking Paths" (1941); various works by Edgar Allan Poe and H. P. Lovecraft; Peter Straub's *Ghost Story* (1979); Arthur Machen's *The Great God Pan* (1890, 1894); Tennessee Williams' *Suddenly, Last Summer* (1958) and Gore Vidal's film adaptation of the play (1959); Lewis Carroll's *Alice's Adventures in Wonderland* (1865) and *Through the Looking-Glass, and What Alice Found There* (1871); Daniel Myrick and Eduardo Sánchez' *The Blair Witch Project* (1999); the works of Carl G. Jung and Joseph Campbell; Joan Lindsay's *Picnic at Hanging Rock* (1967); Mark Z. Danielewski's *House of Leaves* (2000); Joseph Payne Brennan's "Canavan's Back Yard" (1958); Angela Carter's *The Bloody Chamber* (1979); Karl Edward Wagner's "Sticks" (1974); Shirley Jackson's *The Haunting of Hill House* (1959); Henry David Thoreau's *The Maine Woods* (1864) and *Walden; or, A Life in the Woods* (1854); Charles Hoy Fort's *The Book of the Damned* (1919), *New Lands* (1923), and *Lo!* (1931); Joseph Conrad's *Heart of Darkness* (1899, 1902); Algernon Blackwood's "The Willows" (1907); and M. R. James' "The Ash Tree" (1904). Also, the section of *The Red Tree* titled "Pony" originally appeared in *Sirenia Digest* #2 (January 2006).

I would also like to thank my agent, Merrilee Heifetz of Writers House, and my editor, Anne Sowards, for their support of this book; Sonya Taaffe, for many helpful conversations, and for proofreading, translation, and invaluable feedback; Carol Hanson Pollnac, for her assistance with research, including that first trip to Moosup Valley; William K. Schafer, for all his continued support; Harlan Ellison, for the pep talks; Dr. Richard B. Pollnac (University of Rhode Island), for reading the first draft and offering comments and proofreading; Byron White, for more things than I can mention; and the staffs of the Peace Dale Public Library, Providence Athenaeum, Providence Public Library (Central Branch), the URI College of Continuing Education Library, and the Robert W. Woodruff Library at Emory University. And, most of all, my partner, Kathryn A. Pollnac, without whom I'd have stopped writing a long time ago.

AUTHOR'S BIOGRAPHY

Caitlín R. Kiernan is the author of nine novels, including *Silk, Threshold, Low Red Moon, Murder of Angels, Daughter of Hounds,* and *The Red Tree*. Her award-winning short fiction has been collected in six volumes, including *Tales of Pain and Wonder; To Charles Fort, With Love; Alabaster;* and, most recently, *A Is for Alien*. She has also published two volumes of erotica, *Frog Toes and Tentacles* and *Tales from the Woeful Platypus*. Trained as a vertebrate paleontologist, she currently lives in Providence, Rhode Island.

www.caitlinrkiernan.com
greygirlbeast.livejournal.com